Praise for *Anthrax Island*

'A first class thriller with an international cast of characters led by the inimitable and unstoppable John Tyler. Tense, intriguing and deadly. This debut is going to be huge'
    Mari Hannah, author of *Without a Trace*

'Uncomfortably well researched and brimming with pace it's that rare thing: a thoughtful and intelligent thriller. Absolutely brilliant'
    M. W. Craven, 2019 CWA Gold Dagger award-winning author of *The Puppet Show*

'I LOVED IT! Marshall has an obvious talent for storytelling. Fans of spy fiction will love this. Fans of detective fiction will love this. Fans of thrillers will love this. Bloody hell – everyone's going to love this! I wish I'd written it'
    Russ Thomas, author of *Firewatching*, a Waterstones Thriller of the Month pick

'*Anthrax Island* makes brilliant use of a unique setting, and at times reads like Agatha Christie by way of John Carpenter's *The Thing*. Enthralling'
    Mason Cross, author of *Presumed Dead*

'*Anthrax Island* is an exhilarating thrill ride with so many twists and turns that it's impossible to predict what's going to happen next. A classic mystery with a contemporary twist, *Anthrax Island* is a joy'
    Chris McGeorge, author of *Inside Out*

'Smart, rocket-paced and super twisty this phenomenal debut thriller is like a cross between Jack Reacher, Bond, and *And Then There Were None*. A real must read!'
    Steph Broadribb, author of *Deep Down Dead*

'Absolute belter! Seriously, if Hercule Poirot and James Bond had a baby and sent him to the Jason Bourne School for Badasses he would grow up to be John Tyler. Cars, cash, poison, guns, thrills, chills and murder – this book has the lot'

S E Moorhead, author of *Witness X*

'A genre-busting debut. It's like the bastard son of Agatha Christie and Ian Fleming watched *The Thing* on repeat before bashing out a pacy, locked-room, action-adventure thriller'

Trevor Wood, 2020 CWA John Creasey (New Blood) Dagger award-winning author of *One Way Street*

'*Anthrax Island* combines the fast paced thriller narrative of the old masters like Alistair MacLean or Lionel Davidson with the heightened paranoia and claustrophobia of John Carpenter's *The Thing*. A cracking read'

Martyn Waites, author of *The Sinner*

'A nerve-shredding thriller packed full of atmosphere and tension from a writer to watch'

Doug Johnstone, author of *The Big Chill*

'Fast-paced and action-packed, with a compelling and complicated protagonist, *Anthrax Island* is a crackingly good read. Impossible to put down'

Sheila Bugler, author of *I Could Be You*

'Marshall explodes onto the literary scene with *Anthrax Island*, a novel of high stakes thrills, compelling mysteries and charisma to burn. If I come across a more thrilling and enjoyable read this year, I'll be amazed'

Rob Parker, author of *Far from the Tree*

'A gripping debut thriller with a claustrophobic and highly original setting'

Alex Walters, author of *Lost Hours*

'Intense claustrophobic locked-room style tension, in as harsh and hazardous a setting as you'll find, makes for a stunning entrance for the John Tyler series into the ranks of must-read action thrillers'

Robert Scragg, author of *End of the Line*

'*Anthrax Island* is so evocative, you feel like you are on the island with the action going on around you. It's pacy, action packed, clever and full of classic one liners. Sure to be one of the breakout books of 2021'

Chris McDonald, author of *A Wash of Black*

'A deadly virus, an unknown killer on an island surrounded by inhospitable seas and a flawed protagonist we can't help rooting for – *Anthrax Island* is a cracking thriller from a brilliant new writer'

Marion Todd, author of *What They Knew*

'My heart was in my mouth from the first page to the last!'

Alison Belsham, author of *The Tattoo Thief*

'Dark, engaging, utterly atmospheric and totally consuming. I can't wait to read the next book'

Parmenion Books

D. L. Marshall was born and raised in Halifax, West Yorkshire. Influenced by the dark industrial architecture, steep wooded valleys, and bleak Pennine moors, he writes thrillers tinged with horror, exploring the impact of geography and isolation. In 2016 he pitched at Bloody Scotland. In 2018 he won a Northern Writers' Award for his thriller *Anthrax Island*.

ANTHRAX ISLAND

D. L. MARSHALL

San Diego, California

Canelo US
An imprint of Printers Row Publishing Group
9717 Pacific Heights Blvd, San Diego, CA 92121
www.canelobooksus.com

Printers Row Publishing Group is a division of Readerlink Distribution Services, LLC. Canelo US is a registered trademark of Readerlink Distribution Services, LLC.

This edition originally published in the United Kingdom in 2021 by Canelo.

Published in partnership with Canelo.

Correspondence regarding the content of this book should be sent to Canelo US, Editorial Department, at the above address. Author inquiries should be sent to Canelo, Unit 9, 5th Floor, Cargo Works, 1–2 Hatfields, London SE1 9PG, United Kingdom, www.canelo.co.

Publisher: Peter Norton • Associate Publisher: Ana Parker
Art Director: Charles McStravick
Senior Developmental Editor: April Graham
Production Team: Beno Chan, Julie Greene, Rusty von Dyl

Map by Daniel Jarrett.

Library of Congress Control Number: 2021952570

ISBN: 978-1-6672-0125-2

Printed in the United States of America

26 25 24 23 22   1 2 3 4 5

For Louby

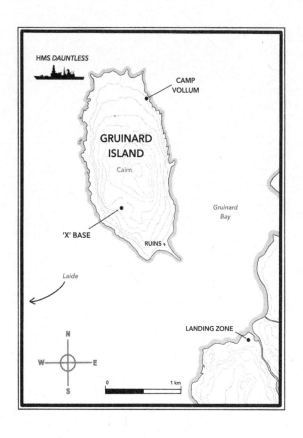

Chapter One

My first view of the island was through the fogged lens of a gas mask, though a thousand feet was too high to fully appreciate the horror below. As we lined up for a second pass I pressed against the helicopter's window, knocking the mask against the glass. A bleak hill, storm-lashed cliffs jutting from angry waves, no real features in the pale dawn, even less life. My stomach knotted.

The Royal Marine opposite leaned against the bulkhead, swinging casually from a cargo strap like he was riding the Tube. I nodded at him, pointing a finger downward. He got my meaning, leaning into the cockpit to talk to the pilot then dropping into his seat as the helicopter banked. I pulled out my iPhone to fire off one last message and felt a tap on my shoulder. I turned to Bates, the burly Glaswegian corporal in the seat next to me. He held out a huge paw, beckoning. I handed him the phone and turned back to the window, watching the murky sea pound the rocks as we swept across the bay.

Too dangerous to set down on the island itself.

The helicopter lurched, I gripped the seat base; it'd been a long, bumpy flight north from HMNB Clyde, the naval base at Faslane, and I'd been gripping it most of the way. The Marine opposite smirked. I closed my eyes, steadied my breathing, concentrated on the thudding rotors. A minute or so later the vibrations changed, followed by a jolt that clouted my head against the restraints. Banging, muffled shouting; my eyes were still screwed shut when a rush of cold air swirled around the cabin. I opened them to see the smirking Marine jumping out

I

of the door with my bags. I took a deep breath, unclipped myself, and climbed down after him, relieved to feel spongy grass beneath my boots.

The pilot kept the power up, rotors whipping the drizzle into a frenzy. I could see twice fuck-all through the stream of droplets on the visor; the world was a crazed mosaic, blurred crags and jagged pines. The roar of the turbines was muffled by the thick rubber over my ears, disorientating me further. I hunched low as I jogged away, arm up in a vain attempt to keep the mask clear, but slid on the wet grass, almost ending up on my arse in the mud. A powerful arm caught me, yanking me sideways. I strained to see a Picasso representation of Bates yelling something unintelligible but I got the gist as he dragged me, slipping and sliding, down the narrow track to the beach.

Smirking Marine was already jogging back towards us. Bates slapped me on the shoulder, yelling something encouraging as I stumbled across the rocks, just reaching the sand when the turbines' pitch increased. Turning as the Merlin helicopter rose from the grassy plateau, I flicked a farewell salute, watching it bank away, climbing rapidly towards the lightening sky to clear the mountains inland. It receded into the distance, the gas mask damping the sound long before the dot disappeared over the snow-capped peaks.

I stood there, alone on the beach, listening to my amplified breathing, organising my thoughts. I felt claustrophobic, desperate to tear off the stifling plastic suit, to taste the cool salty air. I could have done, there was no danger here on the mainland – but they'd spent ages taping the hood of my hazmat suit to my gas mask, and I didn't fancy replacing it in these conditions.

I pulled a clump of tissue from my pocket and after rubbing the visor I could see my destination more clearly, though it didn't improve the view. Murky waves stretched seamlessly to the grey horizon. The island was nothing more than a dull, grass-covered rock, gravel spits jutting from beneath a hill at its nearest point, foaming rocks on the other side. Inhospitable, malevolent even.

A dark angular structure poked out from the long shadows behind the island, a huge prowling shark floating in the murky dawn. I'd had a look at HMS *Dauntless* when we'd overflown her; why the Royal Navy had sent a Type 45 Destroyer to this tiny island had puzzled locals and crew alike. They'd been told it was part of her sea trials following a refit, though anyone could see the current conditions wouldn't test her.

I trudged through the damp sand to where they'd left my gear; a toolbox and a kitbag of personal belongings. Gruinard Bay embraced the island, stretching round through windswept fields and twisted trees, dark mountains and darker sea. The tiny crofting settlement of Laide clung to the hillside further along the coast, a herd of white cottages dotted across the meadows sweeping up from the waves. The ruins of its tiny medieval chapel were just visible, reduced to a pile of rocks through the streaked visor. Somewhere below Laide was a jetty; it would have been far easier to meet a boat there, but the crossing was far shorter here, plus those in charge hadn't fancied landing a military chopper in the middle of the village. I didn't blame them; God forbid the press got hold of what was going on.

The drone of an outboard motor floated across the bay, I watched a speck grow into a small dinghy. As it buzzed closer I could see a figure hunched at the helm, a Navy boatman bent double to avoid the worst of the freezing spray.

As they approached I swung the heavy kitbag onto my back. Tape ripped somewhere near my ear as the hood pulled away from my gas mask, the breeze tickled my hair. I shuddered, patting the tape back down. Reality kicked in, dropping heavy through my intestines. Despite the frigid air, sweat tingled my fingertips inside the rubber gloves. Was I crazy for taking the job? *Wouldn't be the first time.* Low risk, they'd said. Easy cash. I don't know if they'd been lying or mistaken, either way I'm selectively naive when I need the money.

The outboard snorted as the helmsman beached it on the sand. He made no attempt to leave the dinghy, a moment of impasse as we regarded one another over the grumble of the motor. I could see now the guy wore overalls with a simple filter over his mouth; total overkill for his task, I thought, yet totally inadequate if things went tits up.

'Tyler?'

I nodded and picked up the toolbox, wading through the foam.

'Get a wriggle on,' he added.

I briefly considered tipping the bastard out, but instead threw my gear into the dinghy and grabbed the side, dragging it back into the sea, turning it round on a wave. Tiny leaks in my suit soaked my jeans, filling my boots. Like air conditioning, it took my temperature down several degrees – something I hadn't thought possible. When I was waist-deep, the helmsman twisted the throttle, which I took as a signal to haul myself in, facing him and the receding beach. Huddled in the grim trees, a lonely whitewashed cottage watched us leave, curtains twitching. A postcard-perfect scene ordinarily, but, armed with the knowledge of where I was headed, the dark pines and granite outcrops scowled down. I'd seen a graveyard up there as we'd landed, which suited my mood perfectly. I shivered. My feet were going numb, but if trench foot was the only thing I contracted in this godforsaken place I'd consider myself lucky.

The Navy man shouted above the outboard.

I lifted a hand to my ear. 'What?'

'I said, I drew the short straw,' he yelled. 'Taking you out.'

'Still longer than mine, mate.'

'So you're the technician?'

I glared... I'd been hoping for a quiet ride.

'Wouldn't catch me on that island,' he continued. 'Not a chance, pal.' He opened the throttle and the little boat skipped across the bay, smacking into waves, spraying sheets of freezing water across my back. 'I heard the doors on the shitty decon chambers are knackered? They're trapped inside?'

I didn't reply, still glaring.

'You Army, then?'

The guy wasn't going to shut up, so I shook my head. 'My company manufactured those shitty decontamination chambers.'

'Civvie?' he asked.

I looked over my shoulder. Closer now, I could see the island's features, though *features* is an exaggeration, there wasn't much to see. Resilient grass and scrubby heather, punctuated here and there by stunted trees bent crooked by decades of Atlantic gales.

'You've heard the stories?' The Navy man was grinning now behind his stupid mask. 'Vanishing tourists, weird lights at night. Fishermen that don't return. Watch yourself.'

'It's not the ghost stories that scare me.' I looked back at the bluffs and low cliffs. No circling gulls, and I knew that if he shut off the outboard there'd be no sound other than the slap of the waves.

'Messed up, didn't they?' he asked. 'Not having a technician on site. Typical Army.'

I shrugged. 'Wouldn't know, I'm just a civvie.'

In fact, I did know. There *was* already a technician on the island who could easily have fixed the doors on the decontamination chambers, were it not for the unfortunate fact that he was zipped up inside a body bag.

Chapter Two

Anthrax.

I've worked in some awful places, got myself into some terrible situations, but those seven letters instilled more terror than anything I'd come across in twenty years in the job. I watched the diseased mud close over my boots with each step, realised I was holding my breath even though I trusted the filters on my gas mask. My skin itched, I tried to scratch but the suit made it impossible.

The outboard buzzed away, leaving me alone again. I passed a low mossy wall being slowly consumed by grass; the crumbling remains of a sheep pen. Beyond it stood a dilapidated crofter's cottage, scant shelter for the spirits of its long-dead tenants. Mist danced through the ruins and skipped out across the overgrown pasture. Several times I caught my boots in rabbit holes, but saw no trace of their occupants; no flitting shapes, no droppings on the mud. The filth of decay, the lack of people or wildlife, the cloying silence; the island was dead.

I trudged upward through the mire, ankle-deep mud sucking at my boots, lurid yellow gorse clawing at my plastic-clad legs, each step forward accompanied by a backward slide as the land emphasised who was boss.

As I finally crested the hill, skin crawling, blood rushing in my ears, breath roaring in the gas mask, my temporary home materialised from the drizzle.

X-Base they'd called it in the briefing. Sounded like the title of a Hammer Horror film, but I knew it was a throwback to what happened here in the Forties. From where I was standing it was just a jumble of bright orange prefab cabins, with a huge radio antenna jabbing the sky. They looked like oversized portacabins, each marked with huge numbers in brilliant white.

Situated on a plateau near the south-western coast, this was one of two facilities on the island. The other, much smaller, base had been set up on a beach a kilometre to the north-east. The Navy boatman had been half right; whilst some of the scientific team were trapped inside X-Base, the rest had been outside on the island when the decontamination chamber had failed the previous day. Thankfully, that second camp had its own functioning decon chamber so they'd been able to cram in there, rather than spend a night outside. Beyond the base I could just about make out the dinghy pushing through the swell, carrying its soggy helmsman back to the anchored destroyer.

I stopped halfway down the hill for a breather. I could see now the huts were sitting on legs a couple of feet off the ground and were all connected like a train, a big semicircle like in the old westerns, wagons pulled in tight against attack. Main difference here was that the enemy was silent and invisible.

I counted ten orange huts, forming a U shape – three stretching away in a line, four in a row at the far end, another three running back towards me. Each connected to the next with a small plastic tunnel, all on those shiny stilts a few feet off the ground.

At one end of the complex an orange hut connected to a separate, smaller block, which I knew was the entrance. I ploughed through the bracken towards the odd one out, nothing fancy here, the end cabin was propped on breeze blocks instead of the other huts' integrated legs, with a few metal steps up to a door. No windows, corrugated steel walls, matt green paint job; to the untrained eye it looked like a shipping container. No coincidence, though I knew different thanks to a familiar logo adorning the door: Rafferty-Nath Decontamination Systems. Familiar because the RNDS logo was stitched onto the T-shirt beneath my suit.

The military love their acronyms; they'd christened this the HADU – Hazardous Agent Decontamination Unit. Contrary to appearances, the portable decontamination chamber was state-of-the-art, privately built to the MoD's demanding specs, though despite all that expense, somewhere here lay the failure that'd stranded the team, the reason I'd been sent to the island.

I knew what the problem with that 'shitty' decon-chamber door was – a keypad at the top of the steps wasn't responding. I reached up, gave it a tap just to be sure. Dead. Below the steps was a removable panel. I crouched, rummaged in my toolbox and pulled out a screwdriver. The tip slid across the steel on the first attempt. I tried again but my hands were trembling inside the gloves. One minute I was too hot, sweat matting my hair and running down my neck; the next, too cold, boots full of seawater soaking my jeans. A month's worth of beard itched beneath the gas mask. I was hungry, I was tired, I hadn't eaten or slept since the call-out last night.

I wiped the mask, steadied my breathing, focused. After several more attempts I managed to regain control of my hands and get the cover off, propping it next to the hut. A red light glowed, the main power was on, no problem there. I threw the switch off, the light faded out. I swung open the fuse box and the cause of the problem was immediately apparent. One of the fuses had gone.

I don't mean blown. I mean *gone*.

Chapter Three

There was no sign of the missing fuse, nothing to suggest why it had been removed. After replacing it, the door functioned perfectly.

I left the toolbox in a wooden shed not far from the entrance, a store for 'dirty' items that couldn't be brought safely inside the base. The kitbag joined me in the first room of the HADU, a small shower with nozzles sticking out from the walls and ceiling. CCTV cameras monitored safety protocol at all times. A red LED winked and I wondered who was watching me.

Someone sure as hell is.

The doors slid shut with a pressurised hiss. I hit a button on the wall, dropping the bag and holding my arms up as jets of bleach assaulted me from all angles, pelting my mask like hail on a windscreen and finding all the tiny holes in the tape around my suit. A few seconds' roaring deluge and the spray shut off automatically. I threw my mask on a bench and tore myself out of the protective suit, pushing it into a chute for incineration. After pulling out a sealed plastic sack, I stuffed the kitbag in too.

I poured the seawater out of the boots, dunked them in a tub of bleach, placed them upside down on a rack. Running a tap, I splashed clean water across my face to wash the stinking chlorine from my eyes. I blinked away tears to inspect a line of hooks running along the short wall, leaning closer to read the names scrawled on strips of tape above them.

Some had clothes hanging from them, most were empty. One stood out: A. KYLE

My predecessor didn't need his hook any more, so I dipped the gas mask in the bleach and hung it up.

The next room housed a couple of normal showers and toilet cubicles. I tore the plastic bag open, dumped out the contents, and pulled out a new rucksack, some clean clothes, dropping a pair of scuffed Adidas shelltops to the floor. The rest of the contents were stuffed into the rucksack. With another glance at the ever-present CCTV cameras, I lugged it into a cubicle, locked the door, sat down.

The bundle of clothes I'd just stuffed in the rucksack spilled out again as I rooted through, unrolling a sweater to reveal a brick-shaped parcel, tightly bound with bin bags and tape. Lifting the top off the cistern, I dropped it into the water then stuffed the clothes back in the bag, gave the toilet a flush, left the cubicle for the next shower.

I turned up the heat as high as I could take, practically scalding myself clean. As I scrubbed, my aching limbs stretched, pulling at old wounds that seemed to be causing me more aggro these days, rather than fading away. I was in decent shape for someone approaching forty but a far cry from the peak specimen I had been, deteriorating too quickly for my liking.

When I finally got out, the clock above the door said 8 a.m. I'd spent hours stewing in my own sweat and felt better for the shower: human again.

Almost, anyway. This was a last-minute rush job and I'd languished between assignments, allowing fitness levels to drop and my usual stubble to grow into a beard almost as wild as my hair. As I dressed, joints clicked, healed bones creaked, ligaments popped. Oil and dirt was ingrained in calloused hands, embedded in dents and scrapes, scars and burns glowing pale against suntan and tattoos. All reminders of similar jobs... of danger money. It'd felt like a good idea back in Yorkshire, and Christ knows I needed a decent payday, but here, on the island, I wondered what new scars would be added.

Pulling on my T-shirt, I stared at my reflection in the mirror, rubbing dull eyes. Deep furrows surrounded them, dark circles beneath. The jagged scar bisecting my right eyebrow itched like crazy.

Always does that at the start of a job.

I grabbed a hip flask from the rucksack, took a swig, washed down my concerns with visions of the cheque for all this over-time.

Time to see what lay on the other side of the door. Pocketing the flask, I breathed deeply, reaching for the entrance to the base. A skeletal figure pounced as soon as I pulled it open.

'Tyler, you made it.' Glancing at the small porthole in the door, I wondered how long I'd been under surveillance. He extended a hand. 'Dr Donald Clay, project head.'

Right. The handshake was limp, the cheap, ill-fitting suit incorrectly buttoned – guys like Clay are never really in charge. I guessed he was about to hit retirement based on the wispy hair and sunken features, but he could have been decades younger, a dull life in the civil service can do that to people.

'I must say, I don't approve of civilians on site –' his lip curled at *civilians*, despite the fact he wasn't Army either – 'but Porton thought differently. I see you fixed the HADU.'

'Nah, decontamination's still not working, but I came in anyway.'

He looked at his clammy hand in horror, the sarcasm initially lost on him. His eyes hardened as he found it.

'Civilians…' he muttered again, rubbing bony fingers into a tightly stretched scalp. 'Stay away from the labs and we won't have a problem. How much do you know about our operation?'

'I know it's top-secret.' I couldn't help it. 'Must be why you painted it bright orange?'

He shot me a dark look, the sentence hanging between us. Maybe I shouldn't have antagonised him so quickly, but I'm a firm believer in starting as you mean to go on.

'Okay, I don't know much, but I've signed the Act.' Official secrets were nothing new, it'd be interesting to see what he told me.

'I can't share much, but I'll give you the tour before you start.' He saw me glance at the winking light above the door, the CCTV camera watching us.

'What do you know about anthrax?' he asked.

'I skimmed the Wikipedia article on the way up.'

'Civilians,' he said again, condescendingly. 'We take decontamination seriously here. Everyone is monitored to ensure no one carries anything into the base, accidentally or... otherwise.' He pulled the door open. 'I trust you left your tools in the shed?'

'Believe it or not, we take decontamination seriously at Rafferty-Nath too.'

He glared again as he turned, he must have heard me mutter about decontamination being our whole fucking business, but chose to ignore me.

I followed him into the tunnel connecting the entrance chamber to the first hut. Thick opaque plastic wrapped over circular hoops, forming a short passageway – like being inside one of those polytunnels on my dad's allotment. Drizzle tapped softly as we walked through.

'Other than your HADU there are ten huts. You'll keep to the first six, the communal areas and bedrooms.'

'And the other four?'

'Are off limits. The base is transportable, with each hut connected either end by these link bridges. Allows the layout to be reconfigured to suit the terrain. Here they're arranged in a sort of a U shape, you may have noticed from the air. As you say, bright orange; obviously it wasn't designed for a Scottish island. Chaudhary can tell you all about it.'

'Chaudhary?'

Clay stepped off the walkway into the first hut. We emerged into a narrow corridor with a door on the left and another connecting bridge at the far end.

'Chaudhary is our facility specialist, I'll introduce you in a minute, but first you must meet PDBRG lead bacteriologist, Dr Marie Leroux.'

Yet more acronyms, this time Porton Down Biological Research Group, the department responsible for the survey and clean-up operation. He opened the door, coughed, and moved aside. I stuck my head into a lounge area; pop music blared from a radio on a shelf overflowing with stacks of board games and dog-eared paperbacks. The woman lying on a sofa peered out from behind a smartphone, did a double take, and jumped up. She pushed her hands through a springy afro then, clearly embarrassed by a stranger's presence, smoothed down a T-shirt several sizes too big and crumpled as if it'd been slept in.

Clay introduced me as the new technician, I walked over to shake hands. As we did a strange look flashed across her face, she stared so deeply into my eyes I had to blink and look away.

'All fixed?' she asked, with more than a hint of a French accent, reeling me back in.

'All fixed. How come you got to keep that?' I pointed at her phone.

'No SIM, I just use it to record data.'

Clay frowned at me.

'Don't panic,' I said with accompanying eye-roll. 'They took my smartphone off me, God knows why.'

I was looking forward to being phoneless for a while; no pinging texts hounding me for payments or telling me I was over my overdraft, as if anyone who's over their overdraft doesn't already know it.

'It's standard practice.' Clay continued to scowl.

Considering *I* was the one digging *him* out of a hole this seemed a pretty tepid reception. He'd made it obvious they didn't want outsiders here, much less a tech like me. Unfortunately for him, Rafferty-Nath owned the decon chambers; the military weren't qualified – or contractually allowed – to work on them. Clay knew there was nothing he could do about it, but the prick's ego wouldn't make it easy. I could see we were going to get along brilliantly.

'I've got to get moving,' said Marie. 'I have work to do.'

Clay turned to her. 'Hang on, Marie, I need you to take Mr Tyler to Camp Vollum.'

Marie looked less than impressed at the prospect of chaperoning a newbie, which suited me; I was hoping to have an unescorted wander. 'Only the bank calls me Mr, and I can find my own way around, cheers, Clay.'

'It's *Doctor* Clay, and you have work to do. We've got five colleagues at the other base suffering from cabin fever.'

'The other HADU's out too?'

'Not yet,' Clay snapped. 'They were stranded outside yesterday when *your* door here failed, and couldn't get back in. They spent the night up there.'

I was about to reply that I knew all this, but thankfully it clicked just in time: their disposable suits had been destroyed entering that base. 'So because they decontaminated to get in, they can't leave?'

'They don't have enough spare suits up there, which is where you come in. More importantly –' he lowered his voice and gestured between us, though clearly Marie could still hear – 'we have a disposal issue to deal with.'

'We?'

'Or rather, you. Take it to the beach for transportation to the ship.' I had no idea what he was talking about. Clay's eyes were cold. 'He was one of your lot, it's only right you handle it.'

Over his shoulder I could see Marie grimacing. My intestines tightened as the penny dropped; he was talking about my predecessor. About Andy Kyle's corpse.

Chapter Four

I'd assumed the body had been stored here, in the main base. I ran a finger across my eyebrow, pushed my knuckles into my eyes. 'You realise I haven't slept in thirty hours?'

Clay's expression said he did realise, and didn't give two shits. The good news was this could work to my advantage; an opportunity to get to grips with the geography of the island, so when I sighed, it was just for effect. 'Guess I'll have a kip later, then.'

'Good man.' He turned to Marie, still lingering in the doorway. 'You go and get ready. Is Chaudhary in the kitchen?'

She nodded, adding a lukewarm smile for me. 'See you in a sec.'

I watched her saunter up the corridor, maybe for a little too long as it provoked a grunt from Clay.

'Three women here,' he said, 'though all fairly competent.'

'Are any of the men?'

He grunted again, switched off the radio, and led me along the corridor. We followed in Marie's wake, floral perfume temporarily displacing the clinical bleach all the way through the tunnel into the next hut. Clay stopped and opened the door.

'The dining room – or as the captain calls it, the mess.'

'And I didn't bring my dinner jacket.'

This time he muttered something about millennials under his breath as I peered into a room with all the joys of a morgue, shiny furniture and wipe-down walls. I could imagine him at work, shirtsleeves rolled up, opening cadavers, stitching together his own monster.

Onward, another link bridge, another hut. I looked back, a clear view all the way through the cabins and link bridges to the entrance.

'Each cabin has a corridor running down one side,' Clay said, 'so we can cut through easily. You'll get used to the layout.'

The layout was fine, it was the inability to swing a cat that worried me. The walls were already contracting.

Clay opened the next door. The sounds and smells of frying food hit, making my mouth water. Clouds wafted around a shiny stainless steel galley that looked like it'd be more at home on the destroyer anchored in the channel.

'Dasharath Chaudhary's an American, but don't let that put you off,' Clay said under his breath. 'Chaudhary, this is our new technician, John Tyler.'

A giant of a man, as wide as he was tall, turned through the cloud of smoke. He beamed, wiping grease from a chubby hand on a T-shirt that barely covered his belly, then thrust it out.

'Call me Dash,' he drawled. 'We were wonderin' when you'd get here. Clay showin' you around?'

'Just the bits I'm allowed to see,' I said as I shook his hand, grateful for a friendly face. 'Door's fixed, you're free to leave.'

'Buddy, I'm used to Phoenix; it'd take a fire to get me outside in this weather.'

I glanced round the kitchen; similar size to mine at home and I don't live with nine other people. 'You don't get cabin fever?'

'Not when the alternative's that cold and wet.' Dash nodded towards the rain-streaked window. 'What's the matter, you don't like my ice station?'

'Ice station?' He didn't look old enough to own a house, let alone this base, though as I get older everyone else seems to get younger.

Clay clicked his tongue.

Dash grinned. 'Dr Clay's sore cos we're taking it back soon. This here's our latest Antarctic research outpost.'

16

That explained the bright orange paint job, the stilts, the unnecessary windows on what was supposed to be an airtight bioweapons lab. 'Dunno how to tell you this, mate, but have you checked a map?'

He was in his element, explaining that the facility had been developed by Miskatonic University for their research in the Antarctic mountains. They needed new outposts for their archaeology programme, and this was the concept they'd come up with. He waved his arms, wafting smoke around his head and sending Clay into a coughing fit. 'The modular construction allows it to be set out any which way, as many units as required. Labs, living quarters, kitchens…' He tipped the pan, a concoction of pancakes and mushrooms tumbling onto a plate, then poured half a bottle of maple syrup over the lot. Suddenly I wasn't hungry any more.

'Must be more money in archaeology than I thought,' I said, though I couldn't see Bradford Uni stretching to a facility like this.

'Department of Defense are behind it. The current administration has a bee in its bonnet about Antarctica, don't ask why. The scientists want the funding, big money comes from the military, so…'

'What Chaudhary has omitted is that we're doing him a favour,' Clay cut in. 'The Americans needed a hostile environment to test the airtight design…'

'And you Brits needed a rapid solution for your clean-up problem,' Dash countered, jabbing a fork at the pile, shovelling a mouthful. 'So a word in the right ear, some old-fashioned transatlantic cooperation, and we've turned our latest portable polar outpost into a research lab.'

'With a little help from us at RNDS.' I winked. 'How's it working out?'

'Designed to stay sealed in Antarctica, so a rainy Scottish island is no problem.'

'Which is more than can be said for your HADU.' Clay was scowling. 'Can we rely on it?'

I went straight for a lie. 'Looks like the fuses worked loose during transport.'

'We can't have any more setbacks at this late stage, we're pushed for time as it is.'

'Give the guy a break,' Dash mumbled through a mouthful. 'It's hardly his fault. Besides, he fixed it quick enough.'

'I didn't see any air tanks,' I said, swerving the subject. 'Where's the supply?' I was already thinking of ways my experienced predecessor could have been exposed to the lethal bacteria outside.

'No tanks. Air comes in through there.' Dash pointed his fork at a vent on the wall. 'The ducting runs through heaters under the floor. We've added filters for the nasties, obviously. Vents operate continuously, otherwise the air would get stale quicker than you'd think. Most of the water's filtered too, sucked straight from the sea. You know, down at the pole we bore a well, melt the ice under the base. Best drinking water on Earth…' He waved his fork, grease dripping onto the worktop.

Clay coughed again. 'You can educate Tyler on the technical aspects later, he has work to do. And do be sure to clean up after yourself this time.' He was already holding the door open.

'Hey, John!' Dash shouted. I stuck my head back round the kitchen door. 'You a poker player?' he asked.

Clay answered for me. 'No poker tonight, Mr Chaudhary; Gambetta's already on the warpath.'

I wondered about this comment as he ushered me away, along a corridor that was different to the others, longer, curving through ninety degrees. We turned the corner, into the base of the 'U' formation, Clay continuing the commentary.

'These are the dorms. Two rooms per hut, two beds per room. Stick to your own.' He pointed all the way to the far end of the base where a similar connecting tunnel curved away. 'Comms room towards the end, though you shouldn't need it. The following labs are off limits. In fact, you've probably no reason to go further than this; you're bunking in here with Demeter, our lead bacteriologist.'

I followed him into a small room, a bed on either side – both taken – a couple of bedside tables and a tiny wardrobe the only furnishings. The huts were split into two rooms here, half the size of the common areas. It wasn't even Ibis standard, comfort wasn't a priority. I've slept in worse places, but only ones with names like Kabul, Aleppo, Mosul and Lancashire. He pointed to the bed on the right. The covers were thrown back, strewn with clothes. Three words flashed through my mind.

Dead man's shoes.

'Did Kyle spend much time in here?'

He nodded. 'Kept to himself. Understood his position.'

My expression clearly said it all.

'Square peg in a round hole,' Clay continued. 'An odd-job man, no reason to get to know him. We're doing very important work here, you understand? Square pegs keep to themselves.' He smiled weakly, steepling his fingers.

'I'll try to remember that.'

The smile warmed up. 'Good. Well, I'll see where Marie has got to and then you can be off to collect the, erm… yes.'

'Where are my spare suits?'

He slid out a cardboard box from under the bed, spilling packs of disposable contamination suits in polythene bags. 'These are yours, one size fits all.' He walked to the door. 'Just make sure you check that other HADU. We don't want any more mishaps, do we?'

With that parting shot he left the room. I dropped my bag on the bed, creeping to the door before it closed, watching him make his way through the next two linked huts. He paused near the far end – which I guessed was the comms room he'd mentioned – and knocked on the door. I ducked back as he gave a nervous glance up and down the corridor before disappearing inside.

I let the door close and leaned against it, taking in the room. In contrast to mine, Demeter's bed was immaculate. A photo on the bedside table was sitting at such perfect right angles to the wall he must have used a set square. I crossed the room and leaned in close. A grainy image of a young woman on the bonnet of a Lada. Given the clothing and the fact it was in black and white it was probably an old picture of his wife, though you never can tell.

I opened the top drawer. Tissues, a couple of packs of repulsive-looking cigs, and a paperback. The cover was in Cyrillic but I recognised it as *The Master and Margarita* by Bulgakov, cause of one of many failed GCSEs. I flicked through the pages and tossed it on the bed.

Pulling the hip flask from my pocket, I took a long draw. I've worked in some fucked-up spots around the globe, but somehow being this close to home made it worse. The island was bad enough, but the suits, the gas masks, the canned air in the base: only an hour since landing, already I was choking. What the hell was it like for the crew of a real Antarctic station, stuck in here for months at a time? *I'd go stir-crazy.* To top it off there was a permanent smell, a taste even, of bleach in the base, like living in a hospital ward with OCD cleaners. I wasn't sure if it was drifting from the HADU, the clothing, or whether it'd already soaked its way up my nostrils and lodged there. Constantly switching between the rubber gas mask and fake chlorinated atmosphere would be torture, amazing how you take fresh air for granted.

I looked around the room again, eyes landing on the wall next to Kyle's bed. Near the floor was the grill that was obviously the air filtration. Dash had said it ran through pipes under the floors. Had something failed, bust a joint and split apart, sucked in contaminated air? The base was made to withstand the harshest environment on Earth, but this was a road-test; finding weaknesses and flaws was the whole point. I doubted it though; why would it have affected Kyle and no one else, not least Demeter, his roommate?

I'd been briefed, but was I out of my depth? The hip flask made a metallic sloshing sound as my hand trembled slightly. I flexed my fingers and tried to slow my breathing.

Heavy shoes pounded the corridor. I replaced the book, sliding the drawer shut just as the door opened. I pushed the flask down into my pocket, turning, but it wasn't Marie who strode in.

'Aha, our new tech has arrived!' His eyes crinkled as he forced a smile. 'Captain Greenbow, project head.'

He and Clay clearly disagreed on that point. *Noted.* I also noted the use of rank despite the civvie status they were keen to remind me of. *He'd probably bust a nut if I saluted him.* Looked the part too, polished brogued Oxfords, carefully pressed barrack trousers, spotless olive wool jersey. Tufts of grey sprouted from beneath the perfectly angled bright green beret of the Intelligence Corps; discretion would be wise around the captain.

I'm no fan of the Army. Not a dislike, not at all; more a mistrust, carefully cultivated over the years. And not of the people themselves, but the institution; I always seem to be on the outside, never in the clique. On these bases there's a hierarchy: Army, civilian contractors – camaraderie above all else always with me at the bottom. After a while it ends up making you feel either expendable or dependant, and I'm neither. I'd give Captain Greenbow the benefit of the doubt but I have a low tolerance and the counter was already ticking.

'Quite a view.' He nodded at the rain running down the window, the dull moorland and sea beyond.

'Hardly a picnic spot.'

The folds around his eyes wrinkled. 'When we're done – who knows? Perhaps this time they'll finish the job properly.' He picked up my rucksack, peering in. 'You're off to collect our unfortunate friend Mr Kyle?'

'Just suiting up.' I tore open a polythene bag, pulling out fresh overalls. 'Did you know him well?'

Greenbow inhaled deeply. 'Terrible thing. Tragic. Wouldn't happen to any of my team. Civilian, you see, not good with procedure…'

The benefit of the doubt evaporated. 'Square peg?'

He tried another smile but it didn't quite work. 'Speaking of which, you don't mind?' He held out my rucksack.

'Knock yourself out.'

He pulled out the clothes, spreading them around on the bed. The bag clinked with them removed. His eyebrow did a Roger Moore.

'Don't tell me it's a dry base?' I said.

He delved again, then, apparently satisfied, set the bag on the bed.

'Clay was worried you'd brought a phone.'

'I wouldn't get a signal anyway, my network's shit. You were saying, about Kyle?'

'Was I?' He looked amused. I didn't answer, gave him room to continue but instead he said simply, 'Baby blue,' nodding at the disposable suit I'd unravelled. Same colour as my car, though as a motorsports fan I'd have called it Gulf Blue. 'Everyone has their own supply of suits, makes identification outside easier. Techs, blue. Naturally, Army wear green. Yellow for the scientists.' He picked up the photograph on the bedside table. 'Our Russki has a sense of humour; his suits are red.'

'Like a game of fucking Cluedo,' I muttered.

'Except here, no murder has been committed.' I looked up into the same smile. The scar above my eye itched. 'Remember that,' he added.

The door opened and a gas mask poked around the frame, followed by a baggy yellow suit. Based on Greenbow's info I guessed it was Marie.

'My escort's here, Captain.'

He replaced the photograph on the bedside table, addressing Marie. 'Ensure you educate Mr Tyler on our procedures. We don't want another civilian casualty, do we?'

She nodded.

'And Tyler?' he added.

I turned.

'Perhaps leave the flask.'

I sought a response but there was none, so I simply made another mental note, pulling the door closed behind me.

As I did I saw Greenbow smile again – the hollow, mirthless smile of a wolf.

Chapter Five

Marie led the way, trooping off along the well-worn track. I hadn't been overly enthusiastic about rewrapping myself in the stifling suit and gas mask so soon but she seemed pretty comfortable. It made me wonder how long it took to get used to it.

Thankfully going back outside had been a far simpler process than coming in. After suiting up we'd pulled on our boots (mine still pissed wet through with bleach – seems I probably *was* destined to contract trench foot), then helped each other tape the top of them to the legs. Gloves next, then the gas mask and hood, all seams wrapped in reams of tape. Marie had shown me how the team dunked their gas masks in a bleach and formaldehyde solution and carried them inside – keeping their masks close as a safety precaution, in case the integrity of the base was suddenly breached. I'd have to remember that when I returned.

I looked up from a decomposing rabbit I'd been tapping with my boot to see Marie staring, waiting for me. I jumped back onto the muddy track, catching her up.

'You a local?' she asked.

'No. Reminds me of where I grew up, though. You're French?'

'Was it the name or the accent?' She laughed and started again up the track. 'Biarritz, which is very different to here.'

'I learnt to surf there.' I smiled briefly behind the respirator at the memory of a school friend's stag do, my brother nearly coughing up a lung after inhaling too much seawater, then a

24

few hours later nearly throwing up the other lung after drinking too much Izarra. 'Wouldn't have thought they had much call for biological weapons specialists down there?'

'Which is why I moved.' She laughed again. 'Have you done a job like this before?'

I shook my head. 'Not as full-on. Some military jobs, Europe, the Middle East, but it's mostly private stuff. Asbestos roofs, chemical factories, shit like that.'

'They told you much about the island?'

'Just the basics about X-Base, the secret anthrax tests back in the war—'

'X-Base! You English, so dramatic.' She threw her arms in the air. Bit rich, I thought, coming from a Frenchwoman. She carried on up the track, continuing to wave her arms around. 'And you did these things in your own back garden, as you say. You'd think Churchill would have chosen somewhere safer.'

'Like the French nuclear tests in the Pacific? Go ask the Polynesians and New Zealanders about safety.'

She shrugged. 'Not my line of work. I prefer working much smaller scale, opposite end of the spectrum.'

'Bacteria?'

'They're what make this island special.'

I turned to look back at the base, fading in and out of the mist and rain. 'And I'd assumed it was the weather.'

'It's such an interesting place.'

'Interesting's not the word I'd use.' We followed a row of rotten wooden stakes set into the ground, skirting an ancient bomb crater. I ran my glove over weathered wood and rusted wire. 'I thought the island was decontaminated years ago. Why the panic?'

'We thought so too. You know a lot about anthrax?'

Was everyone going to quiz me? I shook my head. 'I know it's nasty stuff.'

She tapped a filter of her gas mask. 'Not something you want to inhale. *Bacillus anthracis* is the bacteria which causes the disease anthrax. Named after the Greek word for coal.'

'From the black skin lesions?'

She nodded, sidestepping a pothole half hidden by moss and heather.

'But people should be okay if they've been vaccinated?' I asked.

'Not always effective, I'm afraid.'

'Well, I've not been vaccinated anyway. Not enough time, they reckoned. Expendable, more like.'

'You're lucky. Anthrax vaccines are the suspected cause of Gulf War Syndrome.'

'But it's treatable these days?'

'If caught early the fatality rate drops to about forty-five per cent.' She turned, cocking her head. 'Want to take the risk?'

She spoke nice and slow, like she was addressing a classroom of ten-year-olds, explaining anthrax isn't a virus, like flu; it can only be spread through the physical spores, but can be passed on to other animals if they eat the infected meat – including humans.

Apparently occupational exposure is the most common way of catching it – people's jobs bringing them into contact with the spores through handling infected animals. Grazing wild animals spread the spores to livestock. Infected farm animals pass it to humans, either through a break in the skin, causing the skin disease, or by them eating the meat, causing the intestinal version.

'Not too many sheep knocking around now, we should be okay.'

'It's not a joke. This island is unique, millions of active spores surround us right now. There've been cases where medieval graves have been dug up, causing outbreaks hundreds of years after the cattle were buried.'

'Outbreaks, even in this day and age?'

'The spores are resistant to most cleaning agents, they're incredibly difficult to destroy.'

Of course, I knew most of this – but I'd decided it was probably beneficial to play the dumb outsider, soak up as much

26

info as I could. 'So the previous clean-up job was a total waste of time, then?'

'We believe the rodent population created a reservoir of bacteria that survived the decontamination in the Eighties. Over decades these have evolved into hardier spores, tougher than the original strain. Rabbits were reintroduced years ago and seemed to be doing well. Then sheep started dropping dead.'

'What makes you think you guys will do any better this time around?'

She turned, her eyes creased up into a smile. 'They didn't have *me* here in the Eighties, I wasn't born.'

She accelerated on up the hill, holding an arm up against the savage wind buffeting us now we were nearing the top.

'I'm not a sheep,' I shouted, catching her up. 'I don't plan on eating the grass. Why the suits?'

'The most dangerous form of the disease is pul-mon-ary.' She pronounced the word carefully – I wasn't sure if it was condescension or an effect of English being her second language. 'Inhaled spores can cause anthrax disease of the respiratory system, and that's usually fatal.'

Her foot caught, she pitched forward. In the cumbersome gear it was difficult to reach her, before I could help she was on her hands and knees.

'Y'all right?' I asked, reaching down.

She swiped away my hand with a barrage of French swearing, pushing herself to her feet. 'Exactly the point. I'm now covered in hundreds of spores. *This* is why we wear the suits. If I'd hit my head and knocked off my mask I'd probably have inhaled them too – so like I said, I'd have a forty-five per cent chance of dying, very horribly, very soon.' She said it flippantly but I caught the fear lingering in the darkness of her eyes.

'So here's a question.' I started to brush her down, as if that would clean off the bacteria, but she pushed my hand away again. 'What's with the pound-shop outfits? If it's so dangerous, how come we're not dressed like on TV?'

'You're talking about a full hazmat suit?'

'Yeah. We're basically wearing wellies and washing-up gloves.'

She started walking again. 'American movies usually show level-A protection, which is vapour-resistant. We don't need that. This is a level-B, it's sufficient against bacteriological agents.'

'Tell that to Andy Kyle.'

She mumbled something, motioning for me to keep walking, through waving thistles and long grass, past a pile of boulders, an ancient stone cairn.

'I suppose MoD cost-cutting has nowt to do with it?'

'The camp is just over this ridge.'

It hunkered at the foot of the hill next to a narrow break in the cliffs, a miniature version of the base we'd left except with just three orange huts instead of ten. Once again entry was through another of our green HADU decon chambers, which was tacked to one end. Behind it the land rose again, broken off by the cliffs, which dominated this side of the island. Unlike at X-Base, here the sodden mud was criss-crossed by a yellow grid. A thicker pipe ran from the camp, down a steep break in the rocks to a small pebbly beach, then stretched out to a tiny raft in the sea.

'Pump, for the seawater,' Marie said simply.

'What's that?' I pointed at what looked like a large covered skip with a drainpipe sticking up from it.

'Incinerator. There were lots of dead animals lying around when we got here.'

'You missed one back there.'

Our suits flapped in the increasing wind, the sea rolled the tiny raft up and down. The distant mainland looked just as desolate as our island, and now we were out of sight of the destroyer the feeling of isolation was increased. The landscape alone didn't bother me – the bleakness wasn't too different to my native Yorkshire moors – but the strangling gas mask and tiny bacteria crawling over everything put a damper on it. Marie tramped down the path and I followed, watching my feet carefully now.

Faces pressed against the windows, monitoring our approach. An aerial whipped back and forth in the wind; Captain Greenbow or Dr Clay must have radioed ahead. No doubt these people were eager to get back to work.

With the exception, perhaps, of one of them; the person I needed to have a quiet word with.

The one who'd deliberately sabotaged that door.

Chapter Six

As we approached the second base there was one person whose face wasn't pressed against the drizzle-scored windows: Andy Kyle, whose face was instead pressed against the inside of a body bag. He was next on the to-do list – moving his body to the beach, where it would be collected and transported out to the ship.

'…so you'll have to stay out here, okay?'

Lost in thought, I wasn't sure how long Marie had been talking. She marched up the steps and turned.

'Stay outside?'

'Clay told me you don't have clearance.'

So Donald Clay was that kind of administrator – I'd suspected as much. I shook my head, passing her the bag of spare suits. 'How am I supposed to get Kyle's body?'

'I'll ask Hurley to bring it.'

It. Not bring *him.* She tapped in the code and stepped inside, attempting a nervous little wave as the door slid shut behind her.

Unlike back at the main base, these huts were arranged in a straight line. I knew two were research labs, the third a communal hut – no bedrooms here. I walked down one side of the HADU and along the first section, hugging the walls for no particular reason other than I don't particularly like questions or people. I ducked under the first hut's window, sliding alongside the tunnel connecting it to the second, all identical to those at X-Base. The last hut looked the same but for a thick wire drumming against the cladding as it snaked up to the roof. It connected with the swaying antenna mast, to which someone had tied a fluttering scrap of ribbon.

Then it was just the rocks, the narrow track down to the pebbles, and the dark sea. The pipe ran out to a raft, a simple platform of a few plastic barrels lashed together. I watched it bob on the swell, recalling the geography from the maps I'd studied back at Faslane a few hours earlier. Our island was sitting in a huge oval bay, and here at Camp Vollum we were up on the north-eastern coast. Staring back at me were the other islands in the bay, guarding the way out to the North Atlantic.

The Summer Isles, they call them – bloody joke as far as I could tell, but I wasn't laughing. I wondered if these were the same Summer Isles that featured in *The Wicker Man*, but the weather made it unlikely – apart from the odd human sacrifice, that had looked like a pretty cheery place to live. This, by comparison, was a cold, desolate family of squat brown islands and beyond them, the craggy headland at Polglass and Polbain lost in the mist. Vague pines faded in and out of view as the drizzle constantly remoulded the landscape.

HMS *Dauntless* was sitting out of sight round the north-western tip of our island, guarding the widest channel between the Opinan headland and Priest Island – guarding against what, no one knew. For the briefest of moments the clouds parted, sharing a watercolour of diamond-encrusted heather twinkling in the sunlight. As I was appreciating the sparkling waves and spectacular landscape, the drizzle started up again, the mist rolled back in, and the sea reverted to churning black.

On the other side of the huts I met a mass of pipes and a chunk of machinery. The large pipe coming in from the sea was coupled to one side, no prizes for guessing this was the pump Marie had pointed out. Scores of smaller yellow hosepipes spewed in all directions, connecting to long hoses trailing off across the grass, creating the grid pattern I'd seen from the hill.

I was about to inspect the hoses when the hairs on the back of my neck stood on end. I looked up at the huts, straight into

31

a face at the window. It backed away suddenly, melting behind the steamed-up glass, leaving me with a fleeting impression of dark hair, heavy brows, staring eyes. I watched the window for a while but it didn't reappear.

'Tyler?' A muffled shout from the far side, by the door. I jogged to the entrance. Rounding the corner, I almost ran into the back of someone.

Impossible to tell who was in the suit but I knew the voice belonged to the one person I trusted on the island. I tapped her on the shoulder.

Chapter Seven

She jumped a mile, spinning to face me, eyes wide. 'Jesus Christ!'

'Well, I am your saviour. I'm guessing you're Alice?'

'And you must be John Tyler. I'd expected someone... taller.'

'We need to have a chat.'

The door opened, another figure emerging.

'Not here,' she snapped.

The new person walked down the steps, tall as Dash but minus the girth, stretching Clay's 'one size fits all' comment about the suits as far as it could go, but from the way he walked I could tell it wasn't fat doing the stretching: he was built like a brick shithouse.

'John? Thanks for sortin' us out.' The accent told me this was the other American on the island, Evan Hurley. He flicked a hand back towards the door. 'You here for the stiff?'

'Evan, for fuck's sake!' Alice exclaimed.

He held his hands up. 'Sorry, he was your colleague, right? Gave us the creeps having him in there with us, but he's bagged and ready for ya.'

I looked past him, at the door I thought he'd propped open with a bin bag. I took a step up, seeing it was much bigger and thicker than a bin bag. It was a body bag.

Chapter Eight

Hurley turned out to be decent company, if a little liberal with the gallows humour.

Fortunately, given the atmosphere I'd encountered so far, I was happy to talk to a real human being. He was all set to help me carry the body down to the sea until I explained the tide was on the turn, the currents too strong for a launch from *Dauntless* to land here. Instead I explained I'd be meeting the boat down the sheltered southern end of the island, where I'd been deposited. He dug out a wheelbarrow from under the huts, helping me bundle in the morbid bag of Andy Kyle, ready for his last ever trip to the beach. After promising to show me how to lighten Dash of cash at poker later (apparently something of a hobby for Hurley), he and Alice plodded away to continue their work.

The wind had picked up, blowing across the Minch from the Atlantic, adding to my struggle around the low rise to the centre of the island. Being uninhabited, there were no paved paths, just endless mud. I swore aloud time and again as the wheelbarrow skidded, digging in. I cursed Kyle for dying, the cause for my being here, and I cursed him for being overweight, the cause for my aching arms and legs. But at that moment I mostly cursed austerity and the penny-pinching British government; if this was an American-run operation I'd have at least been given a Jeep.

Wellies, washing-up gloves, wheelbarrows. Welcome to twenty-first century Britain.

The skinny tyre bounced on a rock, jumping over the grassy summit. I followed a second behind, sighing with relief as I saw what was left of the island stretching out below. Even on this more sheltered coast the channel we'd crossed from the mainland was livelier, furious dark swells topped with white crests pummelling the rocks at the shoreline. Through the mist and drizzle I made out smoke drifting from the cottage near our helicopter landing site. They had a good fire going, probably cooking breakfast right now, which reminded me of my stomach and a place down past Glencoe that served great stovies.

At the bottom, the coarse grass gave way to rocks. I wheeled down, searching for a place to complete my task. I didn't know much about the tides or currents, there was a far better reason I'd brought the body here rather than the shore nearest the ship, or that cove near Camp Vollum.

Below was a short drop onto the pebble beach, where I'd be partly hidden from prying eyes. It meant having my back to the sea, but I'd take that risk – I'd heard the approaching outboard easily enough earlier. I instinctively looked at my wrist but my watch was still in my bag. Didn't make a difference, I had no idea when the message would get through, and when that launch from the ship would be coming to collect the body – I could be waiting hours or minutes. Best crack on; I had things to do before they arrived.

I pushed the wheelbarrow to the edge of the drop then tipped it on one side, dumping the bag onto the beach, wincing as Kyle's head bounced, though I don't think he minded.

I pulled the body up into a hollow the tide had washed out, undercutting the land. With another glance, satisfied I was alone, I set to work.

I've had no formal medical training. Some basic first aid and a few choice bits learned here and there but I'm certainly no pathologist. Still, I felt compelled to check Kyle's body for myself before consigning him to the relevant authorities. They'd determine the cause of death soon enough, but how long would that take?

When you're starting a new job, first thing to do is find out why the previous person left the position. My needs were immediate.

I unzipped the bag, pulling it apart. Kyle had died yesterday morning, less than twenty-four hours ago, but hadn't been kept refrigerated. Thankfully, sealed in the bag, any flies usually associated with a day-old corpse were absent, but I was glad to be wearing a respirator, a barrier between living and dead.

Still dressed in his protective suit, I could only see the skin of his face. All colour had leeched away, leaving it glowing white, highlighting the stubble on his cheeks. Flecks of vomit crusted his lips and spattered the hood of the suit. Someone had cleaned him up but it was clear he'd puked into his gas mask. I pulled the hood back, revealing the same light stubble on his head. My head itched. If I'd been clever I'd have shaved my hair off for this job, life in the suit would be more bearable.

Rigor mortis wouldn't wear off for a while, which made it easier to roll the body on one side, then up onto the other. The pale blue suit looked intact and unmarked. Marie had said he must have had an accident – I'd been puzzled but thought better of asking too many questions so soon after my arrival.

Anthrax isn't a lightning-fast killer. Marie had explained the differences between the types of death you could look forward to. I reconciled these with the pictures and notes I'd studied during the short briefing, ticking them off in my head.

Pulmonary – he breathed it in. Rare in humans, results in several days of flu-like symptoms followed by respiratory collapse. Usually fatal if it gets that far, but sometimes treatable if it's caught early. I wasn't an expert but this seemed to me an unlikely candidate for Kyle's death, for several reasons. Firstly, there would have been a gas mask between him and the anthrax, which would have had to come off for him to inhale the spores. If he'd knocked off his mask he'd have known about it – ergo, any resulting flu-like symptoms would have been picked up early and he'd have been eating Rice Krispies in a military hospital right now.

Gastrointestinal – rare, usually contracted through eating infected meat. Highly dangerous and a much quicker, surer killer, but again I discounted this for similar reasons. If he'd fallen, knocked his mask, and swallowed a gobful of dirt, he'd certainly have known about it and sought help.

That left the most common and likely form of the disease – cutaneous, which basically means infection through a cut. It's easier than you'd think – you may have a cut you don't even know you have, or a scratch you don't think is serious. So if Kyle was infected through an existing cut, he wouldn't have known when the infection happened – there'd have been no single 'event' or accident to trace it back to. He wouldn't have needed to fall over, knock off his mask, or eat some dodgy meat; the spores just drifted in on the breeze and fell upon a tiny innocuous break in his skin. To me this seemed by far the most likely explanation, only problem was that Kyle had been wrapped in a protective suit.

Had he skipped a vital part of the decontamination procedure? Skimped on the tape on his cuffs or boots? Regardless, if this was the method by which he'd contracted the disease, there'd be telltale signs. Those coal-black lesions on the skin at the site of infection.

I was about to unzip his suit when something caught my eye – the way the suit creased across his leg as I moved his body. Bending lower I could see it – a tiny slit in the suit just under the right knee. I stuck my finger in and pulled. The flimsy material ripped easily, exposing joggers beneath, with the same slit. Again I hooked a finger through and pulled. A line ran across Kyle's pale flesh, a deep slice just below his kneecap. The wound was clean but darker than the surrounding skin, puckered where the flesh had shrunk away. No black lesions, nothing to suggest it was out of the ordinary.

Actually, that's bollocks – it was definitely out of the ordinary. What I mean is nothing suggested the wound had been infected with anthrax.

It *was* in a likely accident location. I could picture Kyle stumbling, hitting the ground with his knees, catching on something – a branch, a thorn, even a sharp rock. Or falling into the edge of a piece of machinery?

I took some time to remove the rest of his clothes as best I could with his stiff limbs. The skin down the back of his ribs and legs was darker. Hypostasis – the blood had pooled in the lowest points as he'd lain, either on the ground or in the huts. I prodded and pressed, inspecting as best I could. Aside from a Saltire tattoo on his shoulder and some chewed nails, I couldn't find any other marks on his body.

There was no point re-dressing him. The ship's doctor would assume he'd been partly undressed prior to sealing him in, so I just bundled the clothes by his feet and zipped the bag back up.

I thought of the scenarios by which Kyle could have acquired the cut, but discounted them all. The cut *must* have happened yesterday – the suit would have been new on when he'd left the base after breakfast, and the cuts appeared in the same place on the suit, the trousers, and the skin beneath. Still, it was definitely out of the ordinary. I did say I'm no pathologist – but I do know even small cuts bleed.

Unless they happen a fair while after death.

There'd been no bloodstains on his skin or the inside of the joggers. I stood and stared at the body bag, thought about the mounting questions, the lack of answers.

A flash in the corner of my eye, a glint of light on the hillside above, interrupted my thoughts. I tried to focus through the streaked gas mask but the movement was gone. Behind me, over the mainland, a lighter patch of sky proved the sun still existed somewhere above the clouds. I looked at the hill again, wondering what would reflect that sunlight, out amongst the dreary grass and heather.

All I could think of was the eyepiece of a gas mask. Someone had been watching me.

Chapter Nine

I was cold, I was hungry, I hadn't slept in over thirty hours –
this was all pushed into the attic of my mind as I walked back
to base.

That the cut had appeared sometime after death was beyond
doubt. But was it an accident – the result of rough handling of
the body – or something else? There was no corresponding hole
in the body bag (I'd checked) so it's not like it had happened
when I'd bundled him around. If deliberate, then why?

As I started down the slope towards the base those thoughts
in turn were pushed out by a pale blue figure making their
way to the shed. Yet again Clay's 'one size fits all' comment
was stretching it in more ways than one, but this could only be
Dash. I didn't fancy getting roped into anything, so I slowed,
hoping he'd disappear. Someone else slinked along the side of
the base. Dash hadn't seen them, he was still waddling towards
the tool shed as they jogged up behind. I was closer now, could
see the newcomer moved like a man. Yellow suit. Too short
for Hurley, too tall to be Clay. I thought back to Captain
Greenbow's Cluedo game, process of elimination told me this
was Gambetta, the Frenchman I hadn't yet met.

He must have shouted something, as Dash stopped to turn.
Gambetta was angry, gesticulating wildly, stabbing a finger at
Dash. I picked up the pace. Dash's reply clearly wasn't to his
liking as Gambetta responded by shoving him roughly. His
weight got the better of him and he splatted heavily in the mud,
the Frenchman turning to walk back round the side of the base

before he hit the ground. As Dash got to his feet, brushing himself down, he spotted me running over.

'You okay?'

He shrugged. 'It's nothing, you know what these Eurotrash are like. Emotional.'

'Surely we've got enough on without you two—'

'Don't worry, I've got plans for him. You're new, John, you'll figure everyone out. Hey, mind giving me a hand? Gotta run some checks on the generator.'

I shook my head. 'I'm heading back inside.'

'Well, if you're at a loose end later...'

I flicked a wave, heading back towards the steps, but after checking Dash had disappeared I instead ducked round the side of the huts, following in the direction Gambetta had taken.

I found him round the back, leaning against the second hut. He'd pushed his gas mask up his forehead and was sparking up a cigarette, gazing at the churning sea. It'd been ages since I'd quit, but the island was frying my nerves so much I could have joined him.

I was about to speak when he turned and beat me to it. He took a drag and spat smoke in my direction, eyes narrowing. 'You are John Tyler, the new technician?'

I didn't ask who he was or give him the pleasure of letting on I already knew. 'Taking a risk, aren't you?'

'Leave science to the scientists,' he replied, balancing his Zippo next to a pack of cigs on the windowsill.

My heart was hammering, I clenched my fists to stop them shaking and took a step closer. 'I don't pay my taxes for the NHS to treat wankers who can't wear a mask.'

'You think the anthrax spores will jump up off the ground? You're as retarded as they said.' He flicked the cigarette at my mask, showers of tiny sparks and ash exploding across the visor, then reached up to pocket the lighter and cigs, leaning back against the hut, one leg propped up on the wall behind him.

My right eye twitched, fuzziness creeping in at the edges of my vision. I swept out with my right foot, hooking it behind his ankle. Before he knew what was happening he was pitched sideways onto the ground.

He rolled away, hastily pulling his mask down, glaring at me as he crawled backwards through the mud. '*Batarde!*' he shouted. 'I could have got it on my face!'

I took a step forward, drawing my leg back, ready to smash my boot through his ribs, stopping myself just in time. 'You touch Dash again and I'll make sure you do.'

He got to his feet, eyes daggers. 'Technician is a dangerous job here.'

He almost added something else but thought better of it, glaring, chest heaving, fists clenched at his sides. Finally he turned, stamping away towards the bluffs.

Clay and Greenbow had been bad enough, but here was a new contender for biggest arsehole on the island. But did that justify my reaction? I watched him go, inhaled deeply, tried to feel my heartbeat, willing it to slow down, using the techniques they'd taught me. When he'd disappeared I turned and walked slowly in the opposite direction, back to the entrance.

As I went through the decontamination ritual I tried to calm myself, putting Gambetta out of mind and instead thinking about my hasty inspection of Andy Kyle's body, about who could have been watching me. Who else had been outside? I'd no idea where Alice and Hurley had gone. I couldn't imagine Dash getting back in time without having a heart attack. Unfortunately my thoughts circled back to Gambetta as I decided he was the most likely candidate.

The late-night drive up to the naval base, the dawn briefing, the hellish helicopter flight, the adrenaline comedown – I was dead on my feet. It all caught up with me at once, I took a moment to rest on the bench in the HADU, almost dozing off right there.

The lounge was closer than my room and mercifully empty. I ignored the curling magazines and made straight for the radio. I flicked it on, stretched out on one of the sofas, closed my eyes. Kate Bush wailed, appropriately about wild windy moors. The gusts attacked the windows with increased ferocity, hurling rain and sticks against the glass like handfuls of pebbles, despite the triple glazing. I shuffled and pulled the hip flask out of my pocket, the sofa pulling me in deeper. Wasn't long before I was imagining it was ghosts banging at the window.

Chapter Ten

'You've been drinking?'

With great effort I hauled up one eyelid to see a silhouette filling the open doorway, a bulky mass with a gas mask propped on its head. Her hair was longer, no makeup, a few years older, but undoubtedly the same woman from the picture I'd studied in the dossier.

'I'm off duty, Alice.'

'It's not even lunchtime, John. You wanted to talk?' She rustled into the room, squeezing herself into a chair.

'Sun's over the yardarm somewhere.' I swung my feet off the sofa and rubbed my eyes. 'Besides, I would have thought alcohol's pretty much a requirement in this shithole.' I picked up my flask from the floor, took a swig.

Revulsion creased her face. 'How long have you been hiding in here?'

There was a scuffle outside the door. I held a finger to my lips, motioned for her to stay where she was, crept to the door, grabbed the handle. Alice tensed. I pulled it open. Clay nearly fell into the room. He stumbled, regaining his footing.

'What the bloody hell are you doing?' he screamed.

'Do you usually hang around outside doors?'

'That's not the— ah, there it is!' He skulked across the room, snatching up a pen from the sideboard. 'And why aren't you completing the grid sampling, Alice?' Frowning at her, he switched off the radio and stormed from the room.

I raised my eyebrows at Alice.

'He's all bark.'

'Where can we go where we won't be disturbed?'

'Nowhere at the moment,' she snapped. 'I'm late and I don't want to raise suspicions.'

I poked my head out of the door. Clay walked through the tunnel towards the first bedroom hut, glancing behind him every few steps.

'Don't go too far,' I said.

Alice nodded, placing a gloved hand on my shoulder as she squeezed past me, heading back outside.

I bent to retrieve my hip flask despite the protests from my knees, and went the other way, to my room. The dishevelled bed, whose last occupant was lying on the beach not far away, beckoned. I climbed in without even peeling off my clothes.

Chapter Eleven

My eyes snapped open but the room was dark. Another thud. I lay still, ears stretched, muscles tensed, heart pounding. Crazed half-sleep thoughts, the hangover of a nightmare flashing through my mind as I clicked into defence mode, instantly I was back in that burning 4x4, eyes stinging, ears ringing.

Something in the room fell over, accompanied by a bout of muttered cursing I didn't understand. Still, swearing sounds like swearing in any language, my heart slowed, panic subsiding as I remembered where I was. The room wasn't completely dark – the blinds were closed, but my eyes had adjusted.

'Who are you?' A thick accent, which my sleep-fogged brain took a second to identify.

It was Russian – this was my roommate, Demeter. The blinds flicked open, revealing a mess of grey hair receding from an enormous forehead so wrinkled it seemed to be melting from his skull. His bed creaked as he sat back down, stroking a heavy moustache, which may have been Stalinesque at one time but had since evolved to cover his mouth. *How the hell does he get a decent seal on his gas mask with all that hair sticking out everywhere?*

I slid my feet onto the floor and stuck my hand out. 'I'm John.'

He eyed it suspiciously, I realised it was still trembling. I clenched a fist, pushing it into the mattress, taking a deep breath.

'I thought you were ghost,' he said from somewhere beneath the moustache. 'This is Andrei's bed.'

'And I thought you were a scientist.'

He laughed but there was no cheer in it. 'This island... There are things out there, in the mist. Andrei knew. They watched him, they took him. Now I feel their eyes on me.'

'I think you're pretty safe in here.'

'A locked door is no protection from the Reaper.' This all seemed utterly bizarre coming from supposedly one of the foremost researchers here, I wondered if my earlier thoughts about going stir-crazy in here were true. He looked down at his feet for a while, inhaling deeply, then looked up, eyes shining. 'I am old, superstitions grow the closer we get to death. John Tyler, you are Andrei's replacement, yes?'

I nodded, realising what else was strange about him; he was wearing a bright red NBC suit. 'Did you not decontaminate?'

'I changed, I go back outside soon. I wear all the time or we will never be finished by next week. I work, I work. I work enough for all of these *duraks*.'

'What time is it?' I yawned, grabbed my watch from the bedside table. Don't bring anything of value, they'd said, but my scuffed Bremont Supermarine goes everywhere with me. Only midday – I felt jet-lagged, the darkness had been entirely a product of the weather and the blinds.

Demeter was watching me. 'When I was your age I didn't need watch. My office in Moscow was so close to Spassky Tower, I could tell time by chimes.' He smiled at the memory, I know from working with Russians this was akin to having a corner penthouse. 'That was before I moved to Biopreparat at Sverdlovsk, and ha!' He threw his hands in the air.

'You worked at Sverdlovsk? You're not to blame for the accident, I presume?'

'Pah. More *duraks*.'

I'd read about the incident, a biological Chernobyl, they'd called it. The city has been renamed back to its original title of Yekaterinburg, but during the Soviet era it was named for the country's party leader, Yakov Sverdlovsk. An industrial city north of the border with Kazakhstan, the fourth-largest city in Russia, and one of the country's first industrial centres. Infamous for a few reasons.

It's where Tsar Nicholas II and his family were transferred to in 1918 by the revolutionary government, held prisoner in the Ipatiev House. Three months later they were taken into the cellar and shot by a hastily assembled execution squad, and when that failed, the children were stabbed with bayonets.

During the Second World War, owing to the city's location and relative difficulty to attack, major industrial complexes and technical institutions had moved to the city wholesale. Made sense Demeter had worked there.

In May 1960 a CIA U-2 spy plane had departed its base in Peshawar, Pakistan, to photograph the military installations. Interestingly, the first U-2 flights over Russia had been flown by British RAF pilots, to give Eisenhower deniability in the event that a plane was shot down – thus avoiding potential nuclear war. The Soviet Union had been aware of the encroaching flights since the mid-Fifties, but the U-2 had flown too high for the missiles of the time, and Eisenhower had felt safe enough to switch to American pilots.

On this occasion a Russian MiG-19 scrambled to intercept the plane, but couldn't reach the required altitude, so a newly manufactured – and therefore unarmed – SU-9 was ordered to ram the spy plane in mid-air. It missed, thanks to the huge difference in speed. As the U-2 was over Sverdlovsk it was hit by an S-75 Dvina surface-to-air missile. (Interesting postscript: eight anti-aircraft missiles were launched that day – and one of them hit the intercepting MiG-19, whose unfortunate pilot was killed.)

The American pilot, Gary Powers, was unable to activate the plane's self-destruct system prior to ejecting, and the aircraft was captured almost intact near the city. The ensuing political scandal had set ongoing talks between Khrushchev and Eisenhower back considerably.

So it was to this infamous city and those military factories that Demeter had been sent to work for the motherland, and it was a story linked to his work I'd come across on the internet the previous night.

Shortly after the Second World War, the Soviet Union set up a biological research facility in Sverdlovsk under the mysterious moniker 'Military Compound 19', using information captured from the Japanese germ warfare programme in Manchuria. By the Seventies, Compound 19 was churning out enormous amounts of 'Anthrax 836', the most virulent strain of anthrax in the Soviet arsenal, destined to grace the warheads of ICBMs pointed at Western cities. Key to the warheads' lethality is the form the anthrax takes; it's deadly however it arrives, but in order to be delivered most effectively to a population it's best used in aerosol form, dried to a fine powder.

One Friday afternoon in March 1979 a technician performing maintenance removed a filter. It'd been covering an exhaust vent over the driers. He dutifully left a note for his supervisor, but the supervisor must have had a case of Friday-afternoon syndrome, as he made no entry in the logbook. When he went off shift the next supervisor didn't notice anything untoward, so turned the machines back on.

No one knows how many people were infected, how many died in the following days. The authorities blamed tainted meat, but no one was fooled. It was a few hours before the filter was found and replaced; a few hours of pumping the most virulent strain of anthrax the Soviets had, straight into the atmosphere.

It's just a damn good job the wind had been blowing away from the city that day.

There've been a ton of incidents like this, it was far from the last. And when the wind's blowing the wrong way, like Chernobyl, we all suffer the consequences – even here in remotest Scotland.

Not that I think lives over here are worth any more than Russian lives; far from it. People are people, I don't go in for the political stuff. But that just makes it worse when those who do cause issues for the rest of us.

'Do you miss it? Russia, I mean.'

'Sometimes... I miss weather. I miss cold, real cold. I miss fishing on Iset with Gregori. My son is older than you now, he works for mining company in Verkhnyaya Pyshma. I used to take him to visit Ipatiev House, do you know of it? Yes, you know it. You are taught about butchery of Romanovs at hands of Bolsheviks. You learn nothing of butchery of Gapon's workers, or demonstrators of 1905. *Nicholas the Bloody*. Bah, it matters not, house was demolished long ago. If I return, I will still never see it again. They even changed name of city.'

He gazed out of the window. The drizzle had upgraded to heavy rain, obscuring the glass.

'But yes, I long to see Gregori.' He grabbed a carton of cigs from his drawer and stood with a squeak of gratitude from the bed. 'It is nice to meet you, John Tyler. You be careful outside, yes?'

It sounded like friendly advice, but the way everyone was acting it could have been taken as a threat. I mumbled the same in return as he pulled his gas mask on, tightened the straps, and left the room without a backward glance.

Rather than get my head back down I decided to sort my gear. Pulling the cardboard box of disposable suits from under the bed, I tipped them onto the floor, kicking them back under. I put the empty box next to the bedside table, opened the drawer, and began packing Andy Kyle's possessions into it. A couple of paperbacks, Alistair MacLean and something by Dickson Carr. Some chuddy, a box of matches. Three packs of cigarettes, which I almost kept but thought better of it and tossed them, together with two crushed-up empties, into the box. I praised the gods when I found a chipped enamelled camping mug and a small tin of Yorkshire Tea, and left those in the drawer. Last was a dog-eared old map of the area that I figured could come in handy, so dropped that back in the drawer too.

His wardrobe held nothing interesting, mostly sports attire with a few RNDS polos like mine thrown in. I folded and packed his clothes on top of the cardboard box, sliding it across to the door. Andy Kyle's worldly possessions – those on the island, at least – took up a small box in the corner of a small room.

If I died here my possessions would take up even less space, I wasn't planning on a long stay. After dropping my clothes in the bottom of the wardrobe I extracted a few other things from my rucksack. A pair of optimistic aviators, vintage Ray-Bans which had survived jobs from Iran to Sierra Leone but were now bent, possibly thanks to careless packing but more likely Greenbow's search. They were fairly pointless here anyway, but you never know. A washbag that even included a bottle of Acqua di Parma – again, fairly pointless here, but again, you never know. A Lenser torch, the little one with the warning sticker that says it can blind you – probably the second most useful thing I'd brought. Finally out came two bottles of blended Scotch, supermarket own-brand vintage, to be stood on the floor by the bed.

Time for a brew, kick-start the grey cells before I go find Alice. The mug looked clean enough so I tipped some tea into it, replaced the tin in the drawer, and headed for the kitchen. I had a thought and stopped outside my door, placing the mug on the floor. In my wallet was a crumpled petrol receipt from my fill-up at Tebay services. I smoothed it, folded it in two, slipped it under the door. Giving the paper a couple of seconds to unfold, I opened the door, peering round. The paper had been pushed across the floor by the door. I repeated the process then picked up the mug. Less cliché than the old hair-across-the-door trick, but just as effective. Demeter wouldn't be back for a while; if anyone went in my room, I'd know about it.

Spices and the crash of utensils enveloped me as soon as I stepped into the kitchen, far more welcoming than Dash's heart attack on a plate. Marie turned from the hob, pulled her baggy T-shirt down and leaned against the counter.

'You weren't out long,' I said.

'And you're just in time for lunch,' she said, pointing to a pan. 'You like *thiéboudiènne*?'

'I'm only after a brew. A cuppa. Don't look at me like that.' I held up my mug. 'Tea!'

'Ah!' She glided across to click the kettle on then cocked her head. 'What are those?' She was pointing at my arm, at the series of small tattoos that ran from my left wrist to disappear under the sleeve of my T-shirt, tiny black squiggled outlines.

'You seen *Saving Private Ryan*?'

She nodded.

'Remember that guy who collects jars of sand, scoops one up from every beach he lands on?'

She tilted her head and looked again. 'That's France.' She beckoned me over, took my arm, placed a finger just under my elbow. 'Here's Biarritz.'

Her eyes sparkled. 'Oh! They're all countries.'

I pulled my arm away and shook my head. 'They're jobs.'

Her mouth creased up. 'Looks like you've worked in a lot of places. Good memories, eh?'

'Not always. Speaking of which, can I ask you summat?'

She took a pack of tomatoes from the fridge. 'If it's about Captain Greenbow, yes, I believe he does iron his underwear.' Her eyes shone again. 'Don't let him get to you.'

'I suppose he was like this with Kyle?'

She smiled and nodded. 'You're not special, he's the same with everyone, as if it's our fault the project is overrunning. The only person here with a rank, and doesn't he love to use it.'

A woman after my own heart. 'I had a question about procedures, actually.' I slid the mug across the counter and opened a cupboard, scanning for biscuits or chocolate; I needed the sugar. 'After what you were telling me about anthrax I'm worried about decontamination. How can I be sure I'm clean?'

'I thought RNDS were the decontamination experts?'

I shrugged. 'I'm just a technician, machines are machines.'

She put the tomatoes aside and popped up to sit on the counter. 'Well, you can either kill the spores or physically remove them. The best way is like we do in the HADU, a mixture of formaldehyde and bleach, which does both.'

'What if I don't have any to hand?' In the second cupboard I spied the cans, and wondered whether I could be bothered to cook. 'Any more pans?' I asked.

'In here.' She tapped a heel on the cupboard next to her. 'It's the spores that are dangerous. You *can* just wash them off with soap and water – but the problem is making sure you're properly clean. Under your nails, in your hair, they're microscopic, so a shower doesn't cut it.' She saw the can in my hand and turned up her nose. 'Mushy peas are disgusting at best, and those are probably out of date.'

'This is Yorkshire caviar! And all of your five-a-day.' I put them down and continued scanning the cupboards, pulling open a pack of custard creams and tipping a few onto the counter.

'Ingrid's going to kill you.'

I looked at the packet in my hand. 'Not if you tell her Clay ate them. Anyway, anthrax; what about sterilising. Boiling, or fire?'

Gambetta smoking outside and those packs of fags in Kyle's drawer had started me down a path; inhalation was a great way to introduce anthrax into the system. A little of the right dried-up dirt sprinkled into a cig – that had to be plausible? I crammed a custard cream into my mouth.

'Anthrax is extremely resistant to heat. It's the reason it was developed as a weapon – explosives don't kill it, they just spread it around. Works well in bombs. It can be destroyed but only with very high, prolonged heat, like in our incinerator – the kind of heat that would kill you long before the anthrax.'

My mind automatically put that information in a folder somewhere – doctored cigarettes *were* a possibility.

The door bounced off its stops, we both jumped. A ruffled Greenbow filled the doorway, shiny-faced and gasping for breath.

'Tyler, where the hell have you been?'

I frowned, swallowing the last bits of biscuit. 'Bed.'

'You were given a job to do.'

'Thanks to you lot I haven't slept,' I replied. 'I did the job, then got my head down.'

In the corner of my eye Marie slid off the counter and turned away.

'The job was to deliver the body to the boat.'

'It's waiting on the beach.'

'Well I've had the bloody watch officer from the *Dauntless* on the radio. He's had the bloody motor launch on *his* radio, and they're telling me it's not there.'

'Then the idiots have got the wrong beach.'

Marie was slicing tomatoes now, pretending not to be interested. I looked past her, to the window. We were sheltered on this side of the base but still the rain was pretty much horizontal – not that it made much of a difference physically, thanks to the protective suits, but it wasn't good for the soul.

'Tell them I'll be there in half an hour.'

'Fifteen minutes, you can run all the bloody way.'

I'm English, I can't be seen to be running anywhere, but no point arguing, and he marched away before I could anyway. I looked back at Marie and blew out my cheeks. She gave me one of those straight-mouthed *I'd hate to be you* kinda smiles.

'See you later then,' I said, sweeping up the biscuits and stuffing another into my mouth.

'Good luck.' She followed it up with another tight-lipped smile.

I hung back from Greenbow as I headed to my room to grab a new plastic suit. Pausing outside my door, I waited until he'd disappeared into a room a few huts along then dropped to my knees but I couldn't see the paper I'd pushed under. I opened

53

the door slowly, just wide enough to squeeze my head through, and my heartbeat picked up. The wad of paper was sitting on the floor another few inches from the door. In the last five minutes or so, someone had been in my room. Greenbow, looking for me, or someone else?

Chapter Twelve

The dinghy was pulled up on the spit next to the upturned wheelbarrow. A fed-up looking guy was sitting on the inflatable sidewall, gazing out through the spray off the sea. This time he was wearing a full NBC suit complete with a more suitable gas mask.

He turned as he heard me jump down onto the pebbles. 'Not only did you make me come all the way round the island, but you've made me wait half an hour in the freezing cold.'

I pointed to the scooped-out hollow fringed with over-hanging grass. 'I left him here.'

'Well I haven't moved the bloody thing, have I?' He trudged across the beach. 'Fucking civvies.'

The same jobsworth who'd brought me across this morning. 'Your luck with straws hasn't improved.'

'What?'

'Never mind. You see owt when you arrived?'

'Fuck-all.'

'But you knew where to land?'

'Yeah, they said, fuck knows why you couldn't have taken him to the northern shore like you were told. Saw this.' He patted the wheelbarrow. 'Even checked under the bloody thing.'

'You see anyone up there?' I gestured behind me.

He looked at the hillside and shook his head. 'You were supposed to be waiting.'

'Why, do corpses usually wander off on their own here?' I looked about the beach. 'Tide must have taken it.'

He paced round the beach, turned to the sea, hand to his mask, staring as if the body bag was about to materialise.

'You may as well get off,' I said.

He walked back to the dinghy, grabbed a radio handset, speaking rapidly. It crackled, a heated discussion kicking off as he waved his arms furiously. I only caught a couple of words but someone on the other end was unhappy. He stamped back and forth on the pebbles then kicked the side of the dinghy, throwing the radio onto the bench and climbing in after it.

'You're in the shit, pal. Gimme a push.'

I thought again about tipping the bastard into the sea, or worse, holding him under until it washed off his stupid grin. I dragged the dinghy off the pebbles, he pulled on the starter.

'Come and see us again.' I waved.

He flicked a finger and revved the outboard, turning the little boat away from the beach. I watched him shrink against the already darkening sky. The seas were growing, waves colliding, spewing foam into the sky. When the boat finally disappeared around the rocks I inspected the depression where I'd left the body, spending a good ten minutes kneeling on the pebbles, pacing the surf line, studying the flattened grass above. Shadows lengthened as the sun began its early afternoon descent. By then I'd confirmed what I already knew.

The tide didn't touch this spot, someone had deliberately moved the body. Probably the same person who'd been watching me. No body, no post-mortem, no evidence.

Chapter Thirteen

As I reached the top of the ridge, X-Base spread below, I could see Gambetta having another crafty cig. I wondered whether it was best to try to make amends in the hope of gaining some info, or avoiding him altogether. Partway down the hill I realised it wasn't Gambetta. Or rather, it could well have been – they were wearing a yellow suit – but whoever it was, they weren't having a crafty cig.

The figure peered through the window into the base, then knelt to retrieve something from the ground. They could have been doing anything, it wouldn't have been suspicious were it not for the fact that, whatever they were doing, they were doing it right under the first window of the dorm blocks.

Which was my window.

I quickly backtracked over the hill, crouching close to the ground. The figure stood, and with another furtive glance around, set off along the track.

I skirted the hillside, one eye on the figure and one on the ground, avoiding potholes and rusty wire trailing across the bracken. I was careful to stay low, slowly rising now and then to watch.

We crossed the island in this way and after ten minutes or so we were approaching Camp Vollum, with its sparse cover. I threw myself on the ground, shuffling backwards, working myself into the undergrowth as far as I could. In the distance, high up on the cliffs beyond the base, I could see a couple of colourful blobs wandering back and forth. Below them the mystery figure crouched, adjusted his or her course, making their way to the incinerator. They threw something in, slammed the lid shut, and knelt at the base. After standing hands on hips for a while they walked to the other side of the incinerator, waited another thirty seconds, then hit a button. A jet of flame shot out of the chimney, dying down, smoke rolling after it into the dirty sky.

Their back was to me, attention fixed on the incinerator. I circled behind the huts, keeping them between us, and took off down the hill at a sprint. Seconds later I hit the wall of the base, panting loud into the rubber mouthpiece, back pressed in hard next to the window. I was sure no one had seen me. I slowly crabbed along the side to the edge, when my breathing steadied I peered round. The figure was nowhere to be seen. I rolled back behind the hut and screwed my eyes shut, thinking fast. They couldn't be far. I crouched, looking under the base, all the way to the steps at the far end, nothing.

A pair of boots appeared on the far side of the incinerator, the mystery figure had walked round the back of it. A glove appeared next to the boots, fiddling with something near the ground, turning a valve – switching off the gas supply.

Suddenly the boots ran towards the base, towards me. I held my breath, not moving. *Surely they can't have seen me?* The boots stopped for a moment, then stalked towards the corner, straight for me. I crept backwards, staying low. They were coming up quickly now, round the end of the base. Round this side.

Flinging myself flat, I rolled underneath the base, lying on my back in the mud, holding my breath, watching the pair of boots now standing where I'd been moments before. *Did they see me? Hear me?* The blood rushing through my ears certainly seemed loud enough.

They crept on, inches from my face as they stalked the perimeter of the base, all the way round to the entrance. I slowly let out my breath – they weren't interested in me. Just like me, they were avoiding being seen. Which meant I'd been right to be interested in what they were doing.

I rolled over, crawling on my elbows through the mud under the huts, acutely aware of the microscopic killers inches from my mask. Sliding all the way to the HADU, I peered out from below the metal steps leading to the door. The boots were moving away now, back up the hill, back to X-Base.

I waited another minute before dragging myself out. Jogging across to the incinerator, I reached to swing open the hatch on the top. The incinerator was nearly as tall as me, the hatch too high for me to see inside. I gripped the top edge, jumped, hauled myself up. The thick steel was still warm, the heat of the brief fire rising from the opening. I slid across and peered in.

It was difficult to make anything out, especially through the wet lens, just piles of ash as black as the interior. I leaned in further and was about to give it up, when my eyes adjusted enough to see the dim light catch on something resting against the far end. I'd no idea what it was but it didn't match the rest of the organic remnants, it looked man-made. I pulled my head out and swept every direction. Mud, grass, empty moorland. No inquisitive faces at the windows to worry about. I turned back, dangled my legs over the edge, and carefully lowered myself in.

I'm not religious but this was my best guess at what hell would be like. Volcanic, black as night, stifling, crunching underfoot, ash and bone relics of a filthy apocalyptic wasteland. I was grateful for the suit and mask that protected me from what must have been a godawful stench, could already feel sweat running down my back, soaking into my T-shirt. My boots slid; I realised the soles were starting to melt in the hot ash.

Careful not to snag the suit, I bent to retrieve the object. As soon as I touched it I realised what it was, but I held it up in the hazy light from the hatch to be sure, passing it from one hand to the other as it seared the gloves. On one side, the side that had been face down into the ash and not blasted with heat for long enough to burn it away, was an orange Yorkshire Tea logo. This was Kyle's tin, and I wondered why someone would throw it in here for all of a second before the whole picture made sense. That's what you get for being sleep deprived, normally I'd have spotted it a mile off. The brown flakes of tea that could easily hide a minute amount of dried soil. Anthrax-filled soil, which, as Marie had said, wouldn't be destroyed by boiling water. Slurped down first thing in the morning without a thought. And now the evidence – just like the body – had disappeared.

A shadow fell across the interior. I looked up at the hatch in time to watch it slam down, extinguishing all light.

I dropped the tin, jumped for the blackness where the hatch had been, couldn't find it. My gloves moved across the ceiling, pushing in vain against solid steel plates. I shouted, still walking the ceiling with my hands, feeling for the edges, trying to stay calm, fear slithering up my spine when I couldn't find anything. I shouted again, still couldn't find the hatch.

No need for panic, it was just the wind blowing the hatch over. A simple accident.

Then I heard it. Hissing, coming from the floor. The gas had been turned on.

Chapter Fourteen

I slammed my hands against the side of the incinerator, shouted as loudly as I could, but the hissing continued. Whoever was outside had surely heard me, but was ignoring me – I had to assume it was intentional, I was wasting energy and more importantly, time.

I dropped to my knees, wrenching the gas mask from my head so I could hear the hissing gas better. Bile rose in my throat as the smell hit – rancid burnt meat, mixing with the unmistakable rotten-egg stink of propane. My gloves scrabbled through swirling ash until I found where it was coming from – a nozzle near the floor, a pipe through the steel wall. I put my thumb over the end but it was hopeless, the pressure too great. I stood and kicked down at the pipe but the wellies were useless against the metal, plus my boots slipped and found another nozzle next to it, another next to that – pipes continued around the floor.

The gas wouldn't ignite, not yet – not enough of it. But that ratio was quickly rising, any second now whoever was outside would hit that button. Fear and panic took a back seat, replaced by the familiar hit of adrenaline and action. *Where's the ignitor?*

Click. My thoughts made real, a tiny blue bolt of lightning flared on the far wall, just like the clicker on your gas hob or a spark plug in your car.

Click. Spark.

The gas still hadn't reached critical saturation point, they were too eager, pressing the ignitor prematurely. Stifling now, seconds left, I launched at the far wall.

Click.

I tore off the gloves, fingers searching frantically. Propane was heavier than air, the ignitor would be lower. I crouched.

Click. Behind my head. Russian roulette, how many clicks left before sudden searing heat? *Will I cook instantly or slowly? Will my lungs burn up on the first breath?*

There! I got a hand on it. Choking now, difficult to breathe, but it'd be a hell of a lot harder if that ignitor clicked again. I stuck my finger between the points. No click this time, no lightning flash, but an electric shock pulsed up my arm, jerking my hand away. I thrust it back, holding my breath, eyes screwed shut against the burning fumes. My arm jerked away again, felt like I'd been smacked with a cricket bat, but back it went, preventing the electrical arc, knowing if it clicked and produced a spark, that would be the end.

With my other hand I pulled a strip of duct tape from my suit and stuck it between the points, wrapping it round and round, getting another shock from the live contact in the process but managing to stop it sparking. The tape ran out, I tore off another strip, wrapping the lot in sticky plastic. No conductivity, no spark, no ignition.

I gasped, breathed a couple of lungfuls of gas, retched violently. Still no click, no heat, but vomiting made me gasp and breathe. I heaved again, a vicious cycle, not enough air available to quell the choking. Head spinning. Lack of oxygen, lightheadedness, which I knew would be followed rapidly by loss of consciousness, followed rapidly by death. I found the gloves, pulled them back on and stood tall as I could, kissing the ceiling, managing to find a fetid mouthful of air. Hardly any left, the incinerator was nearly full of gas. They'd be wondering why it hadn't ignited, might have gone off to get something else to do the job; a match dropped in now would go off like a bomb.

As I pressed against the ceiling, snatching what air I could, my fingers found a slim edge. The hatch. I pushed but it didn't budge. I jumped, pushing with all I could muster, and it opened a crack. Something grated on steel as it slid across the roof. I jumped again and this time the hatch swung open, letting daylight in but not the heavy gas out. I stood on tiptoes and choked on the sweet, cold air.

Until I remembered where I was. *Anthrax Island.*

I dropped back down, holding my breath, screwing my eyes shut, found my gas mask easily enough, the only thing in the detritus larger than the bones. It was covered in hot ash, ash that could still be filled with active anthrax spores. I looped it onto my arm and leapt, my gloves sliding off the metal and landing me back in the ash. I stood as tall as I could, feeling the rain on my face, taking a moment to steady my breathing and gather my energy before jumping again. This time I managed to grab the sides of the trapdoor, hauling myself out, scrambling onto the lid, swaying against the chimney pipe.

A concrete block was sitting on the roof where it had slid off the hatch; one of the spares from the stack under the hut, definitely ruling out an accident. I shook out the gas mask but no good, it was covered. I held it up into the rain and scanned my surroundings. The moorland was empty. Still no faces at the windows.

Panic turned to rage, as I dropped down to the mud my fists were clenched, expecting trouble, eyes on the horizon for a target. Nothing. Adrenaline was still shaking my hands as I knelt by the pipework to twist the valve, shutting off the gas. I bent lower to check under the hut. Empty. Whoever it was had scarpered.

A couple of minutes, that's all. No one expects an attempt on their life, I hadn't expected it here, but I'd been foolish. I knew how quickly things could turn, but my gung-ho attitude had nearly meant my funeral, skipping to my cremation.

It had been no accident, the question was: an attempt to scare me, or a serious shot at murder? I'd thought it could be a message, a warning, until the ignitor had started up. No way would you play that game if you didn't seriously mean to cook someone.

Attempted murder, then. Gambetta getting revenge? Surely not.

Someone had been watching me on the beach with Kyle, assumed I was suspicious about his death. I didn't know a lot, but someone thought I did. They'd ditched the body, ditched the evidence, and tried to ditch me.

Could have been anyone on the island.

The body was gone. The tea was gone. I was very nearly gone, strike three. Did that put me out of the game?

Chapter Fifteen

All evidence of the past twenty minutes was balled up with the filthy suit and crammed down the chute, or washed down the shower plughole. With it went the raw rage. I was furious, but tempering it with curiosity and caution. I was the outsider here, it would be difficult to take action until I knew who to take it against. I decided that since I was alive I wasn't on strike three just yet, but I'd definitely been caught on the back foot, and needed a plan. Until I had one, I'd keep what happened to myself.

Clay was waiting for me in the decontamination chamber. Or perhaps he'd just come in and decontaminated ahead of me. Looking at him, I couldn't seriously consider him running all the way here but regardless, as was his style, he pounced as soon as I left the shower cubicle.

'Tyler, I thought we'd lost you.'

'Do these showers have a reputation, Donald?' I grabbed my towel from the hook, wrapping it around my waist. His eyes travelled across my body, taking in the tattoos and scars. His mouth flapped open and it looked as if he were about to ask about the particularly nasty scar on my chest that sliced right through a tattoo, tearing a wing from a stylised parachute, but thought better of it. Instead he asked the question to which he already knew the answer.

'You transferred the body, then?'

'It's gone,' I said ambiguously, feigning indifference.

He straightened up onto tiptoes, succeeding in looking me square in the nose. 'I knew you were going to be a problem. The

HADU's fixed, you're no longer required. You'll be leaving.' I turned to scoop up my T-shirt. 'This evening!' he added, spit gathering at the corners of his mouth.

'Fine by me, I get paid either way.'

'Not if you're in breach of contract.'

'What contract?' I laughed. 'I'm a technician, not a bloody undertaker. Besides, we both know I'm not going anywhere; you still need me.'

'You're no more useful than Kyle.' The spit was really flying now. 'We'll take our chances.'

'And if the doors fail again? Or something else?'

'We'll get your company to fly out a better tech.'

Clay wasn't getting it. 'Thought you were shipping out next week, where you gonna find one in time?'

He flushed. 'Kyle died because he was lazy, and you're shaping up no better. Chaudhary will have to manage.'

'You'd compromise the whole operation just to score points?'

'You've been boozing since you arrived, Tyler. I wouldn't be surprised if you'd tipped that body straight into the sea. Do I have to tell Captain Greenbow to detain you?'

The nerve in the corner of my right eye twitched. 'Let's get on the radio right now, I can tell 'em all about your quest for a scapegoat to cover your lack of enforcement of safety protocols.' My palms felt cold, clammy, fingers tightening at my sides until my knuckles burned. 'Gambetta removing his mask for a fag, people wandering around inside in hazmat suits, God knows if they're coming or going. You're at pains to act like you're in charge, well Andy Kyle died on your watch.' I tensed my right arm, drew it back slightly, and focused on the bridge of Clay's nose.

The door swung open and Hurley entered the chamber, he'd been wearing a hazmat suit when I'd met him but given his physique it wasn't a difficult assumption to make. He'd a good couple of inches on me, built like a rugby forward, with enough muscles stretching his T-shirt to have lent Clay some and still be left with plenty to bench-press me. He could have lent Clay some hair, too, he looked like an extra from *Point Break*. I'm stereotyping, but he wasn't the picture of a typical lab monkey.

'What do you want?' Clay snapped.

'Captain wants you in the radio room,' Hurley drawled, flicking a thumb over his shoulder at the corridor beyond.

'Then he should come to find me, I am not at the beck and call of lackeys. And what the hell are you doing?'

'Going up to help Demeter.' Hurley was seemingly immune to Clay's demeanour.

'I do wish you people would realise we're working to a strict deadline.' He turned to me. 'Pack your bag.' He whirled and slammed through the door.

'Fucking prick,' I muttered.

'Someone's not in the good books.' Hurley grinned as he kicked his shoes off.

'You'd think I'd killed someone.'

Hurley's grin vanished when he saw how tense I was. 'You look like you're about to.'

I relaxed, flexed my fingers, smiled. 'Just tired.'

'Well Demeter will be pleased, it'll take the heat off him for a while.'

I raised an eyebrow and let him continue.

'Clay was chewing him out earlier. The guy's an asshole but generally toothless, he's just stressed about the approaching deadline. On the plus side it sounds like you'll never have to see him again.'

'I can do without him or Greenbow.'

Hurley shook a disposable suit out of a polythene bag. 'El Capitan's all right, he's just playing soldiers, you gotta know how to take him. You've already made an impression on the French contingent, though.'

'He's a wanker too.' Which was possibly an understatement, considering he might have just tried to kill me.

Hurley laughed. 'I meant Marie. Finest ass on the island.'

'I don't know about her arse, but she seems like the only person here with her head screwed on, present company excluded.'

He nodded, working his way into the suit. 'I do a bit of work in Paris, she's helping me with my French.' My ears pricked up, he mistook my interest for something else and winked. 'That's not a euphemism. Don't be fooled by those big brown eyes, though, you don't get to be a biological weapons expert without a killer instinct. Ingrid's more my type, met her yet?'

I shook my head.

He cupped his hands to his chest and jiggled them up and down in a gesture I hadn't seen since school. 'Gotta love a Viking.'

'Yeah, I heard she has four PhDs?' I'd just survived an attempt on my life and my fuse was shortening, I needed more important information than his preferences in women. I'm not a prude but I've never understood the need for some people to immediately engage in quote-unquote bants with total strangers, especially the macho pricks I come across in my line of work.

He looked crestfallen, I realised he was just trying to connect with the new guy. I inhaled deeply, reminded myself I could do with allies. I smiled and changed the subject. 'You guys get your survey finished?' I wanted to steer him towards who could have been watching me earlier, who else had been wandering the island.

He shoved his feet into his boots and began taping them up. 'Rain stopped play, isn't that what you guys say? Pissing it down, that's another one. Cats and dogs. You guys have so many phrases for your shitty weather.'

I pulled on my shirt. 'Only for the rain; don't they reckon Eskimos have three hundred words for snow?'

'Good point. Anyway, no. It's a mudbath out there, and Clay says tomorrow's not looking much better. We should have been doing this in summer.'

He was nearly ready, taping up his gloves, so I tried again. 'I think I saw Demeter earlier?'

'Down the south end of the island? Probably. He's crazy, out there in all weathers.'

The south end of the island – where I'd left Kyle's body. 'I think Gambetta's the only other person I saw braving the rain?'

'Doesn't matter to him if he's digging dry dirt or wet dirt,' he said. 'Well, I'll catch you later, John.' He pulled his gas mask down and pushed open the exit.

I gave him a nod, echoing Demeter's words to me. 'Careful out there.'

Chapter Sixteen

When I'd finished dressing I locked myself in the toilet cubicle. Hurley had confirmed both Demeter and Gambetta had been outside earlier, so they'd moved to the top of my list of suspects, with Greenbow just behind and Clay trailing a fair way after. Things had got serious, quickly; time to move up a gear.

I opened the cistern and extracted the parcel I'd placed in there a few hours ago. Removing the tape carefully to avoid any noise, I ripped apart the bin bags. I said the torch was the second most useful item I'd brought to the island; wrapped inside, in a sheet of greaseproof paper, was the most useful. I ran a finger across the letters stamped along the side:

HECKLER & KOCH GMBH 9MM X 19
VP70Z

The pistol's futuristic looks contrasted with its battered and scratched frame; I've tried countless handguns but this one goes everywhere with me. If you're an enthusiast you might ask why – I'm sentimental, but there are practical reasons too; the polymer frame keeps the weight down, it's hugely reliable, and the eighteen-round capacity is more than most. It's also simple to maintain – the takedown lever makes it very easy to strip in the field.

The drawback is that it only has a double action, which makes for a very heavy twenty-pound trigger. Crunchy, like a staple gun, but you get used to these things. I felt its comforting weight, familiar in my hand, muscle memory sliding out the magazine to double check even though I'd loaded it myself a few hours previously. Nickel glinted in the toilet's fluorescent lights, Speer Gold Dot G2 hollow points, like the FBI use. I slid it back in.

Wrapped in the paper was another magazine – this one loaded with full metal jackets on the off-chance I needed penetration rather than obliteration – and a lightweight inner-waistband holster, which I clipped inside the top of my trousers. The rubbish was balled up and dropped back in the cistern.

I pushed the safety behind the trigger to make it safe, tucked the pistol into the holster, reassurance pressing my hip, and tugged my T-shirt down over it. I felt better already, as if treading familiar ground. I'd already been searched, so from now on wherever I went, it would go too. Let them try again.

Chapter Seventeen

Someone was sat at a table in the dining room as I walked past the open doorway, a woman in a hazmat suit, hunched over an iPad, stirring a bowl absent-mindedly. Not Alice or Marie. I backtracked and walked over, arm outstretched. 'You must be Ingrid? Heard a lot about you.'

She looked up from the tablet and shook my hand but her smile wasn't reflected in her eyes. 'You're Andy's replacement?'

'John.' I nodded, pulling out a chair. 'Do you mind?' She shook her head and I sat down opposite her. 'Another woman after my own heart.'

'Sorry?'

I pointed to a stack of biscuits next to the bowl, she slid one towards me.

'Custard Creams are the best thing about this country.' Her face brightened. 'I have a stash but I've had to hide them, Clay's already eaten half a pack.'

'What a bastard,' I said, putting the biscuit in my mouth without a trace of guilt.

She pushed the iPad away and leaned in, winking conspiratorially. 'Third cupboard from the left, behind the granola. He won't check there.' Her face dropped again, she looked down into her bowl. 'Andy liked them too.'

'Did you know him, then?'

'Not really, he pretty much kept to himself.'

'I'm hearing that a lot. Wondering if anyone knew the guy?'

She tucked a few stray blonde strands into her hood and gave her bowl another stir. 'I guess Demeter? Sharing a room and everything. He seemed okay, but I only spoke to him over breakfast. You know; work, the weather.' She gave another nervous little semi-smile. 'Did you know him?'

'I did, his family are devastated.' I don't know if he even had a family.

She nodded. 'Hanna, my sister, she's with Médecins Sans Frontières in Sudan. I'd be destroyed if anything happened to her.' She blew on a spoonful of spicy-looking rice. 'You have siblings?'

My brother's face flashed up, a mental image forever burned into my memory, him behind the wheel, relaxed, smiling, joking. Skipping tracks on the old Discman balanced on the dash, Beastie Boys kicking in just before... I shook my head. 'Nope.'

'With Hanna in Darfur my parents don't have any worry left for me. But then Scotland doesn't sound quite as dangerous, does it?'

'Maybe it's that complacency that killed Kyle.'

She swallowed her rice and shook her head. 'No, he was careful, he'd scrub himself in the showers for ages. I can't understand how he was infected.'

Yet again, the same sad little smile. She wasn't sure either. I didn't speak, gave her room to continue.

'He was worried,' she said finally.

'What about?'

'Said someone had been following him.'

'It's a pretty small island.'

'Watching him. While he worked.'

I shuffled forward. 'Was this yesterday, when he died?'

Every time she shook her head her hair tumbled loose from her hood. 'Since we arrived. I talked to him yesterday morning, he said he had an odd feeling. I saw him later in the morning heading inside, he wasn't feeling well.' She looked into her bowl. 'He never came back.'

'Who found him?'

'Gambetta. He said Andy probably stopped for a rest and never got up. Heart attack, most likely.'

'Did Kyle say who he thought had been following him?'

'I asked but he didn't know. Just glimpses, shadows. Really freaked him out.'

'I've already had the haunted-island shit.'

She picked at some pieces of fish and scooped up another spoonful. 'Easy to be a sceptic in the sunshine but here on the island – you gotta admit it has an atmosphere. Echoes of what happened in the war.' She chewed thoughtfully, tried a little laugh but it came out as a cough. 'No one really believes it's haunted, it's just… Andy had a bad feeling and now he's dead. Probably the anthrax, if that's what it was, of course – illness can give you feelings of dread, impending doom. Coupled with the mood here it's enough to send anyone over the edge.'

It wasn't hard to see why this place could send someone doolally. 'Seen anything weird yourself?'

'Thankfully I stick to my nice warm lab.'

'Doing what, exactly?'

She paused, spoon halfway to her mouth, considering, then lowered it again. 'Staring at tubes of mud.' She chuckled. 'I specialise in isolating different strains of pathogens—'

The door burst open and Ingrid jumped, dropping the spoon and banging her knees on the table. Clay was back.

'Tyler, Captain Greenbow's office, now.'

I sighed and stood. 'I'll catch you later, Ingrid.'

She slid another Custard Cream across the table to me and smiled, warmly this time.

Chapter Eighteen

It wasn't apparent why Greenbow needed his own office with space at such a premium. Like all the huts along the back row of the complex, this one was split into two rooms – his office and, next door, his bedroom. Kudos for Greenbow for having two rooms and therefore an entire hut of his own. Suppose that answered the question of who was really in charge.

A typed piece of paper was sellotaped to the door in front of me.

'*Captain Greenbow*'.

Was that really necessary in a base this size? Probably typed it himself; the image of him sitting there in his uniform printing it, cutting it out, made me smile. I waited in the corridor, straining to hear what was being said further along in the radio room. Someone was having a heated discussion with the ship. I considered going to listen when Greenbow's door opened and I found myself face to face with the one person I wanted to talk to, albeit privately, one-on-one.

'…and if you lie to me again, Gambetta, I'll bounce you off this island,' shouted Greenbow.

Gambetta ignored him, glaring at me from beneath heavy eyelids, tortoise-like mouth clamped around an unlit cigarette. He shoved me out of the way, striding down the corridor.

'*De rien*' I muttered, fists clenched at my sides.

He whirled round, looking me up and down, fishing in the breast pocket of his shirt. Pulling out his Zippo, he lit the cigarette, exhaling clouds of blue smoke in my direction. He took the cigarette between thumb and forefinger and pointed it at me.

'You be careful,' he said in that Gauloise-marinated voice. He jabbed the cigarette at me with each syllable, sprinkling the shiny floor with ash.

'*Vous ne pouvez pas fumer ici!*' I said, *You can't smoke in here!* I added my favourite French insult, '*On t'a bercé trop près du mur?*' *Was your cradle rocked too close to the wall?*

'Tyler?' Greenbow shouted from the office.

Gambetta ground the ash into the floor with his shoe. 'You be *very* careful, *monsieur.*' He sneered and turned away.

I'd barely stepped into the office when Greenbow flew into a tirade of abuse not normally seen outside a parade ground. I closed the door behind me, parking myself against it. He managed to talk a lot without really saying anything, ranting about deadlines and timetables, procedures, but mostly about the disappearance of Kyle's corpse.

Let him vent, I wasn't angry any more, I knew the drill. Back to that hierarchy; despite me technically not being subordinate to anyone, he had to assert his authority, show me he was a shark, I was a minnow. All just static noise; my mind was blunted but working overtime, still trapped in that incinerator, thinking about the figure I'd followed across the island. A bastard of a headache had moved in behind my eyes and another had just begun to grind its way into the base of my skull. I wasn't sure which was from sleep deprivation and which was the comedown from the adrenaline. Of course, there was always the possibility of the early effects of anthrax poisoning, but I put that straight out of mind.

Greenbow was asking something so I nodded. I could feel my eyes glazing over, the lids on pulleys, the more effort I put into hauling them up the harder someone else pulled them down. I had to look around the office to occupy them, drag my mind into the present.

I focused on the details. Same utilitarian room as all the others in the complex, but the captain had brightened it up with

76

a couple of massive prints of military oil paintings. I think he was aiming for 'gentleman's club' but it came off as the portacabin office of a used-car salesman. I stared at a massed charge of red tunics and huge grey horses hanging above Greenbow's head, desperately trying to dispel the mental image of him tugging himself dry to Kipling and the Band of the Irish Guards. He slammed his palm on the birch-effect-laminate desk and I jumped, much to my disappointment, though thankfully it cleared the image.

'Consider yourself lucky you're still here.' I can honestly say I didn't feel lucky. 'Sea's too rough for an extraction, you've been given a stay of execution – though if it was up to Clay you'd be swimming back to the mainland.'

So that's how it was, apparently I was staying because a storm was coming in. Nothing to do with the fact my employer would have argued against me leaving, and must have won.

'When can I speak to command?'

'You bloody well can't!'

'I need to report to my manager on the shortcomings here, I've never known such a slack operation. You can bet it'll all be going into my report. I'm looking forward to Kyle's inquest.'

Greenbow faltered. 'You've been here a matter of hours and already surpassed your predecessor in stupidity. Be sure it doesn't happen again.'

'Make sure another body doesn't go missing? You're planning on there being more?'

'Well I wouldn't be surprised if you got yourself killed. You're dismissed.'

I hesitated in the doorway; there was something else, something he wasn't saying. I considered bringing up the incinerator, but decided to keep quiet as something had just flashed into my head. Instead, I closed the door, then jogged all the way back to the dining room.

Hadn't Ingrid told me that she specialised in identifying and isolating new strains?

The room was empty. I ran back to the kitchen, nearly colliding with Alice. She shielded a bowl of cereal, sidestepping out of my way.

'John,' she said, concern in her face. She reached out to touch my arm. 'What's happened?'

'Where's Ingrid?' I asked.

'Just left. But come on, I need to talk to you.' She put the bowl down.

'Not here.' I nodded at the door. 'Too many ears. Outside the main entrance in half an hour?'

Alice nodded but looked annoyed.

'And get hold of some binoculars.'

Alice's annoyance changed to confusion but I didn't elaborate. Instead I turned and slid a tin mug out from behind the toaster. It hadn't all been destroyed; I'd spooned the leaf tea straight into it an hour or so ago, then shoved it away when Greenbow had interrupted me. Had he inadvertently saved my life? I grabbed a plastic sandwich bag from a drawer, tipped the contents in, tied it shut.

'Taking a packed lunch?' she asked. 'It'll go nicely with the Scotch.' The derision in her tone was dulled through the spoonful of cornflakes.

I flashed her a look and left the kitchen before she could say anything else, just as Gambetta entered. I swerved, looking back to see him staring after me intently.

Chapter Nineteen

My mood had rubbed off on the weather. Thankfully I'd quickly changed into more suitable clothes; warmer trackie bottoms and a thick green army jumper that Greenbow would be proud of. 'Jersey, Heavy Wool', it's imaginatively known as in his profession. My brother had taught me a neat trick he'd used in the Army, looping a bootlace through the neck seam so it could be drawn in nice and snug. I thought about him again, about what he'd have done in my position. *He wouldn't be in my position.* I pulled the bootlace tight round my neck, zipped up the protective overalls, felt the comforting pistol holstered at my side, stumbled down the steps.

The change of clothes didn't keep me as warm as I'd hoped, I'd underestimated the latitude. Wind screamed relentlessly across the heather, no cover to prevent it pushing the grass and weeds flat into the mud. The path was slippery, rain saturating the ground until it had refused to absorb any more. Ingrid had left deep plodding prints. I took off after her at a pace. She had a head start and I tried to work out how far she'd got, deciding she'd be on the downslope over the hill.

I pushed on, but the faster I ran the more I slipped. The world was a blur of brown and sickly yellow through the streaked gas-mask visor. Occasionally a rock loomed into view, reminding me of what Marie had said earlier about slipping and smashing my face – a decent way to contract anthrax and a swift trip to the military hospital.

I met Dash coming the other way as I marched up the centre of the island but the wind was too strong for conversation.

Near the top I used the elevation to look back at the ship. She was rolling now, the huge blocky radar mast that dominated her silhouette swaying noticeably. White tips danced on waves that surged, rather than the gentle swell of the morning. Way below me, Dash was struggling towards the generator shed in the middle of the base. A solid sheet of rain swept in, swallowing the ship, the island's coastline, X-Base, then me. If I were a superstitious man I'd have considered the weather an omen, an augury of impending doom. I'm not, but I patted my pistol through the suit just the same, shivered, and ploughed on.

Finally I cleared the top of the hill to see Camp Vollum. For all the joking it was a good job the huts were painted bright orange – the driving rain and gas mask had conspired to reduce visibility to vague shapes and colours. I estimated the base was a good few hundred metres away but about halfway to it a pale yellow shape bobbed like an untethered buoy on the waves. I shouted but Ingrid couldn't hear, so I started jogging again. I caught up just as she reached the steps, calling her name.

She turned, shocked when she saw it was me, and stepped down. I pulled the plastic bag from my pocket, walking closer but still needing to shout over the wind and rain.

'I need a favour.'

She nodded but looked unsure.

'Your speciality is identifying different strains of anthrax, yeah?'

'Yes?' Confusion showed through the visor.

'Can you test this, see if it's contaminated?'

Her eyes narrowed as she peered in the bag. 'Soil? Where from?'

I hesitated. 'I just want to know if it contains anthrax. How lethal it is.'

She looked from the bag to me, wondering why an engineer would request analysis of a sample. 'Is this to do with—'

'I wouldn't ask if it wasn't important.'

She nodded. 'I don't see why not, I mean, it is what we're here for. Should have an answer in a couple of hours.'

'Thanks a lot.' I started to walk away. 'Oh, Ingrid?'

She paused at the top of the steps.

'Keep it between us, okay?'

She punched in the code, disappearing inside.

I set off back to base, careful of my footing in the mud. So carefully focused on my boots that I only caught the movement in the corner of my eye. I turned to the hillside but whatever it was dipped below the horizon, just a flash of movement. Had someone been watching us? Gambetta? I briefly contemplated giving chase, confronting him, but there was no way I'd catch up. Plus, it could have been anyone.

But thinking about Gambetta and his cigs had flashed another thought into my head that needed further examination.

Anything you took outside couldn't come back in unless it was already sealed inside your suit with you. So with decontamination closely monitored – how had Gambetta got that Zippo in and out?

Chapter Twenty

I needed to speak to Alice but she'd be out soon, no point going in and changing, so I headed round the corner in the direction I'd seen Dash take. I found him sheltering in the shed from the worsening wind.

He turned as I pushed through the door. 'Hey, wanna lend a hand with the generator?' he asked.

I shook my head. 'Sorry, Alice has roped me into helping her.'

He looked at the open doorway, the driving rain. 'Rather you than me.'

'Tell me about it, day like this I might even prefer to be sealed in that base.'

'You and me both, buddy.'

'You serious about what you said earlier, though, about not getting claustrophobic?' I asked. 'I'm already feeling trapped.'

He dropped a screwdriver into a toolbox and leaned on the shelves. 'It don't bother me none. I've worked in polar bases, you don't wanna crack open a window there, I tell ya.'

'What about here? If I just need a quick breather?'

'You mad? You know why we're here, right?'

'Well, the anthrax spores are in the soil. It can't be a big risk opening a window?'

He went on a mini rant about protocol and security but then explained that the modular construction of the base wasn't just there to make transportation and deployment easy, it was there to combat the biggest danger in polar regions. Fire.

You might think it's the cold; that's a danger, but fire in an Antarctic base is a death sentence. There's no water to put a fire out, it's all frozen. You can't count on fire extinguishers, they don't work in extreme cold, and you'd need a roomful of them to put out anything more than a chip-pan. The best you can do is stand back, grab the marshmallows, watch it burn itself out. That's when you realise that if your base burns you're left with a very long walk home. A base in the Antarctic is a lifeboat, without its shelter you'd be an ice-pop within hours. And if you left the base quickly, in the middle of the night without your cold-weather gear, good luck…

X-Base – or 'US Outpost 32', to give it its correct American designation – would replace 'US Outpost 31', which had burned to the ground (should that be burned to the ice?) a while ago in mysterious circumstances. The theory with the modular construction of this replacement base was that the compartment on fire burns itself out, the plastic bridge burns, and hopefully the fire doesn't jump to the next compartment – which means you're still left with shelter until help arrives. In order to allow occupants to escape a burning compartment, all windows on the base slid open sideways – wide enough for a person to climb through. Crime isn't a consideration in the Antarctic, safety outweighs it a million times over, so the windows opened from both the inside and outside using the same key.

'But here we don't have to worry about fire,' he said. 'I've got pumps and hoses ready to rock, no freezing here. So the windows stay locked and sealed.'

'What if there's an emergency?'

'Take it up with Greenbow, he's got the keys, security is his business.'

Presumably he didn't have all the keys, or not at all times. If briefly opening a window was minimal risk, and if Gambetta had got hold of a key, he could easily be using it for a smoke. More worryingly, it was likely how the tin of tea had been dropped out of my bedroom window.

Dash was closing up his toolbox and preparing to head back into the gale.

'You a superstitious man?' I asked.

'What's that got to do with anything?'

I looked out the doorway at the clouds rolling overhead. 'So far three people have told me the island's haunted.'

He laughed. 'Ghosts ain't my thing. Weird place, though. Islands usually are, don'tcha think?'

'Ever feel like you're being watched?'

'It's the respirators and this weather. Bad combo. Nothing like stealing your senses away to make you paranoid.'

Paranoia hadn't slammed that lid shut and tried to BBQ me alive.

'Like why people are afraid of the dark,' he continued. 'Dull the senses, you'll start seeing things that aren't there. You sure you can't lend a hand with the generator?'

'Maybe later.' I tried one last go. 'Kyle reckoned he was being followed.' I didn't tell him I thought the same. I stepped aside as he pushed past, and as he did I could tell his eyebrows were raised under the mask.

'Demeter's the worst for that crap, guy's a fruit loop.' He gestured outside. 'I really gotta make moves. Want in on the poker later?'

I nodded and followed him into the gale, which made further conversation difficult, so I slapped him on the shoulder. He waved, heading for the generator shed as I set off round to the entrance.

Alice was already outside, carrying a toolbox.

'Where can we go?' I asked.

'Follow me.' She didn't wait for a response, marching away in the direction of the beach.

After a few minutes the toolbox's weight was showing. I offered to carry it but she scowled and soldiered on – a mixture of stubbornness and pride, I guessed. She reached the top of the hill when suddenly her feet flicked out from under her. She'd slipped on a patch of mud and lurched backwards, dropping the toolbox, arms flailing.

I dived forward, catching her about the waist, fighting to avoid slipping myself.

'I'm-quite-capable,' she spluttered, grabbing my arms anyway.

We stared at the beach below. The tide was fully in now, waves sloshing over the pebbles and pummelling the black rocks. As I'd suspected, the water came nowhere near the over-hang where I'd left Andy Kyle's body. Alice pushed away from me.

'You were right to flag it. Kyle was murdered,' I said.

'Of course he fucking was,' she replied.

Chapter Twenty-one

We stood there silently, Alice and I, staring out across the waves whilst the rain belted and the wind howled. She handed me the small pair of binoculars I'd asked for and I tested them on the cottages on the mainland, scanning the treeline and the graveyard. They'd do. Finally I asked the obvious question.

'Why the hell are Clay and Greenbow ignoring Kyle's murder?'

She looked at me as if I were stupid. 'Tax year end, funding-bid time. The government don't fund departments scandalised by murder.'

I raised an eyebrow. 'Even the Tories?'

'Okay, so it'd make things difficult. An accident – especially a private contractor rather than someone from Porton Down – is more convenient. No one wants anyone throwing spanners.'

'Hence why you couldn't use the radio, with all comms monitored.'

'If Greenbow learns I'm an MI5 informant I'll be booted off the team faster than you.'

I looked at the driving rain, the thrashing waves, the endless mud. 'Would that be so bad?'

'Some of us actually like our careers.'

'So you pulled the fuse instead. You took a risk, you know. If anyone had checked, it would have been obvious it was sabotage.'

'I shouldn't have bothered. You managed to lose the body, the only proof Andy was murdered.'

'Nearly lost me, too.'

She cocked her head, eyes narrowed behind the mask, but I didn't expand on the statement. Finally she threw her hands up. 'Look, Clay clocked you swigging the moment you arrived, though I'm not surprised you drink so much. I don't want to end up the same, you can tell your masters I'm through with the cloak-and-dagger shit.'

I put the binoculars back to my mask and scanned the distant beach, sweeping in and out of view in the downpour. 'If you want out, I need information.'

'I don't have any – Andy wasn't important.'

'Nice, I'll make sure his mum knows that. Obviously someone thought so or he wouldn't be dead.'

'None of us had met him before last week.'

I lowered the binoculars and gave her a hard look. 'If you say he kept to himself I'll throw you in the sea.'

'Look, he didn't really have anything to do – he was only here to maintain the HADUs.'

I resumed my inspection of the coastline. 'Greenbow's military intelligence – you sure he doesn't know why I'm really here?'

'Intelligence in name only, he's too absorbed in his own little empire. He's convinced Andy's death was an accident. When I told him we needed another technician he refused.'

'And pulling the fuse was the only way to force his hand, to get someone sent to the island?'

'Like I said, I shouldn't have bothered.'

I put the binoculars in my pocket and looked at the jagged rocks. Our suits flapped in the wind like the luffing sails of a yacht, the waves crashing below reinforcing the image. The wind had upped its game to a gale. The rain let up long enough for me to see the distant pines on the mainland bending. Just as quickly, it rolled back in to envelop the island.

'I'd put Demeter at the top of your suspect list,' Alice said.

'Really? He's odd, but not a killer.'

'Obviously you know best,' she snapped.

'Specialised in weaponising bacteria, didn't he?'

She detected my tone. 'You do know what we *do* at Porton Down? And you say he's not a killer… Captain!'

We both spun – Greenbow was standing not ten feet behind me, flapping green suit almost camouflaging him against the drab vegetation. The wind had masked his approach. In this weather, with everyone squinting in the fading afternoon light through blurry rain-lashed glass, it was probably easy for him to wander the island unseen, keeping an eye on people.

'What brings you two up here?' he asked – conversationally, but there was an implication somewhere behind it. Had he heard us talking?

'Giving Tyler a crash course in grid sampling,' Alice said, turning back to me. 'Like I said, we need this section mapped before dark.'

Greenbow surveyed the spit of land jutting out to sea. '*Dauntless* says a storm's coming in. Don't get swept away, eh, Tyler? We've had enough accidents.'

I ignored him, addressing Alice, catching up with her diversion. 'So you want me to start here?'

'Like this.' She set the toolbox down and opened it up, producing a long ball of garden string and some metal tent pegs. She tied the end of the string around one of the pegs and pushed it into the ground.

'Follow me.'

She walked in a straight line, unravelling the string. To my dismay Greenbow walked alongside us. After a while the string ran out, she tied the end round another peg and stuck it in the ground.

'The string's twenty metres long,' she said, gesturing at the line running parallel to the beach, back to the cliff edge. She produced a tiny clear tube from her pocket – the kind you'd piss in for a doctor – and a tape measure. 'Like I said, we've done this across the whole island, so just this section left.' She unscrewed the lid, which had a slim spoon-like tool attached to the inside. She used it to pick up some mud next to the peg, dropping it in the tube. It left a trail as it slid down the inside of the glass. 'Take a sample every five metres and label the tube like this.' She screwed the cap on tightly and pulled out a marker pen. 'Line one, sample one – got it?'

'High-tech.'

'I'm sure even he can manage this,' said Greenbow, turning to Alice. 'I'm heading to Camp Vollum, I came to tell you you're needed there too. Gambetta wants to re-run the soil composition data.'

Alice continued the instructions. 'When you've done this line, move each peg three metres down the hill and start again, line two. And so on until you hit the beach. There are more vials in the shed.'

'Should keep you out of trouble,' added Greenbow.

She started to walk away, which was irritating – thanks to Greenbow we'd have to wait until later to finish our conversation. I could feel his eyes on me as I bent to root around in the toolbox.

'Come to my office when you're finished,' he said when I finally looked up.

He trudged away without another word, leaving me alone with my test tubes. I'd be visiting his office far sooner than that. His appearance had been annoying; I wanted to know what more Alice knew about Demeter, but he obviously suspected something. On the upside, I could spin him being out here to my advantage.

I picked up the toolbox and walked along the string.

Chapter Twenty-two

I'd diligently taken samples for all of five minutes before heading back to base. Greenbow hadn't been kidding about the storm, the wind had increased still more, something I hadn't thought possible. It whipped around the side of the base, threatening to push me over as I leaned into it. The benefit was that it had cleared the mist, the downside was that visibility was even worse as the rain fired horizontally across the exposed ground. I stabbed at the keypad and stumbled into the HADU.

The binoculars had come in useful – as far as I knew the team were now all outside, except one person. As I'd returned I'd watched the others before leaving the binoculars out of sight under the steps. Demeter and Marie were occupied with the pipes on the cliffs, Alice and Hurley were helping Gambetta, Demeter, Greenbow and Ingrid were inside the other base. Dash was still tinkering with the generator. Only Clay had remained inside, and I figured he'd be in the radio room.

Which meant there was a good chance he was on the other side of the CCTV lens watching me as I decontaminated – a perfect opportunity.

I needed to test a theory, and for that I was set on getting into Greenbow's office one way or another. Using just a couple of items from my washbag I was pretty sure I could pick his lock, but I was rusty and fairly confident there was an easier way. This wasn't a security-conscious bunch, no way would Greenbow take his keys with him. Not in an already secure base on a military-controlled island.

After dressing I went straight to the lounge, to the radio on the shelf, turning it on, volume all the way up. Eighties classic rock echoed around the base. I left the door open and quickly crossed through the link bridge back into the HADU, pressing myself against the door, under the camera, careful to stay out of its line of sight. I didn't have to wait long.

I peered through the porthole to watch Clay storming down the corridor. He marched straight to the lounge, seconds later the music stopped. He reappeared, flustered, slamming the door and stamping back up the corridor.

I was already moving, counting down from thirty as I crossed to the line of hooks on the opposite wall. Greenbow's gear hung at the end. Nothing in the shirt pockets. *Twenty-five.* I unfolded his trousers. Nothing in the pockets. *Twenty.* I carefully refolded them and stared. Fifteen seconds before Clay made it back to the radio room and the CCTV screen. *Maybe I was wrong; lock-pick it is, then.*

Greenbow's polished shoes were sitting under the bench. I slid them out, one jangled. Inside was a key ring with three keys on it. I pocketed it, slid the shoes back under, then made my way out of the HADU.

I'd have bet Clay would be back in the comms room, but equally he could have been anywhere in the base, looking for me. Between the HADU and my bedroom I could easily make an excuse, so I strolled casually but quietly through the base. No signs of life.

I passed my bedroom and crept further through the corridors, along the link bridges. Dangerous territory now – I was ready with some bullshit about looking for Greenbow, but just as Clay had said, I had no business being here. Static burst from the radio room ahead and I paused, not breathing. No other sounds. I was outside Greenbow's bedroom now, loitering would be impossible to explain so I changed to speed rather than stealth to reach the next door.

A flash of colour outside caught my eye. At first I thought Dash was looking in, but no, it wasn't outside. It was out the window, but I was looking across at the last section of base, the labs. Blurry through two sets of streaky glass, I could only make out vague movement. Clay was making his way from the labs at the far end of the base towards me.

He was moving steadily past the windows, not rushing – he hadn't seen me. I looked at the keys. Only one was a door key, the others were too small. I stuck it in the lock, tried to turn it but it jammed. I risked a glance over my shoulder but couldn't see Clay any more. I could hear him now, though, plastic shoe soles tapping plastic flooring, getting louder.

I took the key out and steadied my hand, pushed it back in gently, all the way. This time it turned. Clay's shoes rapped on the link bridge at the far end of the corridor. I pushed the door and slid inside, closing it behind me, letting the handle up slowly, careful not to let the latch click.

I remained motionless until a slamming door told me it was clear; Clay was back in the comms room. I let out my breath and looked at the door key. A simple five-tumbler mechanism, I could probably have picked it in under a minute anyway but was grateful for Greenbow's assistance.

I looked around his office. Gloomy in the dimming after-noon light, but just as it had been when I'd seen it earlier. I fought the urge to mess up the papers on the desk and looked out the window, checking no one was about to wander past and look in. Empty dismal moorland and vast swollen sky. I closed the blind, checked the keys again, looked at the short filing cabinet behind the desk. I half wanted to pick it with the paperclips on the desk for my own entertainment, but ego usually equals trouble.

It was the second key I tried; the drawers slid open easily. Nothing but a couple of large-scale maps of Scotland in the top. The middle drawer was just packs of paper, ink cartridges, Sellotape, an empty notepad. Top-secret stuff indeed. I found what I was after in the bottom drawer; the window keys, in a lidless Tupperware overflowing with Post-its and pens with no lids. I tipped it out and placed the keys in a row.

Lounge, dining room, kitchen, my room, Marie's room. Three more bedrooms. Greenbow's office. The last bedroom and radio room. Three labs.

Assuming there was a key for each room, which seemed logical, there were two keys missing. I looked again at Greenbow's key ring, this third key was one of them.

Which left one key unaccounted for.

I'd suspected Gambetta had used a window to get his lighter and cigs inside, avoiding the HADU's CCTV; he must have the key. I was pretty confident someone had opened my window to drop the tea tin outside, hence why I saw the figure creeping under the window. In my book that meant Gambetta's guilt for the incinerator trick was pretty nailed on.

No, not necessarily, there are other explanations. Gambetta could have shared the key with someone else. It could have been Captain Greenbow, or he could have willingly given someone a key. A third person could have broken into the office just like I had, and then returned the key after. Too many explanations, not enough facts. I stood and stared at the keys as if they'd yield an answer. My gut said Gambetta was the man I'd been sent to find, but men's organs aren't always the best decision-makers.

As I bent to tidy up, the papers on the desk caught my eye; my name, scrawled across on a red cardboard folder. I carefully moved an L-102 expenses form out of the way and opened the flap.

Paperclipped sheets of paper, a B-107 form topped with a photo of a burned-out Toyota Landcruiser, half its front end missing. I swallowed hard, sweat prickling my face, eyebrow scar on fire. There was a ringing in my ears and I was back in the dirt, in the fire, in the blood. Face down, breath ripped away. Somewhere the Beastie Boys are playing but it's distant, muffled, like it's under water. So are the shouts, the cries, the screams. The sporadic gunfire. I'd been specifically told to come this way. This road's been swept, they'd said. I could feel my fists clenching at my sides. They'd told me it was clear.

I was dizzy, could feel myself swaying, had to force my knees to lock, focusing on the stupid fucking painting behind the desk.

'Captain?'

A knock at the door. I blinked several times, shook my hands out. *Shit.* Clay knocked again. 'Captain, are you in there?'

I looked at the door. No bolt showing by the mechanism, I hadn't locked it after me. If he turned the handle…

Surely he must know Greenbow hadn't returned yet, via the CCTV. Maybe he was due back?

His shoes clicked away, I finally exhaled. I gathered the keys back up, put the tub back in the drawer then, deciding to even out the odds a bit, reached back in and pocketed one.

No noise outside the door. I waited for my heart to slow then eased the handle down and pulled it open. The corridor was empty. I silently closed the door behind me, locked it, then set off back towards my own room.

Steps again, coming from in front, moving towards me. I picked up the pace and grabbed the nearest door handle, throwing myself into a room and closing the door behind me.

The steps moved on. What the hell was Clay up to, doing rounds like a security guard? Looking for me?

I was in the next hut along from mine, one of the other bedrooms. I waited by the door as the steps faded, then grabbed the handle.

A light blazed on, the room lit up. I froze. No one spoke, nothing moved.

Slowly I turned, hands open at my sides, an automatic reaction. 'Sorry, I think I'm in the wrong room. I'm not used to all these doors…'

Nothing but an empty room, a lot like mine. I was alone. One of the bedside lamps glowed, it'd somehow turned itself on. Ingrid's words came back to haunt me. *Ghosts. Echoes of what happened here.* Cold trickled up my spine. I stared at the lamp for nearly a minute, not daring to move. The wire snaked under the bed – where it was stuck into a timer plug.

The island really did have everyone strung out. This was Dash's room; I remembered what he'd said about life in the Antarctic, about the perpetual winter night and the need to create time breaks to keep your sanity. *I'm an idiot.*

I opened the door and slowly peered out into an empty corridor. I only had to make it as far as my room, a straight run. I shut the door and jogged it, closing my door behind me. I crossed straight to the window to test the key. I cracked it open an inch – confirming the locks and keys *were* all the same. I opened a bottle of Scotch from next to the bed and poured a good third outside, cheap fumes blowing in with the rain and searing my nostrils. I closed and locked the window, mopped the rain up with a T-shirt, grabbed a pair of socks and another disposable suit, and made my way to the HADU.

'Tyler!' A shout from behind me. I turned, Clay was approaching. 'What are you doing?'

I held up the socks. 'My feet are freezing.'

'Where have you been?'

I put on my best frown. 'In my room.'

'You weren't in there a minute ago.'

I shrugged and pulled open the door to the HADU. 'Getting a drink.'

I let the door close before Clay could get to it, turned, and nearly collided with Greenbow.

'Shouldn't you be gathering samples?' he growled.

I held up the socks again and repeated the story about my feet being cold. He smirked. 'Not acclimatised to this sort of work, are you? Get a move on, then.'

He picked up his shoes and tipped them, frowning. Clay barged through the door.

'Captain, I'm glad you're here. I don't know what Tyler is doing—'

'Helping Alice,' barked Greenbow, cutting Clay off. He thrust a hand in his shoe and cast his eyes about wildly.

'But—' Clay tried but Greenbow held up his hand.

'Who else has entered the base in the last hour?'

Clay blinked. 'I'm not sure.'

'You've been monitoring the entrance?' He pointed at the camera.

Clay flushed. 'Yes. Marie came back briefly, then Tyler. But I've been in the labs as well…'

I sat down on the bench and removed my trainers, pushing them under the bench and dropping the keys with them at the same time. They jangled as they hit the floor. Greenbow spun.

I made a show of moving my trainers and reaching under, holding the keys out. 'Are these anyone's?' I asked.

He snatched them and bent to put his shoes on, glaring at Clay. 'Just want to ensure everyone's following correct decontamination procedures.' He paused for a moment, staring at me, then pushed through the door with Clay protesting in his wake, leaving me to suit up in peace.

Chapter Twenty-three

The clouds were a black duvet above, depositing an inexorable torrent of water, which bounced from every surface, creating rivers criss-crossing the well-trodden paths across the island.

Rather than complete the survey, I retrieved the binoculars and went to find Alice, catching her outside Camp Vollum. Marie and Hurley stuck to her like glue, giving us no opportunity to talk, though things had moved on quickly and I wasn't sure she had anything of value to tell me any more. Gambetta, true to form, wasn't far away; tinkering with the pumping equipment, looking busy whilst eying us suspiciously. I spoke to Dash again by the incinerator for a while, watching the others carefully. Demeter came by to discuss soil densities before heading up onto the cliffs to continue whatever he was doing up there. At that point Gambetta lost interest in us, skulking after the Russian, disappearing into the rain. Helping Demeter run some tests near the cliffs, finally doing something useful, Hurley remarked. I almost followed to confront him about the key but decided I'd nothing to gain; neither a lie nor the truth would advance my thinking.

I meandered back and forth, looking busy whilst watching the team, and as afternoon turned to early evening I slipped away alone, taking care I wasn't followed.

I walked back up the hill towards the beach, searching for a decent vantage point overlooking X-Base, somewhere overgrown, back to the sea. I crawled along the ridge until I found a depression that would suit my purpose then pressed myself into the heather, burrowing in, tearing clumps of mud and grass to cover me like a ghillie-suited sniper, settling down to lie in wait. Eyes trained on the base, watching through the binoculars.

Shadows lengthened as minutes ticked round an hour. I counted people entering the decontamination chamber. It was impossible to tell some of them apart in the suits, but through the binoculars I scrutinised the windows of the base carefully, the common areas, seeing flashes of the team, striking people off in my mind – Hurley making a drink, Gambetta reading – I kept a tally of who was inside and who was still out wandering the island. More of the rooms lit up, including bedrooms and the radio room further down the base, but the angle meant I couldn't see who was in there.

Cold seeped upwards from the streams trickling beneath me. Twilight lent the crashing surf a menacing resonance, booming but muffled under oppressive rain. The island would be impossible to navigate at night, particularly in this weather. Anyone out now was using a torch, which made it easier to pick out the others – including anyone approaching in this direction.

No one did.

During the surveillance I thought about my conversations with the others, when I'd taken the opportunity to learn a little more about my French friend. Apparently he'd been brought in to look at the effects of the anthrax on the geology – whether the resurgence of the anthrax was due to its seepage into the substrata through groundwater, or whether the contamination remained surface-borne. He didn't seem to have made too much headway with the research so far. Hurley had said he didn't have much time for him, despite the fact they looked friendly enough. Marie had said similar, though I'd noticed her talking animatedly to him.

I wondered if Greenbow suspected Gambetta was DGSE. The *Direction Générale de la Sécurité Extérieure* – France's intelligence service. A fair guess, given his recent secondment to the project, his hobby of wandering the island keeping tabs on people, and his complete lack of discernible skill in relation to decontamination of anthrax-infected land. Definitely top of my list of suspicious persons, I thought as I adjusted the binoculars and scanned the dark horizon.

I used the time alone to go back over my theory.

Kyle's tea had been inside the base, he'd been infected inside the base. The anthrax was outside the base. Somewhere there had to have been a crossover. It was difficult to take anything in and out, unless you wanted it contaminated. You'd have to carry it under your suit, like my gun. If you were outside, that meant breaking the seal to get at it (I'd gambled that if I needed to tear the suit to use my gun, I had bigger and more immediate problems than anthrax).

It was difficult enough to take things out, but impossible to bring anything *into* the base. All tools were stored in the shed, remaining on the 'dirty' side. Torches were hung on racks by the door. Vials of anthrax samples – much like those I'd collected for Alice – were brought in but rigorously controlled and signed in by two people, for obvious reasons. I'd watched them do it – at each base, containers of heavily chlorinated water, kept in lockers in the decontamination chambers, were used to transport tubes of soil samples to the labs. They had to be signed in, catalogued and stored by either Ingrid or Clay – and all of them could be accounted for at any time by either of them. Let's not forget, this was a weapon of mass destruction, after all.

Until I'd seen Gambetta earlier I'd wondered how the murderer had smuggled the toxin inside, because – unlike my gun – a vial of anthrax, like Gambetta's lighter and cigs, would be on the outside of their suit with nowhere to hide it.

The missing key had confirmed the simplest of explanations, and the reason I'd been lying here alone, waiting for complete darkness.

Chapter Twenty-four

I pulled myself out of my bracken hide, brushed myself off, and headed for the bright lights of X-Base. It was a straight run, no need for a torch, no cliffs for me to walk off.

After a trip to the shed I paused by the steps, safe in the amber glow of the lamp above the door. It highlighted the rain around me, but beyond the pool of light the island was absolutely black. I strained my eyes but there was nothing. I strained my ears but the rain pounded on my plastic hood. I thought I heard a helicopter roar overhead at one point, but the already muffled sound was swallowed by the storm before I could pinpoint it.

I rounded the HADU and started down the far side of the complex. I needed to do this quickly, before I was seen.

The windows around the outer perimeter belonged to the various rooms, facing the open moorland. I slowed, ducking under the glow from the first window – the common room. Again under the next window, the dining room, and round the corner at the end of the kitchen, passing the curved corridor to the first sleeping hut – mine.

As far as most people knew the windows were all sealed, but it would have been easy enough for someone with a key to have slid a window open from the outside, dropping a vial of contaminated soil into their bedroom, avoiding the CCTV.

I didn't like the idea of people being able to come and go without detection, bypassing everyone else and the CCTV, so I set about remedying the lax security. I could have pocketed all the other keys from Greenbow's office, then maybe confronted Gambetta in front of the team, but I didn't want to involve anyone else just yet. Fortunately, there was a far easier way to secure the windows, without alerting anyone.

I was crouched alongside my bedroom hut. There were two windows, as each hut contained two rooms. Both dark. I knew from my recce that Demeter was still outside somewhere so ours was a good window to start with. I stood up, peering in. Thanks to the hut's stilts and the relatively small windows (less surface area means less heat loss in the Antarctic) my chin only reached the bottom of the window frame. As far as I could see, the room was empty. I clicked on my torch, shining it through the window to be sure. Demeter's bed was the opposite of mine – again perfectly made, the effect of years in relative captivity on a military base in the Soviet Union, I presumed. My opened bottle was standing upright on the bedside table, the unopened one lay on the bed. I switched off the torch.

I turned my attention to the window frame itself. Each window was split into two staggered panes – one pane sliding sideways across the other in a track. It meant only half of the window area opened, but it was still plenty big enough for even Dash to climb through.

It was the outer pane which contained the handle and lock, so the outer pane which slid open. I traced my finger down the joint between the two frames. As you'd expect, it was close, airtight. I reached in my pocket, pulling out a screwdriver and a self-tapping screw I'd swiped from the shed. I jabbed the screw into the inner frame, pushed the screwdriver as hard as I could, turning, grinding until the screw finally bit into the plastic. I kept screwing it in until just the head stuck out. I coloured the end of the shiny brass screw with the black permanent marker I'd used to label Alice's vials, and stood back. The screw was invisible.

There was no way the window would open now – milli-metres, at best, until it jammed on the screw head blocking the track. One down. It stood to reason the killer would most likely have used their own bedroom as the means of smuggling the anthrax in (you wouldn't drop something onto the sofa in the common room or the kitchen worktop, and leave it there for ten minutes while you decontaminated), so I wasn't as concerned with the public areas at the moment; the lounge, dining room, kitchen, labs – I didn't want to be seen screwing windows shut, for obvious reasons.

The clouds parted, orange base glowing in the faint light. I looked up to see a thin sliver of moon watching me, the last of it before the darkness of early December and the coming of the Oak Moon, the time of the Dark Lord, if you're into that sort of thing. I'm not, but I shivered all the same.

I felt something else, close by, a presence, just a whisper. The same phantom had followed me for so long now. My hands were clammy in the thick gloves, my heart raced, I felt dizzy, had to reach a hand to the wall to steady myself. It would be satisfied soon. I got my breath back and turned through 360 degrees to empty black. The Moon scowled and slid back behind the clouds, leaving me alone again.

Chapter Twenty-five

In less than ten minutes I'd worked my way back, even managing to do all the labs, radio room, and dining room undetected. Only the kitchen and lounge had been occupied. I was a little concerned with how Dash would react when he found out I'd screwed nearly all his windows shut, but reasoned it was worth the risk and, though no one seemed to be acknowledging it, we had other things to worry about. Now anyone wanting to bring anthrax – or anything else, for that matter – in or out of the base would be forced to run the gauntlet of CCTV camera in the HADU.

After dropping the screwdriver off, I climbed the steps, walking straight into the first shower, this time scrubbing quickly, glad to be back inside. I spent considerably longer in the second shower, sitting on the floor, letting the hot water flush the cold from my bones and wishing more than ever I was back on the mainland. I was getting too old for this, maybe not physically, but… I held my head in my hands, gripping tightly to stop them shivering.

My mind wandered; an old coaching inn on the shores of Loch Ness, a pie and a pint of something local, without having to choose a seat with a view of the exits. Craving a different kind of normality, for something else to become familiar, to push out the other. Someone went out, toilets flushed, doors banged. When I realised I was stalling, I finally left the cubicle.

Chapter Twenty-six

Unexpectedly, there was a party atmosphere in the common room. The term is relative, you understand; still, drinks were flowing and smiles seemed to have replaced ill tempers as I hovered silently in the doorway. Marie was deep in conversation over an iPad with Alice, both of them cradling wine glasses. Dash was sitting at the table in the corner. I gave him a nod, but he was engrossed in a handful of cards. He must have been playing with Hurley, who was absent – another set of cards were lying face down on the table opposite him. From the look on his face, he was wrestling with the idea of sneaking a peek. I realised Gambetta was absent too, and for a brief moment I panicked that I'd miscalculated, that he could have been watching me all that time, so I was relieved when someone mentioned he was in the comms room for the 7 p.m. radio check-in.

Clay was slouched in an armchair, a magazine on his lap and a tumbler of Scotch clasped in a bony claw. He yawned, with the effect that his already inhumanly long head increased in size twofold. With his ears jutting out and his jaw hanging open he looked for all the world like Nosferatu. Greenbow was missing. My watch said seven – he'd be wondering why I hadn't been to see him yet.

'Winning yet, Dash?' I asked.

He jumped, dropping Hurley's cards. 'It's about to turn in my favour.' He smiled, leaning back in his chair and rearranging his hand.

'Not been swept away by the tide?' asked Clay, voice slurred.

'Wouldn't want to miss your ninetieth birthday, would I?'

He scowled. 'We're celebrating my team's achievements.'

Marie put the iPad down and jumped off the sofa. 'The upgraded decontamination procedures work!' she exclaimed, walking over to give me a hug before I could protest. 'The worst-affected areas are showing clear!' Her accent had grown noticeably thicker; probably a correlation with the almost empty glass in her hand.

'John, grab a glass!' said Dash. Alice looked decidedly uncomfortable with that but remained silent.

'He only drinks Scotch,' said Clay, waving his own glass and spilling it down his sleeve. He refilled it from a hip flask extracted from the folds of his cardigan, then added, 'In fact, go and get the champagne from the kitchen.'

Was he ordering me around now? Between him and Greenbow I was beginning to lose my patience. Not much longer, I told myself. I held my tongue, backing out of the room.

As it turned out there was a bottle of prosecco in the fridge. No stemware in the cupboard so I grabbed five tumblers. I'd just returned to the lounge as Hurley jogged up behind me.

All eyes turned to him eagerly.

'Did Ingrid radio in the final results?' asked Alice.

'Yep, she's still finishing up at Vollum. Gambetta's filling them in on his data. Ford passes on his congratulations.'

Clay nodded his approval. Ford, I knew, was the head of PDBRG, his boss back at Porton Down.

'So what's the verdict?' asked Alice.

Hurley crossed the room, retaking his seat opposite Dash. 'Still stuck here for the duration, unfortunately. He wants more tests running.'

'But he was pleased?' asked Marie.

'*Mais oui, il était très heureux,*' Hurley said, beaming like a puppy that'd just sat for the first time. *Yes, he's dead happy.*

Marie laughed. 'Better, but it's "trezeureux" – don't pronounce the "h" and when a word ends in an "s", run the words together.'

'Well, he was pleased.'

Clay looked at the bottle in my hand. 'Yes, well, champagne!'

'Prosecco, I'm afraid.'

'Same thing, give it to me, you illiterate northern imbecile.'

Clearly *someone* was still pissed off about being put down by Greenbow in front of me earlier. 'It is most definitely not the same thing, Clay,' I said, holding the cork and twisting the bottle. Now don't get the wrong idea, I'm not stuck up my own arse – I just hated the man.

I filled a glass and held it out to Clay, who snatched it from me. 'Yes, well, of course a drunk *would* know.'

'Says the man with a glass in each hand, eh?' I said. 'You stupid old bastard,' I added under my breath, filling another for Hurley. Marie took one for herself and handed another to Alice.

'I hope you didn't bring a glass for yourself,' said Clay. 'Didn't Greenbow want to see you as soon as you returned?'

I crossed the room, pouring the last glass for Dash then swigging the remnants from the bottle. 'Just on my way there. Have a good evening.'

Chapter Twenty-seven

KEEP CALM AND SOLDIER ON, the mug on Greenbow's desk said. *Dickhead*. I'd love to see how calm he'd be if the shit hit the fan.

'Ironic, isn't it?' I said.

'What's that?' Greenbow tapped his pen in time to 'The British Grenadiers' piping out from a tinny Bluetooth speaker sitting on the filing cabinet.

'*Scotland Forever!*' I tore my eyes away from the filing cabinet and pointed at the print hanging behind his head. 'By Lady Butler; I've seen the original in Leeds. *Scotland Forever!*, hanging on a wall on a beautiful Scottish island that'll probably be a patch of contaminated Scotland forever, thanks to people like you.'

He stopped tapping, laid the pen next to a small stack of Rich Tea biscuits, and picked up his mug of tea. 'I didn't take you for an art lover.'

'School trip.' I saw the red file on the desk in front of him, the one with my name on the front.

'Coincidentally, you bring me straight to the point.' He took a sip of tea and tried to hide a wince. 'Where *did* you school, Tyler?' There was an edge to his voice and it wasn't because he'd just burnt his mouth. 'Halifax?' He rolled the syllables in disgust and leaned back in his chair, staring down his nose.

''Alifax, it's a silent H.'

He glared. 'Your brother was in the Parachute Regiment?'

I kept my mouth shut.

'Justin Tyler. Spent some time in 1 Para until –' he put the cup down and opened the file, shuffled some papers, and looked up – 'insubordination, disobeying orders. Related to you, that's not hard to believe. DD in 2002.' He pulled out another piece of paper and waved it around. 'Since then, illegal combatant. Black-market profiteering. Arms trading. Allegations of war crimes. A fitting career for someone deemed unfit to serve, until –' he shuffled again, extracting a photograph, tossing it on the desk – 'he died in a godforsaken desert a decade ago.'

I already knew what photo it was but couldn't avoid another glance. The blown-up Landcruiser. Another photo peeping out showed a hand, blood seeping into dirt, all bleached out by Middle Eastern sun. My legs were going again, I took a step backwards to lean against the wall, flexing my hands.

Greenbow hadn't noticed. 'And little brother,' he continued, brandishing the papers still, 'little brother *John* Tyler failed to reach even *those* dizzying heights. Dropped out of university. Dropped out of a naval application. Dropped out of society, it seems.' I held my breath. Someone had been doing some research. 'Screwing your way around Thailand on a two-decade-long gap year, no doubt.'

I let out the breath. 'You said you had a point?'

He picked up the pen and started drumming again as the music changed to 'Balaclava March'. 'This, Tyler, is my point exactly. You're an oik, a nobody. You're not even a qualified engineer.'

'Well—'

'And that being the case, I don't understand what you're doing on my island.'

'Square peg?'

'Quite.'

I felt my mouth twitch, almost slipping into a smile. Unless he was holding back, he didn't know anything. Whoever had fed him this crap hadn't dug any deeper than publicly available records. Did he suspect I'd been in his office? No, he'd already had the file.

'I'm here because I know a shitload more about those HADUs than you know about soldiering. I'm guessing this is your first time in the field—'

He slammed his pen on the desk, one of the Rich Teas teetered and fell, smashing across the floor. He composed himself, wiping up a couple of drips of tea, steepled his fingers, and inhaled slowly in that same way Clay kept doing. Different clothes and approaches, similar mentality.

'Do you think I'm stupid?'

There was a very easy, one-word answer I could have given. 'I think you're the same officer I've met a hundred times before. Stupid isn't the first adjective I'd pick.'

He pointed accusingly. 'How do you know Alice String?'

Was he fishing? 'When Rafferty-Nath tendered for the military contract we worked with specialists from Porton. She was one of our contacts.'

'There's more to it than that.'

I piled on the lies. 'There's some... history. It didn't end well.'

'You surprise me. Do you think the drinking played a part?'

I didn't have time to invent a reply, he leapt up, chair scraping across the floor. He was around the desk and in front of me before it fell. Dark eyes bored through mine. I was acutely aware of the pistol in my waistband, and shoved a hand in my pocket to cover it.

'Why did you lie, Tyler?'

'About?'

'The door. The malfunction.'

I shrugged. 'Happens with new technology; this is a test—'

'There was no bloody malfunction!' he shouted. 'Did you imagine I wouldn't know? The fuses were the first thing I had checked!'

I had no immediate answer. His unblinking eyes continued to drill into me.

'Your clearance is revoked,' he hissed. 'First light, you're on a helicopter, and if they've any sense they'll march you straight to a misconduct hearing. Until then you're confined to quarters.'

'You wanna know why I didn't tell you?' I matched his stare. 'You have a saboteur on the island.' I kept hold of his eyes until he moved away to look out the window. 'You've got a saboteur,' I repeated, 'and let's not forget the dead body, and I value my life, thanks. I'm not about to go around shouting about the fact that someone purposely disabled the HADU, whatever the reason might be.'

'You should have come to me.'

'And risk ending up like poor Andy Kyle? No chance; like I said, I value my life.'

'There's no saboteur, Tyler. I agree the fuse was purposely removed, but I'm sure there's a legitimate reason.'

'Look, I just want to do my job and go home, the sooner the better.'

He ran a finger down the window, tracing the path of the rain. 'Your wish is about to be granted, believe me.' He'd be gutted when he learned he had no chance of getting me kicked off. He removed his beret, working his fingertips into his forehead. 'Whatever your politics, this country is in a state. We're a country divided, polarised, seems we're imploding at every opportunity.' He turned from the window, picking and forming his words slowly. 'And there's been ample opportunity recently. Thanks to world and domestic events, there's been a huge power shift. We can no longer count on the United States, and most of Europe is watching us eat ourselves, though they know there's a good chance they're next. Russia knows that right now we're the weak link in the West, they continually test us, probing for gaps. A hacked department here, an encroaching flight there. On top of that, funding's been slashed, seven departments set to merge this year alone. Workload at Porton Down Biological Research Group is dwindling. Sure, there'll be an occasional ex-KGB spy poisoning that demands our expertise but really, will that support us? What do these people do when they're made redundant? Not much call for analysing biological weapons on Civvy Street. Somewhere in Westminster, lists of surplus departments, surplus people, are circulating. I don't want PDBRG to be on any of those lists, you understand?'

'I think so.'

'Let's not forget that this base is on loan from the Americans, as are two of our colleagues.'

'And?' He was rambling, I was hoping he'd get to the point soon.

'And after all the delays we've suffered on this project we can't afford another foul-up. We've convinced the Americans your friend Mr Kyle's death was down to his lack of training. He was, after all, not one of us.'

'You're covering it up?'

'Understand this, Tyler; there's nothing to cover up. He simply had an accident, didn't take sufficient precautions. All I'm doing is ensuring the bigger boys know there were no failings on our part.'

'And the missing fuse?'

The hard stare was back. 'Perhaps we'll never know why Kyle removed it. It was probably faulty, he was halfway through a repair when his illness overcame him. That's what the record will say. This is important; I need you to agree that's what happened.' He perched on the desk, still staring at me, but the anger had gone.

'I'm just an oik so I don't really understand what you're on about. I'm not sure that's what my record will say.'

'You mention this to anyone – I mean anyone – and I'll have you up on charges. Count yourself lucky you're going home tomorrow instead of to a cell.'

I nodded, though I knew full well I'd be staying until the job was done.

There was a knock at the door. 'Come.'

Alice opened it but remained on the threshold. 'Captain, Dr Clay is asking for you.'

'Stay in your room,' he said to me, switching off the speaker and ushering us into the corridor. 'I don't want to see you until morning.'

Alice raised her eyebrows but I said nothing. The three of us walked together through the connecting passage into the next hut. At the far end of the corridor Hurley strode towards us, bottle in hand. Demeter shuffled behind him, finally in from the cold.

Alice stopped when we reached her bedroom, tapping my arm. 'In here while I grab my stuff.'

I hovered in the doorway, leaving Greenbow to march onward. He stood aside to let Hurley and Demeter pass, and as they crossed I slid into the room.

Alice smiled warmly. 'Sounded like you needed rescuing.'

'Greenbow knows something's up,' I said. 'But I don't know if he's stupid or clever.'

'Stupid,' she replied, stuffing a jumper into a rucksack. 'What did he say?'

'He saw us talking. I fed him some bullshit, pretty sure I threw him off the scent. If he asks, we worked together previously on the design for the HADU.' She frowned. 'Okay, I might have implied a bit more than that. But more importantly, he checked the fuse on the doors.'

'Shit,' she whispered. 'Well, it doesn't take a psychic to work out something's rotten here.' She looked past me and dialled her voice up an octave. 'Viktor, how's that southern quadrant looking?'

Demeter threw his hands up in despair, shuffling off again as Hurley entered.

'Fizzy wine's all gone, probably a blessing,' he said. 'I've got some real alcohol – in the form of Kentucky bourbon – in my room. Hold this.' He handed me the empty bottle and clapped a hand on Demeter's shoulder, nearly knocking his gas mask off. I crossed to the door and watched them walk together as far as Hurley's bedroom. Demeter plodded on alone, stopping at the radio room. I felt sorry for him. He hunched, a smaller, deflated version of the vibrant man I'd seen that morning. Not surprising, considering the poor guy had been out on the cliffs for hours in the freezing rain. I remembered yesterday he'd come in, decontaminated, changed straight into a fresh suit before grabbing a snack and heading back out. You couldn't fault the man's work ethic.

'Demeter works too hard sometimes,' Alice said, reading my mind. 'Barely has time to eat, hardly sleeps.'

'You know he was on about spirits this morning?'

'Spirits?' She frowned.

'Of the island.'

'I told you he was the one to watch. One of these days he's gonna snap.'

I shrugged. 'Maybe he already has.'

She nodded, grabbing a magazine from the bedside table and pushing it into her bag. 'I'm telling you, he's bookies' favourite for offing Kyle.'

At the very far end of the corridor Demeter knocked on the door to the radio room. Alice looked up, saw me watching.

'He'll be making his report with Gambetta,' she said. 'Speaking of whom, did he tell you what he saw this aft?'

'Gambetta? I'd be the last person he spoke to.'

'He's okay, you know, once you get to know him. You just got off on the wrong foot.'

I smirked when I remembered literally knocking him off his foot was our first meeting. It faded just as quickly when I wondered again whether that almost got me killed.

Along the corridor Demeter banged harder on the door to the radio room. The reply mustn't have been to his liking as he shook his head and shouted something back, breaking into muffled Russian cursing. We ducked in as he looked round, then back out to see the door open. He stuck his head in, gesticulating wildly, pushing the door roughly, barging his way into the radio room. The wall shook as the door slammed behind him. At the same time the other door in the hut opened and Hurley popped his head out, grinning, obviously enjoying the argument going on next door. Regardless of how Alice felt about Gambetta, I hoped Demeter was tearing him a new one. Age wouldn't matter, I was sure the tough Russian could hold his own, wouldn't be intimidated.

'Alice, come choose your poison!' Hurley shouted.

Great choice of words.

Alice tapped my arm and nodded in the other direction. I followed her gaze down the corridor to see Greenbow waiting, looking back.

'Probably better if Greenbow doesn't see us together right now,' she said.

Next to him, Marie poked her head out of her room, saw us, then withdrew it sharply, slamming her door. I was anxious to get into my own room; I needed to change, the pistol felt conspicuous without the baggy suit. I couldn't risk anyone noticing it, could do without the questions right now. I left Alice to it. Greenbow turned and disappeared round the corner in front.

I'd just reached the connecting tunnel into my own hut when there was a sharp crack. Time stopped as it echoed around the base, bouncing between the plastic walls and on down the corridors. An unmistakable sound, from behind me.

I spun, hand automatically moving towards my gun. Back up the corridor Alice was already running for the radio room.

I took off after her, shouting at her to stop, reaching under my jumper, flicking open the holster's safety strap.

Hurley was frozen in his doorway up ahead. 'Was that a—?'

'Gunshot!' I shouted, tearing along the corridor towards them.

Hurley dashed from his room as I approached his door. I sidestepped but we collided, I slammed painfully into the wall, cracking my elbow on the window ledge. Hurley fell, flailing, his bulk taking me with him. I struggled to pull myself free. Down the corridor Marie had reappeared and started walking towards us. Alice grabbed the door handle to the radio room.

'Wait!' I shouted, pushing Hurley off.

She looked at me, turning the handle, throwing open the door to the radio room, stepping inside. I got out from under Hurley, scrambling to my feet. Alice screamed, backed out of the room, hit the wall, leaned against it, breathing hard.

I checked she was okay, turned my attention to the doorway. I could already see enough to know it wasn't pretty. I withdrew my pistol, held it down low, and stepped into the room.

Chapter Twenty-eight

At point-blank range, a 7.65mm hollow point bullet makes a hell of a mess.

The far wall was painted in blood. It dripped from the desk, pooling on the floor, a dark mirror spreading in all directions. It ran down the window, flickering in the strip light, reflecting murky pink flashes across the walls. A whiff of burning hung on the blood-scented air, almost chewable. I screwed my eyes shut, fighting back bile.

The radio on the desk crackled, spitting static. I gripped the doorframe, opening my eyes. The handset was dangling by the wire, clanging against the leg of an upturned chair. Holding my pistol down in front so Alice couldn't see, I stumbled around the spreading red slick to switch off the set. I lifted my jumper, pushed the pistol into the holster, looked back at her in the corridor. Sweat beaded across her paper-white face.

'Is he dead?' she asked.

The question seemed ridiculous given the size of the hole in Gambetta's head, but it wasn't the time for sarcasm so I just nodded. She sank to the floor.

Hurley appeared, sliding down next to her. 'Where is he?'

Since Gambetta was laid out at my feet I assumed he was referring to Demeter.

'No idea.' I shrugged. 'Room's empty.'

'Gambetta's dead!' he shouted, then shot off down the corridor, spreading the news. 'Demeter's killed Gambetta. He's gone out the window!'

More shouts sprang up from further along the base.

'He's outside!'

'Gone out the window!'

'Lock the doors!'

I gave my best shot at a sympathetic smile to Alice. She rocked, eyes darting, settling on the body, drawing her legs under her chin. Clearly corpses were a novelty to her. I've never been good with empathy, but I guessed Marie would be along soon to absolve me of that responsibility.

'I'm shutting the door.'

She nodded.

I closed it, leaning back, massaging my eyes. Lack of sleep had taken its toll on my critical thinking but my senses had sharpened. No fear now, the scent of blood had awakened something deep within. Time to work.

I took in the details. I'd not been in this room before, but like all the other huts, the walls and floor were seamless grey plastic. *It'll make the clean-up easier.* Government-issue shelving ran the length of the walls on either side, spots of blood already drying on cardboard boxes piled high. A TV was positioned on the shelves, angled towards the desk; the CCTV from the main entrance, but it was switched off.

Standing behind the door was a filing cabinet similar to Greenbow's. I gave a handle a pull but it was locked. The only other furniture was the desk under the window and the upturned chair next to the body. I couldn't see a gun, which ruled out suicide – though it was obviously murder.

Gambetta lay on his back in the middle of the room, one arm pointing at the shelves, the other submerged in blood by his head, as if he'd had an arm up, trying in vain to protect himself. The amount of blood was staggering; I hoped his watch was waterproof.

I knelt to inspect the wound. The shot had entered his left eye, the other stared at me. His face was bloody and not from the gunshot, a stream still trickled from his nose and a cut on his cheek. I touched my fingers to his neck out of habit, obviously, no pulse.

The bullet had removed a good deal of his skull before slamming into the ceiling above the window where a hole punctured the plastic cladding, surrounded by a splattering of matter I could only assume was brain. I traced the path of the bullet, concluding Demeter had fired from the hip.

Where the *fuck* was he?

We'd been in the corridor right outside when he'd entered, seen them arguing, heard the shot, entered a few seconds later to find it empty. Except, of course, for the warm body in the middle of the room.

It was obvious how Gambetta had been killed. It was equally obvious who'd killed him. What wasn't obvious was how he'd escaped the room. There was nowhere to hide and I began to doubt my own memory, because despite their assumptions I knew he couldn't possibly have escaped out the window. Just a short time earlier, I'd screwed that same window shut from the outside.

I pulled the hip flask from my pocket. Had I really screwed this window shut? I thought I'd done them all, but had I been mistaken? I took a swig and crossed to the window, avoiding the pool of blood.

The missing key was still sticking out of the lock. *Fuck.* That must be it – I'd misjudged it somehow, a random error on my part allowing Demeter to escape. I gave the handle a pull, it opened millimetres then stuck fast. I *had* screwed it shut. The sound of rain intensified as droplets sprayed inside. I noticed more water on the floor, from where the window had been opened previously. Demeter must have wrenched the window open to make his escape, but the screw had dug in and held, preventing it opening further. I pushed the other way, shutting it with a click, then crossed to the door, avoiding the blood again.

It opened before I reached it, Greenbow edging into the room. Marie and Alice peered around him, moving back as he shut the door. The grip of a pistol protruded ominously from a holster on his belt. Browning Hi-Power, standard issue; he'd taken his time getting here because he'd gone to tool up first. I stepped aside, revealing the full extent of the mess. Greenbow recoiled.

'So,' he said, eyes widening as he took in the scene, 'Demeter *was* our saboteur, eh?'

'Dr Scarlet, in the Radio Room, with the pistol.'

'But why kill the frog?'

I didn't answer.

'And he's definitely gone?'

'Nowhere else he could be hiding,' I said. No reason to complicate matters. Yet.

'Out the window, then.'

'Any idea how he got hold of a key?' I asked, pointing at the window lock, wondering if it was the one Gambetta had been using or yet another missing key.

'I… no…' He struggled to take it in, realising the implication. 'I need to check.'

Greenbow was pale, making no attempt to move from the door, and I realised that for all his bluster he'd probably never been in this kind of situation before, never seen anything as grim.

'Shot at close range,' I said, 'beaten, too.'

'Beaten?'

'Punched, or hit with something. Broken nose. There are fresh cuts and marks on his cheeks that would've turned into nasty bruises if the bullet hadn't got in the way of his circulation. Look at his knuckles.'

'What does it mean?'

'He was fighting with Demeter.'

'We need to report this,' said Greenbow.

'That'll be difficult.' I nodded towards the smashed radio. 'I'm guessing whatever his motive, he's destroyed the radio to cover his tracks. Is the TV normally off?' I pointed at the CCTV unit.

He held a hand to his mouth. 'I think that's the least of our worries.'

I crossed to the shelves to pick a thin screwdriver from a rack, looking at the hole above the window. I stood the chair up in the blood slick under it.

'Don't touch anything,' said Greenbow. He'd gone fully green and had no intention of helping.

'I doubt we'll be getting a forensics team in here for a while, let's see what we can find out.'

I stood on the chair, digging the screwdriver into the jagged hole. The low-velocity round had expended most of its energy pulverising Gambetta's skull, tumbling its merry way through the air rather than punching neatly into the ceiling. As a result the dull metal was visible just beneath the plastic. I stabbed at the cladding, tearing it back, finally popping the misshapen lump out. I tossed it to Greenbow, who had to remove his hand from his mouth to catch it.

'What do you think?'

'A bullet?'

'Small calibre. If I was forced to guess I'd say 7.65 mil Browning?'

He shrugged, throwing it back as I climbed off the chair. I placed it on the desk next to the radio. 'Where's everyone else? Right now?'

'Dash has sealed the door. Hurley is checking the rooms. Clay is still in the common room. Marie is taking Alice there, she's shaken up.'

'I'm not surprised. We need to get back there, right now.'

'Yes, yes…' His voice tailed off as he put his hand back to his mouth, only too eager to leave.

I followed him from the room, and as he went to his office to find what I already knew – that the key had come from his drawer – a couple of fresh questions whirled in my head. Why would Demeter want Gambetta dead? I wasn't overly enamoured with the guy but unless I knew for sure he was responsible for the incinerator stunt I wouldn't have blown his head off. There was no long-standing grudge between them as far as I could see, they'd been talking together fine earlier.

But the far more important question right now, the one only I was pondering, was; if I'd planned to murder Gambetta in that room, how would I have got out?

Chapter Twenty-nine

The rest of them were waiting in the common room, Alice, still pale and fidgety, sandwiched between Marie and Hurley. Having piled tables against the door to the HADU, Dash now stood guard at the window, fairly futile given the darkness and lashing rain, but I suppose it helped morale. Clay looked worse for wear, though still managed to clutch a glass of Scotch. Away from the blood and gore Greenbow had regained his composure. He stood in the centre of the room, cleared his throat.

'Owing to the unprecedented situation, I am assuming military command of X-Base.'

Clay murmured but Greenbow was undeterred. I decided to stay quiet, see how it panned out; I could always jump in if needed.

'As you know, we have a murderer on the island. For reasons unknown at this time, Viktor Demeter has killed Eric Gambetta. I've inspected the body for myself – Gambetta has been shot at close range with a pistol. Demeter is obviously armed. Fortunately, as I am also armed, there is no cause for alarm.'

'Why?' cried Marie. 'Why would he do this?'

'I haven't yet determined the underlying motive. However, we know he and Gambetta argued, and it looks to me like he gave him a good hiding before shooting him. He then destroyed the radio to cover his tracks.'

'Where the heck is he?' asked Dash, eyes flitting between Greenbow and the door.

'Knowing the shot would raise the alarm and rouse my attention, he fled the room via the window.'

'But how did he get out the window?' Dash persisted.

Greenbow coughed, clearly embarrassed. 'Somehow he evaded security. There are two window keys missing from the locked drawer in my office.'

Two? My ears pricked up, but I realised I had the other missing key; all keys accounted for.

'Makes sense he's disappeared,' said Alice, looking at Hurley. 'Remember what Gambetta said? When he came back for radio duty, he told us what he'd seen this morning.'

'What did he see?' I asked.

'Off the eastern cliffs.'

'Spit it out!'

'Divers. He saw divers out in the bay.'

Chapter Thirty

I'd seen Gambetta returning to the base earlier that evening, while I'd been on stake-out outside. According to Alice he'd wasted no time telling her and Hurley what he'd seen before reporting to Greenbow, getting him to call it in. Divers, one on the rocks below the cliffs with more heads disappearing beneath the waves.

The *Dauntless*' brief was simple: keep everyone clear of the island, no exceptions. Even locals had been escorted away smartly – so how had a group of divers got close?

Worse, Gambetta had thought they were armed.

I'm no diving expert but even I know that sport divers don't tend to go out tooled up. It was conceivable there were military teams training up here; I remembered from the briefing that there was a US task force on exercises south of here, their Marines playing war games in the mountains on the mainland. Too far away, no reason for them to be this far north. And our guard dog would still have warned them off, allies or not.

He'd said they'd been wearing dark, military-looking gear.

It raised the question; had Gambetta been killed because he'd seen something?

'The weapons he described sound like AKs.' Hurley turned back to the window, tracing a finger along the glass. 'Russians.'

'As I said earlier, there's no evidence of any divers,' said Greenbow. 'Armed or otherwise.'

'Where would they have come from?' asked Marie.

'This coastline's got a million inlets and bays,' said Dash. 'Could have come from anywhere.'

'Easy enough to park a sub right next to us.' Hurley turned back to the room. 'In from the north, slip through the deep channels. Deploy a Spetsnaz combat swimmer team right out the torpedo tubes without even surfacing.'

He looked at me for backup, I shrugged.

Greenbow shook his head. 'There's absolutely no way a submarine, Russian or otherwise, could make it into these waters with the Royal Navy's latest destroyer anchored out there.' He muttered something about an overactive imagination.

'2010!' Hurley waved a finger at Greenbow. 'A Russian sub was caught sitting right outside Faslane, your most sensitive naval base, waiting for Brit subs to float past. Only a couple of years ago a Russian sub pack had to be scared away from the Scottish coast.'

'You said it yourself, they were caught…' said Greenbow, but from the look on his face it was himself he was trying to convince.

'What about the new Borei class? Twice as quiet as the latest US subs.'

'Commandoes could be crawling over the island as we speak!' said Alice. 'What if they come for us?'

There was a smash of glass.

Everyone leapt, looking for the source, Clay slumped in his chair, broken tumbler glistening in a pool of Scotch at his feet. His head lolled as he slurred thickly.

'Nonsense, Demeter is… I'm…'

'You're drunk,' said Greenbow. 'Go to bed.'

Clay dry-retched. A strand of thick saliva escaped his lips, slowly reaching for his cardigan.

'I'm… I'm going to bed.'

He struggled to stand. Alice and Marie took an arm each, half helping, half dragging Clay from the room.

'Bloody fool,' Greenbow said.

'So now what?' Hurley asked.

'We radio the ship.' Three pairs of eyes locked onto me.

'The captain just said Demeter destroyed the radio?' said Dash.

'Presumably to aid his getaway,' I said. 'But we do have another, and we're wasting time.'

'Camp Vollum!' Dash shouted. 'I'd forgotten about Ingrid!'

'If Demeter *did* sabotage our radio to cover his escape he's probably on his way there now. He was suited up, he has a head start – we need to stop him. Captain, you and I should get up there; the rest of you stay here.'

'You can't go up there, Tyler. You don't have clearance.'

'I think we're way past that.'

'He's right,' said Dash.

Greenbow contemplated it for a second, weighing up the risk versus the threat from Demeter. 'Fine, but you stay with me at all times.'

I nodded.

'I'll come too,' said Hurley. 'If Demeter's there you'll need all the help you can get.' He was already racing down the corridor, and wouldn't get any arguments from me. I followed, Greenbow close behind. I grabbed a fresh suit from under my bed, then a second for the return trip; I was learning. I checked my pistol again, adjusted the holster, snatched my gas mask from the side table, kicking over the almost empty Scotch bottle on the floor.

Both Greenbow and Hurley were already racing back towards me, suits in hand. We met the others in the HADU.

'Be careful,' Dash said, somewhat unnecessarily, as he hastily wrapped duct tape around my boots. 'I don't care what Greenbow says, there really could be unwanted visitors on the island.'

Hurley nodded. 'You guys stay safe. Don't let anyone in, make sure you barricade the door after us.'

'Either way, Demeter's long gone,' I said. 'There's no point him returning.'

'Then why did he take two keys?' asked Dash.

It wasn't the time to tell them the other key was in my pocket. I was about to push my trainers under the bench when something caught my eye. What looked like a folded piece of paper had been jammed into one of them – I must have been walking round on it since I'd come back in, hadn't noticed it when I'd dressed.

'Hurry up, Tyler,' said Greenbow.

The other two were suited and ready, Greenbow's thick, gloved finger stuck through the trigger guard of his pistol. He was watching me like a hawk, whatever was in my shoe would have to wait. I pushed the paper deeper in as I slid them under the bench.

Greenbow marched to the door with Hurley in tow. I gave my seams a quick test to ensure everything was covered, shooting one last glance at the others. Alice and Marie had returned from Clay's room, already helping Dash slide a table towards the door, ready to seal themselves in. I gave Alice a wink, earning a smile of encouragement and a mouthed, 'Take care,' in response.

The wind screamed around the huts, a solid sheet of rain waiting to assault us as soon as the door slid open. I swore at the clouds as I was nearly blown off the steps but that only made them try harder. The weather meant communication was impossible as we struggled along what was now a river pouring from the hillside. Hurley went first, his light suit just about visible in the faint moonlight, bobbing as his head darted side to side. Greenbow followed, gun outstretched warily, not so sure of himself now we were outside. I brought up the rear, keeping one eye on them, the other on the island. We kept our torches off – no sense giving any unwanted visitors an easy target – which made for slower progress than I'd hoped. I envied Greenbow's camo-green suit, almost invisible in the night, should have insisted we all wore them.

I thought about Demeter, about the mysterious divers that Gambetta claimed to have seen. If an extraction team had been sent for Demeter then perhaps the destruction of the radio was the motive, and Gambetta had got in the way.

It made sense Demeter must have killed Kyle too. Poisoning his roommate's tea would have been easy, but what linked the two victims and their deaths, and the radio?

Had his defection all those years ago been a ploy, a long-term strategy by Russian intelligence services to get someone inside Porton Down? The public may have thought that sort of stuff had disappeared with the Berlin Wall, but I knew the Cold War was still there, tectonic plates of twenty-first century diplomacy barely hiding the magma beneath the surface, so it wasn't too hard a leap to make.

But why the sudden violence? If he'd wanted to escape, why hadn't he slipped quietly away on any number of other occasions, when it would've been so easy to just vanish? I decided the island itself held the key.

Most importantly for now, how the hell had he escaped from the room? I couldn't see his powers stretching to teleportation. What about invisibility? I looked around, peering into the storm. Where was he?

Chapter Thirty-one

Wiltshire, early 1940s.

Despite emerging victorious from the Battle of Britain, the country is still under attack by the Luftwaffe. Their lightning advance across Europe may have faltered at the Channel, but the Nazi war machine has dug in, with Hitler boasting that his impenetrable 'Atlantic Wall' stretches all the way from Norway to Spain.

Unfortunately for him, a wall only deters people on the ground.

Whilst the Luftwaffe still leap over the Channel to bomb major cities (though for the most part without the enthusiasm they had during the Blitz), the Royal Air Force is bombing German cities with increasing ferocity, including burning them to the ground with incendiary devices.

This was the stuff I'd learned at school, forgotten, and re-learned when I was old enough to be interested in anything other than girls and grunge. I'd heard of the island before, of course, about what had happened here. The briefing pack had coloured in the detail, and as we slogged up to Camp Vollum I thought over the history, tried to wrap my head round how it could be relevant to our current situation.

Those fire-bombing campaigns against German cities incense Hitler, who demands appropriate retaliation. Of course, this being Hitler, appropriate usually means the maximum possible overreaction.

Churchill understands this only too well, and whilst he knows the RAF are able to spare the country from the worst of the air raids, he also knows that regardless of how many Hurricanes and Spitfires are built, pilots trained, regardless of the latest developments in radar, and regardless of how many anti-aircraft batteries are deployed – one or more bombers will always get through. You couple that with the latest reports about rocket-powered aircraft and flying bombs that can outpace any allied fighter aircraft, the result is that if Hitler wants to drop a bomb anywhere on mainland Britain, he can still do so – 'finest hour' or not. It seems victory in the Battle of Britain has bought the country time, but the Nazis, at least in this early stage of the war, can afford to play a longer game.

A natural train of thought follows, in conference rooms and labs and military briefings on both sides of the North Sea. If a single bomber can always be guaranteed to get through and land at least one bomb on a target, even if the rest of the squadron fail, how can you maximise that bomb's effectiveness? Conventional high explosive development has reached its zenith and now physical size is a limiting factor – planes just can't carry bigger bombs. Spies report German research into atomic bombs, which can pack a vastly bigger punch with a smaller package, but they require exotic raw materials, extensive development and testing, and the physicists who'd either been drafted or escaped to Britain and America. So what else can the Nazis be up to?

Churchill instigates an investigation into the feasibility of an attack on Great Britain using bacteriological weapons. Enter Porton Down.

Porton Down had been set up during the previous war, its original purpose being the scientific investigation and further development of chemical warfare. A sparsely populated site near Salisbury, Wiltshire was chosen – a few farms and cottages moved on. Named the 'Royal Engineers Experimental Station', it began researching chemical agents such as chlorine and mustard gas. By the end of the First World War the tiny huts had grown into a large camp. All gas defence and respirator research had also moved to Porton from London.

The site had almost closed in 1919, but the War Office decreed research must continue and the establishment of a permanent base was begun. Wooden huts were replaced with concrete, civilian scientists were recruited, and the pace of research accelerated.

And at what a pace. The Manhattan Project, the US Atomic Program that spawned 'Little Boy' and 'Fat Man' – the bombs that flattened Hiroshima and Nagasaki respectively – is regarded as being the father of the modern Weapon of Mass Destruction.

If that's the case then the British – and Porton Down – are the grandfathers.

Chapter Thirty-two

A soft glow escaped the blinds somewhere in Camp Vollum. It looked like a peaceful haven in the storm; I hoped it was, that we weren't too late. I looked over at the incinerator and shuddered. A heck of a lot had happened in the last few hours.

Greenbow mounted the steps, faltering at the top.

'Hurley, open the doors.'

Hurley climbed up after him, staring at the keypad. 'I don't know the code. I assumed you had it.'

'I never have need to,' said Greenbow.

'I thought you were in charge?'

They both stared at the keypad. I rolled my eyes.

'23-15-63,' I said.

Hurley punched in the code and the light above the keypad blinked green. Greenbow pulled open the door, stepped inside. With one last scan out over the blackness, I followed.

This was my first time inside Camp Vollum. Unsurprisingly the HADU, and therefore decontamination procedures, were identical. After the first spray-down we carefully disposed of the suits, skipping the next showers in favour of speed.

All three huts here were deathly quiet – no gunshots, no one attacked us. Ominously, no one came to greet us either.

Greenbow dipped his pistol in the bleach, wiping it off on a towel. He held it warily.

'Anthrax has dropped down our priorities, Captain. If I were you I'd grip that gun more firmly.'

He held it outstretched, shaking.

'If you're going to hold it like that, don't walk behind me.'

He was reluctant to venture into the base, Hurley was about to slam through the door when I stopped him.

'Quietly.' I gestured for him to follow, Greenbow slinking behind us, still shaking. 'Captain, pass me your gun.'

'Absolutely not.'

KEEP CALM AND SOLDIER ON, wasn't it? 'Then do me a favour; put the bloody safety on.'

I gripped the door handle, opening it slowly. The noise increased, rain performing a drum solo on the plastic link tunnel. At the other end the door was open, total darkness beyond.

I crept forward into the corridor. Hurley followed, Greenbow a respectable distance behind, still holding the gun out. I brushed my hand against my hip, touching the reassuring handgrip of my own HK. I contemplated removing it but didn't want to overplay my hand. I also didn't want to risk switching the lights on, navigating by the dim moonlight darting in and out of the swiftly moving clouds. When we reached the door to the first room I tapped Hurley.

'Check it out. I'll stay here.'

Hurley nodded, gripping the handle. He burst into the room, quickly followed by Greenbow. After a few moments' scuffling they reappeared in the doorway.

'Lab's empty,' Hurley whispered.

I nodded, motioned to move on. Again the rain hammered on the plastic connecting tunnel, into another dark hut. We followed the same procedure but this time when Hurley opened the door to the room, a chink of light sliced the floor. It grew to a dazzling triangle stretching up the far wall as he opened the door wider, sticking his head in.

'Empty,' he said, the light somehow telling him that there was no need to whisper. I poked my head around the door to find a laboratory, with what looked like shiny white kitchen cabinets down the far wall. Various apparatus of no interest to me adorned the worktops, rows of white filing cabinets filling the near wall. Nowhere Demeter could be hiding. I shut the door, plunging the corridor again into darkness. Greenbow was apparently satisfied with our search; he remained in the corridor, reluctant to come any further. I grabbed the handle into the final hut, waiting in silence while our eyes readjusted. After a few moments I eased open the door.

There was a different sound this time. The familiar barrage of rain on plastic but also a screaming, howling sound that could only have been the wind tearing through an open window somewhere. I had a clear view all the way through to the far end of the base. Where every other hut had a door at each end, this last hut had a window – presumably the configuration could be adjusted as required. I stepped off the bridge into the hut, started to walk forward but my shoe skidded. The temperature plummeted, my stomach with it. I pulled out my torch, motioning to Hurley.

The beam illuminated a scene reminiscent of the radio room. Greenbow immediately backpedalled.

A pool of blood had spread across the floor, seeming to cover most of the corridor. It fanned across the windows and mixed with mud and rain running down the far wall. The sorrow I felt was the first genuine emotion I'd experienced here. Splayed out on the floor, in the spotlight of the torch beam, was Ingrid.

I didn't need to feel for a pulse. Just like Gambetta, she'd been shot in the head, the bullet removing the back of her skull. I knelt to study the wound and heard a tinny scratching. A pair of earphones swam in the puddle next to her head. I bent closer; a German singing about balloons. Tracing the wire down to her belt revealed an iPod. I tapped it, stopping the noise, then touched my finger in the pool of blood by her head.

'What the hell are you doing?' asked Hurley.

'Took us just over ten minutes to get here, right?' I rubbed my fingers together.

'I guess.'

'Gambetta was shot at quarter past.' I stood, wiping my fingers on my trousers.

'So?'

'So we're about ten minutes behind Demeter.'

'You're losing me, buddy. What's the significance?'

No point explaining it right now. Instead I pointed up at the door. 'This is the comms room, right?'

Hurley nodded. 'And break room. This is where we slept last night, before you fixed the door at X-Base. Poor Ingrid. Why would Demeter want to kill her?'

'The same reason he killed Gambetta,' said Greenbow, still hovering in the link tunnel fidgeting with his sidearm.

'Demeter was standing where you are now,' I said. 'He shot Ingrid as she left the common room.' My brow crumpled up as I noticed what was wrong. 'No range at all but he still managed to miss the first time.' I pointed at two distinct holes in the far window, the source of the screeching wind.

'How do you know he didn't shoot her twice? Her face is a mess.'

'The shot killed her instantly. Why fire a second time if she was already dead?'

'I guess maybe he squeezed a couple off in quick succession? Double tap?'

'So he did miss first time?' Greenbow added.

I reached for the door handle. My hand stuck to spots of congealed blood.

'Careful, he could still be in there,' said Hurley.

Given my suspicions, I seriously doubted it. I eased the door open and looked in on what was essentially the same common room as that in the main base. After swinging the torch beam around a few times I could see it was empty so I stepped inside, flicking the light on. A few items of clothing were scattered on the sofa, a mass of empty food wrappers piled next to a microwave on the sideboard. Next to them was a radio identical to the one back at the main base. I do mean identical – this set was also completely destroyed. I walked closer, running my hand through torn wires spilling from the back of the set. The speaker had been completely smashed in.

A TV set on the shelf displayed the entrance chamber. I grabbed the remote and clicked rewind, thinking it might reveal clues about Ingrid's murder – but an error message flashed up.

'So we're too late.' Greenbow shuffled up behind me, pistol still shaking.

'We were always going to be. How does this CCTV work?'

'Continuous recording, each forty-eight hours has a memory stick for audit purposes.' He pointed to a stack of memory sticks. 'They get overwritten after a couple of weeks.' He switched his gun into his other hand, pulled a box from the shelf, passed it to me. I opened it, skimming through neatly labelled memory sticks of CCTV footage.

'I can't find one for today.'

'It'll be in the recorder,' he snapped.

It wasn't. Whether the memory stick had been removed or never been in there, I'd no way to tell, and Greenbow was no help.

I returned to the corridor and, satisfied the base was otherwise empty, switched the light on – to find that Hurley had disappeared. I looked again at the windows, at the rain being driven through the neat holes, running down to mix with the puddles of mud and blood on the floor. The holes had punched straight through each pane of glass, which I guessed was laminated safety glass, otherwise the whole lot would have shattered.

'Where's Hurley gone?'

'Checking the labs to see if anything's missing.'

How had Demeter got past us? I envied Greenbow and the others, unburdened with the knowledge that the window in the radio room was sealed shut. How easy it was for them to believe he'd simply jumped out the window and then come here.

'We should get back,' said Hurley, creeping towards us along the corridor. 'It's not safe.'

Greenbow nodded. 'There's nothing we can do here.'

I agreed. 'Let's suit up.'

Greenbow led the way back to the HADU, only too happy to be leaving; proximity to real death and danger was too distasteful. He could still hardly grip the gun, his arm was shaking that much.

A few minutes later we were back out in the storm, trudging back to the main base. Convinced that Demeter had somehow fled, they had their torches on this time. I didn't – a marksman could easily have picked off one of the dancing lights. For the same reason, I hung back, putting some distance between us. It might sound callous, but I reckon putting self-preservation first is the best way to stay alive.

Fortunately there were no shots, and a few minutes later I was passing the dark stone cairn, dropping over the other side, within sight of the main base. It was in total darkness; no lights shining from the windows, just that dismal amber glow by the main door. Silhouetted against it, Greenbow and Hurley marched ahead, marked only by their torches sweeping side to side. They'd built up a couple of minutes' lead. I started down the slope, buffeted by the gale. No respite from the wind and rain; shouldn't have mattered much, clad in the waterproof suit, still, it slammed into the mask, blinding me. I turned, walking with my back to the wind.

Lightning flashed as the storm moved in from the open ocean behind me, and in the following black lull I saw it.

A light out in the darkness, off to the left, far from the base.

I stopped, knelt to wipe the visor, shielding it from the rain, staring hard. I could just about make out where the charcoal sky hit the coal-black ground. Right where they touched was a tiny bright pinprick. Hurley and Greenbow were below me, nearing the steps to the HADU. Everyone else was barricaded in the base. There was no one else on the island. No one except Demeter.

Thunder rumbled over the waves.

I reckoned the light to be over by the beach, near the ruins of the old cottage. Right where I'd left Kyle. Another dead body, more spirits swirling in the fog. I thought of Ingrid again, easy to laugh off in the daytime, when the sun bleaches everything clean. Easy to be sceptical when you're reading about it, or watching a film, safely protected by a page or screen. I said I'm not a superstitious man, but that doesn't stop an overactive imagination.

The light was gliding slowly towards the base. Pitch black night, unfamiliar territory. Ancient land, rich with legend. Stories bounced round my head, including recent history, strange wartime experiments. All topped off with the knowledge that somehow Demeter had killed Gambetta and passed straight through a solid wall, had killed Ingrid not far away from where I squatted, and now I was out here on my own. I felt a twitch in my arm, a tremble in my hand. I balled it into a fist.

Get a grip.

I've seen more than my share of real horror on jobs, know that nothing in the spirit world can begin to compare to human cruelty. I'd faced real devils before, ghosts were nothing.

I looked again at Greenbow and Hurley, who'd reached the base. One of their torches bounced up the steps while the other hovered and disappeared around the side, towards the sheds. Neither seemed to have seen the phantom light, which by now would be hidden to them round the other side of the huts.

There was a whisper somewhere behind me, I turned to empty moorland. I squinted at a black shape, a crouched person or the pile of boulders marking the summit of the island? As I stared, the darkness swirled, forming a figure that became unmistakable, one I hadn't seen for years, one it was impossible to see out here. I screwed my eyes shut, lifted my head to the rain, breathed deeply, forced myself to be aware of my emotions.

Fear, paranoia, they come first. Worse under stress, worse when I'm tired. *Be aware of it,* they'd said. Picture it, pry it out, don't let it grip, don't let it slow me. *Concentrate.* On the decisions. On the experience. On the *tools.* My right hand was still trembling slightly. I calmed it by resting my fingers against the heel of my pistol through my suit. When I opened my eyes there was no crouching figure, no whispers, just an old pile of rocks.

But the light was closer now. If I discounted ghosts – which I had to, imagination or not – and natural phenomena – which I had no knowledge about and couldn't possibly determine – what else could a light mean all the way out there? What if Gambetta really had seen divers coming ashore? I'd been sceptical, but Dash's words came back to me, the island could be crawling with Spetsnaz.

Either way, whoever the light belonged to couldn't possibly know I was watching them. I had the advantage.

'Fuck it,' I said to no one, taking a bearing, setting off quickly, jogging diagonally across the springy bracken on a course to intercept. Another glance at the base, a slice of light disappeared as the door shut – which meant the other two were now inside. I was alone out here, just me and the mystery light. It wasn't too comforting to think that for all Greenbow and Hurley knew, I could have fallen and injured myself. I could have been lying on the ground with a smashed mask, suffocating on anthrax. Worse, I could have been jumped by Demeter. I made a mental note to thank them for their concern then put it out of mind, concentrating on the light, which was now only a hundred metres or so away, still floating towards the base. I slowed, adjusted my angle, creeping forward on an intercept course, still without much of a plan.

It was closer now. This was no ghost, or natural phenomenon. A conical beam lit up the rain; undoubtedly a torch. It bobbed along, not deviating from the path, when suddenly it snapped off. The empty space was swallowed by the black.

I flung myself down as quietly as possible, pressing flat into the grass. Boots squelched in mud, approaching slowly. Then something else, rusting in the undergrowth. The familiar whisper of branches on plastic, another suit moving parallel to the path. Then more, all coming towards me. I stared hard, saw a shadow, an impossible blackness, a shapeless absence in the dark that could only be a figure. Another off to one side, as my eyes adjusted there was another, more fanned out across the moorland. Impossible to tell how many.

It was around this time I regretted discounting Gambetta's divers.

A tiny, dim red light hovered nearby, almost imperceptible, a star on a dark night from the corner of your eye. Infrared. *Night vision.* There was a shout from my left, something swept quickly through the bracken.

I'd been spotted.

I leapt to my feet, snapped my torch on, whipped it round. Shouts as dark figures swarmed, jerking in the strobe of the whirling torch. Gas masks spinning, gun barrels moving, confusion everywhere. It wouldn't last long. I pointed my torch at the nearest figure, straight into the night-vision goggles hanging in front of their gas mask. The rifle spun in their arms as they threw their hands up to their face. I chucked the torch at them and launched after it, driving an elbow below their ribs, grabbing for the rifle. A muffled scream as they fumbled, pressing the trigger, an automatic stream of bullets hammering the sky, deafening next to my head. A green tracer round ripped into the clouds like a laser. Lightning flashed in response, briefly illuminating the figures rapidly surrounding me. I pulled the rifle, dragging it from their grasp, at the same time kicking out and knocking them onto their back.

A rifle butt appeared in my peripheral vision, a blow aimed at my head from one of the other figures. I ducked, rolled backwards across the mud, came up on one knee, rifle ready. My finger tensed on the trigger, taking up pressure, left hand feeling for the torch clipped under the barrel.

I found it, flicked it on, illuminating several soldiers clad in camo overalls and gas masks. Rifles swung towards me. Trigger fingers flexed. I was outnumbered and outgunned, with a couple of seconds to live.

Chapter Thirty-three

It took me half that time to put two things together.

Firstly, the rifles trained on me, the one in my hand – SA80, a bullpup automatic rifle, very distinctive. Secondly, the muted green Union Jacks on the shoulders of the soldiers' NBC suits.

'Bates!' I bellowed.

'Stand down!' came the unmistakable Glasgow patter from just behind my right shoulder. 'Friendly!'

It was the corporal from the flight up, and his section of Marines. I turned, nearly clouting my mask on the barrel he had levelled at the back of my head. The other guns lowered, torches clicked on, suits rustled as everyone relaxed. I felt a quick pang of regret as a sorry-looking Marine picked himself up off the ground, clutching his ribs. Bates flicked his night-vision goggles up onto his helmet and glowered.

I was livid. 'I gave you clear instructions.'

'You don't give me orders, son, not here.'

'Like fuck.'

'There's been divers reported in the bay, and no contact since the seven o'clock radio check-in. I'm securing the base, we evac at first light.'

'Reported by who?' I narrowed my eyes.

'Frenchie on the radio. Chopper's been up but—'

'There were no divers, it was a misunderstanding.' I still wasn't entirely sure, though I couldn't fathom why Gambetta would have invented it. Either way, no one could check with him now.

'You've had your chance, it's out of your hands.' He started to walk past me.

'Nothing's changed.'

No point telling him *everything* had changed, that the shit had hit the fan, the 'Frenchie' on the radio was dead along with another of the team, and there'd been a failed attempt on my life.

He turned, frozen in a flash of lightning. 'Even without trespassers, the biggest storm in years is coming in, a dead body's gone walkabout, and now you're keeping radio silence.' Thunder rolled off the distant mountains. He gestured for the others to follow him.

I raised the rifle. 'Let me do my job.'

'Let you earn your blood money, you mean. Meanwhile you're risking the lives of everyone on this island.'

He started to walk away again. If the Marines went in now it'd be over. Yeah, everyone might be safe, but how would I catch Demeter or make sense of everything that'd happened? And, okay, he *was* right, how would I earn my pay?

The gunshot tore across the moorland, freezing the Marines, seeming to stop the rain in mid-air. Flashes of lightning as Bates turned again, fists up. The thunder rolled in quicker now, scoring every movement. I lowered the rifle, aiming squarely between his cold eyes staring out from the mask. I glared back through a wisp of steam rising from the barrel.

'Can't let you go up there,' I said, finger twitching.

'It's true what they say, you're a fucking nutjob, Tyler. I have orders. I know you've made a career out of not giving a fuck about those, but I do. Secure the base, seize any anthrax samples, await evac to escort you off the island.'

'There're things you don't know.'

'All the more reason for us to go in. You've lost control.'

'You go in now, we'll never get the truth. You got a radio?' His eyes involuntarily flicked to the guy next to him, at the pack slung across his shoulders. 'Let me speak to the ship.'

'Orders, Tyler.'

'And a good soldier follows them. But a fucking great soldier knows when to read the situation on the ground.' He was wavering. 'You don't wanna be the one who fucks this up. Five minutes,' I added.

He slapped the guy next to him on the shoulder. 'Not a second more.' He looked around his section, held his fist up. 'Hold here,' he barked.

I lowered the rifle. 'Gimme that night vision.'

Bates took a knee, balancing his rifle across his legs. He detached his night-vision goggles and threw them to me.

'What's your name?' I asked the radio operator.

'Jarrett,' he replied, charging his rifle.

'Right, Jarrett, follow me.' I didn't wait for a reply, marching off up the hill I'd just come from. I wanted some shelter from the weather to use the radio, and needed to be out of sight of the base when we did.

Navigating in the black and white of the infrared goggles, I found my way back to the path, following it up and over the hill. From there I could see the crooked fingers of lightning stabbing the nearby islands. I needed to get this done quickly, didn't want to be up here in a storm for longer than necessary.

When I'd first come this way with Marie (Jesus, had it only been this morning?) I'd noticed the crater depressions in the ground, like bunkers on a golf course, filled with heather instead of sand. As we descended the other side of the hill I scanned the moorland. No more than ten metres away was one of the deeper hollows I'd seen. I slid down into it, sinking into the undergrowth, thicker here out of the wind and rain. Jarrett crashed down beside me, hunkering low. I was amazed at the difference it made – with the rain skimming above us, the shelter from the wind meant we could almost talk normally.

'Right, Jarrett, get the colonel on the blower.'

Chapter Thirty-four

Fifteen minutes later I was stepping out of the shower and dressing quickly. It'd taken every centimetre of good favour I had owed, but I'd convinced HQ on board the ship to give me until ten in the morning. I'd managed to convey the genius of Demeter, the unanswered questions, the reason we had to let this play out a little longer. It was a gamble I had to win, because in the morning Bates' section of Marines would be back to quarantine the lot of us, and if that happened there'd be no effective resolution.

Or payday for me, though I hadn't mentioned that.

The base looked abandoned. The door swung open silently onto darkness, broken intermittently by explosions of lightning as the clouds raced overhead. The wind played a frenetic drumbeat along the roof, drowning out all other sound as I crept into the first corridor. Tables and chairs were lying discarded all the way along; they hadn't bothered barricading it.

I kept the lights off, could just about see the door to the common room was shut – I placed my ear against it, but still couldn't hear anything over the storm.

Had Demeter come back whilst I'd been alone outside? What had happened to the others?

Another thought dropped through my guts like a laxative, a thought far worse because it was more believable. After killing Gambetta, had Demeter ever left the base at all?

As I reached for the handle the door trembled. I withdrew. The handle turned, slowly, almost imperceptibly. I slid to the wall alongside the door, heart slamming my ribs. The handle pointed straight down and hung there as the person on the other side decided what to do next. Friend or foe? I held my breath.

The door creaked open, an arm appeared holding a pistol. I stepped forward, pulling the arm out of the room. At the same time I pressed my thumb deep into wrist, into the well just below the palm of the hand, digging in hard. The stranger's hand sprang open. I caught the gun in my other hand, still pulling them into the corridor. As their head came towards me I extended my arm backwards, smashing my elbow through the face. There was a muffled scream as the stranger went limp, dropping to the floor. Still holding on I stepped over their body, pulling them with me, twisting their arm behind their back, my other hand aiming the pistol into the darkened room beyond. I took up the pressure on the arm, knowing any more would tear the ligaments in the rotator cuff, rendering the offending arm useless. They screamed again, louder, more urgently. I thumbed back the hammer on the pistol, ready to shoot the next face that appeared.

'Stop!' a woman shouted.

The strip lights in the common room blazed. I blinked, momentarily blinded, letting off the pressure on the trigger. When my eyes cleared I was aiming down the fixed sights of a Browning Hi-Power, right at Marie.

Other faces appeared around the frame. Hurley and Alice. Behind them cowered Dash. I lowered the gun, let go of Greenbow's arm. He clasped his hands over his face, trying to stem the flow of blood from his crushed nose. Whimpering, he crawled to the wall.

'You bloody maniac,' he said thickly. Blood leaked from between his fingers, spilling to the floor.

I remembered the dressing-down he'd given me earlier and fought to prevent a smile. 'You came at me with a gun, what did you expect?'

I held out the Browning. He snatched it with a bloody hand, pointing it at me, arm shaking.

'Captain, what are you doing?' Marie asked.

'Why were you trying to catch us off guard?' he asked.

'I didn't know what I was walking into,' I said.

'Captain, put the gun down,' said Dash.

'What have you been doing out there?' Greenbow's eyes narrowed, still peering over the pistol, one hand on his nose.

'Thanks for noticing. Nearly broke my ankle on that bloody hillside. I could have done with a hand pulling my foot out of that rabbit hole.'

Greenbow eyed me suspiciously.

'Seriously, you didn't hear me?'

'Couldn't hear a thing over the storm,' said Hurley sheepishly.

Greenbow didn't move.

'Why would I give you the gun back if I wanted to kill you?'

He looked round the others and made up his mind, shoving the sticky pistol back into the holster. 'Hurley, didn't you realise Tyler was missing?'

He shook his head. 'I was checking the sheds, remember?'

Greenbow glared at Hurley. 'Come with me. The rest of you stay here.'

They strode away down the corridor.

Marie rushed from the doorway, grabbing me. 'Are you okay?'

'I could do with a drink.'

'We thought you were a gonner,' said Dash. 'Thought maybe Demeter had got you.'

I uncoupled myself from Marie, looking round her. The furniture in the common room had been piled by the door.

'Planning a last stand against the Russians?'

'Taking no chances,' said Dash, shrugging. 'Thought it'd be easier to defend one room if he came back.'

I walked over to the sideboard, picked up a half-empty bottle of vodka, took a swig. It burned, I coughed, vodka splashed down my shirt. My throat was still raw from the gas in the incinerator.

'If he ever really left at all,' I muttered under my breath, taking another swig, managing to keep it all in.

Chapter Thirty-five

Through the heavy insulation, the rain still hammered away steadily, as if a mob of angry villagers were outside hurling handfuls of pebbles against the fibreglass walls. We could feel it as well as hear it as the storm intensified.

The door opened. Everyone jumped, my hand went to my holster, but it was Hurley returning, flopping into an armchair. Greenbow followed a few seconds later, red toilet paper sticking from his nostrils, darkness spreading across his cheeks. He'd be cultivating a nasty pair of black eyes by tomorrow.

'How's the nose?' I asked.

His eyes would have shot daggers, were they not still streaming. He sat down in a chair by the door, cradling his pistol and his arm.

'So what do we think?' Hurley asked. 'Any theories?'

I inhaled deeply, looking round the group. Clearly it was all they'd been talking about, but as the latest addition to the discussion they were seeking my input.

'I get why Demeter smashed the radio after killing Gambetta – to slow us down. I can't see why he killed Ingrid, unless it was so he could destroy the radio there too. Best guess is so he could make a clean getaway from the island. And if Gambetta is to be believed, after killing him that getaway headed straight for the cliffs to meet those divers and hitch a ride back to Russia.'

When said aloud it almost sounded feasible.

'I thought Demeter killed Gambetta and *then* went to Camp Vollum and killed Ingrid,' said Marie. 'Wouldn't that make more sense, if he was being extracted from that side of the island?'

'Ingrid was shot long before Gambetta.'

Dash shuffled to the edge of the chair. 'What makes you say that?'

'Two reasons. Firstly – we were all here when Demeter shot Gambetta. Just after radio checkpoint, 7:15. I was in the room straight after – the blood was still pumping out of his brain, for God's sake. Time of death is nailed on.'

'Get to the point,' growled Greenbow, adjusting the toilet roll in his nose to catch a fresh dribble of blood.

'We were, what, ten minutes behind Demeter?'

'I reckon, but I still don't see the significance.' Hurley was leaning in now as well.

'Ingrid's body was still warm – it takes hours for a body to cool – but the blood on the floor was cold and congealed – it had been pooled for longer than ten minutes.'

'You're well informed for a technician,' Greenbow said.

'Common sense, Captain. Ingrid checked in with the ship on the radio at seven, but her blood was cold when we got there about seven thirty-five. She must have been killed just after her check-in.' Too late I realised I'd divulged information I'd gleaned from Colonel Holderness on the radio, information a technician couldn't have known, but fortunately they didn't pick up on it immediately. I pressed on before they did. 'It means she was killed first, with Demeter making his way back to X-Base immediately after to kill Gambetta. It's significant, because it probably means there's a different motive than just killing Gambetta.'

'Which is what?' asked Hurley.

'Maybe we have it backwards. I think Demeter killed them *in order* to destroy the radios. Maybe they tried to stop him.'

'It's a bit thin,' said Dash. 'He had a gun; I'd have stood back and let him get on with it.'

'Hmm.' Greenbow studied me carefully, brows furrowing as the cogs behind them whirled.

'You said you thought Ingrid was killed before Gambetta for *two* reasons?' said Dash.

'This reason is much simpler.' It was time to share information; I needed help. 'Demeter didn't escape out the window.'

If a storm wasn't raging you could have heard a pin drop. I was content with the open mouths. It seemed like ages until someone spoke; in the end it was Hurley.

'Bullshit. You were in the room seconds after he shot Gambetta.'

'True.'

'You said he escaped out of the window!' said Marie.

'Did I?'

'He couldn't have got past us in the corridor,' said Alice.

'I didn't say I knew *how* he got out of the room, I just know it wasn't through the window – so there's no way he could have got to Ingrid immediately after.'

Greenbow snorted, then winced and touched his nose. 'Nonsense. Demeter was already wearing his suit and gas mask – he knew exactly what he was doing. One of the missing keys was still in the lock, for goodness' sake. He shot Gambetta and jumped outside.'

'I think that was his plan, that's why he was suited up and ready, but I'm telling you for a fact he didn't.'

I left the room without waiting for the others. I'd walked through several huts before I even looked behind. They were following in a line, and I was struck how our numbers had dwindled.

Alice and Marie clutching each other, Greenbow clutching his pistol, Dash clutching a bag of crisps. Hurley with his fists ready at his sides. Discounting Demeter, there were seven of us left, and that included Clay sleeping it off. I led the way past the bedroom huts to the end of the corridor, the door to the radio room, and stood aside.

No one wanted to enter. Alice and Marie looked as pale as Greenbow. Finally Dash pushed forward. He put his crisps on the windowsill then opened the door.

The smell hit me again. Not a rotten smell – Gambetta hadn't been dead long – but the tangy, metallic taste of blood, copper and iron weighing down the air. Stifling, almost unbreathable. It made my teeth ache, my insides itch and my ears ring.

'Jeez, what a mess,' Dash said, lifting a hand to his mouth. He stepped in gingerly, avoiding the slick floor, eyes shifting nervously between the body and the door. I followed. Greenbow positioned himself on the threshold, pale as before.

Something had changed. I studied the floor. The blood around Gambetta's arm was smudged – his fingers now pointed at the window rather than the shelves. And hadn't he been wearing a watch?

Someone had been in here, must have been whilst we were up at the other camp. Alice, Dash, Marie, or Clay.

'John, you with us?'

Dash was staring at me. I shook my head. 'Sorry, miles away.'

'I was just replaying it,' he said. 'Demeter entered the room. We heard 'em both arguing. He smashes the radio, opens the window to get away. Gambetta tries to stop him. Bang. Bullet through the head, Demeter's out the window, *au revoir*, Gambetta, *do svidaniya*, Demeter.'

'A solid theory,' I said, walking to the window and stopping abruptly to point at it. 'Where's the key?'

'What do you mean?' asked Hurley, stepping into the room.

'Captain, you said yourself, there was a key in the lock. Did you take it back?' I scanned the floor even though I knew it couldn't have fallen, that it must have been removed on purpose.

He walked across the room to inspect the lock. 'I did not,' he said simply, pulling out his own keys. 'I always have a key on me.'

I took them, inserted the key. Greenbow stepped back. 'Don't open it, Tyler.'

I turned the key.

'Don't do it!' Dash shouted.

'There's no risk,' I said.

Greenbow fumbled with his holster and pulled his Browning. 'Get away from the window.'

'Captain, put the gun down!' screamed Dash.

The room exploded in chaos, everyone shouting at everyone else at the same time; Greenbow shouting at me to get away from the window, Hurley and Alice shouting at him to put the gun down, Marie and Dash imploring me to listen to the captain. I had to shout twice as loud to be heard.

'I SCREWED THE FUCKING WINDOW SHUT!'

I yanked the handle. It slammed with a thunk, there was a collective gasp then a moment of silence, cut short by a crash of thunder and a blast of arctic wind. The window had barely opened a centimetre. I gave it another pull, then pushed it shut again.

'I screwed all the windows shut earlier,' I said at a more civil volume. 'Sorry, Dash, you can invoice me.'

'What the... why would you do that?' he asked.

'Long story, but I had a feeling someone was bypassing the HADU.'

'Outrageous!' said Greenbow, thankfully sliding his pistol back into its holster.

'Bollocks,' I said, pointing at the corpse. 'I found him having a fag outside this morning. Who's to know what else was going on?'

The room descended into chaos again, this time strings of expletives, followed by whats and whys. Dash started up about compensation and repairs but was interrupted by Greenbow.

'How dare you take matters into your own hands!'

Hurley stepped back out into the corridor, blew out his cheeks, whistled. 'Well that puts the fox in the henhouse, now don't it?'

'You see the problem?'

'So Demeter enters the room, shoots Gambetta, and then...' Dash tailed off, a frown creasing his face.

Greenbow's anger lost out to confusion. 'What are you thinking, Chaudhary?' he asked.

'Well, if he never left the room...'

Greenbow looked exasperated. 'We all saw him enter...'

'We heard them both arguing!' said Hurley.

'And we were all outside when he shot Gambetta,' Greenbow continued. 'Then we were in the room in – what was it, Alice, ten seconds?'

'Less than that,' said Hurley. 'But not so's makes any difference, because he couldn't have got past us either way.'

'There must be a way,' I said. 'Sleight of hand and all that. This isn't haphazard, this confusion; I think he planned it. Misdirection. We're looking over here while he's over there. Come on, Dash, what are you thinking?'

'I know how he disappeared,' he said, eyes dropping to the floor.

Chapter Thirty-six

'Why the hell didn't you tell us about this before?' I asked.

'It wasn't relevant,' said Dash. 'We thought he'd gone out the window.'

I dropped to my hands and knees. The floor was marked, scratches along one edge of the panel.

The base was heavily insulated, all electrical, heating, and ventilation conduits running internally. Essentially each hut was a protective cocoon, everything on the inside. Made total sense; if any systems failed they could be repaired from inside the base, no need to step foot outside into what could be a minus-sixty-degrees-centigrade gale. Temperatures here on Gruinard were balmy in comparison, but the danger outside was just as real – so the theory was still sound.

As every hut was a separate self-contained unit, each had its own utility compartment, accessed from a small trapdoor near the door. I hadn't seen it when I'd first entered the room, hidden as it was around the side of the filing cabinet. Even now it was difficult to see, the edges fitted so perfectly.

Kneeling on the floor, shaking my head, I looked at Greenbow. 'Pass me the gun.'

This time there were no complaints; he'd no desire to stick his head down there. He handed it over, retreating to the doorway. Hurley pushed through and crouched next to me. Dash passed him the screwdriver from the shelf. I positioned myself at the front of the trapdoor, aiming Greenbow's Browning squarely at the hatch. It rattled and I gripped it harder, forcing my hand still.

'You okay?' asked Hurley.

He must have mistaken it for fear. 'Just hurry up, I wanna keep my head on my shoulders.'

Hurley coaxed the screwdriver into the thin gap, levering upwards, arm outstretched, expecting the worst. I kicked the flap fully open, aiming the pistol into the blackness. No Demeter. Dash passed me a torch. Holding it alongside the pistol, I flicked it on. A plywood hollow under the hut dropped a couple of feet to a dusty floor. The beam illuminated scuffs in the dust.

I didn't fancy sticking my head in, but reasoned if Demeter was still hiding down there he was in total darkness. I lowered my hand down and shone the torch around. To my relief there was no gunshot, and my hand was still attached when I pulled my arm out. With a glance at Hurley I put my head in the hole.

The crawl space extended under the whole hut. The light reflected off plastic pipes clipped to the underside of the floor, which, as Dash had explained, carried air, heat, electrical wires, all sorts of technical gubbins. It reminded me of that bit in *Alien*, and unfortunately that's exactly what went through my head as I slowly turned through 360 degrees. I completed the turn, swearing loudly, nearly dropping the torch. Dash cried out.

There, in a corner, huddled in a foetal position, was Demeter.

I caught my breath, holding the beam steady. 'Demeter, don't move.'

He obliged. I realised that, as he hadn't been moving before, I had not advanced the situation. I could hear the others whispering above.

'Okay, come out. Don't try anything, I've got a gun on you.'

Cheesy; like something from a gangster flick. It didn't do the trick, Demeter still ignored me. I could just make out the breather of a gas mask poking from the red hood, a modern-day plague doctor huddled in the shadows.

I slid in head first, ending up on my belly, reaching out with the gun to prod him.

155

The red collapsed. I shrank back. The gas mask rocked over on the floor. Empty.

I prodded a bit more and something else fell out of the crumpled suit. I pulled it towards me. A small blob of melted plastic, a charred metal USB connector stuck out on one side. The missing data stick from the CCTV system? I prodded a few more times before remembering this suit might have been outside and thus be covered anthrax spores. I dropped the melted USB stick.

'John, you okay?' Dash called.

I looked back at the hatch. He and Hurley peeped over the rim, Greenbow's face a respectable distance behind.

'Part of the mystery solved. Found Demeter's gear.'

'Is he down there?'

'You'd know if he was.'

'Fair point.'

'I'm coming out.'

I rolled onto my back, sliding towards the opening, careful to stop my jumper riding up and revealing my holster. The others moved away from the trapdoor. I had a sudden claustrophobic moment as I remembered the incinerator lid slamming down, and shuffled quicker. Fortunately I reached the hatch without incident, and was about to climb up when my torch reflected off something out of place. A plastic tube, just like the ones Alice had given me to collect the samples, wedged up under the pipes next to the hatch. It looked like it contained mud, but there was no identification sticker.

'John, you okay?' asked Dash again.

'Give me a second.'

I pulled it out and something else dropped down. A sandwich bag, wrapped tightly round a tiny quantity of brown dust. Tea. This was what was left of the sample I'd given Ingrid to test, presumably swiped from her lab.

I quickly stuffed both into my pocket, then climbed out of the hole.

Chapter Thirty-seven

'So we know the full story now, don't we?' Alice said.

We were gathered in the corridor outside the radio room, door closed.

'Let's not get overexcited,' I said.

'He must have been hiding down there all along,' said Dash.

'Every hut has those crawl spaces?' I asked.

'Yup,' Dash replied.

'Then we need to check the rest of the base.' I handed Greenbow his Browning and looked around the others. 'Do we have any other weapons?'

'This is a scientific base, only El Capitan has a popgun,' said Hurley.

'It'll have to do. We need to check every room, top to bottom – including these underfloor spaces. And from now on, no one goes anywhere on their own.'

Greenbow scowled, put out by my initiative and assumption of authority, but didn't challenge it – I presume through lack of his own plan or a sense of self-doubt, so maybe he wasn't that stupid after all. 'Right,' he said, 'Dash, Hurley, with me. We'll check the labs and common rooms. Alice, Marie, check the bedrooms with Tyler.'

Childhood memories of Saturday mornings flashed into my head, my brother and I cross-legged on the floor watching *Scooby Doo*, and while I wouldn't have normally minded going off with Daphne and Velma, I didn't fancy our chances if we encountered Demeter. Still, the captain wasn't the only one who was armed. The other three marched to the other end of the base, the labs, to work backwards.

Four huts across this section of the base, and in one of these was the radio room that we'd already checked. To converge on the others we made our way to the other end of the corridor, starting in the first bedroom hut – mine. As we entered I saw Alice turn her nose up at the dregs in the Scotch bottle, the full one next to the bed. She started going through Demeter's things.

'Marie, chuck me that pen, will you?' I asked, pointing at the bedside table. I caught it, turning my attention to the floor. The trapdoor was in the same place, but this time beneath the drawers.

'Are the rooms set out identically?' I asked.

'*Oui*,' said Marie.

Alice shrugged. 'Mine's the same.'

'Then I doubt he's hiding in one of them.' I pointed to the drawers. 'Unless he somehow managed to pull the furniture back after – but we'd best check.'

Even in this clean environment, grime had accumulated along the edges. No need for caution here, clearly the drawers hadn't been moved. I dragged them across the floor then jabbed the pen in, levered the hatch up, shone my torch around, verifying that it contained nothing but pipes and dust.

As I pulled my head up there was a gasp behind me. I closed the hatch and turned to see the two women perched on the Russian's bed.

'Have a look at this,' Alice whispered, handing me a crumpled piece of paper.

I sat on my own bed to study it. A scrappy note, torn across, no sign of the other half.

Viktor

Rendezvous East Coast Gruinard – February—

Your son cannot escape justic—

on the island. The west wil—

held accountable—

at Yekaterinburg—

Call—

Even with three quarters missing it was impossible not to get the gist of a blackmail note. I held it up to the light, turning it over. Huge childish block letters in blue ballpoint. The paper looked to be torn from a sheet of plain A4. Scribbled in haste. Doubtless an expert could have subjected it to numerous tests to prise more clues from the page, but those are skills I don't possess, and this was an island in the middle of a storm.

'Where was this?' I asked.

'Hidden in this book,' Alice replied, holding up the battered copy of *Master and Margarita*. 'Like a bookmark.'

I frowned, thinking back to my arrival. Hadn't I thumbed through it? The note was crumpled but the paper looked fresh. And 'note' was ringing a little bell in my mind. I massaged my knuckles into my eyes until colours exploded across the inside of my eyelids. The note in my shoe, it was still there. I couldn't read it now, in front of anyone.

'His son lives in Russia. You think he's been taken?' Alice asked.

'More likely they're just threatening,' I said, more interested in who would have crammed a note into my shoe.

'With his expertise, the Russians would jump at the chance to get him back.'

I lay back on my bed, took a sip from my hip flask, closed my eyes. 'So Demeter is blackmailed to return to Russia. For whatever reason, they're prepared to go to any length. And you said it yourself earlier, Demeter is tired. He's nostalgic for his homeland, and to see his son again.

'Here he sees an opportunity to go through with it, away from Porton Down, from the ever watchful eyes of MI5 and GCHQ.'

'But why murder Andy?' asked Marie.

'Maybe he found the note? He was his roommate after all, probably suspected something. Confronted Demeter, threatened to go to Greenbow. Andy had to be disposed of, but in a way that looked accidental, to buy Demeter time. A vial of anthrax emptied into his tea.'

'His tea?' asked Alice.

'Or whatever.' I shrugged. 'He was poisoned.'

'Sounds plausible,' said Alice.

'Motive, means, opportunity. All stacks up.'

'Then what?'

'He has a rendezvous with a sub this evening, under cover of darkness. But the divers have been spotted – so the witnesses have to die, along with the radios, to stop us alerting the Navy to their presence. Covering his escape. First poor Ingrid, then he comes here to destroy this radio too.'

'And to kill Gambetta.'

'It might have been his motivation all along. Remember we saw them together on the cliffs? I bet Gambetta suspected something, maybe confronted Demeter about it. We'll never know, but whatever the reason, Demeter shoots him.'

'Then disappears,' said Marie.

'He tries to escape out the window but it's shut, so he gets under the floor instead.'

'Could he do that? I mean, quickly enough?'

'He's quicker than he looks. It fits – we saw them arguing, remember? Maybe they'd argued on the cliffs, they saw the divers, Gambetta put two and two together and knew Demeter was defecting, that he'd need to destroy the radio, so he didn't want to let him in the room. Demeter knocks him over the head, smashes the radio before Gambetta can raise the alarm. He's not to know the window's screwed shut. He's struggling with it when Gambetta recovers. They fight, and – BANG – that's that. Demeter assumed the window was just jammed, that if he hid under the floor we'd think he'd got away. Down the hatch just in time for us to walk into an empty room.'

'Almost empty. I don't think I'll ever forget that.' Alice shuddered.

'So what happened next? The captain, Hurley and I went off to Vollum to find Ingrid dead. What did the rest of you do?'

'We hid.'

'You what?'

'You'd gone off with the only weapon and there was a madman loose on the island!'

Marie picked up the story. 'Not to mention Russian frogmen. We stacked the furniture against the door and turned all the lights off. We thought we'd be safer, if there was someone out there.'

'You hid in there for nearly an hour?'

'Yes, until you got back,' said Alice.

'No, I got back after the other two, remember. Did you hear them come in?'

'They knocked on the door.'

I thought about this for a second. 'Okay, so Demeter waits for the base to go quiet, then emerges from his hiding place and creeps down the corridor, slips away into the night. You didn't hear him because you were all cowering behind a barricade in the common room.'

Alice looked at her feet. 'So where is he now?'

'Now? Those divers will have brought a spare dry suit and rebreather. A ten-minute swim and he's sipping vodka on board a super-quiet Borei-class en-route to Severomorsk, and with no radio we can do fuck-all about it.'

They sat in silence, mulling it over. I could tell they believed the series of events as I'd just told it. Everything tessellated perfectly.

Which is why I was uneasy.

In my experience, if you throw the jigsaw pieces in the air, they rarely fall together that snugly on the first go. How had Demeter got a window key? Had Gambetta given it him? There were no others missing. Where was it now? Who'd taken it from the comms room, and who'd moved the body? Why had a vial of soil been hidden under the floor?

And lastly for now, the fact that two bullets were fired up at Camp Vollum was really niggling at me.

All I knew for sure was that I didn't believe a word of what I'd just told Marie and Alice.

Chapter Thirty-eight

Despite my doubts about Demeter sticking around, we checked the other rooms anyway. The bedroom next door to mine belonged to Ingrid and Marie. Actually, Marie had just been upgraded to single occupancy due to the recent unpleasantness. So had I, come to think of it. Silver linings, and all that.

I'd had to wait outside while she ran around the room collecting underwear, tidying God knows what, despite assurances that I'd seen such sights before. She was crying when I finally entered, and one look at Ingrid's still rumpled bed on the other side of the room reminded me why – and made me more determined to get to the bottom of this mess.

Alice comforted her while I checked the floor for a hatch only to find there wasn't one. Lack of quality sleep must have stripped the teeth from the constantly whirring gears in my brain, as it took me a while to realise that the dividing wall between the rooms extended above the floor only – the hatch in my room next door actually provided access to the crawl space under the whole hut. With nothing more to check, we proceeded to the next hut.

The next bedroom was also single occupancy – Alice's, for the sake of modesty, being the only other woman in the base. Again I had to wait outside while she tidied, and then we were in. The hatch was in the same place as the other hut, covered by the drawers, and again the dust told me it'd be fruitless. After a quick check, which also confirmed the space ran under both bedrooms, we moved on.

Considering Gambetta had sauntered around in a permanent state of dishevelment, the room he'd shared with Dash was the model of order. The lamp was still on, watching me carefully, threatening to reveal my trespassing in here earlier. While Alice checked Dash's things, I opened Gambetta's bedside drawer. Nothing of interest – just the obligatory packs of fags. No hints of a personality, no private items and I was beginning to think the man was a robot until, hidden under a pile of clothes in a bottom drawer, I found something of great interest to make up for it.

A lightweight Galco shoulder holster, tailored perfectly for a suppressed Walther PPK, the French-produced gun made famous by fictional secret service agents. It lent further weight to my suspicions about Eric Gambetta being DGSE.

There was nothing terribly ominous about that. This was a joint operation after all, a combined study into decontamination procedures. MI5, MI6, GCHQ, DI, NATO, CIA, DGSE – nosy acronyms were in endless supply, soaking into all aspects of government. Every department, every single project being undertaken in one place, was represented on an office wall somewhere else in the world.

Gambetta being DGSE wasn't ominous. The missing pistol, like the missing key, was. Had he been murdered with his own gun during a struggle? If so, how had Demeter shot Ingrid beforehand?

I stuffed the holster back into the drawer.

We didn't encounter anything else of interest in the room – like a bedroom in a show home, it was a sterile environment that was, other than the faint odour of cigarette smoke, devoid of atmosphere.

We continued into the next hut. Door one was Greenbow's bedroom.

'Nice of him to reserve a room for himself,' I said.

'Clay wasn't best pleased,' said Alice. 'He's sharing with Hurley next to the comms room.'

'Shows who's really in charge here. Greenbow has a bedroom *and* an office.'

Marie sniggered.

A glance was enough to tell me nothing could be gleaned from the room. Marie attacked the drawers whilst I set about the wardrobe. Like the previous room, it was fastidiously tidy, but unlike it, this screamed information about Captain Greenbow. Two pairs of black brogued Oxfords, polished to a mirror shine. Five identical green jumpers (Jersey, Heavy Wool) folded in the drawers. Two full uniforms hung up; no.2 Service Dress and no.10 Mess Dress. Why Greenbow had brought his parade uniform and formal evening dress was beyond me.

'Not much in here,' said Marie as she rooted through the drawers. 'Boot polish. Spare laces. Tissues. Band of the Irish Guards?'

I turned to see her holding up a couple of CDs. I was mildly amused to see Alice next to her inspecting a well-thumbed copy of *The Man Who Would Be King*.

Yet again the trapdoor revealed nothing.

We bypassed door two, Greenbow's office (locked, plus we'd already checked beneath it from his bedroom). Thank God there was only one more hut to check, the one we'd all started in – housing the radio room but also a dorm shared by Clay and Hurley. We'd already checked under it, where I'd found Demeter's suit, but needed to check the bedroom. We'd left it to last to avoid disturbing that foul drunken creature.

Marie knocked on the door. 'Dr Clay?'

No answer.

'He's pissed as a fart, just go in,' I said.

After a moment's uncertainty Marie opened the door. It was pitch black inside, blinds drawn. I stepped into the room as Marie fumbled for the light switch.

It stank, the air heavy. I started to tell Marie to wait, grabbed her arm. Too late; the strip lights buzzed on.

She screamed, pulling away, stumbling backwards into Alice's arms. She buried her face, shuddering.

Dr Donald Clay was dead.

Chapter Thirty-nine

Clay lay in bed, tongue hanging from a distended jaw, neck bent horribly backwards as if he'd been electrocuted. Bony fingers clutched at his chest, one leg jutting out from the blankets.

He'd clearly suffered, but other than the stretched limbs and wild eyes there were no outward signs of violence; no blood or gunshot wounds to be seen here. I threw the covers back, wafting the stench around the room. Stains had spread across his clothes and the mattress beneath him. He'd lost control of everything, violently. Dried vomit crusted on his chest.

The signs pointed to organ failure, probably a heart attack. Possibly a seizure of some kind; we established I'm not a doctor.

I pushed his leg into bed with my shoe – rigor mortis takes a while to set in – but was careful not to touch him. Although I doubted it was anthrax, until I knew what the cause of death was I wasn't taking risks.

'He's dead!' Alice exclaimed. She'd left Marie in the corridor.

'Was he a big drinker?'

'He liked a Scotch but I wouldn't call him an…' She shot an uncomfortable look at the flask in my hand.

I wiped my mouth with the back of my hand. 'Alcoholic?'

'Yes. Not that I know of, oh God, I've known him for years!'

'*Mon Dieu*, I didn't like him but…' Marie had snuck up behind me, and was peering over my shoulder. 'I can't believe he's dead.'

'So not shot, then,' Alice stated.

'Could be natural causes,' I said, though I didn't believe it.

'At fifty-five?' Marie wrinkled her face.

'Give over! He was never fifty-five.'

'He did say he felt ill when we put him to bed,' said Marie.

'And we thought it was the drink,' I said. 'Our numbers seem to be dwindling.'

I picked up his pillow off the floor. It was a wanky down-filled one. Obviously the standard-issue synthetic pillows were for the plebs.

I told Alice and Marie to wait outside as I pulled the blankets over his head.

I opened the bedside table, just tissues, a tin of toffees, a washbag, a book on gardening, which seemed about the most pointless thing anyone could bring to this barren rock. I took a toffee and looked in Hurley's cabinet, which was entirely empty so I turned my attention to the wardrobe where, thanks to the lack of hangers, all the clothes seemed to be folded at the bottom. I had a quick feel when something caught my eye. A small hole in what I presumed were Clay's trousers, unless Hurley was partial to M&S cords, but strangely it passed through the other side too. I picked them up, held them up to the light. Four holes, all the way down the leg; something had happened to them while they were folded. I dropped them, crouched by the wardrobe, pulling out more clothes until I reached the bottom and a similar-sized hole through the solid wood base. I stuck my little finger through but it just wiggled in the void beneath. The wardrobe was bolted to the floor so I'd exhausted that line of enquiry.

I stood, unwrapped the toffee, added the hole to the growing pile of questions in my head.

Chapter Forty

Greenbow had of course demanded to see the body, but predictably spent all of ten seconds in the room, forming no opinion of his own, adding nothing of value. The other group had checked the labs without incident then gone on to check the kitchen, dining room and common room. Each time the same result; nothing in the under-floor areas and nowhere else to hide. After that we'd convened in the common room for a stiff drink. I cradled my flask, turning things over in my mind, occasionally lifting my head to listen in on the debate.

I didn't tell them about the gun missing from Gambetta's room or the hole, there was already enough for them to discuss. The note Alice found, it was generally agreed, backed up the sub theory – proof positive that Demeter was indeed headed back east, taking his knowledge of Porton Down with him in a mirror of events years before, when he'd arrived in Britain carrying the secrets of Sverdlovsk. A redefection. This in turn was further proof that he'd killed Gambetta (we already knew that, but it was nice to have supporting evidence), Ingrid, and Andy Kyle. Alice recounted the theory we'd discussed, careful to present it as mine in case of rebuttal – but she needn't have worried; it was swallowed down as easily as Andy's poisoned tea.

They decided Clay had died of natural causes; an unfortunate coincidence but not outside the bounds of plausibility. All sewn up nice and tight.

I didn't have the answers but at least I'm clever enough to know when I'm not clever enough. In contrast, these were scientists with IQs far loftier than mine, but in a herd, with shit dripping from the fan, they were truly gormless.

The storm had intensified and the facility that had seemed so permanent that morning felt rickety in the gusts. Dash assured us there was no danger to X-Base itself, and I believed him – it had been designed to cope with those Antarctic winters – but the same couldn't be said of the shaky outbuildings that had been erected in the compound. The tool shed looked dangerously close to blowing over, rocking crazily against the generator shed next door. This in turn was sturdier but taking a real pounding, and it worried me that while we were safely ensconced in our warm huts, our lifeline – the generator – was protected by a thin sheet of plywood.

I left the common room at the earliest possibility, on the pretence of going to the toilet. That's where I headed, but not to use the facilities in that way. That lockable cubicle kept my secrets once again.

Demeter's note had reminded me about my own note. I removed my trainer. The paper was creased flat, worn at the edges from a couple of hours' walking.

At first I thought it might link to Demeter's note, but the handwriting was different. Besides, this was helpfully signed.

John

Sorry I didn't catch you! Heading back to Camp Vollum now, will find you later, but thought you'd want to know as soon as possible. Your sample contains anthrax – unknown strain. Related to Vollum 14578. Much more virulent than 1B. Similar effects but highly aggressive, rapid replication. Much enhanced virulence would cause illness far quicker than Vollum, hours instead of days. This aggression likely counteracts vaccine. I'm naming it the Gruinard strain.

Gruinard strain likely mutated from Vollum 1B-1942. Passed through indigenous wildlife, mutated over forty years.

Replication rate suggests death through massive organ failure would likely occur within two to five hours, no external signs other than distress.

I'm guessing your sample links to Andy Kyle – given what we know I'm pretty sure it's what killed him.

Soil analysis shows it was taken from the area that's now decontaminated, so this is likely a unique sample. Will talk to you when I come back later.

Ingrid X

I leaned back and closed my eyes. I hadn't known Andy Kyle. Clay and Gambetta I couldn't give two shits about. Ingrid though, that was different. She was entirely innocent, here to do her job. She didn't care about any of this, wasn't involved, just living her life. A lump began to crawl up my throat.

I opened my eyes, focused on the back of the stall door. There'd be time for sentimentality later, I knew all about storing things up, had to stay in the present.

A new, far more virulent strain of anthrax, here on the island – a more aggressive strain than anything previously known. This changed things. A new strain as aggressive as this would be valuable. If someone wanted a sample, without anyone finding out – wouldn't that be a solid motive for murder?

It fell into place. Frustratingly, the killings had followed a classic pattern, based largely around covering up that one first murder – Kyle. It was running wildly out of control, a juggernaut with no brakes – and I was standing right in the middle of the road.

By finding the sample and asking Ingrid to analyse it, I was part of the pattern. In asking her to analyse the sample, I may have sealed her fate. What was certain was he'd tried to kill me once and failed – knowing I suspected something, could he really afford not to try again?

I flushed the note down the toilet.

Chapter Forty-one

The lounge was a sorry scene. Greenbow shivered in an armchair in the corner, pushed back against the wall, wide eyes darting, fingers twitching on the pistol. Alice jumped up from a sofa when I came in but all in all was managing to stay relatively composed, whereas Marie looked about to burst, rocking, tapping her feet on the floor. Dash slouched sideways on another sofa, feet up, staring at the ceiling. Hurley looked the most composed, hovering near the door, cradling a glass, except I reckoned his composure was due in part to the bottle of Stoli on the bookcase behind him.

The wind buffeted the base. Something hit one of the windows in the corridor, just a branch or something, but everyone jumped a foot in the air simultaneously, watching each other nervously.

Only six of us left.

Chapter Forty-two

Oxford University, 1937; the ear of a diseased cow arrives for post-mortem bacterial analysis, ending up in Canadian bacteriologist Roy Vollum's (presumably gloved) hands. He identifies a particularly virulent form of bovine anthrax also deadly to humans, which becomes known as the Vollum strain. Like other forms of the disease, it's more virulent when exposed to more hosts.

A sample of Vollum-14578 finds its way to Porton Down, where it's passed through a series of monkeys, enhancing the virulence to create the Vollum-1B strain. This new strain is found to be highly aggressive.

It's at this point, sometime around 1942, with this terrible anthrax strain isolated, that British research switches away from passively studying the feasibility of an enemy attack, onto planning a biological attack on Germany. Operation Vegetarian is born.

Like something from a science fiction film, scientists at Porton Down come up with a plan for a new kind of weapon, one with a high chance of success and high lethality without damage to German infrastructure, and without risking too many aircraft. Perfect.

As I'd found out, the best way to infect someone (assuming by 'best' you mean worst) is to get them to eat it. I'd already seen up close the effects of gastrointestinal infection. The problem for the scientists at Porton Down, then, is how to get Germans to eat a plate of Vollum-1B. Dropping infected strudel or bratwurst on major cities may arouse suspicion, but fortunately (or unfortunately for the Germans) the scientists think up something better.

There's an oft-used phrase, something along the lines of 'any civilised country is just three missed meals away from anarchy'. The proposed plan plays into that notion perfectly.

Cattle-feed cakes, developed at Porton Down, are to be dropped onto fields on the outskirts of cities. Anthrax bombs will be dropped over herds. Infected cows will be slaughtered shortly after to feed a hungry population. Tainted meat floods the food chain. As well as this, dairy herds are decimated, milk supplies contaminated. Hospitals and health services stretch to breaking point and collapse. Thousands of Germans die slowly and painfully from anthrax infection.

Then comes the coup de grâce. To stem the tide of bacteria, *all* milk and meat, infected or not, is destroyed to stop the spread of infection. War is already here, pestilence has swept through, now the third horseman arrives – famine, riding rampant, all grazing land rendered useless, entire herds slaughtered. What scarce food supplies remain are prioritised for the military. Villages, towns and cities across the Reich starve. Servicemen at the front learn of the plight of their loved ones dying back home. Will is broken. The country is destabilised, the military's back broken from within.

All this has been achieved whilst leaving infrastructure intact.

Other than the huge irony that Hitler himself was a vegetarian, it was the perfect plan. The War Office gives the green light.

Preparations get underway. Linseed cakes are provided by a company in Blackburn, and a London-based soap manufacturer is contracted to process them into inch-sized pieces. By the middle of July 1942, 40,000 cakes are being produced per day. In a secret facility at Porton Down thirteen women with expertise in soap manufacture are recruited to inject the cakes with the anthrax spores.

Cube-shaped cardboard containers are produced at Porton Down for transport in modified RAF Lancaster, Halifax, and

Stirling bombers, and drop sites are chosen in Oldenburg and Hanover. Aircraft returning from conventional bombing runs of Berlin fly over sixty miles of grazing land. In less than twenty minutes one bomber could rain 4,000 infected cakes down onto the fields. In one night just a dozen aircraft could cover enormous swathes of the north German countryside in deadly anthrax spores and no one would be any the wiser.

The cakes are in production and the date is set for 1944. Only one thing remains.

No one really knows how the anthrax will fare in the wild. Will it survive deployment long enough to be eaten? Can it be delivered by explosives, to disperse the spores even wider? Or would bombs destroy the anthrax? It all needs to be tested in the field, somewhere in secret.

A team from the Ministry of Defence and Porton Down arrive in Scotland in mid-1942 to scout possible test sites. The site has to be in an isolated, uninhabited area, easily sealed off from the public, and safe from civilian and spy eyes. Gruinard Island fits the bill perfectly. At that time inhabited only by sheep, it's purchased from a farmer for £500 and immediately placed off limits to all. A team from Porton Down move in, and the island is designated 'X-Base' by the Ministry of Defence.

They lose no time shipping in troops to assist with tethering unlucky sheep to lines across the island, or caging them in wooden crates with their heads exposed. Devices are exploded on the top of poles upwind of the animals, simulating bomb blasts. These test both the dispersal of anthrax, and that it remains virulent after the heat and pressure of a bomb blast. Needless to say it does, and all the sheep are dead within a few days.

Anthrax has been successfully weaponised for the first time, with proof that the laced cakes and anthrax bombs will be effective if dropped across Germany. No doubt some morbid bastards are rubbing their hands in glee as the deadline approaches, anticipating the effects of all that research finally put to use.

But that was that; thankfully for Germany the order is never given. I'd love to think a British sense of fair play fed into the decision, though I know that thinking is extremely wishful. Other than the moral implications there was a huge drawback, which became immediately apparent and was the reason we were here, in a sealed base, nearly eighty years later. Marie had impressed on me the hardiness of the anthrax spores. For decades after the tests a rusting sign on the beach on the mainland had declared Gruinard Island a no-go area, by order of the government. Those spores of Vollum-1B that were grown at Porton Down and dispersed across the island were still just as deadly, rendering Gruinard Island inhospitable for humans and animals alike. Finally bowing to pressure, a team moved in and the island was decontaminated in the mid-Eighties. It was officially declared anthrax-free in 1990, but some of those spores had been far hardier than expected. The wildlife returned and, as Ingrid had proved, the spores had passed through generations of rats or birds or whatever other unfortunate beast had happened upon them, mutating over the years outside the confines of a laboratory. These mutant spores had survived the decontamination procedures, sleeping quietly under the dirt for years until a storm had brought them to the surface, to sit in the grass and be eaten by the reintroduced sheep. Thanks to the island's history, a recent outbreak was reported to the right people straight away, setting alarm bells ringing. A team had headed to the island immediately and tests confirmed the worst: it was teeming with anthrax still, after all this time and after the previous decontamination.

Just as the Vollum-1B strain had been created in the first place, by passing the already virulent Vollum strain through a series of monkeys, much of the anthrax here had passed through indigenous wildlife – but these spores had survived and mutated in ways that couldn't be synthesised in a lab at Porton Down. Almost eighty years of mutations had made Gruinard a unique petri dish.

Here had grown, by accident, a super-anthrax capable of infecting and killing its host in a matter of hours, worth more than plutonium for any government research department. These days, Western democracies' hands are tied by conventions written in Geneva, but of course that didn't make it worth any less. Where did the Novichok come from that poisoned people in Salisbury and Amesbury? And more to the point, how did the UK identify it? Chemical and biological weapons are the great leveller against the superpowers, so while East and West rattle their sabres against their use in places like Iraq and Syria, research continues in secret, because you can only defend yourself from this sort of stuff if you know how it works.

I figured it was this hypocrisy that actually pushed the value of a sample higher. If elements within a 'civilised' country could get their hands on this unique superweapon in guaranteed secrecy – without even their allies and perhaps their own governments finding out – well wouldn't that be worth even more? Wouldn't that be worth *killing* for?

I couldn't let the Gruinard strain get out.

Chapter Forty-three

We talked for a while about the island, its history, piling facts on top of the stuff I'd read in the briefing pack. I was now convinced that this was the true reason for the murders. This was the reason Andy Kyle was killed, the reason Viktor Demeter had left, and the reason he'd killed again to get the sample away from the island. Some of the same unanswered questions remained, but at least I was satisfied with the motive.

Turning from the others, I dug around in my pocket, pulling out the object I'd found hidden up under the pipes in the crawl space of the radio room. I turned it over in my hands, tipping it up, letting the glare of the fluorescent lights reflect off it. I added a new question to the many others.

If Demeter had tested this new strain on Kyle, then orchestrated this mess to smuggle the priceless sample off the island, unique because that area had now been decontaminated – if he'd perpetrated a series of murders to cover up his crime and make good his escape – why on earth was I holding that unique sample in my hand?

Chapter Forty-four

'Unlike some other bioengineered mutations, the original Vollum strain is reliably aggressive,' said Marie. 'It's so bad they still use it today to test vaccines.'

We were sitting around the common room, talking it out, trying to make sense of everything that'd happened. I hadn't mentioned Ingrid's note, or the test tube.

'It's what the Iraqis had in the Gulf War,' said Alice.

'Marie mentioned Gulf War Syndrome earlier,' I said.

Greenbow nodded. 'One of the causes was the anthrax vaccinations we were given. Bloody nasty stuff.'

Alice continued. 'No stockpiles were ever found, of course, but they took plenty of samples from dump sites and found hits for the Vollum strain.'

'Hence why we're here, eighty years later?' said Hurley.

'Exactly, it's ridiculously difficult to get rid of. You know about the Dark Harvest incident?' asked Alice.

'I've never heard of it,' said Dash.

Alice explained, with Greenbow chipping in the odd faintly right-wing grumble. In the early Eighties a militant Scottish group known as the Dark Harvest Commando had demanded the government decontaminate Gruinard Island. They'd bypassed security and left a container of soil right outside the gates of Porton Down, and a second package outside a hotel in Blackpool (not a typical terrorist target, but the Conservative Party conference happened to be underway there). The first sample had been found to contain anthrax. The second hadn't, but was still confirmed to be soil dug up

179

from the island. Cleaning up the island made sense. Discounting the obvious ethical arguments of leaving this patch of Scotland forever contaminated (which, to be honest, I can't believe Thatcher's government gave a shit about), such a huge stockpile of lethal anthrax spores sitting a stone's throw from the coast of mainland Britain was never a good idea. Apart from the danger of contamination, there were other things to think about, as the Dark Harvest Commando had pointed out. Anyone who wanted to get their hands on large quantities of military-grade bioweapon simply needed a rowing boat and a bucket and spade.

'It's just the same now,' explained Alice. 'The Russians were after the anthrax as well as wanting Demeter back. A nice source sample of Vollum strain, they used him to get it, two birds, one stone.'

'And was he involved in planning the operation?' I asked.

'Clay sent the two of us up here six months ago to run preliminary tests, just a day. We collected samples and took them back.'

'And what did the samples show?'

'That the island was actually more contaminated than in the Forties.'

'You think Demeter's been planning this all along?' asked Hurley. 'The Russians got in touch a while ago, threatened his son. He got the wheels moving…'

'He used his influence with Clay,' Greenbow cut in, 'to set the dates and make sure he was on the team. Cunning bastard.'

'Exactly,' Hurley continued. 'For him, the whole trip was a means to get away from the UK *and* get in the good books with Russia.' Hurley looked pleased with himself.

There was a minute as we mulled over the ideas. I wondered who'd handled the samples left in the Dark Harvest incident, whether they'd showed any signs of mutated strains. Had Demeter been in the labs at Porton Down then? He came across in the Eighties – it was feasible.

Dash broke the silence. 'Shouldn't we be focusing on getting off the island ourselves?'

'Why?' Marie asked.

He turned to her, sofa squeaking in protest. 'Our numbers are dwindling, and I'd rather leave before they dwindle down to me.'

There were nods of agreement, but I'd already considered this, had been waiting for it.

'We should stay put, we're safer in here,' I said.

'We need to report the murders,' said Greenbow. 'And Demeter's defection. They could still catch him.'

'You forget Demeter smashed the radios?' said Dash.

'Well what the bloody hell do you suggest?' Greenbow stood to reinforce his authority, but looked unsure of his next move, simply standing next to his chair gripping the seat back. 'We need to do *something*.'

'The boat,' said Alice. 'We'll use the boat to get to the ship.'

Hurley jumped in his seat. 'Alice is right! It's tied up below.'

I knew sooner or later someone would bring up the boat. I couldn't allow anyone to leave, not yet. Everyone spoke at once, I had to raise my voice to be heard. 'We'd be dead in minutes.' They turned. 'Are any of you sailors? No? There's a six-foot swell out there and it'll be worse round that northern shore. That's if we could even get away from the breakers; we'd probably be smashed on the rocks before drowning.'

The mental image shut them up. It had been a perilous journey for experienced Royal Marines and the storm had only worsened since then. With the exception of perhaps Hurley and Marie these were, for the most part, hapless lab-bound scientists who'd probably brought a note from their mum every PE lesson; they had no chance in the great outdoors.

'John's right. Storm's ragin', we ain't goin' nowhere,' said Dash, acknowledging his limitations, and perhaps his mass.

'Once the *Dauntless* realises the radios are dead they'll get in touch,' said Greenbow. 'Our check-in is hours overdue.'

'They'll have already realised, but they can't do any more about it than we can,' I said.

'Protocol says they'll send a launch to check on us.'

'They can't send one in these seas.'

Obviously Greenbow was entirely right; my first bit of luck had been intercepting the Marines before they reached the base. We looked at one another. I could tell they weren't all sold on waiting it out and I wanted everyone where I could see them. I needed to sweeten the deal.

'We'll signal the ship with Morse,' I said.

'In this weather?' said Dash.

'I saw a big battery-powered work lamp up at Camp Vollum. We'll signal from the cliffs, request a helicopter evac soon as the wind drops.'

'Well I'm not going out there,' said Alice. 'Not in this storm and especially not with a killer on the loose.'

The room descended into chaos again, I had to shout this time.

'We'll split up.' I stood to draw a line under the argument. 'A couple of people go to signal the ship, the rest stay here to secure the base.'

'Does anyone even know Morse?' asked Hurley.

'Greenbow does,' I said. I did too, and I wanted to talk to the ship myself, but having the military man with me might be of benefit. 'We'll both go back to Camp Vollum.' I turned to him. 'You'll need to leave your gun with them.'

He shrank back into his chair. 'Alice is right, Demeter could still be out there. I should stay here to protect everyone.'

'I'll go with you,' said Marie.

Hurley, Dash and Alice made no attempt to move. The decision was made. Marie wouldn't be my first tag-team pick in a physical fight, but she seemed to know her stuff and I'd take her brains and enthusiasm for now.

Alice gave me a knowing look that suggested she'd keep an eye on the others and tip me off if anyone acted suspiciously in our absence.

'Right, Marie, let's get suited.' I looked around the others, all happy that affirmative action was being taken as long as they didn't have to be involved.

Chapter Forty-five

The rain stung through the thin suits, pushing us sideways with each step forwards, forcing us to crab-walk through the thick mud. Occasionally a gust would pull at the filter of our gas masks, threatening to tear them from our faces. We had to shout to be heard, and even then it was difficult to understand each other.

'You'd have been safer staying in the base, Marie. You should go back; I'll go up to Vollum on my own.'

'No chance. It's safer to stay close to you.'

Probably the opposite was true; I had a target painted on my back. 'Well I'll do what I can to keep you safe.'

'You worry about yourself,' she snapped. 'I mean, if you're next I want to see where the shot comes from rather than be hiding under a table.'

I smiled to myself, but it turned to a frown when I wondered whether there was another reason she wanted to come out here with me. Suddenly I didn't feel that confident with her walking behind me.

'How well did you know Gambetta?' I asked.

'Not at all, really.'

'He was French.'

'So's Gérard Depardieu, but I don't know him either. Look, before this project I'd met him a couple of times, that's all.'

'Fair enough. Why do you think Demeter killed him?'

'I thought we knew why?'

I mumbled and switched tack. 'What were you talking about this aft? You looked pretty cosy.'

'Did we?' She shrugged again.

I let her overtake me as we started down the far side of the hill, the rain and thunder making further conversation impossible. The wind wrapped the baggy suit tight around Marie, outlining her curves, the only way to tell who was under there. Somehow we made it to the steps without being blown over or having the suits ripped from our bodies. I punched in the code for the door and stepped inside.

It slid behind us with a hiss as the room pressurised, sealing out the storm. We could still hear the rain nailing the sides and roof, but it was quiet enough to hear the hum of the strip lights, until the showers started up and pelted us with bleach.

We moved through, Marie dropping her mask into the tub of bleach and looking at me, eyebrows raised. 'How did you know the code for the door?'

I waved an arm around. 'We built them.'

'Rubbish, Clay came up with the code and apart from me only three people knew it – and they wouldn't have told you. We're a suspicious lot.'

'Ingrid told me,' I said, pulling off my boots.

'No, she didn't. Demeter and I are the only others, and we didn't tell you either.'

'Must have been Clay, then.'

That alarm was ringing in my head again, the one I'd learned to listen to carefully. Marie was frowning, still demanding answers as she pulled herself out of the suit, but I was fully focused on a new line of thinking.

Of course Demeter had known the code for the door; Greenbow had mentioned it earlier, but that was before…

'There were two gunshots… quickly, Marie, come with me.' I pushed my suit into the chute and grabbed her, pulling her inside. No time for showers, if I was right the integrity of the base had already been compromised anyway. We went straight through the corridors, stopping in the link tunnel to the last hut. I felt her hand pull away, tugging backwards, I realised she'd just seen Ingrid's body.

'Don't look.' I left her in the tunnel while I ran to the common room, grabbing a lab coat from the chair. I returned to the corridor, laying it over the body. By now she was cold, her already pale skin blue, translucent almost. The lab coat stuck to the floor where the congealed blood hadn't yet dried. I took Marie's hand and gently guided her into the last hut.

She looked at the coat, trembling. I pulled her forward.

'Look at the window.'

She shuddered again when she saw the bullet holes in the safety glass, her eyes started to drift back to the floor.

'Marie, look at the windows, what do you see?'

'Bullet holes.'

'Okay, now stand here.' I ushered her to the wall. Ingrid's body lay a few metres in front of us, with the window another couple of metres beyond that. I pointed Marie's arm out, aiming an imaginary gun.

'Demeter entered the base and made his way here, the last corridor. Ingrid came out of the common room, where she'd been on the radio. She must have appeared right in front of him. He shoots.' I pointed her arm wide to the right. 'The first shot misses, goes through the window.' I moved her arm to the left. 'He shoots again. The bullet goes through her head, out the back, then through the window there.' This time her arm lined up perfectly with the body and the window behind. 'Makes sense?'

Marie nodded. 'Yes, I guess so.'

'Yeah, Hurley and Greenbow thought so too, but they're wrong. I should have seen before, it couldn't have happened like that.'

'Why not? Seems logical.'

'No, it doesn't. You're squeezing the facts together to make it fit but you're ignoring the things that don't make sense.'

'Like what?'

'Like why the hell Demeter fired in completely the wrong direction the first time. Look.' I pointed her arm to the right again, swinging it away from the common room door. 'Why did he shoot that way? What's over there? Nothing.'

'Maybe Ingrid moved? She dodged?'

'But why would she have been standing there? It's empty corridor.'

Marie knitted her eyebrows together. 'So he must have fired at someone else, or something else, that was in that corner? Something that's been moved?' She was pleased with herself. 'Maybe that's what Ingrid came out to see, and that's when he shot her?'

'Sorry, no. Good idea though – you're thinking along different lines, at least.'

She pouted. 'What, then?'

'Well first, don't you think the position of the two bullet holes is odd?'

She scrutinised them. The one on the left had punched a neat circle halfway up the window – about five centimetres in from the right-hand edge of the pane. The bullet hole on the right was larger and jagged. Here the bullet had pulverised the glass, taking some shards with it, but it was easy enough to tell that this too had hit halfway up the window. This time the shooter had aimed far over to the right, the hole about ten centimetres from the edge.

'I don't see it,' said Marie.

I walked over to the window, fished out the key, clicked the latch, sliding it open. The rain was deafening but the wind took the worst of it away from us.

I backed away from the window, standing next to Marie. 'Now what do you see?'

'I see an idiot who's opened a window to a sealed base, on an anthrax-infested island. Where did you steal that key from?'

'Ignore the key. Come on, this area's been decontaminated, plus you know with all this rain falling there's minimal risk of airborne spores.'

She nodded but didn't seem to share my enthusiasm.

'Just look at the window, Marie.'

She let out a squeak. I held her arm out again, tracing the path of the bullet as it had flown from the pistol, through Ingrid's head, through the first bullet hole – and straight on through the second bullet hole which, now that the window was open, aligned perfectly with the first.

'There was only one shot.'

She looked puzzled.

I said it another way to help the penny drop. 'When Ingrid was shot, the window was open.'

'Why would she open the window? And how, if she didn't have a key?'

'You're a scientist. Theorise.'

Marie thought about it for a moment and said, 'She didn't, so… the killer opened it?'

'Why?'

'To get in or out?' she said.

'And since you need a code to open the door into the base, but not one to get out? And the mud on the floor?'

'The killer came in through the window?'

I could see from her eyes that the implication was hitting. I summarised to speed it along. 'Demeter had the code for the door, but the killer came in the window. The killer had a window key but not the door code.' I stepped over the body and slid the window shut. I repeated it for her. 'The killer didn't have the door code. Demeter isn't the killer.'

Chapter Forty-six

Marie thought about it for a few seconds, looking between me and the holes in the window.

'That's a bit of a leap. We know Demeter killed them.'

'The CCTV data stick is missing. If Demeter killed Ingrid, why did he remove it? He'd know he was the only suspect, and he didn't give a shit about us knowing he was at the main base. Nope, the killer removed the data stick because of what it *wouldn't* show. It *wouldn't* show *anyone* entering the base.'

Marie soaked up what I'd suspected for some time. Then the inevitable challenges came. 'Who?' 'Why?' 'When?' Questions I didn't know the answer to.

I left her, taking the opportunity to grab the high-powered work lamp from the shelves next to the radio, and while I did I pondered some more, because there was of course another explanation. The killer removed the data stick because it showed them – and not Demeter – entering the base. Which would make the killer one of the people who knew the code. If not Demeter, or Ingrid or Clay, both dead – then was it Marie?

When I returned she was still staring at the window. I decided to keep that recent line of thought to myself and concentrated on the other.

'The killer makes their way here and finds the lab lights on. The blinds are shut but they assume Ingrid's in there – the logical place for her to be. They creep to this end of the base, less chance of being heard, and open the window from outside.

'But Ingrid's not in the lab. She's in the common room, still on the radio – she's just finished her 7 p.m. check-in. She puts her iPod on and stands up.

'The killer climbs in through the window. They leave it open and dash inside – as far as they know, Ingrid could have heard it, so they've got to get her quickly before she raises the alarm. They know they can shut the window later. Wellies off but keep the suit on – no muddy footprints. Straight past the common room, towards the lab where the lights are blazing. Gun ready.

'Ingrid doesn't hear the window, or the killer, because she has her headphones in. She steps into the corridor, sees the suited figure right in front of her.

'The killer hears her, turns round, fires – one shot, through Ingrid and the two window panes.

'Then they smash the radio, take the CCTV data stick, close the window. Collect their boots and leave the base by the HADU. They either don't care about the two bullet holes, or more likely don't even notice – we can assume they're still wearing a gas mask streaked with rain, it's a bugger to see.

'Gambetta's next; the killer has to get to him quickly, because if he's on the radio and Ingrid doesn't reply, Gambetta will raise the alarm and the ship will get involved. The plan is to get back to the main base, dispose of Gambetta and the radio, quickly.'

'It sounds plausible,' said Marie. 'But we saw Demeter.'

'All we saw was a red suit.'

'But why?'

I kept it vague. 'Covering their tracks – I don't know why at the moment. All I know is Demeter didn't kill Ingrid. That means he *probably* didn't kill Gambetta either. Once you establish that, it seems likely he didn't kill Andy Kyle or Donald Clay.' *Or try killing me.*

'But the note, his escape?'

'Why would Demeter keep the note?'

'I'm not sure, but that doesn't prove—'

'If he got it a while ago, on the mainland – why bring it with him?'

'Because—'

'And the killer question – if it was written to Demeter, a Russian, from Russian Intelligence, the GU or someone else, why is it in English?'

This time she didn't even bother to open her mouth.

'Someone on the island is trying hard to frame Demeter. He was always the obvious candidate, the first person anyone would suspect.'

'But the divers?'

'There's still another question we need to think about.'

'I don't think I can take any more.'

'If someone's framing Demeter – where's he gone?'

'I think the fact he's missing probably quashes your theory.'

'I don't think so. If he's been set up they'd have got rid of him, too.'

There was only one way to be sure.

I gave Marie the lamp and sent her back to the HADU to get suited up. Meanwhile I had a quick search for anything out of place, anything that might give us a clue to where Demeter might have gone. I checked the lounge, rooting through the clothes discarded by the others when they'd had to sleep in here, opening cupboards, pulling out batteries, torches, books, a first aid kit. I didn't really know what I was looking for, and couldn't find it anyway.

The lab next door was full of equipment, I'd no clue what it was used for but still nowt interesting was jumping out at me. The cupboards were crammed with petri dishes, microscopes, boxes of labels and forms and documents and manuals.

I stood looking out of the window at the bright spot lamp attached to the pump. The incinerator taunted me from the edge of the circle of light.

I'd gone over and over it, was convinced now one of the other five was a killer, had a pile of clues as tall as me, but nothing to string them together. My concern was that their plan seemed to have come to an end. They'd acquired a sample.

They'd tested it on Andy. They knew the authorities would suspect something if an autopsy was carried out, so they'd disposed of the body – setting me up as the idiot who'd lost it. They'd implicated Demeter. Everything had been tied up nicely. I probably got Ingrid killed by asking her to test the tea, she'd had to die.

And Gambetta? Maybe he *had* just been murdered because the killer wanted the radio out of action. Slow everyone down, increase tensions in the base and ensure the authorities didn't get here too quickly. Just enough time for these fictitious divers to disappear, supposedly taking Demeter with them.

Now all the killer had to do was wait it out. Lie low, hide among us, confident there was no evidence to connect them to the deaths. Come tomorrow morning when the storm abated, rescue would arrive in the form of a motor launch or helicopter from HMS *Dauntless*, and we'd all be back on the mainland in time for dinner. We'd be debriefed, of course, but our stories would corroborate and exonerate each other. Captain Greenbow would probably spin the situation around and end up vouching for everyone's innocence. Case closed, the killer is free.

I couldn't let that happen. I needed to smoke the killer out, force their hand. Get them into the open before rescue arrived. That's why I'd asked the Navy to leave us here, keeping their visit from the others, buying time.

I left the room and went next door, into the lab nearest the HADU to finish my search, rifling through the cupboards. I found what I needed in a drawer under a desk; stacks of unused test tubes, vials like I'd been filling for Alice that afternoon. I stuffed one into my pocket then looked over at the cupboards, thinking. The wheelie chair had been pushed away from the desk, spun round and discarded at the far end of the room. I looked up at the cupboards attached to the wall above it and climbed up onto the chair.

It was on top of that far cupboard, right in the corner of the room, that I discovered the thing I was looking for, at the back against the wall. I slid it towards me to have a proper look. It was a big piece of the puzzle, but how did it fit?

The hairs on the back of my neck stood on end, I caught my reflection in the window, froze as I noticed the figure right behind me, an indistinct shape, a shadow of a man. I couldn't look away, the apparition moved towards me, reaching, imploring. Features swam into focus, its mouth opened. My heart pounded, I gripped the top of the cupboard, closed my eyes, breathed deeply.

'What are you doing?'

I opened my eyes, turned to see Marie in the doorway. I shrugged. 'Sorry, miles away.'

I slid the ominous item I'd found back through the dust on top of the cupboard and jumped down, wiping sweaty palms on my trousers.

'Have a look at this,' said Marie, holding up an iPad.

'What is it?' I asked.

'I had a thought. I checked what Ingrid was working on, she signed in a new sample this morning but it's not in the store.' She waved the iPad in my face, as if I'd understand.

'Is that odd?'

'Very. Samples are rigorously controlled. It's a one-off, too.' She ran a finger down the spreadsheet on screen. 'Not from one of Alice's test sites.'

My sample. Diligently, she'd checked it in. Is that how the killer had known, why she'd had to die? Why they'd stolen it, hiding it under the floor at X-Base?

Marie continued, but I wasn't interested. I'd moved on, thinking about something else entirely.

I was wondering why Eric Gambetta had hidden his silenced Walther PPK on top of a cupboard here in this lab.

Chapter Forty-seven

Marie and I were back outside, next to the whirring pump. It spluttered, the huge pipe bucked, shuddered, writhing on the waves. I crouched to run my gloves over it, feeling the rush of water inside, looking out to sea where it disappeared into the void. A couple of floodlights bathed us and the pump in artificial white light, but the surrounding black squeezed it into as small a space as possible, ensuring no light extended beyond a few metres. If you were to step away it'd look like a white canopy of water had somehow been erected against the hut, beyond it, the world ceased to exist. I flicked on the work lamp, running the beam across the hillside to quell the claustrophobia, to prove there was something out there.

Alice and the others had been busy, the ground was covered with pipes in every direction. The beam reflected off a bright yellow grid stretching up to the cliffs overhanging the cove.

Marie explained the generator was powering a pump, sucking up seawater from out on the raft. I couldn't see the barrels floating it, but could picture them twisting up and down in the frigid dark, threatening to tear up whatever it had been anchored to. She gestured to a cluster of huge plastic vats arranged alongside the huts, demonstrating how the seawater was mixed with formaldehyde then pumped through the small pipes across the island. I could see the tiny holes all along the smaller pipes, like garden watering hoses. Apparently it was enough to decontaminate the island, the anthrax being restricted to the top few centimetres of soil, and concentrated mostly in this area. Here the topsoil had already been removed in sealed containers for high-temperature incineration, the rest had been soaking in 5 per cent formaldehyde, 95 per cent saltwater.

'This is the worst affected area?' I asked, shielding my mask from the driving rain.

'We're just downwind from where the explosives were set off in the Forties,' said Marie, shouting above the wind and spluttering pump mechanism.

This was where the Gruinard strain had grown over eighty years and been eradicated in days, leaving just the sample in the vial in my pocket, the one I'd found under the comms room.

The pump shuddered and died.

'Why's it stopped?' I shouted.

'Probably out of fuel.'

'We need to make sure this whole area is thoroughly decontaminated.'

No arguments, no questions, thankfully. 'Make yourself useful, get that restarted.' She pointed to a small generator sheltering under the base, a rugged Petter single-cylinder that should go on in all weathers, coupled to an inverter huddling under a tarpaulin. 'Switch the fuel barrel over,' she shouted.

I liked Marie more and more. I knocked a few sheets of plywood out of the way then turned to watch her confidently turning valves and flicking switches, probably the most competent person on the island. I rolled the empty fuel cannister out of the way and pulled the hose across to a new one. 'So, Biarritz. Anyone, erm, special waiting for you back there?'

'Concentrate on the generator, I don't want to be out here all night.'

I smiled, flipped the lever, pulled the crank. The Petter fired up again immediately, settling down into a rhythmic ticking, barely audible over the rain. I looked over at the pump, saw a couple of lights had appeared in the darkness. Marie pushed more buttons. The electric pump whirred back into life, sucking seawater up, pushing it through the pipes. They untwisted, straining at the stakes as the pressure hit once more. It was both too dark and too wet to see it spraying. We'd just have to trust it was doing its job.

I swung the lamp around again, landing on the incinerator, which got me thinking about Demeter. On this island, where could you hide or dispose of a body?

I walked over to it, resting my gloves against the side. Cold, though it wouldn't take long to cool in this weather. I hauled myself up onto it again, swung open the lid. Clouds of ash swirled up, gluing themselves across my soaked gas mask. I shuddered at the memory, wiping the muck away, and shone the lamp inside.

Just those fragments of bones jutting from piles of ash. All too small to be human, and I could still see the warped tea tin where I'd dropped it. I shivered again, fighting a flashback. The beam found the ignitor still swathed in dirty duct tape. It'd been a good theory but no bodies had been disposed of in here, it hadn't been used since the morning.

'What are you doing?' shouted Marie. Behind her the pump lurched, spluttered for a few seconds, whined, then went back to pumping water.

Marie returned to the pump, adjusting the controls, one hand resting on the bucking pipe.

Where else could Demeter's body be? I jumped back down, walked to the base and dropped to my knees, shining the beam underneath. Nothing but mud and the small generator.

The rest of the island was empty space. There were craters, and I guess a shallow grave was always a possibility, but it'd be a pig to dig the stony ground out here, and far too conspicuous. I'd been trying to ignore the obvious, of course, the booming surf on the rocks. Last time anyone had actually seen Demeter – not counting from when we assumed it was him in the corridor – was late afternoon, over this side of the island. Easy enough for Demeter to have gone the same way as Andy Kyle's body, over the cliffs and into the sea.

The pump choked again, underscored by a flash of lightning.

Marie still had a hand on the pipe. 'There's something wrong with it.'

I scanned the break in the bluffs, the cove beyond. The tide was on the turn. It'd been coming in earlier, when I'd last seen Demeter. He'd been headed up onto the cliffs then, with Gambetta.

Assuming he'd been dumped, if the tide had been coming in when he was killed his body might have been pulled to shore. I skirted the small cove to the bottom of the hill, where the low bluffs morphed into the angular crags that dominated the north-western shore of the island. I shone the beam around the rocks. It illuminated the crashing waves, glowing white geysers spraying the black cliffs, the roar of the surf below blending into the thunder above. There was nowhere the body could be lodged, it'd have been smashed to pieces in no time.

I spent a good ten minutes walking up the hill and back, one eye on the shore. The other was on Marie – it hadn't escaped my attention that we were exposed out here, our lights a beacon for anyone wanting us out of the way. No others appeared in the black and Marie never moved. All the time, my hand hovered near my holster, ready to tear open my suit just in case.

On the way back down the hill I shone the lamp out to sea, watching the waves rise and fall. *The waves, the tide, the faltering pump.* I ran the rest of the way.

The pump was still whining and choking. Marie was leaning against it, watching me.

'Stay there,' I shouted, gesturing in case the wind took the words.

She tapped her wrist impatiently.

I scurried down the narrow track between the rocks, splashing into the sea, looking over my shoulder every few steps to check on Marie. She was casting her torch around nervously, scanning the moorland beyond the base. I grabbed the thick pipe, switched my torch onto high beam, and waded deeper. It dipped and rose on the swell. The sea was above my waist now. I pressed on, out of Marie's torch beam, surrounded on all sides by furious sea, the crests smashing across the gas mask.

A few metres away the pipe dipped under the waves before reappearing further out. It was weighed down, pulled under the water by something large resting on it. A creature from the deep flapped, wrapping a tentacle around the pipe, pulling it back under, rising and falling with the incoming waves.

By the time I'd reached the thing, I had to fight to remain upright; my boots were slipping out from under me every time the pipe rose, lifting me up, water spraying above my head and running down my back where the tape had been torn from my hood.

The thing weighing the pipe down was distorted, broken and bent out of shape, but I could still tell I'd found Demeter.

Chapter Forty-eight

Demeter reached out. His glove had been torn off, a sickly blue hand trailing shredded tape in the foam. Buoyed up by air trapped in the suit, body bent double round the pipe, legs wedged somewhere underneath. His other arm had folded round, trapping the pipe under his body, holding him against it.

I could see why the pump had been faltering. The plastic sections of pipe were tethered with a cable clipped through hoops along its length, and when Demeter's body had been swept onto the pipe it had dislodged one, splitting the coupling open. The open pipe had been thrown out of the sea on the incoming waves, pumping air instead of water.

I grabbed handfuls of red plastic suit and heaved. At first he didn't budge, but with the assistance of a wave I managed to slide my arm under the pipe, wrenching him free. He started to float away but I grabbed his suit again – I didn't want to lose two bodies to the sea. It was easier heading in, pushed along by the waves, though with both hands on the body I couldn't see where I was walking, twice slipping to my knees as I dragged it in.

Marie still huddled in the cone of light from the work lamps. I waved her over.

First there was disbelief, then argument, finally she pitched in. On top of his considerable bulk, his suit was half full of water, but after a ton of grunting we'd succeeded in dragging Demeter up the pebbles, over the rocks, onto the mud. Only then did we stop for a rest.

'How did he get there?' Marie asked.

I turned him over, answering the question. She cried out, scream choked off by her respirator. A lifeless eye stared from behind the shattered visor of his gas mask. I flicked a crab away as lightning illuminated the dark mess of his other eye. 7.65mm lobotomy, just like Gambetta and Ingrid.

'He had some help into the sea.'

'Why did they shoot him?' she asked. 'If he was escaping by submarine, why kill him?'

'There never was a sub, or divers. Demeter's been murdered in cold blood, framed for the others.'

'Could the killer still be here somewhere?' She spun her torch about wildly.

'They never left. There are six people on this island. One is a murderer.'

Marie backed away, into the safety of the spotlights, leaving me alone with Demeter. I stood, watching her checking over the pump, then took the anthrax vial from my pocket, the one from the radio room back at base. The raft briefly flashed in the lightning, held high on a wave, then black, as thunder rolled overhead and the waves broke over the rocks. With four people dead and the contents of Ingrid's note to chew over, the vial in my hand now weighed a hell of a lot more.

Chapter Forty-nine

After I waded back out to recouple the pipe, the decontamination spray worked fine, no more protests from the pump. The seawater was in endless supply, and even at the higher dosage of a 10 per cent solution, we reckoned there was enough formaldehyde in the vats to run for a few hours yet. With the amount of fuel in the tank it was a toss-up whether the diesel generator would conk out again before the formaldehyde tanks ran dry, but either way, and despite the rain, the ground around here would be so saturated, no spores could possibly survive.

I felt a lot safer knowing there was zero chance of any more super-anthrax lying around. Whichever of the team had taken the sample would have been at pains to ensure no one else could get their hands on it. If the underlying personal motive was money – usually a safe bet – then the sample was only worth something if it was unique.

I'm not religious, dead flesh is dead flesh, but it'd felt undignified to leave poor old Demeter lying on the grass, so we'd dragged him under the huts by the generator. I'd done my best to prop some plywood up to shelter the generator and the body, though I suspected the wind would make a mess of it within minutes.

Marie's demeanour had changed since discovering Demeter's body. Given this and the difficulty communicating, we walked to the north cliffs in silence, my hand close to that holster under my suit. We skirted the top of the hill so as not to be struck by lightning, flinching at every crash of thunder, using every flash to scan our surroundings, then looking back at the ground to avoid going arse over tit.

I was overthinking it. One minute Demeter was the *only* person who could possibly have killed Ingrid and Gambetta, the next he *had* to have been framed. My mind was reeling. By the time we'd rounded the island I wasn't sure I'd progressed my investigation a great deal, but I was set on Demeter's innocence. The main thing was, I now had a plan; a solid plan to flush the killer into the open in the morning ready for the Marines' arrival.

The darkness up ahead told us we'd arrived at the northern cliffs, the percussion of waves against rocks louder here, facing into the storm. I leaned into the wind, could just about make out the foam smashing over the exposed bones of the island, but beyond that, black.

Up ahead, two stars wavered in sheets of rain. One floated slightly higher than the other, the only evidence *Dauntless* was watching, waiting, a jaguar ready to pounce.

Marie rustled in the bracken behind me, I turned to see her walking backwards, away from the edge.

'You signal the ship, I'll head back,' she said.

I shook my head. 'Wait for me, it's not safe.'

'Fine.'

I turned back to the lights. Somewhere out there a watchman would be on duty. I held the work lamp out and flicked the light on and off, signalling the prosign for attention.

The answer came back almost immediately, whoever was on watch was keen.

I flashed my brief message and turned to Marie only to find she'd disappeared. The reply came from the ship, I put the work lamp down and started jogging for the base.

After a few minutes I was beginning to think something had happened to her, that she'd got lost or worse. Thankfully, I spotted the dim lights of the base up ahead and, bobbing towards it, Marie's silhouette. I increased the pace, closing the gap as she launched up the steps. I lost my footing and dropped onto one knee, balancing to avoid falling further, shouting her name. She turned, I expected her to come back and offer a hand but instead she vanished into the HADU. The door quickly slid shut behind her. I brushed myself down and followed, pausing on the platform at the top to complete a slow turn, one last check of that impossible black, before I punched the keypad for the door.

Nothing.

I looked down to see the keypad was dark. Power to the HADU had been cut, stranding me outside in the storm.

Chapter Fifty

I punched the keypad again but it was definitely dead, it had worked for Marie so no missing fuse this time, this was manual intervention via the control panel inside.

I sprinted round the side of the base. The lounge windows were dark, furniture piled against them. I kept going to the only other window I hadn't been able to screw shut, the kitchen, praying I wasn't too late. My stolen key turned easily in the lock, I placed both hands on the windowsill and pulled. The aluminium track bit deep into the gloves as I hauled myself up and through, onto the worktop. Plates and utensils crashed as I crawled over the sink and dropped to the floor.

I peeled off my gloves, pushed my mask up onto my head, and tore at the side of my suit, pulling my gun free.

The lights blazed on, Greenbow appeared, Browning ready, flanked by Dash and Hurley brandishing a chair leg each.

'Stay where you are, Tyler.'

'He's got a gun,' hissed Hurley.

'Just let Marie go,' I said, pistol outstretched to match Greenbow's. 'Let her go and we both back out of here.' I automatically calculated the risk, assessing the most efficient way to dispatch the three of them, where to place the bullets, Greenbow first, then Hurley, then Dash. Acute angles, twenty degrees between them, easy.

'Don't listen to him,' said Marie from somewhere behind the wall. I realised she wasn't a captive at all, it was her who'd locked me out.

'Where's Alice?' I asked.

'I'm here—' she started.

'Start explaining,' said Dash.

Keeping the gun up I reached behind me to slide the window shut. 'Marie? Why did you lock me out?'

She directed her answer at the others. 'He knew the code for the door at Camp Vollum. And he has a window key.'

'And a gun,' Hurley said again.

'Of course,' said Greenbow. 'I knew something was off when we went up to Vollum earlier, but it didn't click.'

Dash tensed. 'You were grilling me about the windows earlier,' he said. 'All makes sense now.'

Greenbow shifted slightly as he put two and two together and made thirteen.

'This is crazy, Demeter killed Gambetta and Ingrid,' said Alice, finally finding her voice, peering round him. 'And he's still missing.'

'No, he's not missing any more. John knew exactly where to find him,' Marie said. 'Demeter's dead,' she added to collective gasps. Dash shuffled back.

Greenbow's eyes narrowed. I tensed my hand, finger oh-so slowly squeezing the trigger. Twenty-pound trigger, single action.

The collective gasps had meant this was news to them, which in turn meant the killer was still hidden. The rest of them were innocent, this wasn't a conspiracy of everyone against me otherwise they'd have jumped me. And they certainly wouldn't be acting like this, this was nothing more than paranoid group mentality.

'Everyone out into the corridor,' I said. 'Nice and slow.'

Greenbow and Hurley shuffled almost imperceptibly.

'Just tell them, John,' Alice shouted.

'You killed them,' Greenbow said through gritted teeth. 'You'll kill us all too.'

I shook my head. 'Let's not have any accidents. Gun down, now.'

'John!' Alice screamed.

'Shut her up,' said Greenbow, pointing behind him, presumably at Alice. 'You know the code to the secure door at Camp Vollum, despite not being part of the team. You stole a window key. Two of our colleagues have been shot and you're the only other person on the island with a gun, despite not being authorised to carry one, and now you're pointing that gun at us. We've clearly found our rotten apple.'

Stalemate, I'd no idea what my next move would be but I needed to come up with one before they realised they could easily rush me. I took up about 15lbs of that 20lb trigger, slowly bringing the gun in closer, still aimed at the middle of the three torsos. All I was thinking was, how many shots can I get off before Greenbow pulls that trigger?

Things had taken a dangerous turn, this tight-knit bunch was on a knife-edge. The longer this went on, the more brain cells would be lost to this group mentality. These were the kind of high-pressure situations you read about, that lead to lynchings, or cannibalism, the kind of situations where mistakes are made.

Which is exactly what I was counting on, the reason I hadn't wanted the Marines to evacuate us.

The rain pelted. The strip lights buzzed. The fridge hummed and ticked. The stalemate was finally broken by Alice, who evidently had not been shut up.

'Oh, just tell them,' she shouted. 'He's no more a killer than I am! He's a spy, sent by MI5.'

I hadn't expected this, I was momentarily on the back foot, though in blurting it out, Alice had implicated herself in a conspiracy. There were more gasps, growls, and I'm not sure whether it was because my duplicity had been revealed, or because of Alice's knowledge of it.

'Is that true?' asked Greenbow.

'I work for the government, just like everyone on this island.'

'MI5?' asked Dash.

Greenbow looked nervous. Faced with this new knowledge, he was torn on loyalties and priorities. 'So that's why you're here.'

'It's why I'm *still* here, despite your best efforts. The storm wasn't that bad earlier, the ship *could* have sent a launch to come get me. But, you see, my boss is a funny bugger. When Clay and then you both requested me to be relieved, he sorta thought it'd be worth me sticking around.'

'And a fat lot of good you've done so far,' spat Alice.

'If I remember rightly, you lot were sitting in this room getting sozzled on cheap fizz while Ingrid and Gambetta were murdered. Your colleagues are dropping like flies and you didn't need my help for that. So let's all calm down and have a proper discussion without pointing guns at each other.'

Greenbow lowered his arm slightly. The two others lowered their chair-leg bats. I slowly moved my gun away to the side, other hand up in surrender. Everybody breathed.

'Now, someone help me out of these boots,' I said.

Chapter Fifty-one

The hour or so that Marie and I had been gone had not been kind to the others, it was no wonder they'd pounced. Cooped up with their imaginations and with the storm raging, nerves had frayed to the point that sanity clung by the thinnest of threads. To say everyone was on edge is an understatement; they'd dropped over the edge, dangling by their fingernails – though for one of them it was for a very different reason.

To avoid an unpleasant conversation, I told Greenbow I'd found the window key, realised its importance, and pocketed it. No point revealing I'd broken into his office, it wouldn't do me any favours. His attitude towards me had changed now he realised he was allied with the other authority in the base and that, since we'd been together at the time Ingrid had been killed, in my eyes he was the only person who could be exempted from her death.

Marie had apologised profusely for locking me outside, even though I assured her I'd have done the same. She'd made up for it by helping me clean up before we went along into the HADU to decontaminate properly, paying attention to the areas where I'd ripped my suit. She also made me chuck away my favourite jumper.

Now we were all once again facing each other uneasily in the lounge as I brought them up to speed on the evac plan.

Away from the island, an outsider looking in would find it impossible to decipher fact from fiction. One of these people wanted to remain hidden among us, to make it off the island as soon as possible, when any evidence would disintegrate.

Without understanding the exact time frames, the looks on peoples' faces, the inflection in their voices; without simply *being here*, no one would have a hope of proving what had happened. The powers that be would rule it was a spree killing by Demeter to cover his own defection, double-crossed by his contacts, and that would be the end of it. Away from the island it would be the simplest solution that made the most sense.

I had to prevent that, and to do so I had to prevent everyone leaving for as long as possible.

'So we won't be picked up until tomorrow morning,' I said. 'Can't send the chopper up in this, and too rough for the boat.'

'We can't stay here all night,' said Alice.

'That generator shed's not going to take much more abuse,' Dash added. 'Any more of this wind and it's gonna take off.'

'It'll bloody well have to take it.'

'We've tried to secure the sheds, but they're really getting a beating,' said Hurley.

'Which is why they can't evacuate us – can you imagine trying to land a helicopter?'

'If they won't come to us, we'll have to go to them,' said Greenbow. 'We've got no choice, we must take the boat.'

'They strongly advised against it. That boat we've got is for emergencies only…'

Marie shot me a look.

'Then I'd love to know your definition of an emergency,' muttered Hurley.

'…and like I said before, in these seas it'd be swamped. And if we somehow got out to the *Dauntless*, we'd be smashed against her hull.'

'We'll make for the mainland, then.'

'And be torn apart on the rocks. Look, just a few hours and we'll be off the island.'

'What time did they say?'

'Storm should clear early doors, they're meeting us on the beach at ten.'

The knowledge of an exact time and place calmed them, gave them something to focus on. They knew it was the only sensible option; I'm sure none of them actually relished the idea of taking the tiny boat out there.

After a little more discussion, it was settled; we'd leave the base together at nine thirty the next morning, to be collected at ten. And if my plan worked, one of them wouldn't get that far.

'So what do you think then, Tyler?' Greenbow was still leaning forward in his chair.

'I think we should get some sleep.'

'I mean, about how and why Demeter killed them?' Greenbow asked.

'I'm not sure he did.'

'No one else could have.'

'Jesus, this is Sak,' I said – to myself, I thought, though evidently not.

'What's Sak?' Dash looked at me, then at Greenbow. 'A military acronym?'

In turn Greenbow looked at me, the others followed.

I scratched at a black tattoo on my arm, which had suddenly started itching. Fuck it.

'A job in southern Afghanistan.' I drained someone's flat prosecco and put the glass back on the floor, shuffling, eying them all. 'Transport, working with locals. This was a few years ago, just before the withdrawal, dicey as fuck. Small Daesh squads would ambush vans on Highway One, hijack the gear, food, medical supplies, so we rode along as security.

'Soban Ahmad Karzai was our translator, awesome guy. Five of the most amazing kids and a house on a big plot overlooking the stream on the edge of the village. He was the envy of his neighbours.

'It was dangerous work, especially for him – working with us made him a target, he was probably one of the best-paid guys in the area but I think the real reason he did it was for all the seeds and gardening stuff I used to smuggle out with me.

'Anyway, Soban called himself Sak because half the Americans couldn't get his name right.'

'And is Sak's gardening relevant to our situation?' asked Greenbow.

'One day he didn't turn up. We really needed him that day, so I drove out to his house. All quiet. The door was open. Blood in the hallway.

'Four of those kids had been shot and killed together in the kitchen, clinging to each other in the middle of the floor. I found his wife upstairs stabbed to death. I spent ages searching the house, finally found Sak's body at the bottom of an irrigation ditch he'd been digging for his grapes out back.'

'I was in Afghanistan just after the invasion,' said Hurley. 'I'm not sure it's comparable to Scotland.'

'He and his family were Hazaras – Shiites – so straight away it was obvious it was a Daesh hit, confirmed when they claimed it on a website a couple of weeks later. They'd been abducting Hazaras in the region for months, as well as punishing anyone who worked with the government or Western forces. Sends a message. The police couldn't, or wouldn't, do anything. They're overstretched and what are they going to do about a one-off targeted hit on one family, carried out by persons unknown probably from hundreds of miles away?

'I quit straight after that. Just me and my truck, village to village, tracking down leads, trying to get to the bottom of which Daesh unit had been operating there that day.' I took a swig from my hip flask. 'I'd make a lousy copper, because after months I'd uncovered nothing but sand. It was only when I finally went back to work that I got to the truth.'

'Which was?' asked Dash.

'I was freelancing again in that same village a year or so later. Not sure why, but I stopped off at his house. It was derelict, stripped and looted. I took a walk around the back. The ditches Soban had dug, the ones I'd found him in, had all filled in with mud. All the way to the boundary fence the veg plots were just dried-up weeds.

'In contrast the land beyond the fence was rich, perfect irrigation ditches, onions, tomatoes, grapevines in rows all the way down to his neighbour's house. Then I noticed the shiny Mercedes G-Wagon pulled up next to that house.

'None of it had been there before. Jealousy and money, the two oldest motives for anything. Soban's neighbour had got away with it for a year, he'd never even been considered or questioned because it had been so typical of the low-level hits for that region, the most probable reason for his murder. It was sealed when it was later claimed by Daesh, although turns out they'd just been claiming a freebie.'

'What happened to the neighbour?' asked Marie.

'What do you think, I handed him over to the police and moved on. The point is, Demeter is such an obvious killer; he's Russian, he's an oddball, and we have a note confirming it. The Russian divers make the whole thing nicely open-ended. A likely but ultimately completely unprovable theory can stop you considering other possibilities, things you'd normally be all over.' I'd toyed with the idea of maintaining the Demeter and the sub story, letting the killer think they'd got away with it, but sometimes in these situations I like to throw everything at the wall and see what sticks, shake it up. When people are nervous and on the back foot they tend to mess up. Prod the fire a bit more, I was running out of options and time. 'Demeter is the obvious killer, too obvious. He was framed. Someone in this room is the killer.'

Alice and Hurley shuffled down the sofa with the effect that they were lined up with Greenbow and Dash like a jury. Only Marie was sitting on my side of the room. Alice leaned back, closing her eyes, shutting out the chaos. Marie picked up a coaster someone had dropped on the floor, fiddling with it, refusing to look up. No one spoke for a full minute, even through the insulation the rain hammering on the roof was overpowering. Dash's leg had developed a twitch, drumming against the coffee table. Alice slapped it away irritably. Greenbow studied his gun intently. Thunder rolled, gusts howled, lightning exploded on the other side of the blinds. Somewhere under the floor the heating pipes groaned.

It was Hurley who finally broke the trance. 'Demeter's the only one who coulda killed them. We saw him enter the room. He *musta* been double-crossed.'

'We saw the *killer* enter the room and shoot Gambetta,' I said. 'How do we know it was Demeter?'

'I spoke to him,' Hurley added.

'You spoke to a muffled voice behind a gas mask. What if it was someone in this room?'

Greenbow leaned forward. 'It was Demeter.'

We looked at each other. Chairs squeaked as bums shifted uneasily.

'We can't be sure it was Demeter in that suit,' I said. 'And whoever we passed in the corridor on the way to shooting Gambetta must have arrived *after* killing Ingrid.'

Dash turned on Hurley. 'You kept disappearing, didn't you?'

'I told you, I haven't been feeling well.'

'So your alibi is that you've got the shits?'

'I didn't leave for more than a couple of minutes!' Hurley was bright red.

'That's true, you didn't. You couldn't have killed Ingrid.'

'And what about you, Chaudhary?' asked Greenbow.

He shrugged. 'Like I said, playing poker with Hurley in here most of the night, then I went in the kitchen.'

'On your own?'

His eyebrows rose. 'Me of all people, *running* there and back?' He laughed nervously.

'And, Marie, were you in here all that time?' asked Alice.

'No, I was in my room for a while, reading. But I couldn't have done it, I wouldn't have had time.'

'Who else was in the base?' I asked.

'Other than the people in this room, just Clay,' said Alice.

'Clay couldn't have killed Ingrid, he was stinking drunk,' said Dash.

'Was he really stinking drunk? And was someone with him at all times?' I asked.

Each of us looked at the others.

'We know Ingrid and Gambetta were killed within a very short time window, because of the 7 p.m. radio check-in. Someone in this base slipped away during that time.'

'There is another explanation,' said Dash.

'Go on.'

'There's someone else on the island. I don't mean people from a sub, not necessarily. But someone hiding here.'

'Where? It's one big overgrown field.'

'Caves, down by the sea? That old ruined cottage by the beach?'

'Bollocks. It's a tiny island, we'd know if there was someone else here.'

'It all comes back to Demeter,' said Greenbow.

Hurley got to his feet and stretched. 'So aside from making us all paranoid and ensuring none of us are gonna sleep a wink tonight – what have you achieved?'

I'll be honest, all it had achieved was to dent my faith in my own reasoning. No one in this room could have killed them. I could probably dig up a motive, but no one had the opportunity to get there and back in time, and everyone had been accounted for just after Gambetta's murder – none of them could have been hidden under the floor. I'd gone full circle and found that logic once again supported Demeter being the prime suspect. Just as it always had. Why was I so bent on his innocence?

The note that implicated him, written in English. The improbable sub that had avoided the Navy and their world-beating radar, which only dead people had seen. Ingrid's killer using the window instead of the door. The fact that Demeter himself was lying dead under a hut, washed in on the storm. But were these just circumstantial when compared to the real facts? There were six of us left, and none of the other five had had the opportunity.

I chewed on a nail and thought about Occam's razor, isn't the most likely explanation usually the correct one?

Surely the killer was either Demeter, or an unknown mystery person somewhere out there in the dark?

Chapter Fifty-two

'John, are you okay?'

I opened my eyes to see Marie standing over me, the others filing out the door behind her. I hadn't been aware of my leg bouncing up and down. I was panting. I took a deep breath and held it in my chest, pushing against my ribcage. After a few seconds I coughed and stretched down to the vodka bottle on the floor.

'Tired,' I said simply. Which was true, lack of sleep always made the symptoms worse.

'You don't look well,' she said. 'Maybe leave the bottle?'

I took a swig, put it back down, and pushed my fingers into my eyes. My breathing was back to normal.

'Are you coming to bed?' she said.

A little forward, I thought, though I usually wouldn't argue – but it turned out that whilst lost in my head I'd missed the conversation. To stay together, and to avoid Clay's festering corpse, the six of us would go three to a room. Hurley and Marie would join me in my room, with Dash, Greenbow, and Alice next door. If anything happened we'd all hear it. If people were having doubts about any of the six of us, they'd feel better in a group, all watching each other. There were no arguments, it was a solid plan in the circumstances.

Alice was holding the door for me, concern on her face. As I stepped through she looked at the others then leant in quickly. 'Don't worry, I'll watch the captain. You watch her.' She pulled away before Marie arrived at my side. A strange comment to make but before I could reply she'd already rushed to catch them.

In my room I gallantly took the floor, offering Marie my bed. It didn't seem right her sleeping in Demeter's bed, what with him being dead – although to be fair my bed was only once removed from belonging to a dead man. Hurley dragged his own blankets in, dumping them on Demeter's bed before disappearing to the toilets. Marie and I tried to listen to the others through the dividing wall. I took a tablet from my washbag.

'Are you ill?' Marie whispered.

I swallowed it and laid down. 'Sometimes, when I'm tired… I'm all right.'

'You don't look all right. You need to get off the island.'

How could I tell her that the opposite was true? The itching inside, the tremors and nausea, the faces, they only visited when I spent time with my own mind. It all went quiet when the bullets started flying. A junkie, addicted to a drug that's slowly killing them and constantly playing roulette with instant death.

She rolled over, staring at the ceiling. 'Sorry again for locking you outside.'

'I'd have done the same.'

'But you didn't.'

'Doesn't matter. In a few hours we'll be on the ship eating a nice cooked breakfast.'

'Easy for you to say, you're used to this kind of thing.'

'I can promise you I've never done anything like this before.'

'This is your world.'

'I'm no different to anyone else here.'

She turned her head to me. 'You're nothing like anyone here, I saw it when you walked in this morning. You've seen things. You can wear different clothes, say different things, but you can't change your eyes. Tell me, what kind of person chooses this –' she waved her hand around – 'this shit as a career?'

'No one *chooses* it.'

She rolled back over, quiet for a moment, I almost thought she'd gone to sleep until she said softly, 'I watched you signalling the ship.'

'Get some sleep.'

'I ran to get away, while you were distracted. I didn't realise you'd already finished your message.'

'I told you, all's forgiven.'

'I didn't think anything of it until you told the others about your conversation with the ship.' She sat up in bed, eyes narrowed, at first I thought it was anger but no, more like concern. 'You can't have said more than five words to them.'

More like four. *All well. Be ready.*

'You know Morse?'

'No, but I know *people*.' She chewed her lip then pointed at my arm. 'Which one is Afghanistan?'

I shuffled and turned my arm over, running a finger over the tattooed outline of the country's borders as it curved across my wrist.

'What really happened to that neighbour?' she asked.

I didn't want to lie again but the truth wouldn't help. This wasn't the time to tell her that I could still feel the snap of the man's bones against my boots, feel his pulse panicking through his neck as I dragged him out back to the stream, to his death. Him and all the others over the years.

'Seriously, Marie, you need to get some sleep. Help is on the way, trust me.'

'I'm not stupid. You didn't have that conversation with the ship because you want to catch the killer yourself. You want to *deal with them* yourself, just like in Afghanistan. That seems unnecessarily risky.'

Credit where it's due, she was bang on the money, though the risk was all mine and that's why I get paid the big bucks. Plus I honestly believed it was the best way to ensure the right person was caught. Didn't matter, there was no time to reply as the door swung open and Hurley climbed into Demeter's bed.

'I hope you've brushed your teeth,' he said, 'cos you don't wanna be going in there for a while.'

Marie rolled over. I switched off the lamp and lay back down.

'Greenbow was acting weirdly, eh?' said Hurley.

I ignored him.

'Wonder if that bullet in the wall matches his Browning.'

'Shut up, Hurley,' said Marie.

Truth was, I'd thought the same.

It was the same calibre.

Chapter Fifty-three

Clay's death bothered me, it didn't fit the pattern. We assumed that Andy had been killed to test the anthrax, and the others to cover up its existence. But what about Donald Clay? He'd been an even bigger bastard than Eric Gambetta, but had that been enough to kill him? Had he been killed because he knew something? I doubted he really knew anything that went on.

I squashed the thoughts down, trying to count sheep. Impossible. I'd rather have gone back to those cold caves in northern Pakistan, full of camel spiders and mercenaries with the shits, than stay on that plastic floor. I rolled onto my side. My arm hit something that clinked, rolling away under the bed. The empty bottle of Scotch that I'd poured out the window the previous day. No – I'd only arrived that morning! Jesus, my head was a shed. Marie tutted somewhere above me, thinking I was taking a sip.

No, hang on. My brain was fogged but I knew that when I'd opened the bottle I'd poured a fair bit out the window. I'd wanted an open bottle of Scotch lying around to reinforce the idea that I was a drunk, too incapacitated to be effective.

I'd placed the bottle on the floor by the bed. I thought back to what I'd seen when I'd screwed the windows shut earlier. A half-empty bottle on the bedside table. When we'd then gone room to room looking for Demeter, the bottle had been even emptier, shifting back to the floor.

I blinked even though it was dark, focusing my mind. 'The poison was meant for me.'

'What poison?' Hurley asked.

'Clay, the thieving bastard, has been helping himself to my Scotch. That's what didn't sit too well with him.'

'We don't know Clay was poisoned. He could have had a heart attack.'

'Probably did. Brought on by something in his drink.'

'Like what?' asked Hurley.

'I bet there's a ton of things in those labs that'd kill you.'

'That's true,' said Marie. 'There are a lot of uncontrolled substances in there that would be lethal, before you get to the anthrax.'

I had thought about the anthrax, about whether his killer had used some of the Gruinard strain in the Scotch, in the same way Kyle had been dispatched, but I discounted it. There would be an autopsy on Clay, his body wasn't going anywhere. Whoever had killed the others and hidden that sample under the floor wouldn't want to risk Porton Down isolating the strain from Clay's body, would want to keep their sample unique. Easier to use something else, whatever chemicals or toxins they could get their hands on from the labs, it didn't matter.

'But any poisonous substances would show up in an autopsy?' said Marie.

'So what? Just another of Demeter's victims.'

'Why would someone want you dead?' said Hurley. 'I think this place has got to ya, John. You're paranoid, get some sleep.'

It wasn't paranoia. Someone had wanted me out of the way since the morning, but thanks to the impression I'd created, they'd laced the Scotch to get rid of me. Shit, if they'd poisoned the custard creams I'd probably be lying out there on the hillside somewhere with a frozen heart and a gas mask full of puke.

It could have been tampered with at any time and by anyone in the base. Someone had marked me out for execution even this morning, this was their second attempt. Who'd want me dead? Who'd seen me with the tea sample? Gambetta, but I could discount him since he was lying in the radio room missing half his head. Alice, but she already knew I was here undercover to investigate Kyle's death – it was her who had raised the alarm in the first place. Someone else must have seen. Even this morning that person thought I knew too much.

There was a shout from the room next door, I was on my feet with Hurley at my side, moving on autopilot. More shouts, thuds, furniture breaking, something smashed, Alice screamed; we were out of our room, into the corridor, into their room.

Chapter Fifty-four

We pushed through the door to see Dash straddling Greenbow, arm raised. His other hand gripped Greenbow's, slamming his pistol against the floor. He brought his fist down into Greenbow's face, not a particularly strong blow but with Greenbow pinned, the fight was one-sided. Dash raised his arm again but before he could swing I grabbed it, twisted it round.

'Let me go, he's flipped!' Dash shouted.

Hurley gripped Dash's other hand, wrenching it away from Greenbow. He realised his error as Greenbow, now free, brought the gun up.

'Get off me!' Greenbow screamed, pointing the gun at Dash's head. I stamped down on Greenbow's arm, pinning it to the floor again. A gunshot blasted in the tiny room, the bullet punched into a cupboard. I ground Greenbow's wrist beneath my foot. Rapid shots followed as Greenbow screamed, jerking the trigger, sending splinters and shards of laminate ricocheting around the room. People dove for the floor as bullet after bullet slammed the walls and furniture. Hurley wrapped a huge arm around Dash's neck, hauling him backwards, but as soon as Greenbow's other arm was free, he whipped it round into my knee. I staggered back as he stood, levelling the pistol at Dash and Hurley. Everyone froze.

'You idiots!' Dash shouted above the ringing in my ears. 'He's gone mad, he's gonna kill me!'

'Get away from him!' Greenbow screamed. 'He killed Gambetta!'

'Put the gun away,' I said calmly.

'Tell them!' The pistol didn't waver as he stooped to swipe up his beret. 'Tell them about the watch!' He smoothed his hair down and replaced the beret. It flicked a switch, calming him down, almost returning him to normality, or what passed for his brand of normality.

'Put the gun away, Captain,' I said again, more firmly this time.

Greenbow's eyes flicked sideways. His pistol followed a split second behind, stopping as he finally realised my gun was pointing at him. His mouth flapped open. 'You can't shoot me, I'm still in charge!'

'These bullets don't give a shit about rank, Captain.'

He sidestepped towards the door. 'Tell them where you got it, Chaudhary.'

'He's gone mad,' said Dash, shaking.

'What the hell are you talking about?' I asked.

'He's wearing Gambetta's watch.'

All eyes flicked to Dash. He shook his arm, trying to pull his shirt down, but there it was, the Tag Gambetta had been wearing when he'd been shot, the one I'd seen when I'd checked the room.

'I knew someone had moved his arm. You took his watch?'

'Why did you do that?' Alice said, stepping away from Dash. I noticed they'd all moved back, leaving him standing alone.

'He killed him!' said Greenbow. 'Tie him up.'

'We're not tying anyone up.' I brought the pistol up, just slightly, just enough to remind him.

'I'll see you court-martialled,' he said to me, edging closer to the door.

'That'll be difficult, since I'm a *civilian*.'

Pausing in the doorway, he swept the Browning around the room. 'When the helicopter arrives I'll have you all arrested for aiding a killer.' He stepped into the corridor. 'I'm warning you, anyone steps foot in my room they'll get a bullet between the eyes.'

The door slammed.

All eyes returned to Dash, and so did the barrel of my gun. He looked at each of us in turn, landing on me, on the evil-looking Heckler & Koch in my hand.

'The captain's right,' I said. 'Last time I saw that watch it was on Gambetta's wrist.'

'Look, I'm not a thief. And I didn't kill Gambetta.'

'Convince me.'

The bed groaned as he sat. He sighed, brushing splinters off the sheets, staring at his feet, finally inhaling deeply and looking up. 'It's my watch. I was getting it back.'

'Why did Gambetta have it?' I asked.

'I owed him money, okay? The cards... it was security, 'til we got back to the mainland. Don't look at me like that, he doesn't need it, it was never really his.'

'Where's the missing window key?'

'Which one?'

'The one you took from the radio room.'

'Wait, I thought you took it? Marie said you had a key?'

'Long story, I had a different key all along. So who took the key from the radio room?'

Dash just stared open-mouthed. Hurley and Alice stared back hard. He looked at Marie, imploring.

I lifted my jumper, slid the pistol back into the holster, which broke the tension. Marie knelt to dab Dash's split lip. I'd no way of knowing if his story were true or not, but it was plausible and accepting it was better than holding a gun on him all night.

'He attacked me to divert attention from himself, if you ask me,' Dash continued.

'Don't push it,' I said.

'You think Greenbow's the killer?' asked Hurley, turning to me.

'He's lost the plot, but a killer? Nah.'

'Try saying that when you're on the receiving end,' said Dash. 'He just tried to shoot me. I'd be dead if you hadn't come in, so don't tell me he's not a killer.'

'We should stay together,' said Marie.

I looked at the smashed furniture, the line of bullet holes stitched up the wall. 'In my room,' I said, poking my head into the dark corridor. Greenbow had disappeared.

We returned to my room, double-checking the window was secure. Alice and Marie took the beds, Dash and Hurley on the floor in between. I sat against the door where I could keep my eyes on the window – and crucially, the other four. I envied Greenbow, in his own bed behind a locked door.

In the black, the snoring of the other four turned to whispers in my sleep-deprived mind, the drumming of the rain was gunfire. Shapes swirled in the darkness, forming figures writhing around the room. I screwed my eyes shut, occupying myself by stripping my pistol by touch, laying the components on the floor, reassembling them, the familiarity of process keeping the phantoms at bay. Not long now. Just had to make it to morning then put my plan into action. I turned it over in my mind, fighting to stay awake.

My head rested against the door.

Lines of sheep run in both directions, tethered to wire fences stretching into the mist. Bodies held in crates, bleating heads sticking out through a hole so they can eat if they want to, but none of them do. Poles spear the sky, sudden flashes light the tips, rain cascades out, rolling along the ground in a great cloud. I'm lost in a fog, swirling grey, crows barking in the distance, laughter nearby. Muffled gunshots are swallowed, indistinct shapes encircle me, beckoning, dissolving into the mist, I try to follow but it's like pushing through old engine oil.

The bleating has stopped, complete silence as the fog descends to the mud, tendrils of mist seeping away through the grass, leaving behind rows of sheep heads, hanging from the crates by rotting threads. One after another they drop to the ground then roll over, tumbling down the hillside.

Black oozes from the crates, trickling through the mud, reflecting streams creeping towards me. Noise explodes again as flies swarm from the crates, rising from the gore, buzzing around me, turning the sky as black as the ground. The creeping blackness holds me firm, sucking me down. A glove rises from the ooze, an arm, followed by a gas mask, no eyes. Dark sockets. One of the eyepieces is smashed. The mask droops, the mouth behind it screams, rising to a crescendo. There's another flash, everything is white, searing heat. My brother, staring at me, his head completely motionless but somehow he's shouting, imploring me to help, but I'm powerless. The sound dies away, everything is quiet, completely still as I sink lower. I have no power. No power. There's no power.

Chapter Fifty-five

No power. My eyes snapped open. Pitch black, still paralysed, not sure what's going on, what's real and what's nightmare. Sweat is beaded across my forehead, freezing cold. I was screwed up on the floor, neck bent into the door, solidified, as if I'd been poured there and left to set. No light filtered through the blinds. I tested my fingers, stretched my wrists. The hands of my watch had lost their luminosity. Early morning, I guessed. I gently untwisted my limbs, flexed them, waited for the numbness to give way to agonising pins and needles, side effects of yet another uncomfortable night. As I waited for control of my muscles to return to me, my thoughts flitted between dead sheep, endless mud, sand, burning SUVs, and, God, it was cold. Hurley or Dash snored somewhere and, barely audible, Marie's soft rhythmic breathing to my right.

As good a time as any to put my plan into action. I was about to stand, to quietly get started, gathering what I needed, but hesitated. Something was wrong, and it wasn't simply the hangover of a nightmare. Something felt off-kilter.

I clicked alert, scanning the dim room. Nothing moved. I held my breath, ears stretched for the slightest sound. Aside from the snores, there was nothing.

And then I realised that was the point. No noise.

Throughout my time inside the base I'd been enveloped by a low humming, just background noise, a faint vibration. I don't know what it was – air conditioning, lights, whatever, it was gone now.

And it was far too cold.

There was another sound missing – the wind and rain had finally stopped hammering on the roof, the storm had passed. My eyes had adjusted, dim shapes just about marking the furniture and the other men on the floor.

I silently got to my feet, grabbed my gun, carefully opened the door. Dash snorted and rolled over. I stepped into the corridor, closing the door behind me. The base was deathly quiet. I looked up the corridor but nothing stirred. Was Greenbow still in his room?

From the window in the corridor I couldn't even see the bright orange cabins up either side of the horseshoe. I squinted into the darkness, could only just make out the generator hut. It looked like the tool shed had partially collapsed into it, destroying half the wall. Splintered plywood panels spiked outwards. The little exhaust chimney at the top was still there, but when we'd come back to the base yesterday evening, smoky fumes had been blowing from the top. I couldn't be sure, but it didn't look as if they were now. I flicked the light switch in the hallway. Nothing happened.

I gripped the bedroom door handle, opening the door slowly. There was a groan somewhere in the darkness.

'Who's that? Stay where you are!' A flurry of activity, a light snapped on, blinding me. I threw my arm up, aware of a shape jumping near me.

'Get that fucking torch out of my face, Hurley,' I said.

'John? Where've you been... what time is it?'

The beam swung away. I blinked, when my eyes recovered I could see Alice poised behind the door, an empty bottle held high ready to club me.

'You said no one should leave the room,' said Dash in a questioning tone.

Marie sat up in the other bed, duvet pulled up to her neck. 'What's wrong?' she asked.

I glanced up and down the corridor. 'Power's off.'

Dash leapt up as quickly as his bulk allowed. He flicked the impotent light switch to test for himself, then wobbled into his trousers. 'We need to get it restarted.'

'Why?' asked Alice.

'The base is almost airtight, means the air in these rooms will begin to get toxic. As we breathe it's filling with carbon dioxide.'

Hurley looked out the window. 'The base is huge. Assuming Greenbow's still in here, there are only six of us; surely we can last?'

'We don't know how long the generator's been off, could have been hours already. Without the air circulating around properly, the rooms will become stale quickly. It could be okay, but we really should go outside and get it back on again.'

'What about power to the HADU?' asked Hurley. 'If we don't get the generator on we're stuck outside.'

'Built-in batteries,' I said. 'They should be good for a while.'

'Why can't we just suit up and wait it out?' asked Alice. 'It's nearly six – they're coming to evacuate us in a few hours.'

'That's a last resort,' I said.

Chapter Fifty-six

Dash and I left the others inside whilst we went to check on the generator. The wind had changed direction, noticeably warmer now, and it was refreshing to be outside without being hammered into the mud by the rain. We'd traded one devil for another, though; even if the sun had been up we wouldn't have been able to see more than a few metres. I flicked on my torch and illuminated a vast, endless expanse of grey. It swirled and stretched around and above us as if we were trapped inside a dirty snow globe, muffling all sound. Droplets clung to the visor of my gas mask, smearing everything. Dash's beam found the outbuildings, melting in and out of the fog. I already knew they hadn't escaped the storm. The generator hut leaned drunkenly against the tool shed. We stumbled closer to see the roof had collapsed and the door was bent, embedded in the mud.

'Shit, Dash, if you want this base to stay in one piece down in the Antarctic, you need to build it stronger than this.'

'This is down to your boys. Remember, down there the enemy is the cold – we've got tool huts and generator buildings fabricated that link onto the main base, we don't have the added complication of having to pass in and out of a decontamination chamber. No, this won't be a problem when we ship out.'

'Which is when?'

'Next week. We need to get this base on the ice while it's still summer down there. A few weeks on a container ship – we'll have the decontamination and refit done before we hit the Falklands.'

'Interesting.'

'What is?'

'Speculation. What do we need to get the generator back on?'

'Depends on the problem, let's take a look.'

Around the back we found the split where the plywood cladding had been splintered. I squeezed through easily but it took some coaxing – in the form of pulling and shoving – to get Dash in there. The generator was untouched by the storm – whatever the reason for the failure, it hadn't been physically impacted by the shed partially collapsing around it.

'What do you think, out of fuel?' I asked.

'Shouldn't run out this side of Christmas.'

He pointed at my feet. I was standing on the hose that led up to the top of the generator. I shone my beam over the machinery – this was nothing like the small generator I'd started up at the second camp, more like the kind of thing that sits in the cellar of a government building or hospital. A full-on auxiliary generator, not a portable affair you'd find in a farmer's barn.

'Fuel's pumped out of these –' Dash pointed to a row of plastic drums along the far wall – 'to a header tank up here.'

He rapped a knuckle on the header tank at the top of the generator, which thudded. Full. He pulled off the cap, shining his torch in, swirled with his gloved finger, pulled it out and swore loudly. I waited patiently while he stared into the header tank – this was his domain, after all.

'Full of dirt,' he said eventually.

'Dirt?'

'Move off the pipe. It must be damaged.'

I dropped to my hands and knees to check the pipe. It looked fine.

'Maybe it's broken outside somewhere?'

'Must be. Probably the storm damaged it, blew something onto the pipe. Musta been sucking in mud along with the fuel.'

'Can you fix it?'

'I can fix anything, but it'll take me a while.'

'What can I do?'

'Stay outta my way. You may as well go back inside.'

I pushed back out into the world, but I'd no intention of going back inside just yet – I'd been handed a golden opportunity. Dash had said the base would be loaded onto a ship next week – and at once I'd understood the killer's plan. There was even more reason to flush them out before we were evacuated. Time to put my idea into action, though I needed to be more cautious now the others were awake.

I'd scoped the tool shed earlier, knew it would fulfil my needs. I unravelled an extension lead, wrapping it round my arm and using a Stanley knife to slice the socket end off. I stuffed a few cans of spray paint into the voluminous pockets of my overalls and stole a roll of electrical tape and bottle of paraffin from a cardboard box on the shelf. After a moment's consideration I tipped the rest of the contents onto the floor and took the box too.

I kept my torch off as I walked back to the base. I didn't want to alert anyone that I was coming back in, didn't want to attract attention. Navigation in the double darkness of night and fog was difficult, but following the churned mud I managed to reach the steps.

Protocol was now out of mind – no one was in the radio room monitoring the CCTV. After disposing of the outer suit I packed the things I'd taken from the shed into the box, added a couple of rolls of toilet paper from the cubicles, and wrapped the whole lot in my jumper. I skipped the shower, making a beeline for the kitchen to add a few more things to my bundle. After that I headed to Dash's room, and to that lamp on his bedside table. I swiped the timer plug it was plugged into, the one that kept Dash's sanity at the Poles, the kind normal people leave at home when they go on holiday. Just one last vital ingredient to collect from my bedroom.

Instead of getting it, I rushed to the radio room.

The room stank. The almost airtight conditions of the base had prevented the usual swarms of bugs from feasting on Gambetta's corpse, but not the rot that had started in his internal organs, the necrotic stench of putrefaction. He'd been dead less than twelve hours, but lying on the warm plastic floor hadn't helped. I flicked on my torch to see the discoloured flesh of his cheeks swelling grotesquely. I tore my eyes away, dumped the box on the shelf, returned to my bedroom.

The other three were still there, suited now, ready to go outside.

'Where's the captain?' I asked.

'Still in his room,' said Alice.

'You're sure? Did anyone hear anything at all last night?'

Collective shrugs and shaken heads. 'Why?' asked Alice.

'There's dirt in the generator.' I let the implication float on the stale air, no embellishment.

'Sounds like we'd better check the captain is actually in his room,' said Hurley.

'You read my mind.'

I let the three of them lead the way, waiting by the box of Andy's things, the one I'd packed by the door. As soon as they left the room I pocketed what I needed, and was closing the door when something on my bed caught my eye. I went back in and knelt closer.

A tiny key. I fished in my pocket and pulled out my window key to compare. No doubt about it, here was the second missing window key. Had it fallen from someone's pocket?

'John, you coming?'

Marie had come back to check on me. I dropped the keys and pulled the blanket over them, standing to follow her with a groan from my aching limbs.

The other two were striding down the connecting tunnel to the next huts.

Alice reached the door first, knocking softly. 'Captain? We need to talk to you.'

No reply. I pulled up alongside her and booted the door, it trembled but held. I was about to try again when Hurley shoved me out of the way and gave it a kick, splintering it easily. I crouched, torch and pistol up in case a bullet came our way.

Nothing. Instinctively I flicked the dead light switch, to no effect, then ran the torch around the room instead. Not only was it empty, but it didn't look as if it had been slept in.

'Where the hell is he?' asked Hurley, looking over my shoulder.

'There are only four of us now,' said Marie.

'Greenbow must be around somewhere.' I glanced up and down the corridor. 'Dash is outside on his own. Get out there, stick together.'

'I'm not going outside without you,' Marie said.

I looked at the others, already jogging to the entrance. 'Take this.' I handed her my gun, she took it gingerly, as if it'd go off. 'Safety's here, point that way, squeeze this. Put it in your pocket, don't let on you have it.'

It was a dangerous situation; six of us left on the island, one killer, and at least three guns that I knew of – although Gambetta's Walther was, to my knowledge, still where I'd left it hidden at Camp Vollum. Those are the kind of stats the NRA reckons are safer, but I'd have preferred no guns.

'There's a spare mag under my pillow. Go, I'll be out in a minute.'

'What are you doing?' asked Marie.

'Gotta see a man about a dog,' I winked. The expression was completely lost on her. 'I'll check the labs.'

I watched her jog after the others, still carrying the pistol as if it'd bite, glancing nervously behind every few steps.

Chapter Fifty-seven

I sat in the comms room, back pressed against the door, torch clamped between my feet, trying to ignore the dark, foul-smelling shadow that covered the floor and the grim stains running down the opposite wall. I'd laid the contents of the cardboard box out in front of me; the timer plug and extension lead flex, a couple of toilet rolls, the tape, the paraffin, the spray paint. Then the items pilfered from the kitchen; some foil, all the wooden spoons I could find, and a wooden rolling pin, which did make me wonder who'd thought the scientists might fancy baking. I'd also gone back and grabbed a couple of wooden boards, shelves from a cupboard. Sandwiches were tipped onto the worktop to free up a Tupperware box. Finally, from my room, I took Kyle's box of matches and my cologne.

I used the Stanley knife to strip the last few centimetres of flex, cutting the earth wire off completely, separating live and neutral. I opened up the plug on the other end: three-amp fuse. I tossed it away, the irony of a missing fuse starting this whole thing, the removal of a fuse finishing it, not lost on me.

I replaced the fuse with a tiny fat tinfoil sausage. The circuit breakers in the base would blow, but this wouldn't.

I emptied the matches onto the floor, gathered them into a bunch, using electrical tape to secure them. Back to the flex, I bit away the plastic coating, exposing the wires, taking my time to unwind the strands, trimming them down. I did this on both the live and neutral wires. As I worked, I prayed Dash would get the generator working again.

The live wire was wound around the match heads, twisted together with the neutral wire, then wrapped round and round. After a few minutes work I'd finished, jamming the bundle of matches inside a bog roll then wrapping it up in a second roll, creating one bulky parcel with a flex lead sticking out of it. Perfect.

I poked my head out of the door to check the corridor was still quiet. Crouching in the polytunnel leading to the next hut, I lifted one of the tread-boards on the floor. The tunnel was circular in section, resulting in a gap between the flooring and the metal ribs supporting the tunnel. I laid one of the wooden kitchen shelves on the ribs, placed the Tupperware on top. My bundle sat in it, with the flex winding up and into the corridor. The paraffin was poured into the Tupperware, the toilet roll drank it up, it'd evaporate over time but the reservoir would keep it soaking for a while. Everything flammable was stacked around the bundle. I placed my Acqua Di Parma bottle upside down above the tiny bonfire, followed by the spray cans. I'd brought Kyle's old map to use as additional fuel but decided it was more useful in one piece and stuffed it back into my pocket.

I backtracked to the radio room, paying the wire out as I went, kicking it close to the wall; no one would trip over it and in the dark it was all but invisible. Reaching up to the light attached to the ceiling, I removed the strip bulb, resting it against the wall. Now the corridor would stay dark, and the flex would stay invisible, at least until the sun came round to this side of the base – by which time we'd be long gone.

There was just enough wire to reach the socket behind the door. I pushed it into Dash's timer plug, set it, flicked the switch, and pulled the door closed over the wire.

When the power came back on the timer would begin its slow buzzing revolution. After three quarters of an hour the dial would hit the little depressed numbers, triggering the switch. Instantly the circuit would connect, and in less than a second the wires would get so hot they'd set off the match heads, sparking a miniature fireball. It's called an electrical match, something my brother and I had messed about with as kids.

The small fire probably wouldn't be noticed straight away, but after a couple of minutes flames would get to the plastic cologne lid and that thick glass bottle would go off like a grenade. Around the same time the heat would get to the spray paint cans and – boom – the pressure would be released explosively, flammable gas igniting, expanding to blow a hole through the plastic sheeting.

In the radio room I'd opened the panel under the floor and replaced the sample vial behind the pipes where I'd found it the previous night. When the explosion ripped open the corridor it'd get everyone's attention. It'd get one person's attention more than the rest. The fire would threaten to consume the radio room. I was pretty sure this was a unique sample which meant the killer would have no choice – they couldn't leave it to destruction, wouldn't risk it – so before we were evacuated they'd have to ensure its safety.

A fire would drive everyone outside. All I had to do was stand back and watch their faces, wait for the killer to reveal themselves by going into the radio room to save the vial.

It wasn't foolproof but it was the best I had, given the time and resources available. The killer had been clever. I needed them to give themselves away, catch them with proof. I'd have to apologise to Dash yet again about his base, but he had said they were repairing and refitting on the long journey to Antarctica – and unlike us, the Americans do seem to have limitless resources, so I didn't feel too bad. Besides, he was proud of his anti-fire design, so the way I saw it, this was a good test: if he'd done his job properly it should only threaten this hut.

I just needed the power back on.

I was suited and back outside in no time, almost running into Hurley and Marie huddled at the top of the steps.

'How's Dash getting on with the generator?'

'He's doing well, Alice is with him,' said Hurley. 'We split up to wait for you.'

'Didn't want to leave the entrance unguarded,' Marie said, scanning the fog, one hand thrust in her baggy pocket, no doubt wrapped around the grip of my pistol.

'What with Greenbow being around somewhere,' Hurley added, shining the torch around the fog.

'Agreed. You stay here, I'll check on the others.'

I pushed my way into the shed, almost tripping over them sitting cross-legged on a wooden board on the ground.

'There's a killer on the loose and you're sitting with your back to the world?'

Alice jumped.

Dash shrugged. '*If* they're still out there, what would they want with us?'

'We don't really know what they want.' I scanned the work-bench along one wall, the nuts and bolts and tools spread across it. 'How's the generator looking?'

'Had to strip the carb. Almost got it back together.'

'Alice, go wait with Hurley and Marie, I'll stay with Dash. Keep an eye out for Greenbow.'

She didn't need telling twice, rustling out of the shed. I grabbed her arm. 'Watch them.' I waited until she'd squelched away and lowered my voice.

'Any idea how it happened?'

Dash looked up and wiped the lens of his mask. 'Yeah, I've got an idea.'

'Care to share it?'

'No fault in the fuel lines.'

I stepped round him and looked at the parts on the bench. 'What's your conclusion?'

'How else does dirt get into a fuel tank?'

'Suppose I'm stupid, say it out loud.'

'Easiest thing in the world to dump a handful of mud into the header.'

'Sabotage, then?'

He considered it carefully, holding the fuel filter up to the light. 'I've checked everything else.'

'I thought so. Someone's in a hurry to leave. Can you tell when it happened?'

'Could have been minutes ago or hours. No telling how long it took for the filter to clog.'

I crouched next to the generator, running my glove across the fuel line. 'So it could have been anyone. Including Demeter.'

'Or Greenbow, we don't know where he is.'

'What did you mean earlier about watching Marie?'

'She left the lounge last night. When you guys were up at Camp Vollum.'

'So?'

'So who took the key from the comms room? She was in here yesterday too, who knows what she was doing.' He placed the fuel filter on the generator. 'Fucking respirators, it's so much easier without them.' He creaked to his feet and peeled off a strip of tape, pushing the gas mask up onto the top of his head to inspect a part in the torchlight. 'Just gotta clean this and then—'

His mask fell off his head. Expletives poured forth as he tried to catch it, but in doing so he stepped backwards off the board, onto the mud. His feet slid out from under him. He flailed, grabbing for the bench, I jumped up, tried to catch him but wasn't quick enough. He pulled the bench over on top of him as he collapsed on his back. Pieces of carburettor splatted into the mud all around him. Thankfully he managed to keep his face from going anywhere near the ground.

He screamed, first in shock, then pain, turning to panic. 'Help me up.'

I righted the workbench, pulled Dash off the ground, and saw why he'd cried out. His protective suit hung open on one side of his thigh. His jeans were visible underneath, a dark red patch spreading across them. He tried to put a hand over it but I grabbed his arm just in time, pulling it away.

'You're covered in mud. Sit up on the bench.'

I pulled off my gloves, ripped open his suit, then tore his jeans carefully. There was a cut, small but deep. His leg was smeared with dirt.

'Fell on the knife,' he admitted, voice trembling.

'Any water around?'

He shook his head. Speed was vital. Grabbing the plastic header tank, I wrenched the clip off the fuel hose, holding it above his leg, letting the petrol pour across his leg. He screamed again, pulling away but I held his leg firm.

'What the fuck?' he shouted.

I spread the cut open under the stream of petrol, using clean paper towels to wipe it down. 'You'd rather get anthrax?'

'It'll be fine, it's just—'

'Wanna take the gamble?'

He shook his head, gritting his teeth.

'I know it stings like a bastard, but petrol's a great antiseptic.'

'I don't wanna know why you know that.'

After thirty seconds or so it was clean enough: no mud at least. Petrol's not great for you, but here it was better than the alternative. I wrapped paper towels around his leg and tore pieces of the muddy suit away so it wouldn't touch his leg. 'You need to get inside and into the shower, wash that out.'

He hooked an arm over my shoulder and I half carried him round to the others at the entrance. Alice's beam was casting around like a lighthouse.

'What happened?' asked Marie. 'We heard a shout.'

'Idiot cut his leg. We need to get him inside, get him clean.'

Hurley rushed forward to take Dash's other arm. We mounted the steps, blood dripping onto the metal. The sodden paper towel was hanging down, his leg was completely red. He looked worried, face pale, hands shaking.

'That's a good thing,' I said, pointing at the blood spattering the steps. 'If blood's coming out, anthrax isn't going in.'

Marie and Hurley bundled him into the HADU. I grabbed Alice's arm as she stepped inside.

'Will he be okay?' I asked. 'What's the treatment?'

'Clean the wound up best we can, then an immediate course of antibiotics. Ciprofloxacin, we have it in the medi-kits in the HADU.'

'The immunisation's got to count for something, right?'

'Not guaranteed. Especially as there are some strains on this island that… well, they're exotic, not the strains we'd normally encounter.'

'Get him in the shower while the batteries still have power, and get the drugs. I'll get the generator going.'

She nodded, following the others inside.

Chapter Fifty-eight

Fortunately Dash had been right, he had nearly finished. I'd no experience with generators but have rebuilt enough cars to know the basics; the principles are the same, the parts easily recognisable. The carburettor was mostly reassembled, though I had to give it all another spray and wipe-down since it had fallen into the mud. It took me a good while to find the part Dash had been working on when he'd fallen. I finally dug it out of the mud near the door, cleaned it up, and proceeded to refit the carb to the top of the generator. Fifteen minutes later, and after a good flush of the fuel lines, I finally connected everything back up, flicked the primer, hit the starter. It fired up immediately, roaring on choke before settling into rhythm. I checked my watch before pulling my gloves back on. Nearly seven, dawn was still a way off.

Dash had done all the hard work but I still felt pretty chuffed when I saw the corridors all lit up as I made my way back towards the steps. Now I needed to herd everyone into the dining room for breakfast, because in about forty-five minutes there was going to be a hell of a commotion.

Something flashed in the corner of my eye, or as close to the corner as you get in a gas mask. A glow from the tool shed, through a splintered panel, casting shaking shadows onto the fog. Someone was moving around in there. I tried to look but the crack was too small to see through. Had Dash finished cleaning up his leg and come back out to help me? Hurley, Alice, or Marie?

Or was it Captain Greenbow?

The mud around the door was churned up, and as far as I knew I was the only person to have been in the shed since the rain had stopped. I paused outside, holding my breath, an electric hum from inside just audible through the thick rubber mask. I snatched a quick breath, held it again, gripping the door handle, bracing myself.

I pulled it open, stepping inside. It took me a couple of seconds to realise how stupid I'd been.

A couple of seconds too long.

Chapter Fifty-nine

A torch swung upside down from the roof by a length of string. My own torch beam showed it was tied to a cordless screwdriver, wedged up under a partially collapsed roof truss. The low setting had kept the torch constantly swinging to create the impression that someone was moving around inside. Which meant...

I ducked.

It felt as if the blow split my skull in half. Luckily as I moved it glanced the back of my head, losing most of its energy in pushing me forward, into the shed. I stumbled, dropping my torch, throwing my arms out as another blow slammed into my shoulder. My torch rolled away under a pile of boxes, my gas mask hit the shelves, yanking my head. The screwdriver fell from the ceiling, that torch smashed across the floor, plunging the shed into darkness.

I scrabbled at my mask to keep it on, lashing out with my leg, not aiming at anything but putting plenty of force behind it. My boot connected with something but twisted my ankle in the process. I reached out to the side but grabbed empty space. I scrambled my other hand and closed my fingers around the only object within reach, throwing my arm up as I spun, letting go at just the right moment before I fell backwards.

The paint can hit the shape in the doorway at the same time as my head connected with the shelves. Agony, my vision dimmed even more, I gritted my teeth but watched with satisfaction as their head smashed sideways, the can hitting so hard the lid pinged off. The stuff they'd used to mark up grids on the grass, thick paint, slopped across the gas mask, covering their head and shoulders, the only bit of the figure visible in the slim moonlight. They dropped the wood, clawing at the mask, backing away into the darkness.

I rolled onto all fours, lights exploding like Bonfire Night behind my eyes, blood already soaking into my hair. I blinked rapidly, concentrating on the doorway, wondering why I hadn't received a bullet in the head like the others. I guessed they hadn't wanted to draw attention, which meant they intended to get rid of me quietly. So they could sneak back inside with the others, to wait for the evacuation.

When the wind returned to my chest and the fireworks in my brain died down I managed to stand, swaying against the doorframe and holding my injured foot off the ground. Nothing moved out on the black moorland, no lights in the base, no life. I tried one step and collapsed, only just managing to get my arms out to break my fall before faceplanting in the mud. I'd stood too quickly, could feel blood running down my back. I'd be okay, but a heck of a headache was inbound.

I crawled back into the shed to find my torch, pulling it from under the boxes and shining it around. Yellow paint splattered the door and grass outside. I tried my legs again, this time making it all the way back to the doorway without collapsing. Gripping the frame, I swayed for another second, letting the nausea subside and my eyes clear, then shuffled out.

My torch beam jumped as I limped along, a hamster inside a swirling white ball. The steps of the base appeared. I took one last look around before stepping up, catching something in the light. Since the rain had stopped a while ago, our footprints were easily discernible in the mud. A mess of boots led the way I'd come from, our tracks stirred into the mud between the sheds and the steps, spots of Dash's blood occasionally spattering the grass. But another set of tracks broke away from the others at ninety degrees, heading off into the fog. They must have been made recently, but why had someone headed out across the island? And who?

A closer inspection confirmed the obvious. The light caught on the smudges of yellow paint trailing it, a satisfying drag on the left foot implying its owner was limping more than me. I set off at as much of a jog as I could muster, wishing I hadn't relinquished my pistol, no time to go get it now.

The tracks took me over the hill. Occasionally they strayed from the well-trodden path, exploring the heather to reappear a few metres further on. My attacker was circling. Looking for something? Or checking if they were being followed? There was only one place they could be going: Camp Vollum. Why, I couldn't be sure. Something to do with Demeter's body? Knowing we'd found it, did it contain some crucial evidence? I picked up the pace.

After another few minutes I spotted something in the distance. At first I thought it was a trick of the fog but as I approached I could see it was a dim light. No way of telling how far I'd come but I was pretty sure it wasn't Camp Vollum, which could only mean it was a torch. The killer's torch. I snapped mine off and let my eyes adjust to the murky black. The torch in front bumped along, circling, searching. Closer now. Was I catching up or were they heading back? I stopped, crouched, ears extended. The only sounds were the waves crashing against the cliffs near the camp. I know from time at sea that fog can play tricks with your ears as well as your eyes, but the waves were close. The torch was in between me and the camp, and hadn't moved for a while.

I kept my torch off, moving to the left, away from the path, circling the light. I maintained an equal distance as I moved around it. The booming grew louder, the ground rockier, fog swirling and condensing on the lens of my mask. It reminded me of when I'd landed in the helicopter, had it really been less than twenty-four hours ago?

I was too fixated on the light, tripping, almost falling over. My foot had snagged in the undergrowth, reminding me of Marie's stark warning. Bending to free my foot, I saw it wasn't vegetation, it was a hosepipe; the yellow network still pumping seawater and formaldehyde across the hillside. I continued onwards.

Orientation by sight was impossible but by stopping every few seconds I could estimate my location by listening to how loud the sea was, guessing the distance, triangulating in relation to the torch. I reckoned I'd moved round over ninety degrees, so with the torch in front of me the cliffs were directly on my left. I crept closer.

Either the sun had begun to rise or my eyes had become more accustomed to dim moonlight percolating through the fog. Probably a bit of both, I could just about make out the huts of Camp Vollum below. My attacker was only a hundred or so metres away, near the incinerator. I ought to rush them, throw the bastard in and be done with this place.

I continued my slow creep. The torch didn't move. I began to doubt it was my quarry, possibly a light on the pump? I took a moment to determine my next move. The tracks led in this direction, the killer was here somewhere. Had they gone inside?

No. This was the same trap they'd just sprung on me in the shed, they were trying it again – drawing me in so they could attack. I understood now what had happened; they'd set off down the path, knowing the mud would give away their direction, checking behind them now and again to see where I was. Maybe waiting in the darkness to watch for my torch. When I'd drawn closer they'd left their torch, doubling back, circling round, waiting to ambush me. Probably hiding somewhere they could watch for me. I backtracked slowly, away from the light.

There was movement, a squelch in the mud, but not from down the hill. Something in the darkness, off to my right. I froze. They *had* followed me across the hillside. Again I cursed not having my pistol on me. Given how Demeter, Gambetta and Ingrid had ended up, I was sure my adversary was armed, and wouldn't hesitate to use their gun now. Had they deliberately drawn me away from the base, where the fog would smother the sound of my death? Gun or not, if I could get in close enough I was confident I could deal with them, but would I get the chance?

I crouched and lay on the ground, pressing myself into the mud, training my eyes on the black, just like I had a few hours earlier when the Marines had arrived. What I'd have given for their presence now. I didn't regret sending them away – the risk was worth the reward – but I'd have killed for that rifle and night-vision.

Another movement, my hunter moving slowly. I took solace in the thought that I was better at this; if I'd had my pistol on me they'd already be dead.

I shuffled backwards, heather whispering across my suit. Saturated ground sucked at my boots. I was well aware that I was crawling across what had been some of the most contaminated dirt on the island, and despite the fact it was probably decontaminated, I could still imagine bacteria crawling across me.

There, again, movement. Still to my right but closer now, hard to judge but maybe twenty metres. A dangerous distance; too far for me to use surprise, but close enough that they could easily shoot me. No use lying here in the mud; soon they'd walk over me. Either that or the sun would come up and I'd be laid here like a sunbather on a beach.

They had a gun, but they were injured, and despite my splitting head, the walk over had sharpened my edge, refined my senses. I was pretty sure I could outrun them, and if I set off now I'd be lost in the fog before they could react. Then double back, get to Camp Vollum and retrieve Gambetta's Walther hiding on the top of the cupboard.

The shape moved closer.

If I didn't move I was a dead man. Now or never.

I leapt up, taking off back up the hillside. Immediately there was a sharp crack, but nothing hit me so I kept going. Another crack, something sprayed my suit; the bullet had hit a hosepipe.

I changed direction, sprinting right, towards the cliffs. Another crack followed by lead slapping mud, a flash as their torch beam momentarily found me. They were a better shot than I'd given them credit for, must have started after me, knowing if I got out of range I'd be lost. I couldn't risk looking back so changed direction again, running to the left then going right again, zigzagging up the hill, trying to open up distance between us.

The mud exploded in front of me, I ran through water spray from another damaged pipe. The ground suddenly changed colour. I slid to a halt and strained my eyes; it wasn't the ground that had changed colour – there was no ground. I was on the cliff edge, looking out over the sea. I turned. My hunter was closing fast. Another shot buzzed past my head. I was silhouetted against the sky here on the cliffs, an easy target. My attacker was a good shot and getting closer, and I was running out of island quicker than they were running out of bullets. The mud to the side of me was bathed in light, the beam moved ever closer, and I knew the nasty end of their gun was just behind.

Only one option left, possibly a one-way street to a different death, but one that was less nailed on – and I'd take the possibility of survival over the certainty of those bullets.

I leapt into the abyss.

Chapter Sixty

One of the maps I'd studied at Faslane had been a copy of an old MoD chart that showed the site of the experiments close to where Camp Vollum now stood. Crucially, someone had scrawled on the map by the cliffs, 'Disposal Site'.

A yellowed file in the briefing pack marked *Secret* in big red letters had told me why.

Gruinard Island: 1942. Soon after the covert tests have finished, a fisherman catches a rotting sheep in his nets. No big deal, maybe a foolish solitary sheep strayed too close to the cliffs and fell into the sea. Back over the side it goes, and he thinks nothing of it until that evening, when he sits down for a pint in his local and overhears a conversation between a local farmer and the parson. Earlier that day the parson had come across a couple of dead sheep while walking near the graveyard at Gruinard Bay, and wondered if the farmer ought to check his walls and gates. The farmer says he hasn't lost any sheep. The fisherman turns in his chair, places his pint on the table, chipping in with his own tale of the floater. The mystery passes the time in the pub, but isn't worth losing sleep over.

Until a couple of days later, when another sheep washes ashore. Locals watch with mounting concern as every day, more dead sheep appear on the beaches.

Concern reaches a crescendo a week later, when sheep on the mainland start dying with symptoms consistent with anthrax poisoning. The vet confirms it, and rumours abound.

But strangely, no rumours about Gruinard Island.

That's thanks to an English teacher up on a well-timed bird-spotting holiday. Apparently, a couple of weeks earlier, whilst searching out a purple sandpiper, he'd seen a Greek freighter in the channel, and through his binoculars he'd watched them throwing dead sheep overboard. He didn't think anything of it at the time but given recent events it's clear the dastardly Greeks had sailed all the way to this remote corner of the North Atlantic to dispose of their anthrax-ridden stock, avoiding fines and costly disposal fees.

That's what the English teacher had said anyway, and he was a smart fella; knowledgeable about such things.

The Greeks were never caught, of course. And afterwards no one could remember the name of that bird-watching Englishman, who'd weirdly turned up at the right time in all the local pubs, churning out his tale whenever and wherever there was gossip of dead sheep.

I couldn't remember his name either, but it'd been written in the dossier I'd read. He'd worked for the same shadowy disinformation and censorship department as the 'government representatives' who'd turned up a few weeks later to compensate the unfortunate farmers. The dead sheep eventually stopped, the rumours died off, everyone forgot.

This wasn't useless knowledge; the reason this flashed through my mind was that marking on the dog-eared map. *Disposal Site*. The dead sheep from the island's anthrax tests had been dumped in the sea at the base of the cliffs, with explosives set in the rocks above. They'd calculated that the landslide would bury the carcasses, but the water had been too deep, the shelf too steeply sloped. The sheep had been blown clear out to sea, hence washing up on the beaches.

I figured if it was deep enough for the sheep, it was deep enough for me.

Chapter Sixty-one

I hit hard, feet first, and it felt like kicking concrete, my head snapping violently up as the gas mask almost wrenched my face off. The pain was short-lived as the shock of the freezing water stole my breath and all senses. I sank deep into the churning water, my ankles unbroken; it'd been deep enough.

Just like those sheep forty years before, the underwater current immediately tugged me away from the base of the cliffs. My suit was heavy, turning me over, dragging me deeper. I tore at the straps of the mask, somehow succeeding in freeing myself. Saltwater burned my eyes. The current pulled harder and, blind in the oily black, I couldn't tell which way was up. Panic swelled through me; I needed air. I struck out, pulling as hard as I could. Each stroke sapped precious energy, threatening to keep me prisoner down there.

Just as I thought I was going to breathe a lungful of seawater, my head broke the surface. I sucked at the salty sky, savouring the freezing air in my throat. My body was rigid, pain everywhere. I held on to it, pushed it down, forced my mind silent. Probed my senses. They checked in one after another with damage reports. My ears were ringing, my head was on fire yet numb at the same time, like receiving a football to the face in a winter's PE lesson, multiplied by a hundred. I tested my limbs, flexing the joints, they just about responded. Blood, hot in the water, trickled across my face. It was pouring from my nose down the back of my throat, earthy, metallic. But I was alive.

Not for long. My chest constricted, the cold shutting down the muscles, preventing me from filling my lungs. It was the first time I'd tasted fresh air in two days and I longed for more, but before I could take another breath I was dragged back under. The suit had filled with water, all the way up to the neck. I reached again for the surface, broke through, took a breath, started to sink again. Each time I stopped moving I was sucked straight back down, churning, smashed by currents and waves. My energy was almost expended, muscles seized. I'd already been swept further out. I'd traded the instant death of a bullet for a slower death, dragged out to sea to drown.

A flash on the cliffs above reminded me there was still a chance of that instant death. Above the waves I heard a crack and a bullet sput into the water nearby. Whoever it was, they could obviously still see me through the rolling fog banks – no doubt helped by the bright plastic suit flapping around.

Dragged under again, I pulled the tape from my gloves as I sank deeper. A hand was free, and then I was clawing at my chest, ripping the suit. I slid out of the sleeve then struck out again. This time when I surfaced, the cliffs were twice as far away. I ducked under to pull off the boots, taking the shredded suit to the bottom of the bay.

I was free, and the comparative liberty of jeans and jumper was as good as wearing trunks. That didn't make it much easier; the cliffs had been swallowed by the fog, I was being pulled out further still. I tried to swim in the direction I thought was the island, but the current was too strong. Another gunshot flashed in the murk, dimmer now. They were taking pot shots, they couldn't see me, I was out of range.

I tried to face the direction of the flashes, treading water, pushing my head above the swell, still struggling to breathe in the frozen emptiness. The forecast from the ship had been right; the storm had well and truly departed, leaving fat, rolling seas. As each wave pushed me up I could see only black ocean in every direction. Above, the sky was only slightly lighter and just as blank. Hemmed in on all sides by an utterly featureless wall of fog.

I had to get back to the island. I swam as hard as I could but my limbs didn't respond, freezing up, I was pulled deeper into the void, turned round on the waves, disoriented.

Free of the cumbersome suit, I wasn't worried about drowning, not immediately. The currents were strong; my worry now was being swept away. Hypothermia was a very real threat, slowing my actions, shutting down my mind, seizing my muscles solid. I had to get back to land fast, I'd only be bobbing here half an hour before my body gave out and I slipped beneath the waves, emerging again when expanding gases inflated my rotting corpse.

Assuming the currents were stable I could expect to be deposited back on the mainland sometime tomorrow, just like those rotting sheep. I fought harder, breaking the frigid water's grip on my body, striking out in the direction I thought I'd come from, but it was impossible. The wall was impenetrable, no way of knowing which direction I was facing any more, everywhere waves writhing into black. I struggled onward anyway, positive action preferable to acceptance of fate.

A thought struck me. The currents pulling those sheep.

It made sense that Demeter had been shot up on the cliffs and thrown into the sea, but his corpse hadn't made it to the mainland, instead becoming entangled in the seawater pipe off the beach. A short story by Poe had always stuck with me, 'A Descent into the Maelström'. Spoilers, but it's about a guy who escapes certain death in an enormous whirlpool, surviving only by climbing out of his boat and simply 'letting go'. He's lighter floating on his own; the current takes him away from his heavier boat, which is destroyed in the whirlpool. By disregarding his survival instincts and instead letting himself go with the current, the guy survives. Well, Demeter certainly hadn't been swimming. Could I trust the same currents to take me to where I needed to be? I'd no energy left, so no choice. I lay on my back, shivering, hands already seizing up, trusting my fate to Poseidon.

Chapter Sixty-two

The fog was noticeably lighter in one direction, charcoal grey now rather than coal black. The sun was finally on the rise.

I drifted for long minutes, hands and feet frozen now. No way to measure whether I was being dragged further out or staying where I was. In the distance, a couple of gulls cried, the only sounds of life I'd heard here. To hear them properly, to be outside without the cumbersome gas mask, was bliss – even if I was adrift without hope of rescue. Shivering was painful, the cold chewing down to bone marrow, but at least I knew it was keeping me alive. I told myself over and over: the pain is good. It's when you stop shivering, stop feeling pain, that you should really worry.

The gulls circled closer, laughing, taunting me. I did my best to concentrate on other, warmer things. Childhood holidays. I closed my eyes, kidding myself the gulls were circling the cliff railway in Lynmouth, diving at the brightly painted fishing boats, Justin throwing a toy plane to me as the lighthouse glowed all the shades of autumn in the setting sun.

The gulls got bored of tormenting me, drifting into the distance, taking the memory with them, leaving me alone again in the freezing black. They left behind another sound, something slapping the surface of the water. I craned my neck but couldn't see anything. The sound was constant, getting closer. I pushed my legs under the surface, feeling the current's pull again, and paddled my freezing body towards the noise. A shape drifted in the fog, impossible to discern colour or outline in the pre-dawn, but it was neither sea nor sky and that was good enough for me. Thank you, Poe, the current had pulled me in the same direction as Demeter's bloated corpse, right into the raft.

I was almost carried past it, but at the last minute grabbed for the big barrels. My fingers reacted slowly, numbed with cold, slipping and missing. I panicked, scrabbled, tearing my nails against the plastic, was dragged onward, out to sea to die. I kicked harder and curled a finger through a loop of the strong nylon rope that held the barrels together. The current swung me round, bouncing me against the raft. I didn't feel my finger bend, but heard the snap of bone above the waves. I reached round, grabbing the rope with my other hand, catching my breath. Thank God it was my left hand and not my trigger finger.

The relative happiness in this realisation was short-lived as a wave slammed me against the raft and something below the surface tore my T-shirt, a piece of wood or wire or something sticking out of the contraption, burning its way down my ribs, impaling me, brief agony then nothing. I pulled myself away, felt heat seeping from my left side as I dragged myself round the corner of the raft. I could just about see the beach now but I was spent, clinging to the raft, steadying my breathing, trying to focus. I wasn't shivering any more, couldn't feel anything, the cold, the pain.

I wanted to climb up on top of the raft and lie there until the sun rose, but aside from being exposed to the wind, speeding along my hypothermia, I had to get back to the base.

I could just about see my watch, it wasn't even half seven. I'd only been in the sea a few minutes; it had felt like an hour.

It'd been just before seven when I'd got the power back on; that didn't leave long until the match ignited, and the vial of anthrax went up in flames. The murderer wouldn't allow that – and I had to be there to catch them.

Ever since I'd decided the anthrax vial was the motive, I'd wondered how they intended to profit from it. The problem was the vial itself. When we were taken back to the mainland we'd be isolated. Stripped, scrubbed, handed fresh clothes. Nothing at all could be taken off the island by us, not even a sock, it'd all be quarantined, checked thoroughly, then disposed of or – if valued – decontaminated separately. Even resorting to drug mule methods wouldn't work; apart from the fact that you'd have to be mental to conceal a test tube of anthrax up your arse, or swallow a condom full of it, the medicals we were looking forward too would be *very* thorough. Post-decontamination, the island would be swept by another team, private-sector contractors who would scrub away any trace of our presence. To summarise, we'd be checked, our clothing and possessions would be checked, and the island would be checked, anything left behind destroyed. Presumably there was profit involved, there always is, so how was the killer going to get the sample off the island to collect their fee?

I'd found the answer under the floor of the radio room; the vial shoved up under the pipes by Gambetta's killer. Dash had provided the last clue when he'd told me the base would be transported in its entirety on an American container ship bound for the Antarctic. It'd be cleaned and refitted en route. During that time someone on the crew would quietly remove the vial, as well as the other evidence. The fact that the base and ship were American wasn't necessarily suggestive; the contractors on the crew could be affiliated with any nefarious government or group.

If the killer were allowed to evacuate, there would be nothing to tie them to the crimes. Sure, I could have simply removed the vial – they wouldn't have got paid, there'd be no winners – but four bodies in a morgue and my numerous creditors would consider that a poor ending.

If I didn't get back in time, what then? The fire would start, the killer would retrieve their precious vial. In the rush of the emergency evac they'd hide it somewhere else in the base, somewhere I'd have no hope of finding it but, most of all, hiding themselves from me for good. The fact I knew where it was right now meant I was, despite being stuck in the sea, still one step ahead; finding the vial during the search for Demeter had given me an opportunity I needed to capitalise on, because with my bloated corpse floating around the Atlantic there'd be no one to stop them.

Chapter Sixty-three

It had taken me a while to drag myself to the cove. I'd worked my way around the raft to the thick pipe that led in to shore, then hooked an arm across it, just like Demeter's corpse. Earlier I'd seen the steel cable holding the sections of pipe together, connecting them to the raft where the great gulps of brine were vacuumed up, sucked through the pump to be spat out across the island. I'd curled my aching fingers around the cable and hauled myself in, pushed along by the waves one minute, hauled backwards the next.

My hands were torn and bleeding by the time I'd reached the pebbles, broken finger swelling and useless, but I'd made it, panting and sweating despite the cold. Hot blood still spilled down onto my jeans, every movement pulling at the new wound down my ribs. I allowed myself a minute to recover with my hands on my knees. Truth was, I wanted to collapse to the ground, but I'd just traded the danger of the sea for the danger of infection so remained on my feet.

The sky was mouldy now, sea still black, the land beginning to take on some colour as night finally surrendered. I stumbled up the track, climbed the steps to Camp Vollum, punched in the code for the door, staggered inside.

My torn and bloody clothes went straight in the bin, and I allowed myself a few minutes under the hot shower, swilling blood from various wounds. I was on a tightrope; the need for haste balanced by the acute desire to not contract an anthrax infection. Time was ticking away, every second here another notch on that timer plug, but what if I got back there with time to spare and anthrax burning through my veins? Would it have been worth it? Yes, I reminded myself, it would be if I stopped that sample of anthrax from getting out and managed to avenge Ingrid in the process. I picked up the pace, using a sponge to dab at my wounds with undiluted bleach, thankful no one was around to hear my agony.

When I'd finished, I inspected myself in the mirror. Up top wasn't as bad as I'd thought, a few scrapes and grazes, some itching burns, bleach on raw dermis. There were a couple of nasty golf balls growing on the back of my head, an evil bruise forming across my jaw where the gas mask had almost yanked my head off slamming into the sea, but all in all it was better than the alternative – my head *was* still attached, at least.

My body was another matter, tendrils of blood still ran down my legs. I was sliced right down my ribs, thin skin darkened and contracted like elongated lips, exposing pale flesh and even yellow fat beneath, definitely a case for a shitload of stitches. Even for a clean cut I was surprised it wasn't bleeding more, guessed mild hypothermia had dialled back my circulation. I gritted my teeth and rubbed bleach into it, stuck a few strips of gaffer tape down and wrapped some round my torso to hold it together, start it knitting, at least until the ship could patch me up.

I almost bit clean through a rolled-up magazine as I levered my broken finger against the wall to straighten it, wrapping tape around a few times, splinting it to the finger next to it. The room dimmed, bile rose in my throat, blood rushed like static in my ears. I gripped the edge of the sink as my legs lost their rigidity, held on until the nausea subsided. Waiting for my heart to slow, satisfied with the makeshift first aid, and that I wasn't going to pass out, I made my way deeper into the base.

It seemed wrong to step over Ingrid's corpse, I was glad I'd covered her with a coat earlier. On that visit I'd seen a pile of discarded clothes in the common room. A quick rummage later and I was wearing a baggy pair of cargo trousers and a Pacific

Tech University sweater, which could have been Dash's but the size made it more likely Hurley's. No shoes, and my boots were at the bottom of the bay, so I threw some socks on and taped a couple of T-shirts over my feet. I grabbed someone's shemagh, the type of military scarf you'd see on Brit forces or reporters in the Middle East, and left the room.

I knelt by Ingrid for the last time, ran my fingers over the blanket covering her head. I had to force myself to stand. Plenty of time to dwell after the job.

I checked through the labs, but there was no outdoor clothing. In the second lab I stood on the chair again and snatched up Gambetta's Walther PPK from where I'd put it back on the cupboard. I'd briefly checked it before and knew the magazine was empty, but there'd been one round chambered. I double-checked to confirm, pushed it into my pocket, made my way back to the decontamination chamber.

Ingrid's wellies were sitting on the bench but since they were at least five sizes too small, I ignored them. I didn't ignore the gas mask hanging from the hook above. Adjusting the straps for my bigger head, I slipped it on. It smelled of her – in a non-stalker kind of way, moisturiser or conditioner or something – which made me more determined than ever to get, if not justice, then at least revenge. Finally, I wrapped the shemagh around my head, a *Mad Max* post-apocalyptic Lawrence of Arabia, and punched the button for the door.

Even though I didn't think the killer would have stuck around, I gripped the pistol tightly, hiding round the corner as the door slid open. The sun was still beneath the mountains but the sky was aglow, fog now light grey, the island a dirty watercolour wash. Rotten-looking grass and rusty bracken. A quick glance at my watch told me I had minutes until ignition. I couldn't see anyone in the expanse of fog, which meant no one could see me, so I ran outside, pistol up and ready.

Chapter Sixty-four

I avoided the bracken as I sprinted across the island – no desire to stab my foot on an anthrax-laced twig – sticking to the safer but harder-going mud track. After only a few steps I had to surrender the makeshift T-shirt sandals and socks to the sucking mud, thanking the gods there was no danger of broken glass in this wilderness. The fog continued to blow on the breeze and by the time I'd reached the crest of the hill I could look back and still just about see the camp washing in and out of view; my saviour, the pipe, stretching out into a milky nothing.

I forged on as fast as I could in the terrain, jumping rocks and skirting craters, still holding the pistol ready. As I ran I replayed everything I knew to that point – I couldn't think of anything worse than using my one and only bullet on the wrong person. The doubts I still carried were mainly due to the fact that I still hadn't figured out *how* Gambetta was killed – or more accurately, how they'd shot him, hidden the vial, and then escaped. I was pretty sure that somehow the disappearing trick was the key to everything.

Though everyone on the island had an alibi, one of them had killed both Ingrid and Gambetta, and attacked me. They were clever, but still a cold-blooded murderer.

I approached the stone cairn and the large crater that I'd sat in with the Royal Marine, Jarrett, in the pouring rain the night before, and thought about the report I'd given to the crackling voice on board HMS *Dauntless*. Even though the wind and rain had been abysmal, through the downpour and static the clipped tones of Colonel Rupert Holderness had been unmistakable.

Scottish but educated in a way you'd never know it, the voice was one I was well used to. It belonged to a man I'd first become acquainted with in Iraq, where I'd been making good money with my brother and a few of his ex-special forces mates of dubious reputations. Never been a military man myself – Greenbow had been right about that – but we'd had a particular set of skills that had appealed to Colonel Holderness, and he'd taken us under his wing.

Alice was wrong – I'm not MI5, not by a long stretch. Holderness is head of Section something-or-other in Defence Intelligence, and often finds it helpful to have an outsider, an unknown, on a job that might otherwise prove embarrassing to the British Government. 'Mercenary' is an ugly word; I prefer 'contractor'. He uses the term 'deniable asset'.

A couple of weeks prior to Scotland, I'd been in Syria, showing rebels how to disable Soviet-built trucks with improvised explosive devices made from Soviet-built artillery shells. IEDs – a term I'd first heard in Afghanistan a decade or so earlier, when I'd ended up on the receiving end of one thanks to some shit intel. I'd come away with scars back then, not all physical. My brother hadn't come away at all.

You heard about the old millionaire kidnapped from his yacht by Somali pirates a couple of years ago? The one rescued by French special forces in Eyl? The news didn't tell you they landed in the wrong place and I had to carry him through half the town, pursued by some very angry bastards all the way to the evac point.

The German police who arrested that Belgian would-be suicide bomber a while ago? The news didn't tell you I'd been tracking him for a month. They didn't tell you that when the police arrived he was already tied up on the floor, bomb vest disarmed. I'd been long gone.

You don't know the truth about any of these things, obviously my involvement isn't reported; my income depends on it. Although I did actually make it onto the news once. That footage of the guy hitting the statue of Saddam with a shoe, if you look really hard at the background...

South Ossetia, Libya, Iran, Syria, Yemen, Myanmar; to most people names like this are just dots in an atlas, occasionally read out by a newsreader when nothing interesting is happening to celebs at home. These are some of the tattoos up my arm, the jobs, and well-paying ones at that. I'm a private British citizen, albeit with several very well-made passports that say otherwise, so I can travel where armed forces can't, places the Foreign Office can comfortably deny being involved. And I don't always work for the British; emphasis on *independent* contractor, meaning available to whomever has a problem, if they can afford me to fix it. These conflict zones are pay cheques.

You're now thinking that because I'm a mercenary I've fewer morals than a shark; I've heard it all before. A sniff of blood in the water and we all come running. On the contrary, I do have morals; being self-employed allows me to choose my jobs and methods, but I'm also a realist. I've done lots of bad things, I've done lots of good things, but I like to think I'm a net positive – in my own book. I've sold arms to African warlords and then trained rebels to fight them. I've fought against Russians in Ukraine, then returned to London to take my G.U. friends from the embassy to get a decent suit cut.

A wide variety of jobs, but always requiring someone with no ties to the security services, and usually involving a fair degree of violence.

When a technician accidentally died on an island off Scotland, no one took a great deal of notice. But when the base suffered a malfunction a few hours later, suspicions were aroused in Holderness' office. Clever of Alice to pull the fuse on the door, knowing it'd be picked up on, knowing they'd send an operative in. She'd merely assumed I was MI5 since I'd known who she was, and sought her out.

Holderness himself had flown up to Faslane to brief me, before setting up station on the *Dauntless*. The mission had been simple in concept; investigate the circumstances surrounding the death of Andy Kyle, and monitor the activities of the team. Feed any intel back, let Bates and his Marines do any heavy lifting that might be required. As I now knew, it'd turned out more difficult in practice. I'd been dumped into the middle of a plan already in effect, gaining momentum, far wider reaching than we'd thought.

An explosion shattered the air, interrupting my thoughts, slamming me to a halt. It could have been a pistol shot muffled by fog, only I've heard enough pistol shots to know better. It was the sound of a couple of cans of spray paint and a bottle of Acqua di Parma ripping apart, taking half a plastic corridor with it. The blast died on the breeze, heavy silence swaddling the island again. I dispensed with caution, taking off down the steep section of hill, snagging toes on roots and stones. Halfway down, an ugly sound started up, a howl like a demented sea lion stuck on repeat. X-Base's fire alarm. The fog parted to reveal darker skies, filled with smoke. I knelt to take stock.

Thick black tentacles rolled up into the cold air, mixing with the fog, like tea being poured into a cup of milk upside down. The fire had taken hold faster than I'd expected, flames already licked along the roof of the radio hut. From my vantage point I could see the section after it seemed okay, but only the skeletal ribs of the link corridor remained, plastic all melted. I did feel a brief pang of guilt before deciding the richest nation on earth could afford the repairs. The radio room was ablaze – something near the door had caught, setting off the hut. The power had been knocked off again in that section, I couldn't see if anyone was moving inside.

I gripped the pistol tighter, setting off again, slower now. I was just metres from the base when a figure dressed in green emerged from under the HADU, gun in hand.

Greenbow.

He stood slowly, pistol at his hip, aimed at my chest. He was wound tight, I got the impression he'd fire if I so much as flinched. I held the Walther just as steadily.

'Look here,' he shouted, 'you're making a very serious mistake pointing that thing at me. You need to put down—'

'I don't *need* to do anything, Captain. It's early in the morning and already I'm having a very bad day. I'm cold, wet, I've been shot, drowned, and I'm wearing your trousers without pants.'

'Tyler?' He raised the pistol higher, arm outstretched. 'Why aren't you wearing a suit? Where have you been?'

'I could ask you the same; you weren't in your room.'

'No concern of yours, and you'll answer my questions,' he snapped. I stared at the barrel of his gun, and his finger on the trigger. He stepped forward. 'Why are you out here, and why aren't you suited?'

'There's more going on here than you understand, Captain, things you're not entitled to know. Do something useful, find the others.'

Even through the gas mask I saw his eyes bulge. 'Don't be a fool. I'm still in charge of this operation, and I don't answer to spies.'

I kept my own pistol low, started to close the distance between us. 'If you want to come out of this on the right side, you'll put the gun down. This is your very last chance to get out of the way.'

Behind him the tall radio antenna groaned and started a slow drunken lean to starboard as a puff of smoke erupted skyward.

He narrowed his eyes, clicked back the Browning's hammer. 'This is *your* last chance. I'll count to three.' He started counting, 'One…'

I looked at the idiot, English exceptionalism personified, felt my eye twitch. My knuckles ached gripping that Walther. I didn't have three seconds to spare, and I'd given him enough warnings. I squeezed the trigger, striding forward. The bullet exited the Walther's suppressor with a pop and a click. I was already dropping the empty pistol onto the mud as the bullet was burrowing through the toe of Greenbow's left wellington boot, into the top of his foot. With only tiny bones to shatter the bullet didn't ricochet, drilling straight out of the sole into the mud. Greenbow screamed, buckling forward, bringing his arms down. As I walked past I swung a fist into his stomach and plucked the Browning from his hand, not breaking stride as I mounted the steps to the base.

'You'll want to lie on your back with your foot in the air until the evac arrives.' I winked. 'It'll help with the bleeding, and minimise any nasty infections.'

'Tyler, you're—'

Whatever I was I didn't hear it, as I'd already entered the base.

Chapter Sixty-five

My hands were shaking with adrenaline, sudden explosions of violence always catch me unaware, as if I'm watching with a satellite delay. I rested my hands on my knees until my breathing slowed but when I looked up and saw myself in the mirror I was smiling.

I made a conscious effort to reset my face. It'd been overkill, unnecessary, I was certain to catch an earful from Holderness. No doubt I'd be forced to apologise, would face repercussions. I rationalised it by remembering I'd been warned the captain was an arsehole, and he'd been slowing me down. *Mitigants or a comfortable story – was Bates right about me?* Didn't matter, I had a job to finish.

No time to decontaminate, no point, given the integrity of the base was breached by the explosion. Fuck 'em, they could decontaminate the whole base or incinerate the thing for all I cared.

No time even to find my trainers, I had to get down to the comms room ASAP. I kept my mask on, slamming through the door, Greenbow's gun up in front, into the first corridor.

Smoke had already made it this far, faint wisps rolling along the ceiling. I pressed on, wet feet slapping plastic, trailing mud and blood, running straight for the radio room. Past the kitchen, the smoke thickened. A small explosion echoed down from the radio room, not big enough to be one of the fuel tanks going up, maybe another pressurised can.

I pressed on through the huts, slamming through doors, heading deeper into the smoke. Fire had engulfed the end of the corridor, molten plastic hanging from the ceiling, spewing acrid smoke across the hall. Most of it was sucked outside but enough rolled back to blacken the walls and obscure my sight. The door to the radio room was shut.

I knew who was inside; there was only one person it could be.

Chapter Sixty-six

I brought the pistol up, aiming squarely at Hurley's back. 'Don't fucking move.'

He flinched, the cover slamming down on the underfloor crawl space. He was sitting on the floor next to the panel. I scanned the room, saw a sand-coloured pistol lying on the floor just beyond his reach. SIG Sauer M18, evidently his that he'd somehow smuggled onto the island. He twitched, angling towards it, curling his legs under him as if to stand.

'I said don't move, Hurley.'

He froze.

'Now turn around. Slowly.' I dragged the gas mask off my head, letting it drop to the floor, keeping my gun on him.

'You went over the cliffs,' he said as he slid round. Gone was the good-natured all-American charm, replaced with a sneer that twisted his face and set his eyes glowing. Any doubts about Hurley were instantly dispelled.

'Nine lives. For an agent of the Central Intelligence Agency, you're not that bright.' I moved the Browning to point directly at Hurley's chest. At this distance I couldn't miss, but I was too far away for him to jump me. How the tables had turned.

'What now – you're gonna take me in?'

I didn't move.

'I'll be stateside within the week,' he added.

'The "special relationship" can get fucked. You've murdered people. We don't take that lying down.'

'You'll take it bending over, like you always do. You, Porton Down, your whole fucking annex of a country.'

I clicked the hammer back with my thumb.

'You won't shoot,' he said. 'Wouldn't be cricket.'

'You've killed a Scottish civilian and two scientists from the most sensitive military research facility in the United Kingdom. You've killed a Norwegian scientist and an admittedly detestable French agent. Maybe that's baseball where you come from, cos it's certainly not fucking cricket. Your people aren't gonna want this kind of heat, they'll give you up. Hopefully we'll extradite you to France; their prisons aren't as friendly as ours.'

The room was heating up big-time, trails of smoke puffing under the door. The wall behind me was warping, the plastic had reached critical temperature. The fibreglass exterior shell, the insulation, and the aluminium supports would hold for a while – their melting point was higher – but if we didn't get out soon we'd be shrink-wrapped inside a melting cocoon.

'You're forgetting something,' Hurley said.

'What's that?'

'You don't know shit. You can't connect me to this. I've got a rock-steady alibi. They'll look at the evidence, the testimony of everyone here will back me up. You've gone rogue. It all points to Demeter – shit, your own government are itching to have something concrete on the Russkies, they'll *want* to believe it was him.'

'Demeter's corpse is safe under a hut on the other side of the island.'

'Not any more. They'll shut you up for rocking the boat, man. You days are numbered, not mine.'

'That vial of anthrax in your pocket says otherwise.'

'Your word against everyone else's here. The word of a rogue spy who self-medicates from a bottle to keep the straitjacket at bay and needs to get results to find redemption, even if it means making it up. Like I said, no evidence.'

'I took psychology GCSE too. Easy way to make up the grades.' I smiled, leaning in, emphasising the gun in my hand, my finger gently squeezing the trigger. 'Let's do it the other way, then. I don't need evidence, it won't be your word against anyone's if you're not around to talk.' He was right, though, killing in cold blood is a very different proposition indeed, as I well knew.

He held his hands up, trying a new tack. 'How does a million bucks sound?'

'Sounds good, but not good enough. Give me the sample.'

A blast rocked the hut, blowing the door in, slamming me further into the room. It was the distraction Hurley had been waiting for as he dived for his gun.

I pulled the trigger.

Chapter Sixty-seven

The trigger clicked, dropping the hammer.

The hammer struck the firing pin.

The firing pin slid forward and struck nothing.

No explosion, no tug on the wrist, the slider remained in place. I pulled it back and squeezed the trigger again – same impotent click.

Hurley was moving fast. I stepped forward, lashing out with my foot, kicking his gun across the floor just as his fingers reached it. He grabbed for my leg. I kicked out again, this time aiming for his face, but he was too quick, rolling away. I slid the magazine out of the pistol. Empty! Greenbow, the stupid bastard, he'd emptied his mag earlier, didn't have any more ammo, and I'd wasted my only bullet on him! I should have checked, had been too focused on getting inside. Well, I had even less remorse for shooting him now.

Hurley was on his feet. I threw the useless pistol at his face. He ducked to his left. I knew he would, was counting on it as I was already swinging my right leg up. The top of my foot connected with the side of his head as he ducked. He spun backwards, hands up, but I'd acted instinctively, forgetting my injured feet were bare. Jolts of electricity shot up my leg, I dropped my foot to the floor, limping back. We faced each other across the room, snarling tiger and hunter, each looking for an opportunity. When it came there would be no trading of blows, no noble combat; real fights are won in seconds. Hurley was bigger than me, stronger, fresher, and carrying fewer injuries; this was not an even matching. I glanced at his gun lying in a puddle of Gambetta in the far corner.

He launched, arms raised. Bigger than me but careless, eyes betraying him. I feinted to the right, swinging my left, landing the heel of my palm squarely on his nose. Thanks to my broken finger I couldn't get as much power in it as I'd have liked, but he backed away nonetheless, hands up as blood exploded across his face, spilling between his fingers and running down the plastic suit. He was momentarily blinded. I had to keep up the attack, my only chance was to wear him down to my level. I cast my mind back to the shed earlier, imagined him standing behind me with that length of wood in his hands. Which leg had I kicked? His left. I raised my right and stamped down, if he hadn't been injured before he certainly was now.

The howl echoed off the walls as his leg twisted then sprang back. I stepped forward, preparing a follow-up, looking for a weapon, when something whirled in the corner of my vision.

I ducked instinctively. He'd fallen against the shelves and grabbed for the CCTV unit, which he'd sent flying through the air. A corner connected with my head, setting my ears ringing. I staggered sideways. He'd smashed me on the head with a piece of wood less than an hour before, and through shit luck it'd caught me in the same place.

My legs gave way, I folded to the floor, vision darkening as muffled sounds erupted around me. My head felt too hot and too wet. I forced my eyes open, and when the room eventually swam back into focus Hurley was crawling onto me. I'd no time to do anything about it, before I could move he'd pinned his knees across my arms, hands around my throat. I was barely conscious, unable to stop him.

Blood continued to seep through my hair onto the floor where it mingled with Gambetta's. Shooting stars obscured Hurley's face. I was vaguely aware of flames licking the ceiling behind him. He was saying something but all I could hear was the blood rushing in my ears on its way to pouring out of my head.

Real fights are won in seconds and I'd just lost.

Hurley brought his face closer, staring into my eyes, blood running from his teeth like a rabid wolf. I refused to blink. He didn't notice my fingers clawing at the gore, crawling across the floor, dragging my arm with it until they reached the wall. My fingertips stretched, burning, until they found what they were searching for. I hooked a finger through the trigger guard of Hurley's gun. I pulled it close, wrapping my fingers around the handle. He realised what I was doing and leaned to the side, pressing all his weight onto my hand, which thankfully relieved my throat, allowing me to get a decent breath. I squeezed the trigger, the explosion deafening in the small room. A small hole opened in the ceiling, swallowed in flame. He gripped the pistol over my hand, slipping his finger through the trigger guard, forcing my finger. Pulling with both hands, he turned the pistol over and, pushing down slowly, angled it towards my head.

I had no energy to stop him so did the only thing I could; I squeezed the trigger again, again, again, trying to empty the magazine before the barrel pointed at me. The shots came in rapid succession, millimetres from my face. A bullet ripped my sweater, blood sprayed my face.

Hurley howled, rolling off me, but just as quickly he was on his feet. He cradled his arm, inspecting it. A tear in his suit, a spatter of blood, the bullet had only grazed him. He realised this at the same time as I did, diving for the metal shelves along the wall. I swung the pistol up and fired quickly. A bullet punched a hole through the wall behind him and then the gun clicked empty. Hurley was about to jump back onto me when there was an almighty roar. A section of wall collapsed inward, a rush of flames close behind, licking the ceiling and down the wall, which immediately bubbled, already sagging. Thick smoke billowed in. In seconds the room would become a coffin. Burning globs of molten plastic dripped onto my arm like wax from a candle, sticking like napalm, searing circles into my flesh.

I dropped the gun and rolled over onto all fours. There was a tearing sound, I looked up. The shelving unit teetered above me. Hurley gave it another pull, crashing it down onto my back, smashing me to the floor. I craned my neck, half expecting Hurley to be standing over me, but all I saw was the heel of his shoe as he disappeared down the corridor.

The smoke was choking now, and I was pinned. I tried to reach for the gas mask but it was just beyond my fingers. Gambetta grinned at me; the shelving lay across my back and his corpse. With his contracting skin and lips pulled back from his teeth he seemed to find the prospect of us cooking together hilarious. Fortunately he was fatter than me, bloated from rotting gases. I exhaled, pressing flat, felt a bit of give. Grabbing the leg of the desk, I dragged myself through his black crusted blood. After a few seconds wriggling I'd got enough of my body free to get some leverage, scrambling to my feet. The ceiling was barely visible through the thick smoke, just the middle, a swollen beer belly sagging down, plastic running down the walls like a rain-lashed window. The door hung at an angle, a wall of flame blocking the exit, corridor beyond lost in swirling smoke. I ducked low, fingers searching out the gas mask, but I'd lost it in the mess of boxes from the shelves. I took another breath then grabbed the radio, launching it at the window. It bounced off the triple glazing and crashed to the floor. Screwing the window shut wasn't doing me any favours now. I jumped onto the desk, crouching to avoid the lava ceiling, reaching behind to snatch up the chair. I swung it at the window.

The chair bounced off too, but this time a crack appeared in a corner. The plastic cladding of the ceiling peeled back, another roar of flame singed my beard. I looked up into the aluminium ribs of the hut's ceiling, the glowing fibreglass insultation, no way out there. I swung again – wincing at the pain in my finger and a thousand other places as wounds tore – swung twice, three times more, the middle pane crunched. The glass was laminated and stayed in one piece, but a cobweb of fissures radiated across the window. A piece of insulation landed on my arm, scorching the hairs, burning through skin layer by layer. I swatted it away but it was replaced by another, a blizzard of incandescent snowflakes floating all around me, melting through everything they landed on. I swung the chair one last time and the third pane bent outward, not falling apart but no longer a solid pane of glass. My hair caught alight, burning the tip of my ear. I swiped at it, took a quick breath, almost threw up, smoke roasting my lungs and jamming up my throat. I dropped the chair, crouched, fell against the window, curling into a ball and leading with my shoulder.

Thankfully I'd done enough damage. The window gave way, splintering outwards, dropping away from the frame. Unable to stop I followed it, a jet of flame chasing me out as I dropped the few feet to the ground. Thankfully momentum carried me over the broken glass and onto the soft mud, the impact still taking my breath away. Lucky it did, as I found myself inches from a patch of potentially contaminated mud that I didn't want to inhale.

Though at that point anthrax was lower down my worry list. The fall had pulled the wound on my side, I could feel a piece of tape loosened by fresh blood. I rolled over onto my back to catch my breath, feeling the cool ground beneath me, watching the flames roaring from the window and black smoke rolling up into the raw sky.

No time to rest, Hurley was still close. A voice called out; Dash, round the other side of the base, yelling for help with the water pump. I looked under the huts, could see legs moving and water pouring onto the mud. The flames above receded, a sizzling sound telling me he'd got the hose onto the fire. Without much decent fuel to burn it'd be out pretty soon. But then there was something else, a woman shouting. It had come from the opposite direction, behind my head, towards the beach.

I was back on my feet. In the distance shapes flitted through the fog, Hurley and someone else, either Alice or Marie. She stumbled and he caught her, dragging her onwards into the murk.

I set off at a sprint but my feet were still bare and I slipped on the mud. Jumping into the grass to try to gain traction wasn't much better, the needles of bracken tore at my feet. I set my teeth and carried on. They were lost in the fog as I fell behind, but then came a flash. I threw myself to the ground as the crack of a gunshot whipped across the hillside.

Hurley's Sig lay empty in the hut behind me, along with Greenbow's Browning. *Neither an option.* I'd dropped Gambetta's pistol in the mud by the door, also empty. There was, as far as I knew, only one other gun on the island – my own HK, which I'd given to Marie. It must now be in Hurley's possession. Did that mean he'd taken her, too? Or was she a willing partner in crime?

I had to assume she was with him under duress, and no one else was going to do anything about it. I thought about Gambetta's pistol, briefly considered my spare ammo, wondering if Marie had taken it, but ruled it out; even if it were still there, the 9mm ammunition wouldn't have been any use in the Walther. There were no other options.

It was obvious where Hurley was going – there was only one place he could be headed now. Fuck it, no time to get backup, for a second time I chased the gunman across the moorland armed with nothing but anger.

A sound cut through the fog, a high-pitched revving engine. As we'd discussed the previous night, the dinghy was the only way off the island. The revs spluttered and died. It cranked again, revving higher this time before dying. The sound was close, then the fog rolled on and I was on the crest of the bluffs, above the mooring.

The little boat faced away from the island. Hurley hunched over the outboard, adjusting the choke. I knelt to catch my breath, creeping forward slowly, careful to stay off to the side, knowing his field of vision was narrowed by the gas mask.

Behind him Marie was sitting, gripping the plank bench, staring out to sea. Hurley pulled the cord again. This time the engine caught, settling to a grumble. My fingers curled around a rock the size of my fist.

He adjusted the idle, the screw picked up speed, then, leaving it hanging just above the water, squeezed past Marie to untie the line at the bow. He dropped the rope and was about to tilt the motor down into the sea when he spotted me.

He swung his pistol up and took aim. Marie noticed the boat shift and looked up, turned and saw me.

'Let Marie go,' I shouted above the outboard. 'It's over; everyone else on the island knows the score.'

'They don't know shit or they'd be here with you.' He narrowed his eyes and took a step forward. 'I reckon just one loose end to sort out and I can walk right back there. Tell them all about how you cooked up the whole thing. Now back off.' He turned the gun on Marie.

I threw the rock as hard as I could. He wavered, eyes on my arm, and the rock sailing through the air. He made no attempt to dodge; the pitch was low, never any chance of hitting him. I hadn't intended it to.

The rock struck the outboard with a clang, knocking the spinning propeller down into the sea. The pistol cracked just as the motor bit, churning the water, the boat lurched, Hurley staggered. The gunshot went wide, slicing into the sea behind Marie. He dropped the gun in an effort to stop himself pitching over the side as the boat surged forward.

'Jump!' I yelled, but Marie hadn't needed prompting, she was already over the side into the shallow water, scrambling up the pebbles.

The boat shot across the open water. Hurley scrabbled to sit up in the pitching waves. It was already a good twenty metres away, still going. Marie was struggling against the pull of the tide. I hobbled over to haul her up.

A shot rang out, the bullet pinging off the rocks, burying itself in the grass behind us. I looked back at the sea. Hurley was standing in the dinghy, battling against the waves to get a good aim. He was too far away now for an easy shot, and the swell made it impossible. He fired a couple more times before disappearing into the fog. The revs increased, sound dying away as he made good his escape.

'Thanks!' was all she could manage.

'I said you'd be all right, didn't I? Get back to the base, find the others.'

'What if he comes back?'

'He's making for the mainland, he knows we can't follow.'

'God, you're hurt.'

'It's nothing, just scratches.'

'But the anthrax... You need to get clean!'

'No time! Go, tell the others, wait for the evac.'

She set off up the hillside at a sprint.

Hurley knew he was free. The evac was still a while off, and he was halfway across the bay. He'd be feeling pretty safe. Sometimes people are at their most vulnerable when they think they've won. But it wasn't true; there was another way off the island.

Chapter Sixty-eight

The night before, when I'd sat in the bomb crater in the pouring rain arguing with Colonel Holderness on the radio, I'd asked him to send a second launch to pick up the Marines. Then I'd told Bates to leave his boat hidden further round the bay. I'd had a feeling one of the others might decide to make a break from the island rather than wait it out, and it'd seemed prudent to have a backup plan.

I told you the military love their acronyms; IRC, they call these, Inflatable Raiding Craft. A small black rubber dinghy to you and me, similar to an American Zodiac, it had been dragged up onto the grass, and as I approached I could see they'd filled it with rocks to stop it blowing away in the storm. That didn't slow me down too much, and after a couple of minutes' graft I was dragging it over the beach, out onto the water, drifting with the swell.

The bay was still swaddled in a grey duvet. I pulled Kyle's soggy map from my pocket and took a bearing on the rock spit jutting behind me. Gruinard Island ran north to south, with me off the southern tip. If you took a ruler and drew a straight line on the map directly west from my position, after two miles you'd hit the village of Laide.

That tiny settlement I'd seen the day before, with its white-washed cottages and ruined medieval chapel, was the nearest proper landing and mooring on the mainland. It wasn't the nearest point as the crow flies – that was the beach south-east of here, where we'd landed the helicopter – but there was no reason to head for that isolated spot. It led only to that beach and, beyond it, an empty stretch of road that led back to Laide anyway. To get to the nearest patch of civilisation was a choice between a short boat trip and a six-mile walk, or a longer boat trip with no walk. Not really much of a choice; Hurley would be heading across the bay to Laide.

The outboard snorted, spluttering to life on the third pull – not bad in the damp air – and then I was buzzing across the rolling sea as fast as the little motor could propel me. Occasionally the distant rasp of Hurley's outboard made it through the fog but mostly it was smothered. The upside was I was heading into the wind, which meant he wouldn't be able to hear me.

Hurley.

I don't have an inflated opinion of myself, but there were limited people on the island that would have considered taking me on hand-to-hand in the shed, even if it did involve smashing me over the head from behind. That train of thought had led me to remembering that when checking on Ingrid at Camp Vollum, Hurley had gone off to the labs on his own – where I'd later found Gambetta's pistol hidden on the cupboard.

Then on the way back from Camp Vollum, either Hurley or Greenbow had visited the generator shed before going inside – I'd seen their torch just before my run-in with the Marines. Had it been Hurley, dumping a handful of dirt in the fuel, hoping to hasten our departure? At that point he'd known the anthrax sample was secure, thought the plan to frame Demeter had worked perfectly, and that I'd soon drop dead from whatever was in my Scotch – because even though Demeter had been framed, I still knew about the anthrax strain. He probably suspected I'd collapsed somewhere behind them in the storm. But later when it was Clay who died instead, and with the generator about to pack in at any moment, he realised he was running out of time to silence me, resorting to less subtle methods.

I couldn't prove it, but these suspicions had meant I'd fully expected to see Hurley in that comms room. But how had he killed Ingrid and Gambetta?

As I crossed the bay concentrating on Hurley, with the spray in my face waking my brain up, it all swam into focus.

But it wasn't the time for thinking, it was time for action as the rocky coastline emerged from the fog ahead.

On a clear day Laide would have been visible from the island, an easy trip, but I'd had no way of navigating in the thick fog, so had headed in what I'd judged to be roughly a south-westerly direction. Without line of sight or any navigational aids, if I'd sped directly west to the village it was unlikely I'd have hit the jetty. The current would have made sure I arrived at an uninhabited spot, without knowing if the village was to my left or right. I could have wasted ages heading in the wrong direction.

But because I'd crossed the bay diagonally I knew Laide was definitely to my right (or rather, starboard). I angled the IRC and pushed on, bouncing higher now that I was closer to shore, heading directly into the incoming waves. They broke over the bow, swamping the inflatable, soaking me to the skin, but these rugged little things are constructed with more arduous tasks in mind, and the sea was nothing like the previous night. With the rocks and occasional sandy stretches to my left and endless grey to my right, I pushed the outboard to the limit, bouncing higher. I was almost dashed against the rocks a couple of times, and thought about beaching it on the next stretch of sand, but the thunderous roar warned me away.

After several difficult minutes struggling with the waves, trying to avoid being smashed against the sharp rocks, I was beginning to think I'd gone wrong. Surely I'd come too far, and Laide was behind me somehow – the current was stronger than I thought. Then something caught my eye. Hidden in the fog, for a second I thought it was a person down by the water's edge. No, as I drew closer I could see it was a brightly coloured boat. It had started life similar to mine, a larger rigid inflatable dinghy, but had been dragged onto the rocks. One of its bright orange sides was ripped wide open, sloshing with seawater, a scene from a *Jaws* film.

I throttled back, slowing, immediately swept towards the same jagged rocks. I twisted the throttle again and the boat surged forward, just managing to avoid the same fate. The wreck was the boat from the island, no doubt about that, but where was its passenger?

Then the small jetty was there in the fog in front of me. I kept the throttle on full to avoid being driven backwards. Even then, it wasn't making much headway, just a few miles per hour, so I angled straight for it, preparing to beach on the sloping stones. The boat inched closer, slowing, then surged forward on the crest of a wave, and with a horrific grating I was on the jetty.

I jumped into the shallow water, sliding on the algae-covered stone, racing up the slipway as another wave swelled and cascaded off the sides, carrying the boat with it. The outboard droned away into the fog to join Hurley's boat, driven onto the rocks somewhere down the coast.

I stumbled, fell, collapsed to the stone, breathing hard, no worries about toxins here. I almost gave in to exhaustion and stayed right there. Blood pooled under me, from my head, the tear in my side, from a thousand smaller cuts when I'd smashed through the window. How much blood had I lost? I began to worry I didn't have enough left to finish the job.

Self-pity wouldn't do me any favours, and it certainly doesn't pay the bills. *Get up.* I managed it, limping onward, past the brightly painted boats pulled high up next to the lane that led from the shore. Tall bushes flanked a single-track road, leaving nowhere else for Hurley to have gone. I picked up the pace.

After a minute or so I came panting to a larger road, taking the left turn towards the village, jogging parallel to the bay past the scattered houses. None showed signs of disturbance, most still sleeping peacefully, curtains drawn. The gravel-strewn road took its toll, slowing me to a walk. I hopped occasionally to pick stones out of the soles of my feet, breath clouding in front of me as I gasped in the freezing air.

After another couple of minutes the houses started to thicken. I'd reached Laide, and no sign of Hurley. I paused in front of a bungalow as an elderly chap was backing a shiny new electric BMW off his drive.

'Excuse me,' I said between breaths, hands on my knees, 'you haven't seen a mate of mine up this way, have you?'

'You all right, lad?'

I looked down at my bare and bloody feet, my broken bandaged hand, my sodden, bloodstained, soot-blackened clothes, God knows what my face was like.

'Boat problems,' I said.

'You're damn fools to be out fishing in this weather! Aye, there was a lad in his waterproofs.'

'Did he go this way?' I pointed up the road.

'Aye, 'boot ten minutes since.'

I contemplated commandeering his car, or asking for a lift, but I was close now so I waved my thanks and set off again, past more cottages and hardy bushes until the road widened, a neat hedgerow on my right and cliffs to my left. There was nothing in front of me, not a sound. Doubt snuck in but I pressed on regardless.

A squat white building drifted in the fog. I slowed, caution taking over; there was the small matter of a gun, after all. A sign said this was the village store, Post Office, and petrol station. Flashing multi-coloured light spilled from the window, a premature string of Christmas fairy lights illuminating the fog rolling across the gravel. I stepped over a low wall, crossed the front of the shop, peered through a condensation-painted window.

A man was standing with his back to me. I squinted. Possibly Hurley; he'd shed his outer layers, shivering in shirtsleeves. He was talking to someone. I was about to reach for the door handle when he turned. It wasn't Hurley, but a middle-aged stranger. He saw me at the same time and cried out, rushing to block the door.

I shouldered it, barging it open, sweeping him aside. The little bell above the door jangled and crashed to the floor. A woman screamed, ducking behind the counter. 'I've already called the police!' she cried as a mug of tea smashed.

The man looked about desperately and grabbed a can of beans from the shelves. 'Get out!' he shouted, holding it up ready to throw.

I stepped back, holding up my hands. 'I don't want any trouble. I'm looking for someone; I presume he's been through here?'

'Yer friend's long gone,' said the man. 'And you'd best follow him. Police'll be here any minute.'

'I am the police.'

The man put the can down. 'Well get after him, then, he stole my Landy!' I noticed he wore a Royal Mail shirt.

'Postal Land Rover?'

'Aye, and four bags of post.'

'Came barging in here with a gun,' said the woman.

'Took ma keys and left.' The postie was looking me up and down, as if he'd only just realised what a state I was. 'Hey, just what kind of policeman are you?' he asked.

'The only kind there is right now.' I peeled the ragged sweater off.

'Undercover, like?' His eyes widened as he took in the old scars and new wounds, my body held together by a few strips of duct tape and sheer determination.

'Something like that.' I looked at the woman still half crouching behind the till. 'I presume he used your phone?'

'Your boat go down?' she asked. 'You need an ambulance?' She pulled a cordless from under the counter.

I shook my head, reached over and took it, pulled up the last numbers dialled. I frowned, putting the phone down on the counter. I walked around the aisles, grabbing a 'Scotland' hoody from a shelf, the kind sold to tourists, pulled it on. 'What head start has he got?'

'Not ten minutes. It's a serious offence, you know, inter-fering with the postal service.'

'And so's stealing,' said the woman, pointing at the hoody. 'You gonna pay for that?'

'You'll have to bill the government.' I took a can of Coke from a fridge.

'The government!' the postie said. 'I told you, Annie, you don't mess with the Royal Mail. Robbing the post at gunpoint! They'll throw away the key, and too bloody right.'

'Which way did he go?' I asked.

'Off in the direction of Mungasdale. Heading for Inverness, I'll bet.'

I downed the can of pop in one and pulled out the soggy map, unfolding it on the counter, asking the postman to point out the road Hurley had taken. I took grid references, scribbled them on the map, and picked up the phone again. Time to call in the cavalry.

'Just need to make a call outside, okay? It's local.'

It wasn't local. The call was answered after just a couple of rings. It was quick, no arguments, and a minute later I was in the shop handing back the phone.

'He has ma truck and a gun, how are you gonna arrest him?' asked the postie.

I picked up a Mars bar and winked. 'Oh, I'm not gonna arrest him.'

'Don't you need a licence to kill?' He thought I was joking.

I shook my head. 'Just a gun.' I folded the map and opened the door, then paused to point at his Doc Martens. 'What size are they?'

Chapter Sixty-nine

I left the shop with the postman staring open-mouthed after me. He must have thought I intended to hike the seventy-five miles to Inverness. No need for that, I knew what Hurley's plan was.

I jogged around the side of the building. I hadn't stumbled upon it by chance – I'd done my homework, had a decent knowledge of the layout of the village, the geography, surrounding roads. In those few hours at Faslane with Colonel Holderness we'd agreed a rough plan, which included a contingency. Like I said, I like to have a backup plan.

A dirt parking area ran alongside and behind the shop, opposite the petrol pumps. Tucked up close to the building, next to the bottles of gas and bags of coal, was a filthy Mk2 Ford Capri, which should have been bright blue but was now mostly brown, caked in Scottish mud.

Long and low, hunkered close to the ground on fat wheels under huge flared wheel arches, even stationary it looked tense, ready to pounce. My personal pride and joy, the car I'd driven up to Scotland night before last, which Bates had obviously taken immense pleasure in driving through every pile of horse-shit and muddy verge between here and Glasgow. He'd parked it, making out to be a tourist hiking locally, around the time I'd been on the beach inspecting Kyle's body. I envied the drive he'd had; past Loch Lomond, up through Glencoe, along the northern shore of Loch Ness. Through towns with names like Auchterawe and Drumnadrochit, unpronounceable with my

Yorkshire tongue and all the better for it. What I'd have given to have driven here rather than suffer that flying fucking deathtrap.

I know what you're thinking: why is a spy driving a Capri older than himself? Well, like I said, I'm not a spy – I'm self-employed, and this is my own car. Secondly, if they did, it'd be something mundane and ill-suited to high speed, the government doesn't stretch to custom Aston Martins. Good thing, too, even a bright blue Capri is a damn sight less conspicuous.

I knelt by the rear wheel and crept my fingers under the valance to locate a tiny magnetic box right where I'd asked Bates to leave it. I pulled it free, brushed off the mud, removed the key.

First, I opened the boot, grateful for my foresight in leaving my trusty custom Barbour motorbike jacket in there. It's old, it's battered, I've worn it from deserts to the Arctic and all the oceans in between, which is why I hadn't wanted it on the island getting covered in anthrax. I shrugged it on over the hoody, zipped it up and lifted the boot carpet. Always outnumbered but never outgunned, Bates had seen me right. A short, boxy-looking rifle was sitting on the spare wheel, freshly serviced, gleaming. An SA80, the new A3 version just like Marine Jarrett had carried last night. I left it where it was, concentrating instead on the bundle next to it, which revealed a shiny new Glock 17. I checked it was loaded and slammed the boot.

Next, I popped the bonnet, reconnected the battery lead, good to go. I winked at the engine, kissed my fingers and ran them over the NISSAN lettering embossed across the twin-cam head, a stupid sentimental gesture but she could be defiant sometimes and I needed her good graces that morning.

It worked, the engine roared on the first twist of the key, settling to a burble. As I adjusted the hugging Bride bucket seat, the speakers blasted that old Prodigy tune with the Nirvana riff. While the Neanderthal Bates had been just about able to slide the seat back, I guessed he hadn't been able to work the stereo, he'd been stuck with my music all the way here. I blipped the throttle a few times, she barked angrily at being awoken so early, I gripped the wheel, watching the revs rise and fall. The postie's boots were stiff and too small, pinching my toes, which wouldn't be great for heel-toe pedal action, but beggars can't be choosers. I left the volume up loud; the music was as good a soundtrack as any for fast driving.

I watched the needle of the petrol gauge creep round, pushed the stick into first, and lifted the clutch. It wrenched violently – launching a storm of muddy gravel – out onto the road, climbing through the gears and up the speedometer. I winced, feeling the additional wear on the engine, no time for warmup.

Let loose, the engine howled like a wounded beast, a whoosh and flutter accompanying every gear change with an additional crackle on every downshift, popping and snarling, hot petrol on cold exhaust. Only a two-litre engine under the bonnet, this was obviously not the range-topping V6 model. The badging on the engine gave the game away, but even an onlooker could tell the car was far from standard by the twin black streaks burned into the road – a Nissan SR20DET engine, if you want to get technical, if you don't then you just need to know it's potent. Sacrilege to most Ford fans, this newer Japanese heart had come from a mate's drift car and rather than grumble, the turbo screamed and sucked in foggy air as the needle climbed to ninety. I dropped into second with a crack of flame from the exhaust, burying the brakes, feeling the back of the car lighten, the limited slip differential bite as I accelerated through a corner, heading straight again towards the mountains, sea to my left, endless moor on my right.

A puddle was deeper than I'd anticipated and the Capri drifted, but thankfully the wide tyres chirped and grabbed just enough tarmac to keep me out of the ditch. The road was greasy from torrential rain and hours of fog rolling off the sea; I drove as fast as I dared. It should have been easy to catch a Land Rover but I had to slow and pull over at every farmer's track and dirt road turn-off to check for any signs of Hurley's passing. Didn't want to overtake him without realising.

The Americans. Our allies, but I guess even between friends some things are worth the risk. Their own biological and chemical weapons programme, outwardly disavowed in the UN, was the most advanced in the world. The UK, France, China, Russia, Israel, several Middle Eastern countries and half of Korea; there are a handful of countries that would kill to get their hands on this new strain of anthrax. The United States topped the list.

They *had* killed to get it.

About a hundred and twenty miles south by road lay the village of Spean Bridge, site of the Allied Forces' Commando Training Depot during the Second World War. Special Forces units still train in the nearby lochs and mountains, and somewhere down there a couple of companies of US Marines were currently on manoeuvres. I had no doubt that that was where Hurley was headed. From there he could easily transfer to an American airbase and be stateside before British Intelligence knew what had happened. And there'd be no proof, no way of connecting anything together – and importantly, no way of actually proving the Americans had the new strain of anthrax. Plucked from the soil right under our noses. But it was more than that – he'd get away with murder. And let's not forget he'd tried to cook me, poison me, bludgeon me, shoot me, and drown me – in that order.

Hurley didn't plan to drive the hundred and twenty miles down to Spean Bridge; I'd checked the numbers on the Post Office phone, knew he'd called his contact. A hundred and twenty miles by twisty country roads but only fifty or so by air, no distance at all for a Black Hawk helicopter. It'd seek out the road then fly low, hugging the valleys until it picked up the bright red Post Office Land Rover.

I ground the accelerator deeper into the carpet.

Chapter Seventy

The sun was up now and trying its best to burn off the fog as I tore along the A832. Glimpses of rocky outcrops rising from a sea of brown heather were snatched away as low clouds rolled across the landscape, parting again to reveal pine copses and endless moorland. Occasionally dark distant peaks beckoned me on before they too were swallowed by grey. As I drove on autopilot I thought about Ingrid's murder, how it was key to everything.

Everyone had an absolutely cast-iron alibi for Ingrid's murder, except for two people; Gambetta, who we'd ruled out as we knew he was in the radio room, and Demeter. It was logical and obvious that only Demeter could possibly have killed Ingrid.

It was meant to appear logical and obvious, because it hid the fact that there was one person on the island who we'd never suspected. Because you don't check a victim's alibi.

Gambetta was the only person on the island who could have killed Ingrid.

If the radio operator on the ship was expecting a French voice at precisely seven o'clock and that's what he heard, then he'll swear it was Gambetta, the only French man in the base. Hurley had left the common room for a short while -- not enough time to kill Ingrid, but it had been enough time to cover for Gambetta on the radio.

A random Terrorvision song came on, pulling me back to the road, the rev counter, the speedo. I smiled as I pictured Bates enduring five hours of shuffled iPod hidden behind the dash then switched the stereo off, content to concentrate on the revs, the whining turbo, the crackling exhaust.

I crested a hill with Little Loch Broom racing along on my left. I powered through the cluster of houses at Badcaul and the picturesque village of Camusnagaul, and still I hadn't caught the Land Rover. Doubts crept in again; unless he was a pro racer I should have caught him by now. Had I gone the wrong way? Missed some small turn-off, a hidden farm track? Maybe Hurley knew the area better than I'd thought. Or maybe he'd doubled back and headed directly south through Aultbea. Maybe he had a landing area pre-planned and scouted in advance.

No. His method of transferring the anthrax off the island was to have it hidden in the base when it was shipped away, himself hidden in plain sight among the group of scientists. He hadn't planned this escape, so didn't know the area any better than I did. He thought he'd got away, no one following. This was the quickest and easiest route. He had to be on this road.

The fences racing alongside me were broken by tracks, but each time I'd slowed to check a side track or pull-off I was satisfied that the Land Rover hadn't disturbed them, that it still motored away somewhere just ahead. I did a quick circuit of the Dundonnell Hotel before moving on, the road curving uphill, sporadic trees flashing alongside until soon it was a thick forest clawing out to form a canopy above the road. The tall pines would have obscured any view, even without the fog; no place to land a helicopter.

I used one hand to unfold the map on the passenger seat. Even on the straights the wheel demanded constant attention, minute adjustments as the tyres sought grip, keeping me from bouncing through potholes and flying through the fence. I narrowly avoided a ditch on a corner that tightened more than I'd anticipated, accelerating into the next straight as I split my attention between the map and the road. I almost wished this was a new Aston Martin; I could have done with traction control and satnav.

I stood on the brakes; a shriek of tortured rubber, the aroma of burning brake pads. Throwing open the door, I jogged back along the road. A filthy plastic suit, flapping shreds impaled on the barbed-wire fence. Hurley had disposed of it, probably chucked it out of his window, he was definitely somewhere on this road. I carefully peeled it off the spikes between finger and thumb and carried it back to my car, pushing it into the passenger footwell to avoid spreading spores halfway across the valley. I ran back with a piece of rope from my boot, tying it to the fence as a marker for the cleaning crew.

Another quick look at the map and I was off again. By my reckoning, I'd come about halfway to where this small road joined with the larger trunk road linking Ullapool and Inverness. The trees thinned, replaced by a looming wall of rock in the distance. The road twisted, rising higher until there were no trees left. The last glimpse of countryside reminded me of my native Yorkshire moors, then I was driving through cloud – forced to slow or risk plunging off the road into a muddy ditch or worse as the fog lifted one second then obliterated anything beyond twenty feet the next.

I stamped on the brakes again, sliding sideways across the white lines, switching the ignition off this time. Just the pinging engine, the overworked radiator and red-hot exhaust manifold cooling down. I jumped out and ran a few metres further down the road.

Faint, but definitely mechanical; an engine somewhere on the road up ahead. Distances were impossible to judge but *someone* was driving *something*. I ran back to the car and started her up again, driving slowly this time, winding the window down. Hurley wouldn't be driving recklessly; he had a multimillion-dollar vial in his pocket and no reason to think anyone was on his tail.

A National Trust for Scotland sign flashed past, 'Corrieshalloch Gorge' – I was coming up on the junction, fast. Soon the road would be bigger, relatively more traffic. I flicked off my headlights, it was foggy but light enough; in conditions like that headlights are for the benefit of other road users, and I definitely didn't want to be seen.

I turned a corner and there, fuzzy in the fog for less than a second before it winked out, was a dim red dot. I counted aloud; one, two, three, all the way to eleven – then slowed for a left-hander. Average thirty miles per hour on the twisting road, eleven seconds – my maths wasn't great at the best of times but I guessed I was about a hundred and fifty metres behind the brake lights.

I pressed the accelerator, exiting the bend to see the same dim red dot ahead. I pressed the accelerator even harder, the red dot grew brighter in the haze, splitting into two.

I was worried it'd be a tractor, but a few seconds later, and to my relief, I could see it was a Land Rover – not out of the ordinary in the Highlands, but this one was bright red. I pulled closer, could see it had no rear side windows, a short-wheelbase wagon. The logo on the back panel confirmed it belonged to the Royal Mail.

Chapter Seventy-one

I guessed there couldn't be more than one Post Office Land Rover on this road, hoped I wasn't victimising an innocent postie. We turned a corner, straightened up, the fog grew thicker – now or never. I dropped into third, pressing the accelerator fully to the floor. The engine roared, the turbo whined as it came on boost, and a second later I was right up behind him. He hadn't seen me before, but a puff of diesel smoke from his exhaust indicated he just had, and was accelerating to match.

I closed the distance, less than a metre from his bumper, when red lights glared in my face. The view of the 4x4 was replaced by a crash barrier as he disappeared around a sharp right-hander. I was carrying far too much speed to make it. I buried the brakes, the back end lifted, into second and I flicked the wheel left *towards* the crash barriers before slamming my foot back down on the accelerator, spinning the wheel around to the right. The wheels broke traction, the back end of the Capri slid ninety degrees into the middle of the road, bonnet facing straight into the dismal moorland. I kept my foot planted, tyres arguing and revs bouncing off the limiter as I drifted sideways through the corner. Something jolted me, a spray of paint flecks and a chunk of wheel-arch flashed in the rear view mirror, torn off by the crash barrier, tumbling across the road. I played the pedals, the wheels found grip, I was straight again and pointing at the Land Rover.

I'd lost speed, he was already pulling away, but no way could he outrun me. His only advantage – and it was a pretty bloody big one – was that he could see the corners coming; the closer

I got behind him, the blinder I was. I swept wet hair away from my eyes, felt blood, sticky across the side of my head, flicked my full beams on to dazzle him, and ground the accelerator harder.

I was almost on him again when his brake lights flashed and he turned left. I'd been more cautious, ready for it, negotiating the corner gracefully this time without losing any more parts. As we straightened I was still hovering a few metres off his bumper.

Something appeared out of his window, I yanked the wheel left, losing the passenger wing mirror on the crash barriers but avoiding the bullet that exploded from Hurley's pistol. *My* Speer hollow points from *my* HK, the bastard. The crack of the gunshot was quickly muffled by the fog.

I kept left to avoid any more, digging under the map on the passenger seat, grabbing the Glock. With one hand on the wheel and both eyes on his bumper, I pushed the pistol against the dash, digging the foresight into the spongy material. I cocked it by pressing forward and down on the handgrip, then tossed it into my right hand as I yanked the wheel with my other, pulling into the middle of the road. Sticking the pistol out of the window, I squeezed the trigger three times rapidly, then swung back in behind. Cubes of glass and flecks of red flew past my arm. Another shot replied from in front and this time it connected, ricocheting off the bonnet and shattering the top corner of the windscreen, but I didn't flinch – because when I'd pulled out I'd got a good look at the road ahead, and an opportunity had presented itself. I dropped the pistol into my lap, gripped the wheel, locked my jaw.

Hurley's brake lights flared. I dropped into second gear. The revs jumped, the back end of the car floated, but I kept the accelerator planted, pulling right across onto the other side of the road, as if to overtake. The corner came up fast, far too fast for me to stop, I was heading straight into the gorge, about to fly into it, bracing myself for a short flight through the trees. The gamble paid off as Hurley turned right in front of me, beginning to take the corner; a fatal mistake.

I made zero attempt to negotiate the corner, staying straight, letting him turn across my path. *Je me lance vers la gloire.* I pulled the gearstick into neutral at the last moment as the Capri sailed directly into the side of the Land Rover, connecting at ninety degrees with the rear wheel. I had one of the longest expanses of bonnet on the road, acres of crash-absorbing space behind the radiator to cushion the collision, whereas the Landy took the full impact through the solid rear axle, straight into the chassis.

The Land Rover was lifted into the air and I had a glimpse of Hurley's face, staring in disbelief through the open window, before it rolled up onto the crash barrier.

The seatbelt tore into my chest, whipping my head forward. I was staring at the underside of the big 4x4 – and it looked extremely bloody close. It hung in mid-air for a second then rocked back, I pointed my pistol straight forward, through the windscreen, and squeezed the trigger again and again. My windscreen exploded in a jagged spiderweb, cubes of glass spraying as I emptied the magazine into the underside of the Landy. It fell towards me, a buckled and twisted rear wheel slamming back down onto the bonnet of my car.

An arm flailed at the driver's window, still gripping the gun. I ducked as a bullet ripped into the Capri, punching a hole through the roof and into the passenger seat. I dropped the empty Glock, pressed the seatbelt release, sliding down into the footwell. My engine was still running. I pushed into first gear, full on the accelerator with my other hand, just as another gunshot made more of a mess of my roof, the bullet tearing into the driver's seat inches from my head.

The engine howled. I risked a glance to see the Landy tip sideways, teetering on the crash barrier. The Capri's rear tyres complained, spinning up and sending a cloud of stinking black smoke across the road. Keeping crouched down in the footwell I quickly changed into second, then third. The speedometer climbed, eighty miles an hour stationary, tyres screaming, edging the Land Rover further over the abyss. There was another explosion, not a gunshot this time, a tyre giving way. The car lurched, screeching metal tearing the air. A jolt as the other tyre blew, I raised my head to watch the Land Rover shudder, reach the point of no return, then slowly tip.

I twisted the key, cutting my engine as the Landy groaned and slipped off the barrier, tumbling down the slope beyond.

I leapt from the car. Sounds of twisting metal and ripping bushes echoed up from the gorge. Dirty snowflakes drifted in the fog, scraps of burnt rubber. Twin black channels were chewed into the tarmac beneath the Capri's mangled wheels. I'd have to bill Holderness for a new set of alloys as well as tyres. Stinking, steaming water pooled around my boots. I looked at the front of the car, its concertinaed bonnet. Much as I enjoy rebuilding my cars, I'd probably need to bill him for a whole new Capri.

One foot on the crash barrier, I stared into the grey, listening to glass smashing in the woods below as the stricken Land Rover continued its journey. I ran back to grab the rifle from the boot, pushed the spare mag into one of the ammo pouches sewn into my jacket, and pressed the SA80's stock into the well-worn reinforced shoulder patch. The cocking lever pulled with a satisfying click. I released, remembering to tap it forward with the ball of my thumb, ensuring it was fully home to avoid stoppages, then pushed the safety off and jumped the barrier.

No way of knowing how deep the gorge was, or how steep. I crept quickly but cautiously, rifle to my shoulder, following deep furrows torn in the grass. A shattered windscreen lay against a bush; I hoped the roof had crumpled, saving me a job, but knowing Landys I highly doubted it; I've rolled several and come away without a scratch. A crash nearby, something flapped past my head and I ducked instinctively. Another flash of white in the bushes spun me round. Letters. A postbag appeared out of the rolling fog, spewing its contents into the wind. They fluttered across the undergrowth like birds dancing across the bracken.

As I stalked onward, a red shape emerged from the fog. The rear door, torn from its hinges and bent almost in half. I kept my gun up, advancing slowly down the hill.

The Land Rover finally materialised, lying on its side against a sturdy-looking pine on the edge of the woodland. From what I could see the roof had taken the brunt of the impact, wrapping around the trunk. On what was now the top, the driver's door was shut. No movement. As I rounded the back I looked down each side. Still nothing. I crept closer.

The open rear doorway revealed an empty interior. With one eye on the fog I scanned the ground. A heavy depression marked where he'd dropped down seconds earlier. A few drops of blood spattered the grass, but my hopes of having inflicted a mortal wound were looking slim.

Unlike the open moorland, it was sheltered here under the trees, the ground springy with mossy undergrowth. No footprints, no way to track him. What would I do if I were Hurley?

He'd left the island in a rush, no map, food, or suitable clothing – a death sentence out here this time of year. No way of contacting his evac. He knew I was close, couldn't be sure what backup was on the way. For all he knew the net was closing – every minute he spent wandering the highlands was a minute closer to capture. Hurley only had one play left – head back to the road, keep his rendezvous. The Capri was a write-off so on the face of it, transport-wise, we were in the same boat. No chance of him hijacking another car; wouldn't be much traffic at this time in the morning.

I headed deeper into the woods then turned back up the hillside, towards the road. The wind had died, creaking trees and the nearby river the only soundtrack. I walked parallel to the road, deeper still, eyes on stalks, trying to pick anything out of the murk. The ground grew steeper, the undergrowth denser.

A twig snapped nearby, freezing me to the spot. I dropped to a crouch, ears straining. A dragging sound, shuffling through the bracken, pushing through the bushes, heading for the road. I held my breath, rifle rigid. This was my home environment, and I'd be damned if I'd let Hurley get the upper hand here.

A bush to my left shuddered. I swung around as a shape materialised from the fog. I felt an involuntary twitch in my index finger, a reaction borne of experience. It automatically slid onto the trigger, taking up precisely the amount of play in the firing mechanism, the lightest breath ready to launch a bullet straight between Hurley's eyes.

The fog rolled on and there before me was the largest stag I've ever seen. It lifted its head from the grass, seeing me at the same moment, jaw frozen. For a couple of seconds we regarded each other with mutual suspicion, neither of us moving, then the stag went back to its meal. I was in two minds whether to press on – I'm okay dealing with soldiers, but huge wild animals can be dangerous, less predictable. I was armed, but as a rule I don't shoot anything that's unable to shoot back.

I was about take my chances with the antlers when the stag picked its head up again, sniffing the air. It'd caught a scent, but not mine; I was upwind. We both froze again. Suddenly it reared, turned, bolted back into the fog, the trembling bushes the only evidence it was here.

Downwind. I spun to my right, squeezing the trigger.

A single crack, a shout, snapping branches. A crow barked, taking flight through the branches. I flicked the fire selector down to 'A', pummelled the bushes with a deafening automatic burst, rolling to my left just as a bullet came the other way. Another chewed up the dirt as I got to my feet, running deeper into the undergrowth, into the bullets.

He was shooting blindly behind, I continued, firing again, still on auto. He stumbled, I thought I'd grazed his leg but then my rifle clicked, I was out of ammo and the fog was rolling back. I carried on running through the trees, down the steep hillside, dropping the empty magazine and inserting my spare. Bark exploded as brass and lead smashed into a nearby tree. I replied with a short burst then crouched to listen.

The river was louder now. Nothing else; once again the world was obscured by silently dancing ghosts. A spot of blood on a leaf, another on a branch, Hurley had in a hole in him somewhere. Keeping the sights trained on the bushes, I reached back and flicked the selector up to 'R', single-shot mode. I turned slowly, rifle hard into my shoulder. No trees to my right, just swirling fog, water booming nearby; I was on the edge of the gorge itself.

I walked closer and chanced a look over. Dark vertical walls punctuated by saplings growing out at crazy angles and then nothing but grey. Looking into that abyss made my head swim again. Nowhere for Hurley to have gone.

I followed the edge as closely as I dared until something appeared in the fog, regular, man-made. I slowed. A bit of wall and fence to stop tourists lemming off. A yellow sign told me the cliff was unstable, to stick to the path. I could have done with that advice before I'd leaned over.

But it wasn't the sign that'd caught my eye; it was the thin smear of blood on the stone, diluted by drizzle, revealing where Hurley had rested seconds before.

I pressed on, towards the thundering water, following the well-trodden footpath, looking out for any other tell-tale signs of Hurley's passing. A spot on the ground, a few metres later another on the fence as he'd brushed against it.

A structure loomed, thin and snaking like a modern sculpture, at odds with its surroundings. Twisted steel cables suspending skinny iron latticework stretching out into space, a narrow footbridge to nothing. I moved cautiously towards it, rifle trained on the misty void where the other side of the gorge should be.

I walked round the concrete and iron supports, onto the gravel path, looking straight down the bridge. A smear on the metal handrail, more blood on the wooden treads. Hurley had crossed over, probably waiting for me on the other side. Classic tactic; a choke point, forcing me into an ambush. I had no other options. I could taste the water on the breeze, metallic, full and earthy, drifting up from the waterfall.

I stepped onto the bridge and slid on the slick boards, gritting my teeth as pain tore up my side. I cried out, dropping the rifle with a clatter and landing against the railing, panting heavily. Warm wetness spread under my jacket and a drop of my own red splashed the wood next to Hurley's. I looked frantically at the footpath and trees moving in and out of the fog behind me, at the sheer edge either side, at the wall of fog swaddling the bridge in front. No shouts, no shots, just the thunder of water on rock below.

I struggled to my feet and retrieved the rifle, pushed my hair up, wiping sweat, blood, and drizzle from my eyes. The crow called out again. I was blind, injured and out of energy, my only solace that Hurley was all of those things too. The crows mocked us both from the branches.

And then there was another sound. Quiet at first, difficult to hear over the waterfall, I thought it was a car up on the road. It quickly got too loud; the familiar whump-whump-whump of rotor blades. The crows held their breath, waiting to see what would happen. I didn't, dispensing with caution, lurching after the new sound, away from the bridge. The thumping rotors were close.

I'd been right; the helicopter was approaching from the north. It had flown up the coast then followed the road down to us. Despite the weather it'd have no problem finding us – it would be equipped with thermographic equipment. If he hadn't already, the pilot would soon spot the two cars and try to find somewhere to land.

The footpath narrowed and curved. I staggered along it for a while, putting some distance between me and the bridge, then turned back to it, crouching in the weeds. The helicopter was deafening now. It would aim for the vehicles. Hurley would need to get to it – which meant he'd have to cross that bridge. Like I said, classic choke point.

I crept forward, working myself into a ditch, rifle up, short barrel jutting through the ferns. Freezing stream water trickled underneath me, eating into my legs, but I didn't move. Blood flowed from reopened wounds, warmth soaking into the waistband of my trousers, but I stayed rock-steady. The rifle was sticky with blood against my cheek as I squinted down the sights, watching the little red dot dancing along the bridge, bright against the dirty haze.

The helicopter roared overheard, whipping the bushes, churning the stream. I was worried it hadn't spotted the cars but the pilot banked, bringing it slowly back up the road. It paused to hover over the gorge, shaking the branches of the trees, stirring the fog, kicking up gravel, pulling on the sleeves of my jacket. I thought about the observer looking down through that thermal imager, realised he could probably see both of us but wouldn't have a clue what was going on. The helicopter jinked side to side a few times then backed off, looking for a spot to set down. I remained motionless. I was done in, my arms ached, I started trembling, but I kept my finger on the trigger, kept up the pressure, ready to release a bullet. I was looking down the bridge, at the woodland and rocks fading into the fog.

The pitch of the rotors increased, they were setting down somewhere up by the road. *Time's up.*

The rotors whined, the breeze blew, the fog lifted, for a couple of seconds I could see the trees on the other side of the gorge. A bloodied Hurley limped cautiously down the middle of the bridge, arms outstretched, gun ready, barrel pointing in my direction.

A flash, he'd already fired. So had I. A bullet drilled the bushes beside me, another slammed into the dirt. Too far for accuracy on his part, no point in me hiding, I'd the same chance of being hit wherever I was. I crouched in place, my rifle trading fire with a less accurate pistol. Another flash, the bullet ricocheting off a rock behind me. Grass and dirt exploded across my face as a batch of lead smacked the path centimetres from my head. I didn't blink, just switched to auto and replied with rapid bursts, emptying the last of the magazine into the bridge.

The bullets stopped, the fog rolled back across the gorge.

I jumped up, sprinting into the murk. Seconds later I was on the bridge, walking into the void with the rifle still held high. I'd emptied the mag, but Hurley wasn't to know that; if by any chance he was still alive this would give him pause.

The bridge bowed under my weight, trembling with each step. Deep gouges in the wood showed where my bullets had ricocheted, some had gone clean through the boards, creating splintered holes straight down into the waterfall. Some had gone through Hurley first, sprays of blood and red boot prints; he couldn't be far. A section of safety fence had caught a round and been torn loose, and suddenly the trembling bridge didn't feel that permanent. I crept onward, doing my best to avoid the bullet-weakened planks that creaked and bent under my boots.

I found Hurley slumped over the fence just past the middle, his life force pooled under him and dripping down into the abyss. My pistol lay a few metres away. He wasn't moving.

I advanced steadily, gun first. His postie jacket didn't move, only his hair ruffling slightly in the breeze. A hole in the jacket dribbled blood down his back. I prodded it, but still nothing. Keeping the gun on him I circled, leaning away, pressing myself into the opposite barrier, out of reach.

As I rounded him I could see why he wasn't moving. His right arm hung uselessly, jacket shredded where multiple bullets had pulverised the shoulder and forced him to drop the gun. Another through the torso, a bloody tear in his jeans. A & E couldn't do anything for him, but I didn't feel sorry for the bastard.

I held the rifle with one hand, creeping the fingers of my free hand into his coat pocket. Nothing; I tried the other, but that was empty too. I moved closer and reached into the inside pocket, and there was the vial.

I didn't feel the slice across my skin, or the blood running freely down my arm, it was the flash that caught my eye as he withdrew the knife. My hand automatically sprang open before I could pull the vial clear, the rifle fell. His eyes opened, furious, mouth twisted, ready to slash again. I clutched my fingers, backing away, finally feeling the blood hot against my cold skin.

He swung the knife with his good arm but it was lazy, he couldn't move, propped up by the railing. I didn't give him any recovery time, picking up the rifle and slamming the butt into his face, forcing him back against the rails. I went for the inside pocket but up came the knife again. I swung the rifle at his wrist like a bat, he grunted, the knife fell straight between the planks. His good leg came up into my ribs, I winced. He used his bulk to heave off the railings, pressing all his weight onto me. I slammed against the metal safety rail, felt it dig into my spine, driving the wind from my lungs. I dropped the rifle. He moved his weight closer, edging upwards. My feet left the ground, the railing grating down my back. Near the base of my spine now, he pushed. I felt my centre of gravity edge over the gorge.

I wrapped an arm around his neck and yanked him backwards over the abyss with me. He panicked, letting go of me, leaning away, scrabbling at the railings with his only functioning arm. I grabbed the railing and caught myself, twisting under his arm as he slumped further forward. I used the momentum to heave his legs, tipping them over the rail.

He screamed as he slid further, but couldn't fight back, could do nothing to stop it; he had no choice but to keep gripping the railing with his only good arm. His legs went, dragging his body after, leaving him dangling from one hand. His face was white, eyes boring into mine, fingers locked around the railing. His boots kicked at the bridge as he struggled to get his toes on the lip.

I picked up my HK pistol from the boards where he'd dropped it, hefted it, slid out the magazine. Nickel glinted just like it had yesterday morning; still loaded.

Hurley whimpered, fingers slowly stretching on the hand-rail. I knelt to face him, could feel his breath, panting, shallow, eyes wide with terror. I reached through the railings into his inside jacket pocket, pulling the vial free. I stood, stepped back, watching his fingers extend. He managed to get one foot on the slippery railing and tried to pull himself up. I aimed my pistol at his head and slowly started to squeeze the trigger.

'Don't you want to know how?' he gurgled, blood running from his mouth.

I eased off the trigger and lowered the pistol. He smiled, getting his other foot on the railing and hauling himself upright, ready to climb over.

'Tell it to Ingrid.' I smiled back and slammed a boot into his knuckles, then leaned over to watch him drop into the grey.

The crows were silent as he disappeared from view. No screams, no sound at all as he spread himself across the rocks below.

I slumped to my knees, resting the pistol on the planks, feeling the weight of the last few hours pressing down. I closed my eyes, focused on the crashing waterfall and the wind in the pines, the creaking planks beneath me, anything to take my mind off the blood trickling down my arms, dripping from the inside of my jacket.

'John Tyler?' a voice called from behind me. 'You do get around.'

I turned slowly, staggering to my feet, gun up. A tall man, immaculate in a well-cut suit, was standing on the gravel path. I squinted down the pistol at his crisp white shirt flapping in the breeze. My peripheral vision picked up assault rifles either side of him. The US Marines holding them drifted in and out of the wall of fog.

Chapter Seventy-two

We stared at each other, just a few metres of bridge separating us.

'You're a long way from Langley, Mason,' I said finally, gun still on him but wavering as my muscles burned.

He smiled, made a show of looking around. 'We're a long way from anywhere, Tyler.'

Each of the Marines carried a duffel bag, which they dropped at his feet before taking another step forward to block the bridge.

'You used to take the piss out of my suits,' I said. 'I heard the CIA had finally dragged you behind a desk.'

'And I heard you'd gone back to chasing cards across the Middle East.'

He meant the 'Personality Identification Playing Cards' – packs of cards issued to the US military during the Iraq war to help them identify the most-wanted members of Saddam Hussein's government. There'd been good money to be made tracking them down – bringing them to Mason.

'You're gonna do this, after what we went through in Mosul?' My gun was really shaking now. I flexed my fingers and gripped the gun more firmly so the Marines wouldn't notice and mistake it for fear.

'Business, Tyler, just the same.'

He buttoned his suit jacket to stop it flapping. The helicopter whined somewhere in the distance. The crow regained its bravado, cawing again.

'Hurley's taking a swim?' Mason asked, peering into the gorge.

I shrugged. 'An accident.'

'I never liked him anyway, however, I think you took something from him?'

I glared, fist clenched tightly around the vial. His face hardened.

'Give me my sample.'

'Yours?'

'You took it from an American. I represent his estate.'

'He took it from Scotland. Go back to Virginia.'

There was a rustle in the bushes and a third Marine appeared further down the gorge, rifle trained on me. Another appeared out of the fog in the corner of my left eye. Outflanked, outnumbered, outgunned.

'This'll be difficult for you to explain to Washington,' I said.

'It'll be easier if you're dead,' he replied, casual as ever.

'Maybe, but you'll have to explain the dead Marines too.'

The Marines either side of him visibly flinched. I calculated the odds, wondered how many shots I could get off, whether I could back off the bridge into the fog before those M27 assault rifles opened up. The odds didn't look great.

A radio crackled, the Marine to Mason's left leaned in. 'Aircraft inbound, ETA six minutes.'

Mason nodded, eyes not leaving mine. 'Let's wrap it up.' All four Marines took a step forward.

I thrust my left hand out into space, holding the vial between finger and thumb. 'Shoot me and you lose this.'

The Marines froze.

Mason sighed, weighing things up. After a long few seconds he tapped one of the bags with his foot. 'As we're pressed for time, I can offer an alternative.'

'How much of an alternative?'

'They'd negotiated enough to get away.'

I could feel my energy draining from various wounds, knew I couldn't keep my arms outstretched for long. I nodded. 'I prefer that option.'

A wide smile broke across his face. 'Less mess.'

The Marines breathed. I stood the vial at my feet and slowly backed away, switching the gun onto it. He muttered to the Marine on his right, who shouldered his rifle and picked up the duffel bags, carrying them to the centre of the bridge. I nodded and gestured with the gun. He carefully put them down, picked up the vial gingerly, and reversed off the bridge into the fog.

Mason stepped up onto the bridge and signalled to the remaining Marines. They melted away, leaving us facing each other alone. I looked round, smiled, and finally lowered the gun.

'Dirty bastard,' I said as I limped forward. He ran to catch me, holding his arms out in an embrace, slapping me on the back. I winced.

'I wasn't surprised to get your call,' he said, drawing back, looking me up and down properly. 'Jeez, you really look like death.'

'You had me going, why the theatrics?'

He grinned and pointed toward where the helicopter whined up on the road. 'When those guys debrief they'll say I at least *tried* to play hardball. They don't know you like I do; they don't know you have no loyalties. Apart from this...' He kicked one of the bags with an expensive Italian shoe and I pushed it behind me with a scuffed Doc Marten.

'Well I know you too,' I said. 'Don't lecture me on morality.'

'Hey, I'm a good patriot. I'm working for my country here.'

'Five people dead, Mason; supposedly your allies.'

He shrugged. 'You've done us a favour, Hurley was an asshole. And you know we only specify the ends, not the means.'

'You should have told me – I could have prevented those deaths.'

He held up the vial of soil. 'And stopped me getting this?' He put it in his pocket and took a step back. 'So what now?'

'Piss off before the cavalry show up.'

He smirked. 'We're not the cavalry?'

'Far from it this time.' I hefted one of the bags. 'Out of interest, just how much does it cost to get away these days?'

'That's four million dollars. We should work together again sometime.'

He turned to walk away, I waved the gun to keep his attention. 'You forgetting something?'

He paused, sighed, reaching inside his jacket to hand me an envelope, the information that was worth more to me than the cash. 'I was hoping for your sake you wouldn't ask.' He pointed at the duffel bags. 'If you're going to do what I think you are, I'd advise you to spend that money quickly.'

He didn't look back, throwing up his arm in a farewell wave as he strode off the bridge, evaporating into the fog. I slipped the envelope and gun into my pocket, swung the rifle over my shoulder, picked up the bags, and followed at a considerably slower pace.

I'd made it halfway up the path when the drone of the helicopter increased to a roar, blowing the fog towards me. I caught sight of the underside of the Black Hawk as it accelerated away into the grey sky, then it was gone, turbines muffled by the all-enveloping weather.

I limped through the gate into the parking area, out onto the road, following it back to the cars. I placed the pistol and rifle on the tarmac and opened the Capri's boot, sat one of the bags on the spare wheel, pulled it open.

Mason wasn't kidding. This was what the keys to a bioweapon cost, never mind that five people had to die. I picked up a wad of notes and looked it over. Hundred-dollar bills, banded together in $10,000 bricks. *Retirement funds.*

I did say I was a realist.

Mason and I go way back, though in this life that doesn't necessarily make for preferential treatment; if we were anything like real friends he'd have given me a heads-up, at least some info I could've used to my advantage, but he was right – if he had, he wouldn't have got the sample. When I'd found out it was Mason that Hurley had called on the Post Office phone, I'd simply called to renegotiate the terms of the sale.

Didn't take much; the game was up and Hurley's card was marked – Mason was right, I'd saved him a job and tied up his loose ends. I love the Americans but they're fickle and have money to burn. Makes them easy to deal with as long as you don't trust them – doesn't matter to them who they're paying, they'd sell out their own mums if they could be sure they'd get the goods.

After my call with Mason, I'd phoned the real cavalry.

The thump of rotors again filtered through the clouds, but I could tell this was a different helicopter, the Merlin that had dropped me off twenty-four hours ago.

I looked around frantically. The whole area would be cordoned off, they'd have to retrieve the Landy and they'd also do a sweep for as many shell casings as they could find, empty mags, evidence of our presence – before mopping Hurley up from the bottom of the gorge. Big area to cover. I looked from the forest to the ditch at the side of the road and the moorland beyond. Big area, sure, but a tourist area, no decent hiding places, not without a spade and at least an hour's graft.

Fuck it. The bonnet was trashed so I yanked out the spare wheel, lobbing it over the barrier, sending it crashing through the undergrowth. I tipped out the bag, cramming as many stacks of cash into the spare wheel well as I could. When it was full I stuffed a few remaining stacks into spaces in the bodywork, behind the rear lights, under pieces of trim. I rolled up the bag and crammed it down behind the seats, then replaced the carpet. I locked the boot, pocketing the keys, then sat on the crash barrier with the second duffel bag between my feet, waiting for the helicopter to land.

While I waited I thought about how long it would be before the Americans realised the dirt in the vial was worthless. I'd scooped the mud up from the shoreline behind Camp Vollum last night, while Marie had been sorting the pump – it definitely didn't contain the stuff they were after. There was no way I'd have replaced the real vial of anthrax under the floor, no way I'd risk them getting their hands on it.

I heard the helicopter set down in the car park. I pulled Mason's envelope from my pocket, opened it, sliding out a folded piece of paper. A single name.

I pushed it back into my pocket as a figure strode from the fog with the same assurance as Mason, only this man wore a uniform. The crown and pips on his shoulder indicated he was a colonel in the British Army, but I never addressed him as such.

Rupert Holderness looked at me, bedraggled, bleeding, broken, sitting in the rain on a roadside in the middle of nowhere. 'You've been through worse,' was the extent of his greeting, the same voice a harsh father would use to scold a child for falling out of a tree. I was used to his special brand of sympathy, his coaching and motivational techniques. He stared at my car, rubbing his chin. 'And *that* does not come under expenses.'

I stood, steadying myself on the crash barrier. 'It does if you want this bag.'

His face lit up. 'You played a hell of a close game this time. We followed the Americans in and hung back just like you asked. How much did they pay for the sample?'

'Two million dollars.'

Holderness whistled. 'Less than I thought, but still a job well done.'

'How are the others?'

'They're decontaminating on the *Dauntless*.' He shot me a sideways look as he kicked the wheel of my car. 'Other than Captain Greenbow, they're fine.'

'I can explain that.'

He nodded, seemingly unconcerned. 'So where's the real sample?'

'Destroyed in the fire.'

'Whitehall will be disappointed.'

'I don't see why, since officially we don't develop biological weapons.'

'Always got to do it your way, eh, John?'

'My way's kept me alive all these years.'

'Barely. So, no one has the sample and we're two million dollars up. Another feather in your cap, in any case.'

'The last one.'

He picked at his fingernails. 'How many times have I heard that? Though it is comforting when you remain in character.'

'I mean it this time.'

'Hm. Well, Special Branch are coming to close off the area, and we've got a full bio-response team on the way.'

'They'll want to get down to the bottom of that gorge, there's an American down there that's not feeling too well.'

He raised an eyebrow and looked out over the trees.

'And I'll need my car transported home.'

He wrinkled his nose. 'It's potentially contaminated, the only place it's going is a bonfire.'

My mind raced. 'You don't know it's contaminated. It's mine, it's private property, and you owe me.'

Several hazmat-suited soldiers appeared from the fog, carrying various boxes and pieces of equipment.

'You'll be compensated, as always,' he said, motioning for me to follow him towards the chopper.

I guarantee you won't compensate me that much...

'As a personal favour, then. The car's got sentimental value. Just give the inside a spray.' He wasn't going for it. 'It was my brother's.'

He sighed. 'Whose fool idea was it to go chasing around the Highlands anyway?' After a few seconds' consideration, he barked instructions at the hazmat guys to tear out the front seats and hose down the rest. They started assembling equipment and inflating some kind of containment tent. He turned back to me.

'Oh, and you've managed to infuriate an entire village, we've had to seal off the only place they can buy milk for miles.'

'You owe them on expenses, too.'

He pretended he hadn't heard, gesturing to the hazmats. 'For God's sake, leave the car for now, start with this lout.' He saw my expression and smiled. 'You're not getting on my helicopter until you're scrubbed clean, my boy. Now, tell me what the hell happened on that island.'

Chapter Seventy-three

Same as it ever was.

When siblings fight, one can't gain total victory over the other, otherwise an imbalance occurs. Imbalances upset the status quo, sometimes permanently. Siblings know they need to resolve issues in a mutually beneficial way in order to preserve the relationship.

The Americans were happy because, even though they knew the Brits would be pissed off, they knew we needed them. Mason had seen me take the sample from Hurley with his own eyes, so when they discovered it was worthless they'd have to chalk it up to their own overenthusiastic agent. Nothing they could pin on me, nothing they could do about it now he was dead.

The Brits were happy because they knew the Americans didn't really have the sample, and the whole affair had put our cousins across the Atlantic in a weaker position, diplomatically. Not without cost – but everything costs these days, everyone's expendable.

So the UK had prevailed in a way that allowed both countries to save face because even though they'd need to apologise, America secretly thought they'd won. Britain secretly knew they hadn't. A perfect ending, given the current political climate. Someone in Washington would be forced to add a clause in a trade agreement more favourable to Britain, maybe get a few supportive tweets thrown the PM's way. Essentially, the relationship was maintained, no nasty confrontations or unwanted media attention, which is what could have happened had anyone else been involved.

On top of that, I was personally two million dollars up, plus my hefty fee from the British *and* I was in their good books. On the down-low the CIA still thought I could be bought, which was good for future job prospects with them too. Most importantly, the job had finally given me the bargaining power with Mason I'd so desperately needed to get the information I'd been after for a while. A fairly rosy outcome, given the circumstances.

It's what I do, what I'm very well paid to do. I'm no policeman or judge. I don't understand or give a shit about the ins and outs of the law, it doesn't concern me. I'm contracted to clean up mess but I'm not a detective either, nor am I simply seeking truth. The reason I get paid the big bucks is because I steer the truth – and the mess – to an effective conclusion beneficial to whoever is writing my cheque. Of course, by sheer coincidence that conclusion always happens to benefit me too. Ideals are expensive, they cost a hell of a lot more than scientists. I live in the real world where deals are undone, promises broken.

Okay, I'm doing myself a disservice. I do have my own morals – and being an independent contractor gives me a certain amount of leeway to flex the jobs and my methods. For example, when I'd tipped the real vial of super-lethal anthrax into the sea last night whilst pretending to signal the ship, along with the remains from that sandwich bag. The spores might not be killed immediately but they'd break up beneath the waves, floating away on their own.

Holderness would certainly have been happier with it and it would likely have earned me a bonus but like I said, I have my own morals. The British Government sometimes pays my bills, but that doesn't mean I like them.

Or trust them, but since they'd transferred a big chunk of cash into my account I did at least owe them an explanation, a reason why such a simple job had gone south so rapidly, why a bit of snooping to understand whether a technician's death was suspicious had ended in such carnage dragged across the Highlands.

The flight to the ship was as uncomfortable as the one that had brought me here, though mercifully much shorter. Bates and the hazmat guys had stayed behind to direct the local police and clear up, so it was just Holderness and me. I shivered in an MoD-issue tracksuit and space blanket, still wet following a freezing shower in the middle of the road. I gripped the seat next to him, feeding him details through gritted teeth and screwed-up eyes as he scribbled in his notebook, already working angles for his report.

Holderness laughed when I told him there'd been something nasty in my Scotch, which might sound callous even for him – fortunately he knows I can't stand the stuff, and that my hip flask only ever contains water. We'd thought it'd be helpful to be underestimated.

Holderness didn't doubt that Hurley and Gambetta were guilty as hell, but still hadn't worked out how and why Hurley had killed his partner in crime.

I explained, the windows were the key.

Chapter Seventy-four

As soon as the chopper's wheels touched the deck I was whisked down to the sickbay to be swaddled in iodine and bandages and shots of all sorts of things anthrax-related. Not enough morphine for my liking before my finger was splinted properly, bloody gaffer tape was ripped off, and the slice over my ribs received more agonising staples than I thought necessary.

Afterwards my debrief with Holderness was interrupted periodically by muffled screams from the next room, where Captain Greenbow's foot was receiving much the same treatment. Holderness tutted when I smiled. We didn't make it through the whole story as he was called away urgently, no doubt bogged down with real-world details; crime scenes and jurisdiction, politics and paperwork, bullshit I've always been grateful to steer well away from.

The break gave me time to lie on my allotted berth feeling sorry for myself. My left ankle had doubled in size and my right leg was sliced to bits from jumping through the window. My right hand was bandaged, but fortunately Hurley's knife hadn't slashed particularly deep. The iodine had stained sickly yellowy brown patches all over my skin. I looked at the mirror on the opposite wall, the broken man it reflected, scars old and new all reminders of jobs; assassinations, terrorism, civil wars, news stories of the last two decades condensed into miniature and mapped across my body. Pain, scars, pay cheque, repeat – there had to be better ways of making a living.

Maybe it didn't have to be that way any more. I thought about my pride and joy being hosed down with bleach and formaldehyde and loaded onto a recovery truck bound for Yorkshire. The contents of the boot might finally let me get that place off Russell Square I'd had my eye on. I closed my eyes and, not for the first time, tried to imagine a world where phone calls and emails could be about shopping deliveries, unpaid direct debits, marketing crap. Netflix and a dog and taking out the fucking recycling once a week. Could I learn not to flinch at every car alarm and door slam and JCB digging the road? Could I live in a world where fireworks meant celebrations and helicopters flew over without discharging death? Where conversations never began with questions about languages, vaccinations, or my long-distance accuracy with a Steyr SSG 69?

My reverie was interrupted by knocking. I limped across the room, opening the door.

The young lieutenant saluted. 'Morning, sir.'

'Less of the "sir", uniforms don't suit me. What's the verdict?'

'Doc says it's too early to tell.' He handed me a heavy canvas bag and propped a set of crutches against the doorframe. 'She says to let her know if you start vomiting or develop an itchy rash.'

'Reassuring. Are the cast assembled?'

'Breakfasting in the officers' wardroom.'

'I'll be five minutes.'

Chapter Seventy-five

When I entered the wardroom, five pairs of eyeballs swivelled to lock onto me, only Holderness ignoring me as he lazily pulled apart a croissant. Toast and mugs stopped halfway to open mouths. I didn't look up but could feel the eyes tracking me as I hobbled to a table laden with jugs of weak squash, tubs of sawdusty cereal, a meagre selection of both over- and under-ripe fruit. I put the canvas bag down, spread a napkin out, and pulled out the contents one by one: Gambetta's Walther, Greenbow's sooty Browning, Hurley's charred Sig.

Greenbow glared in the corner of my eye, arms folded, one heavily bandaged leg propped on a chair. He opened his mouth, but Holderness waved it shut with his butter knife. They'd already had words about his foot. Holderness had told me he'd invoked all manner of national security crap to shut him up, told him if he mentioned it again he'd risk his compensation.

'Glad to see you're still in one piece.' That beautiful French accent.

I turned. Marie leaned on the windowsill behind me, now clad in a fetching pair of ill-fitting jeans and a T-shirt, presumably borrowed from a member of the crew. Her face dropped when she saw the guns.

'What are you doing?' she asked, lip trembling slightly.

I was about to reply when Holderness coughed. 'Exhibit A?' He pointed at the table.

'And the other guns too, ready for dabs and DNA,' I replied.

'Fingerprinting?' Greenbow's ears pricked up. 'There's no need to test my sidearm.'

I leaned back against the table, pouring a cup of tea, watching him carefully. 'They're all being taken away for analysis.'

'Procedure,' Holderness added. 'We need to cross all the t's, for my report here.' He held up a pad of paper and smiled.

'But we know Hurley did it, and we have his gun,' said Alice, joining me at the table. 'Why do we care if his fingerprints and DNA are on it?'

I shrugged. 'It's an unusual case, but it's still evidence.'

Greenbow looked around the room, clearly perturbed, making to stand. Alice reached for the guns tentatively, as if exorcising the demons of the last twenty-four hours.

'No touching, they're still loaded,' I said, turning back to my mug of tea. I stirred, watching the brown tendrils swirl and spread through the lukewarm water, replicating like an infection. I shuddered, dropped the spoon, pushed the cup away, briefly contemplating taking up drinking coffee but thinking better of it and pouring a glass of orange instead.

Marie still hovered by my shoulder, face white.

'So why did you take the window key?' I whispered.

She tried to keep her face blank but her eyes darted around the room. No one else was listening.

'I didn't know what was going on,' she whispered back. 'I wanted an escape route of my own, just in case.'

'I can't argue with that, since I stole one too. You took it from the radio room?'

She nodded. 'While you were checking Ingrid at Camp Vollum. I didn't know you'd screwed the windows shut.'

'I suppose I did tell you not to trust *anyone*.'

'Yes, but Hurley? I still can't believe it.'

My throat was dry, a combination of the gas and fire mixed with the anticipation of what was about to happen. 'You gave him my gun and nearly got us both killed.' I coughed, downed the orange juice, and smiled. 'If you'd have shot him instead you'd have saved me a lot of trouble.'

'Sorry.'

'If you wanna make it up to me, I know this great pub in Inverness.'

I didn't catch her reply, I was concentrating on Alice behind me, on her reflection in the coffee pot.

'I told you not to touch the gun,' I said.

She frowned. 'But…' Alice's tongue tripped up.

'But you had no choice, did you? Because you need a way of explaining why your prints and DNA are all over it.' I turned to face her snarl. 'They were already all over it because you used that gun to shoot Eric Gambetta last night.'

Her mouth started working but no sound escaped as she quickly slid the magazine out, backpedalling away. Out of reach, and with my injuries, I was too slow to stop her. I took a step forward but she slammed the magazine back, cocked the pistol.

I dropped my arm and laughed. 'It's over.'

She raised her arm, still trying to speak, when Marie reached round me, smashing the gun aside with the coffee pot, spraying the wall with scalding coffee, splashing back across my face. I raised my arms instinctively, saw Marie launch, grabbing Alice's arm, preventing her from swinging the gun in my direction. Alice whipped it round, cracking against Marie's jaw. I reached and stumbled, wincing as I caught the table to steady myself. There was a brief scuffle, a choked scream, then uneasy quiet. As I blinked the hot liquid from my eyes I saw Marie held prisoner, Alice's head over one shoulder, Gambetta's Walther over the other. Marie struggled but Alice tightened her grip, grinding the barrel into her neck.

'No one move.'

Dash, silent thus far at the other side of the room, quietly placed a chair back down on the floor. Greenbow hovered on one leg, gripping his chair, brandishing a crutch, which he slowly lowered. Holderness remained seated, cradling his croissant.

'Where're you gonna go, Alice?' I asked. 'You're on a Navy ship in the middle of the sea.'

She was silent, unbreathing, eyes narrowed.

'Let Marie go,' I continued.

She looked at Holderness. 'Tell them to get the helicopter ready.'

'Or what?' he asked.

'Or no one's getting out of here alive.'

'There are ten armed Marines outside that door,' Holderness said, still gesturing with his butter knife.

'Then I'll start with him.' She removed the gun from Marie's neck and pointed it at me.

'Go ahead. I've got nothing better to do.' I let go of the table to limp forward, closing the distance between us.

Marie thrashed, lashing out with an elbow.

A silenced gunshot is far from silent. The room held its breath, the pop and mechanical click deafening. It was followed by several more in rapid succession, bouncing between the walls so quickly I couldn't count how many times she fired. Chairs were overturned as Dash and Greenbow dove for cover. I tried to pull Marie towards me but instead she thrust out, driving her fist into Alice's face. I stumbled and fell backwards, dragging Marie with me. Alice continued to jerk the trigger. Her head slammed sideways as a crutch smashed into it, launched by Greenbow from the other side of the room, but she recovered quickly, turning, furiously squeezing the trigger in his direction, the hammer continuing to fall and click long after the magazine was emptied.

The door flew open, Bates exploding into the room. He grabbed Alice, twisting her arm up her back, forcing her to drop the gun. Several of his team crowded the corridor behind him.

'Take Ms String below!' Holderness commanded.

He'd remained in his chair throughout – not through bravery, but foreknowledge. When we'd landed I'd asked him to raid the ship's stores, loading the guns with blanks. Only an idiot would have loaded guns kicking around with a murderer at large.

She spat as the huge Scotsman shoved her out of the door, blood and tooth fragments sliding down the wall. The others recovered, not quite sure what had just happened.

'Thank you, Marie,' I said as we helped each other to our feet. 'And well done, Captain,' I added – sincerely for the first time.

He grunted, glaring at me. Holderness had primed him to make a fuss about the fingerprinting of the guns, but hadn't explained why. I could see he hadn't worked it out yet.

'Right, that's breakfast done,' said Holderness, rising to his feet and striding after Bates. 'John, with me. The rest of you, stay here.'

I pulled away from Marie, following him to the doorway, anxious to finish it. She reached out, grabbed my sleeve.

'I never answered your question last night,' she said.

'Question?'

'There's no one back in Biarritz.'

I pulled my arm back before she noticed it was shaking again, a comedown of sorts. 'That's the real crime. So, this pub in Inverness—'

'Now, John,' said Holderness.

'Hang on,' said Dash. 'Are we going to find out what the heck just happened?'

Holderness looked vaguely amused. 'Nothing at all happened, if you want to keep your pensions.'

I was steered out of the door. Marie gave me a smile as Holderness closed it.

'You missed your calling,' he said as he marched ahead, directing me down a narrow flight of stairs. 'Gentleman Detective.'

'Gentleman being the operative word.'

'Incidentally, the only prints on the gun were yours, probably DNA too. It'd been bleached.'

'She couldn't take the risk, but I *was* about to pull out the shirt.' Everyone had slept in yesterday's clothes, still wearing them when they were evacuated. Her hands had been swabbed on the ship under the guise of testing for anthrax, but in reality those samples were winging their way to a lab in Glasgow to check for gunshot residue. My guess was it'd be a negative after over twelve hours, but her clothes would tell a different story. No getting gunshot residue out of clothing, not without a washing machine and time, two things she hadn't had. The results wouldn't be available for a while, but I'd bet on her not knowing that and panicking; drawing out a rapid confession on the spot is helpful. Letting Holderness wrap it all up before some other agency swooped in would put me in his good books, maybe still yield that bonus.

Holderness led me through the ship's intestines, along corridors and stairways that made X-Base seem like a luxury hotel, past steel doors and circuit boxes and pipes and conduits, never breaking stride or looking back. He didn't notice when I occasionally paused to rest against the wall, breathing deeply, hanging my head to let the nausea pass before limping to catch him.

When he'd picked me up on the mainland he'd been in good spirits, all things considered. His demeanour had changed entirely whilst I'd been getting showered, a cloud had parked itself above his head and now he wouldn't look me in the eye as he finally opened a cabin door and waved me inside. A bonus was definitely off the cards.

'A seemingly impossible crime, Tyler – you made some fairly large leaps.'

'To be honest, I got hung up on catching them red-handed. It was pretty straightforward, really.'

'Glad to hear it. It'll make it easy to write up.' He gestured at the desk, at a pad of paper resting on it. 'Just some more detail for my report.'

'Now?'

He nodded. 'I've a call to make, I'll be back in ten minutes.' He left me to it.

Chapter Seventy-six

I took a deep breath and started writing. Didn't take long to lay it all out, the genius of their plan, how it'd unravelled. The three conspirators, Hurley, Gambetta and Alice.

She'd come here with Demeter a few months ago to scout the island, and it was then she'd discovered the mutated strain. What to do with it? No point handing it over to her superiors, she's employed by the British, which means no profit, just a pat on the back. It's difficult working for two masters and receiving only one pay packet; she wanted out for good.

The French, then – always anxious to keep up an independent array of weapons. Gambetta was their man on the island. I didn't know why or how the Americans got involved, though doubtless I'd wheedle it out of Mason over a beer sometime in the future. Hurley had worked in the CIA office in Paris for a few months, I reckon that's where he'd met Gambetta. The Americans have deep pockets; maybe the conspirators had known they could make a hell of a lot more by taking it to them. So with the base providing the cover to smuggle the sample away, the plan was set.

Gambetta had been a poor choice, as it turned out. He was reckless and had a temper, as I well knew. He'd taken it upon himself to run a test. Kyle was the most expendable person in the base, and sadly the least likely to raise concerns. Someone the authorities wouldn't really care about or dig too deeply into.

Alice was sharper, when she found out, she knew there'd be questions, knew it needed to be covered up, so she took the initiative. She wasn't an agent, but she was on MI5's payroll so it would have looked suspicious if she hadn't reported it. She did the only thing she could do, sabotaging the base, ensuring someone was sent to investigate. Someone who could easily be disposed of if it came to that. No way it could be pinned on her: by initiating an investigation she'd seemingly demonstrated the right allegiances.

The second phase of the plan had been to subvert my investigation by creating a fall guy to take the blame for Kyle's death and my attempted murder. The radios needed to be destroyed to allow the fall guy to disappear, and unfortunately when Ingrid tested the sample of anthrax that had sealed her fate too. Viktor Demeter 'the Russian defector' was an obvious choice. What better way to divert blame for everything than to have Demeter destroy the radios and escape the island – in the process murdering Ingrid and attacking Gambetta – in such a way that it couldn't *possibly* be anyone else? I had to admit, it was a decent plan.

So Gambetta raced up to Camp Vollum, shot Ingrid, smashed the radio, and with Hurley covering his stint on the radio back at X-Base, all of their alibis were solid. Now all Gambetta had to do was get back into the radio room without being seen, to keep that unshakeable alibi intact. The clever thing was how he did it in such a way as to implicate Demeter at the same time; after decontaminating, he handed his pistol to Alice so it couldn't be found on him, and changed into a fresh red suit.

While he did, Alice came to Captain Greenbow's room to fetch us. And as Gambetta came plodding up the corridor in character as Demeter she'd set the stage directions, ensuring Greenbow and I were in the right place at the right time. She ensured we saw him arguing and entering the room, reinforcing the idea that Gambetta was already in there. He'd been arguing with an empty room, yet more misdirection to confirm his own alibi and condemn Demeter.

Once inside the comms room, Gambetta went into over-drive, tearing off the red suit, throwing it and the gas mask under the floor. He took a lighter to the USB stick from the CCTV, because it would have shown that it was him, not Demeter, decontaminating. He smashed the radio, gave himself a couple of scratches and a bloody nose along the way, made it look like he'd been attacked. .

Last thing he needed to do was open the window – which would have been 'Demeter's' escape route. Shout for help, wait for us to arrive, claim Demeter had burst in and attacked him.

And that's the point when two separate things snagged the thread to unravel the plot.

The first was when he tried to open the window and it stuck where I'd screwed it closed. Gambetta struggled with it, starting to panic – because if we came in, how would he explain Demeter's disappearance? His alibi would evaporate. But just as he was desperately thinking of a way out of his predicament, the second snag was occurring. Hurley and Alice had changed the plan – they'd double-crossed Gambetta. He was expendable, and about to die.

He was a weak link, had almost ruined everything by killing Kyle and being too quick to get rid of me. A public death at the hands of Demeter – which we'd all witness – was even better than the original plan, tying up loose ends, further cementing the Russian's guilt, bolstering their own alibis.

Everyone in the base heard the gunshot. Alice in the corridor with me, Greenbow further along, Dash and Marie down the other end of the base. Hurley had his head out of his room, shouting at us purely to keep his alibi intact.

But that wasn't the shot that had killed Gambetta.

Hurley had fired his own gun, that was what we'd heard. Being pushed for time and with limited resources, they'd no way to get hold of blanks, I could picture him trying to open his window just like Gambetta, he would probably have fired outside if I'd not screwed it shut. Instead he'd done the next best thing, opening the wardrobe and firing inside. It worked, the signal to Alice for the next phase – the rollercoaster was almost at the end of the track, just one more drop and timing was everything. At this point we thought Gambetta was dead, but he was actually still struggling with the window in the radio room. Alice ran on ahead. As I hurried to catch up, Hurley came flying out of his room to stall me.

Alice had mere seconds to pull off the perfect murder. She opened the door, stepped into the room. If she'd waited just a heartbeat she'd have found out the window was screwed shut, blowing the whole plan – but she didn't have a single heartbeat to spare.

Out from her rucksack came Gambetta's own silenced pistol, and at that range she couldn't miss. A few minutes before we'd heard the distinctive sound a suppressed pistol makes. I was close, might still have heard it, so she screamed loudly enough to bring everyone in the base running, covering up any noise as she put a bullet through his eye. She dropped the pistol into her bag, then was backing out of the room, into the corridor in full view of everyone. The whole thing took mere moments, and now Gambetta and Ingrid were dead, Demeter the only possible suspect.

Holderness would keep the vial switch out of his report. He'd be sure to let his superiors in Whitehall know, the whole thing would be much easier to swallow that way, but they wouldn't spread the word around too much; let the Americans think they'd won, they'd hardly have the balls to ask for a refund.

There was a knock at the door. It swung open and Holderness stepped into the room.

Chapter Seventy-seven

'Are you all right?' Holderness asked. An expression that I'd come to understand as concern crossed his face. 'You're sweating.'

I hadn't noticed my pen drumming a beat on the table. I put it down, pulled my arms close in to my sides where I could grip the chair, and nodded.

He closed the door behind him. 'I saw your face.' I must have looked puzzled, as he continued. 'When Alice threatened to shoot you. If I didn't know better I'd say you wished I hadn't loaded the gun with blanks.'

I didn't answer because I didn't understand if it was a question or not. He looked relieved to not be having the discussion we'd carefully avoided for years, but I could still tell he was anxious. 'Well, we'll say no more about it.' There was something else. I waited for him to speak. 'So, your, ahem, classic –' he definitely pronounced that as if it were a question, he may as well have done the quotation marks with his fingers – 'car is already on its way south.'

'Straight to my lockup?'

'It'll be in Yorkshire by tonight. How's the head?'

'They glued it together pretty well.'

'Well, you're fairly indestructible, and heads always bleed more than they have any right to. No, ah, ill effects, then?'

One broken bone, forty stitches, a thousand cuts, burns, and bruises. 'No worse than usual, I'll mend.' The bleeding would stop, swellings reduce, but I wouldn't mend, not really. Nothing was healing properly these days, as if my body was slowly packing in, needing twice as much downtime after every job but never getting it, always playing catch-up and slipping further behind. And that's before we get into the other damage, the nightmares, the screaming, blurred faces every time I close my eyes, and sometimes even when they're open. I needed to get out of this game or I wouldn't be playing it for much longer.

He coughed, pulling me back to the room. 'What are your plans, then?'

'I was thinking you could have Bates drive me to Inverness. Browse Leakey's, first-class ticket to London and on to the Eurostar, maybe Biarritz for Christmas. That what you had in mind?'

'Biarritz? Marie's out of your league, you know. Too many brain cells.'

Here we go, the reason for his attitude change. I sighed. 'I told you this was my last job.'

'As you always tell me. Interesting you mention France, how's your skiing?'

'I can hardly bloody walk, and, to be honest, I'm not sure I'll be welcome there for a while.'

'Job in the Alps I'd like you to look over for me.'

'Isn't there an incubation period for anthrax? Even if I wanted to, I can't travel until I've had the all-clear.'

'Mountain air will do you good. I've just spoken to the doctor and to Porton Down. They've given the go-ahead for you to travel on military transport and are fast-tracking the final results. I'll keep in touch.'

I shook my head. 'Get Weatherstone instead, or maybe Groom, if you can afford him; they're always looking for contract work.'

'They lack your *sang-froid*. What else would you do, John, honestly?'

'Get Netflix, take up painting, eat chips on a bench.'

'Painkillers and Prozac and group-counselling sessions at the church hall. You *think* you want out, but really you know it's the only thing keeping you alive.'

Shit, maybe we're going to have that conversation after all. 'I'm ready to take my chances.' I made to stand, but Holderness waved me back down.

'You kid yourself that you don't enjoy it.'

I gave him my best 'conversation over' stare.

Holderness sighed, leaning back against the door. 'I didn't want to do this but you leave me no choice.' He picked at an imaginary piece of fluff on his lapel, something he always did when he had something distasteful to share, when he couldn't look me in the eye. 'I can't protect you if you're out.'

'I've never needed protecting before.' I frowned. 'What's going on?'

'MI5 are flying someone out. Something about a stash of dollars in your car.'

I stood quickly, too quickly for the staples down my ribs, arms raised. 'You bastard, you know how this shit works. You know the things people like me have to do so people like you get the medals.' I caught myself and lowered my fists. 'You'll get a big fuck-off pension and a knighthood when you retire. What will I get? A cheap cremation with no mourners, or worse, left to rot wherever I fall.'

'I turn a blind eye to certain aspects of your work, spoils of war, etcetera, but this is too high-profile, I'm afraid.'

'The contents of my boot are nothing to do with you, or MI-bloody-five; that's my fucking money. Cutting a deal was the best way to cement the vial's credentials and get the Americans off our backs.'

'I don't doubt it, but did you mention it in your report?' He picked up the papers I'd been scribbling on. 'No, I thought not.' His accent was slipping, Aberdeen creeping in at the edges, it always did when he was angry. He straightened, jabbing a finger at me. 'Taking their cash, hiding it from us, that puts you on the wrong side of this affair. Whitehall wants scapegoats on this side of the Atlantic. To an outsider it could appear as though you'd sold the Americans the real sample, and only *told* us it was destroyed.'

I gritted my teeth. 'You know me.'

'Yes, so why did you tell me they'd only paid two million? At any rate, you might need a friend when they arrive in –' he checked his watch – 'ten minutes.'

'A friend.' It didn't matter what I did or said, he already had me. Always would. I was a tool, nothing more, a tool getting blunter through overuse but one that wouldn't be put aside until it had worn down or fallen apart, at which point I'd simply be replaced with the next poor sap.

'Hercules leaves in two hours. The chopper will take you to Lossiemouth.'

I tried to think of a move but my mind was spent and there was nothing more to say. I scratched my arm, at the skin around a cut, the black centre, the redness that had started to swell around it.

There was a knock. Holderness shifted, opening the door. A naval pilot saluted him.

'Warming up, sir, wheels up in five.' It sounded like she'd added a question mark when she'd seen the state of me, eyes widening. I noticed she was carrying my bag.

'Lieutenant Hannah here has packed your gear, and the armorer has serviced that museum piece you call a sidearm.' He straightened my papers and hustled me through the door. 'Few weeks skiing; previous chap ended up falling off a mountain. Usual briefing pack on the helicopter, good luck, Tyler.'

He didn't offer his hand, never did when he thought he might be sending someone to their death. Good job, my hands were drenched with sweat. I wiped them on my trousers as the door swung shut behind me. Hannah, the pilot, was already leading the way to the helipad at the stern. The corridor rocked, bile stung my throat, I had to reach a hand to the wall to stay upright.

With trembling fingers I felt the note in my pocket, the one Mason had given me, could almost trace the ink with my thumb. The information this assignment had finally given me the leverage to obtain, the single name scrawled on the paper.

The man responsible for my brother's death would have to wait a while longer.

Author's Note

A quick glance at a map will tell you that Gruinard Island is a real place. It's a bleakly picturesque oval island about two kilometres long by one kilometre wide. It's right where I said it was, off north-west Scotland – a kilometre's swim from where the A832 meets the sea at Mungasdale, and within sight of the tiny village of Laide. It's pretty remote – a couple of hours' drive north of Inverness, which is in itself a long enough drive north for most people. If you fancy making the journey yourself, then I recommend you do so in summer and not late November – thank goodness for four-wheel drive, that's all I'm saying.

I'd first read about Gruinard when I was doing a bit of online research for a completely unrelated horror novel, and I was immediately fascinated. I love old military sites, hidden haunted bunkers and the like, so I found out what I could. Gruinard didn't make it into the horror novel, but I knew I had to revisit it.

In 1997 the top-secret files relating to Porton Down's experiments at Gruinard were finally made public, along with the horrifying details of Operation Vegetarian – thank goodness that plan was never put into force (that's a whole other book right there…). Yes, the anthrax trials during the war actually happened, almost as described in the story. A top-secret group called BDP (Biology Department Porton) was set up in 1940 to assess the feasibility of Nazi germ warfare and to develop a deterrent. In 1942 Gruinard Island was purchased from a farmer for £500 and a veil of secrecy descended. I don't know if the Ministry of Defence knew what they were doing or how evocative a name they'd come up with when they christened the island X-Base, but every time I see that name I can't help but picture the Hammer Films *The Quatermass Xperiment* and *X The Unknown* – the latter coincidentally taking place near Inverness.

Following the successful conclusion of the tests and for about twenty years after – between the late Forties and late Sixties – scientists from Porton Down regularly collected soil samples, and in all that time the levels of contamination around the test sites did not reduce.

In 1979 responsibility for the testing passed to the Chemical Defence Establishment and a survey was undertaken, which proved the island to still be just as contaminated as in the Forties. In the early Eighties more extensive surveys of the island were undertaken, along with research into possible decontamination techniques. These surveys revealed the main areas of anthrax contamination were limited to about three acres, corresponding to the areas near the blasts and anthrax dispersal sites.

Following Operation Dark Harvest in 1981 (yes, that really happened too) and pressure from Scotland, the government finally started to do something about the island. Actual decontamination commenced in 1986, a huge operation involving the removal of vegetation and the bagging up of the worst-affected topsoil. The contaminated areas were separated into grids with perforated hoses through which nearly three hundred tonnes of formaldehyde diluted with seawater was pumped.

In late 1987 the soil in these areas was sampled and no anthrax was found. Local sheep were grazed on the island and inspected regularly, and when after half a year none were found to have contracted anthrax, the flock were returned to the mainland.

Finally, on 24 April 1990 – forty-eight years since the island had been declared off limits – Conservative Junior Defence Minister Michael Neubert visited the island and ceremonially removed the rusting MoD warning signs. With the island no longer under quarantine, the government sold it back to the family they'd bought it from, for the same £500 they'd been charged in 1942.

At this point I must apologise to Porton Down, anyone linked to biological weapons research, and anyone involved with the decontamination – I'm sure they did a sterling job, this is entirely a work of fiction, after all.

Although some people *are* still sceptical about the decontamination, given the long life and extreme hardiness of anthrax spores.

A study by the *American Journal of Public Health* concluded that anthrax vaccines were one of the contributing causes of Gulf War Syndrome, and that they should only be used in the most dire of circumstances. The word 'anthrax' strikes fear into the public like no other toxin, and its use in terror attacks makes instant headline news. Despite research and improved vaccines, anthrax today remains as potent a threat as it did back in the early 20th century, when it was first isolated and weaponised.

So, despite the clean-up, you still wouldn't catch me camping on Gruinard Island.

Acknowledgments

There are a few people in particular I'd like to thank, whose contributions have varied but are all alike in one respect: without any one of them there would be no book.

Jules, my first ever reader, sitting at my kitchen table for hours going through all those notes on his phone years ago, for what was at that time a very different novel. All that time watching shit old films and Bond marathons was worth it! Bob, my second reader, always encouraging and enthusiastically asking after updates. Fordy, who despite piss-taking borne of a quarter of a century's friendship, has been incredibly supportive. My parents, who always encouraged me to read and always ensured we had shelves full of books.

Jaz Carpet (*nom de guerre*; a wanted man in twenty-three countries – his real name cannot be printed for legal reasons, like those pictures of the SAS with black bars over their eyes). My military advisor who supplied me with some fantastic anecdotes and details, all the cool stuff that adds the spice. As is often the way, anything I got wrong here was my error rather than his, and just means I should have bothered him even more.

Mari, the kindest and officially hardest-working writer out there, always making time and giving so much of herself to others. She told me not to give up and ended up mentoring me, pulling me up, digging out my voice, and driving me forward.

Agent Phil was down with it immediately: he plucked me from a pile, encouraged me, supported me, fought for me – definitely the man I'd call if I was on *Millionaire* with an obscure old film question.

Everyone at Canelo, and in particular Craig, who turned a manuscript into a book. His suggestions lifted it up, his comments were hilarious, and he probably stopped me being sued, which is nice.

Vic Watson and Simon Bewick, the duo behind Newcastle Virtual Noir at the Bar and Bay Tales, where lockdown gave me the opportunity to give the first ever reading of my work and which led directly to the book you're holding. Thank you for the opportunities, the kind words, the support, and for all the great work you've done and will do in future to give people a platform.

The Robs (Rob the nicest dinosaur-fancier you'll ever meet, and Rob who let a stranger tag along at Harrogate and drink his booze), the first real authors to ever ask to read my stuff, and whose words of support spurred me on when I really needed it. Of course the bundt of veracity, 95 per cent pictures of food, 4 per cent memes, the occasional scrap of writing advice. Thank you all for keeping me sane through 2020.

Will at New Writing North and Aki at The Literary Consultancy, huge thanks due for the fantastic work they do to help writers from all backgrounds get the support they need to realise their dreams. Doug, for those insightful comments on an early draft – this book is the result of that advice.

Bloody Scotland, Theakstons Crime Fest, Newcastle Noir for providing opportunities for readers to meet their heroes, but also for the work they do to help readers become writers. Dr Noir in particular for throwing an unpublished northerner in at the deep end on his first panel.

Saving the best for last, Louby; without her encouragement I'd never have started writing, and without her unending support I'd certainly have stopped a long time ago. Thank you for your help, patience, love (very much reciprocated even though I'm not right good with words), but above all else, thank you so much for the endless stream of dubious character names. XXX